The Dar

R.D. Shah spent his formative years in the north west of England before attending Rugby School in Warwickshire. At seventeen he attained his private pilot's licence in Florida and shortly after attended the University of Miami where he studied motion picture & psychology before returning to the UK to work in television & leisure. He has travelled extensively throughout Europe, Russia and the Americas. R.D. holds a scuba diving licence, which he gained along the shores of the Hawaiian island of Kauai. All this experience has prepared him for a career in writing. He lives in Wiltshire with his wife and young daughter.

Also by R.D. Shah

The Harker Chronicles

Relics
The 4th Secret
The Last Judgement
The Dark Temple
The Shadow Conspiracy

THE DARK TEMPLE

R.D. SHAH

10 CANELO

First published in the the United Kingdom in 2019 by Canelo

This edition published in the United Kingdom in 2020 by Canelo

Canelo Digital Publishing Limited
31 Helen Road
Oxford OX2 0DF
United Kingdom

A CIP catalogue record for this book is available from the British Library.

Print ISBN 978 1 80032 031 4
Ebook ISBN 978 1 78863 107 5

Look for more great books at www.canelo.co

Printed and bound in Great Britain by Clays Ltd, Elcograf S.p.A.

Chapter 1

A high-pitched scream shattered the peaceful night air as the figure of a man dressed in a dark black overcoat made its way up to the illuminated porch of a small summer cottage. The warm glow of light emanating from the glass panel above the door belied the reality of what lay inside, and he glanced up towards it as another piercing shriek assaulted his ears.

The man muttered quietly to himself as he approached the gloss-painted wooden door, which he rapped upon three times with a clenched fist. It would all be over soon, he assured himself, and this notion gave him some comfort as the sound of several locks being released could be heard from inside. The door swung open slowly and a woman dressed in a tan, knee-length canvas skirt and a navy turtleneck jumper greeted him with a smile of relief. Her long black hair looked ruffled and, although her eyes were tinged red from sobbing, she looked encouraged by the sight of her visitor.

'Is it time?'

The man offered a reassuring smile and patted her back as she gave him a welcoming hug.

'It is,' he replied and she gently pulled him into the cottage hallway, closing the door behind them. 'Does he suspect anything?'

She was already shaking her head as she started securing the three separate door locks, then she began to usher her guest towards the staircase at the side of the hallway. 'Perhaps, but he wouldn't tell me even if he did,' she answered despairingly, climbing the maroon-carpeted stairs leading up to the first floor. 'Therefore I had no option but to tie him down.'

The woman's distressed voice quivered as she spoke, and he now noticed the thin dark bruise lines under her chin.

'Did he do that?' he asked, pointing to her neck as they both paused on the landing.

She began to nod her head in despair. 'He tried to strangle me earlier today.'

From one of the rooms still above them a screech of pain echoed through the cottage and, grimacing at the outburst, he took the woman's hand and squeezed it firmly. 'This ends now.'

She gave a grateful but uncertain nod and they continued up to the first floor, then headed on to a closed door at the far end of the corridor, from which the heavy sounds of banging and deep moaning were emerging.

'Dr Marceau was here earlier but all he could recommend was to have him committed.' The woman lightly rested her palm on the white, ceramic door-knob. 'But I just can't do that to him.'

The visitor raised the brown leather satchel he held up to his chest and gave it a firm pat. 'Then we don't have any other option, do we?'

She offered him a dismal smile and her eyes dulled slightly. He gently pushed her hand aside, then placed his own firm grip on the door-knob and turned it.

'Then let us finish this.'

With a light push the door swung open and he stepped inside.

The room was a shambles, with clothes strewn everywhere and the wreckage of a large ornamental mirror lay on the floor in front of him with shards of glass splayed all around. To his left a flickering wall-lamp dangled from its electrical cable, where someone had ripped it from the plasterboard, and on the lacquered side table sat a bowl full of water and a stack of facecloths. The commotion abruptly stopped, whereupon the man turned his attention to the queen-sized bed with a brown tufted headboard at the far end of the room – facing the open doorway – where a young boy lay on top of the sheets. The piercing blue eyes that greeted him caused the man to flinch, but he stood his ground and stared back.

It wasn't the belt straps binding the young boy's wrists and feet to the bed or the strange black, pimpled rash which ran across his forehead that caused the man's initial reaction. Neither was it the thick, red, rake marks that ran down the boy's forearms, producing the spots of blood that peppered the bed linen. No, it was the boy's thin smile as he gazed towards his latest guest, and the glassy sparkle in his eyes. The intense glare was as focused as that of a predator, and the unnerving smile said *I know something you don't.*

The boy's chest suddenly began to rise and fall faster and faster, and the penetrating stare was replaced with one of pain as his lips curled, his face contorted and a bellowing scream again began to fill the room.

The woman pushed past to pick up one of the facecloths and after dipping it in the water bowl, she rushed to the boy's side and began dabbing his brow. The gesture clearly had little effect and the boy began lurching forward, as best his bindings would allow, in futile attempts to bite her.

'You need to see this,' she said.

The man pulled himself from the spot and joined her as the boy now began thrashing and twisting his body, with his back arched to breaking point, as the woman rolled back his pyjama sleeve all the way up to the shoulder.

'This appeared just an hour ago.'

At the top of the arm, on the underneath side, a mark no more than an inch in diameter had been seared into the skin and, even before he squinted to focus, the man knew what it was, drawing a perplexed gasp from his mouth. It was shaped like a cross whose tips had been bent at 90-degree angles, all in the same direction, and it appeared jet black where the boy's skin had been burned to a crust.

'A swastika!' he gasped in disbelief as he struggled to take in what he was looking at.

At that same moment the young boy began to calm. 'Please,' he whispered with genuine distress in his voice, 'haven't you hurt me enough?'

He brushed the boy's temple with his hand, then leant close to his face. 'For you,' he said determinedly, 'the pain is only just beginning.' He had barely finished the sentence before a mouthful of spit was launched from the boy's mouth and sprayed all across the man's face. He recoiled in disgust as the boy once again began to thrash about wildly on the bed.

The woman immediately grabbed one of the fresh facecloths and placed it into the man's hands. He wiped his face clean of spittle and made his way to the foot of the bed, where he began loosening the straps of his brown leather satchel. He rummaged around for a moment and then paused, a wide smile spreading across his face.

'There it is,' he uttered in little more than a whisper, then he pulled out an object and held it in front of him.

The boy now stopped squirming and instead eyed the blunt metal implement being thrust towards him. Tears began to form in his eyes. 'Please, don't do this.' But the man ignored his pleas and instead proceeded to search his satchel for several other tools he planned to use. It would be painful, he realised, but wasn't it always?

The woman now moved behind him so she could see, over his shoulder, the young boy still writhing on top of the bed while desperately trying to snap the leather bonds securing him tightly to the headboard. Then suddenly, just like that, the boy fell silent, his body dropping limply onto the bed; his expression peaceful.

This sudden change made the man pause and his shoulders slumped in surprise as the leather satchel slipped from his grip and dropped to the floor with a heavy thud. The woman turned her attention to the man, who was beginning to rock back and forth with a small twitching of his head.

'Is it time to begin?' she asked, reaching out to place a hand on his shoulder even as the rocking increased. Slowly he turned around to face her and what she saw there made her neck muscles tense up in shock as she took one shaky step backwards.

His eyes were now bloodshot red, both pupils were dilated and black, and a thick white froth was beginning to drip from each side of his mouth. His nose wrinkled up in a snarl and he ground his teeth back and forth, with a stomach-churning crunching sound.

'We already have,' he growled, then launched himself at the woman, sending her tumbling to the floor with himself on top, before he slammed her head to one side and sank his teeth deeply into the thick muscles of her neck, tearing away at them with the ferocity of a wolf making its kill.

Amidst the commotion the young boy on the bed lay motionless, with a look of sheer serenity and as the woman's terrified screams morphed into deep gurgling moans a deep voice now hissed loudly from a darkened corner of the room. 'All debts must be repaid.'

Chapter 2

Professor Alex Harker gripped the semi-automatic rifle in both hands and then buried its stock firmly in his shoulder as another round zipped overhead, causing him to sink deeper against the concrete slab that offered him protection from the hail of bullets. He had twisted his ankle during his dive into cover but although damn painful, he was pretty sure there was no permanent damage. Lifting up his gun, he wrenched out its magazine before taking stock, and his heart sank. There were only three bullets left and, with two guards still alive, things were now looking dire. To make matters worse, they had him pinned down and with nowhere left to go… he was trapped.

Harker tapped the magazine back in place and loaded one bullet into the pipe as another four shots whizzed past him in succession. If this was it, then he would go out shooting. He glanced over towards the motionless body of his old friend Tom Lercher, lying face down in the dirt. Tom Lercher – or 'Doggie' to his friends – was the Dean of Archaeology at Cambridge University… or at least he had been before taking two bullets to the chest only moments earlier He was more than a friend, indeed he was family, and to think this was how it had ended for the old boy made Harker's sadness evaporate in an instant, as his blood began to boil.

With a reverential nod to his fallen friend, Harker flipped himself onto his chest and crawled over to the corner of the concrete slab, to quickly steal a glance. He immediately caught sight of the position of the nearest guard, dressed in full camouflage, who was leaning against the thick trunk of a tree off to his right, but he could not detect the other one. That was until a bullet hit the slab's corner just inches from his face, and in that moment, no more than ten metres away, he caught sight of the other killer to his left, dressed in a black boiler suit and resting on one knee at the forest's edge. Both men were barely in sight and he had to act fast.

Harker ducked back out of view as a cascade of bullets pummelled the concrete again with a series of heavy thuds. They had him pinned all right but there was still a chance, only a slim one, but given the alternatives he realised it was a chance he had to take.

Harker rolled over to the other side of the slab and peeked out. From here he had a clear shot of the guard kneeling, and then, God willing and with a bit of luck, he could take out the other one by the tree. He sucked in a deep breath and prepared himself. 'For Doggie' he growled through gritted teeth and then launched himself upwards and over the concrete slab running forward, with the rifle already pointing where he knew his first target to be. Then, for Harker at least, all the sounds faded away and everything went into slow motion.

The first shot was dead on and ripped into the first guard who, still kneeling and aiming at the other side of the concrete slab, was completely taken by surprise and, with little more than a yelp, dropped to the ground like a sack of potatoes.

Two bullets left.

The second guard had now clocked him and was already raising his gun towards Harker, who fired off a shot – but it missed and ended up burying itself into a nearby tree trunk.

Just one bullet left.

The guard meanwhile took aim and fired, but at the last moment the heel of his boot slipped on the muddy ground, sending the shot directly downwards into the earth amidst a puff of dirt.

Harker immediately seized his advantage and, by skidding to a halt with barely a second to spare, he pulled the trigger.

His bullet hit the guard squarely in the chest and the man immediately collapsed in a heap on the ground.

'YES! I win,' he yelled as something thudded against his chest and he looked down to see the familiar pink splatter from a paintball.

Harker gazed up in confusion to see Dr Chloe Stanton decked out in full camouflage outfit and face mask, her gun still pointing directly towards him.

'Actually, I win.' She smiled, then raised her arms up high and let out a yell of triumph.

'Hold on, I thought you were dead?' Harker exclaimed while scanning her for splatter marks.

'Nope,' Chloe called back with a proud smile. Then she did a twirl just to prove that her outfit was unmarked. 'How embarrassing for you.'

Before Harker could reply, an airhorn sounded somewhere in the distance and, as Chloe did a little victory dance, the second guard Harker had taken down sat up and pulled off his mask.

'I really don't like this game!' David Carter complained before letting out a heavy sigh. 'It's not much fun.'

'No, you only don't like it because you lost,' Harker replied with a sarcastic smile, as he removed his own mask and helped the portly fellow to his feet.

'Actually it's because we all just lost fifty quid,' a voice declared in an unimpressed tone from behind them, and Harker turned around to see Doggie making his way over while rubbing his back. 'That was the bet, wasn't it?'

The only person now grinning was Chloe who beckoned everyone towards her and put out her hand. 'C'mon, gentlemen, pay up.'

They were all now smiling by know with the exception of Doggie, who focused all his attention on Carter.

'Honestly, David, you had a clear shot so how did you miss?'

Carter looked insulted. 'At least I didn't get myself shot first, Tom.'

It was now Doggie who looked insulted. 'Yes, I did – but I was protecting Alex from the line of fire.'

Harker immediately burst into laughter at this notion. 'No, you weren't. You pushed me out of the way while making a rush for cover.'

'Exactly,' Doggie replied confidently, 'and in doing so I got shot while taking the heat off you.'

'Priceless, Tom, you're a true hero,' Carter remarked sarcastically, at which Doggie grinned smugly and took a bow. 'Now can we get lunch please?'

Carter turned around to go but had not taken more than a couple of steps before a paintball splattered pink all over his backside, making him jump upwards with a loud cry of pain.

'Oww,' he yelled and spun around to find Doggie pointing his weapon directly at him. 'What the hell was that for?'

Doggie lowered the gun and glared at Carter angrily. 'When I got killed this morning, and was lying on the ground, you walked over and deliberately shot me in the arse. A shot you appeared to take great pleasure in.'

Carter was still rubbing his sore bottom as he took a step forward. 'Hey, it wasn't my fault, just my finger slipped.'

Doggie followed suit and took a step forward, till the two men were within inches of each other. 'Yeah? So did mine.'

'Guys, this is silly. We're all friends remember.' Harker declared, secretly hoping the pair of them were about to shoot it out.

Carter and Doggie continued to stare at each other angrily until Chloe gave a small laugh.

'Wow, you boys take this game really seriously, don't you?'

This comment seemed to relax the two friends and they both turned to face her.

'Of course we do, madam,' Doggie replied flippantly, placing a hand on Carter's shoulder. 'War is no laughing matter!'

Now linking arms with the two older men, Chloe took the lead and dragged them away, whilst Harker lagged behind as many of the other players began to emerge from the treeline and make their way back to the main reception area. Doggie had chosen the location at Paintball Nation centre in Sidcup, not that far from central London and so a perfect venue for all those students catching trains back home to every corner of the UK for their summer holidays.

The University had organised it as an event for both students and professors to spend the day together, *bonding*, in a world gone mad allowing emotions and feelings to trump logic and facts. Away days were common practice and, even though it had been fun, there were other places Harker would rather have been. Still, despite all that, it had provided a glorious opportunity for him to dispense paint-balling justice on some of his more annoying students, which provided a pleasurable bonus. Unfortunately, he himself had ended up being more often on the receiving end than not but, regardless, he had made a few cracking shots and seeing the embarrassment of them being taken down by their professor had been priceless.

The thought drew a smile from Harker and as he watched his friends up ahead still arguing about who had shot the other first, with Chloe acting as referee, he found himself contemplating the varying journeys that had brought them all together.

Since their reunion party back at Mont St-Michel, three months earlier, things had been moving quickly. The final showdown, and complete destruction of the Magi hierarchy, had been received with relief and rejoicing at every level of the Knights Templar, but it had also led to debate on the secretive organisation's future role. Every yin needs a yang, every hero needs a villain and, without the Magi, many now questioned what the Templars' purpose was. What do the victors do once they have won?

With the deliberations still ongoing, Harker and the others had instead focused on their own individual situations. David Carter had accepted Sebastian Brulet's offer to become the full-time curator of the secret vault buried deep within the rocky island of Mont St-Michel, and now he spent his days rediscovering and cataloguing the vast number of relics and historical artefacts that the Templars had been collecting for centuries. The brutal, and rather embarrassing nature of the torture he had received at the behest of John Wilcox and his Magi loyalists had initially proved a serious bone of contention for him. But after gaining his new position within the Templars, and following an intensive course of extra strength pile cream, he had finally put that painful and invasive episode behind him, as it were. Brulet had even presented him with an official badge that Carter now took everywhere with him, and he found great relish in flashing it authoritatively every now and again. In fact the excitement of his work had even encouraged the ex-Cambridge professor to cut down on his heavy drinking; the man had even lost a few pounds and was looking sprightlier than ever. Regrettably his new-found resolve mainly applied during the day only and any phone calls made to him after 7 p.m. were usually met with that slurred and abrasive speech that Harker had come to expect and love. A drunk Carter was always more fun than the sober one.

Doggie had also been given access to the secret vault and now every few weeks he took a trip to St Michel where he was allowed to pore over the wealth of history contained within its walls, although always under the watchful eye of Carter who guarded the place like a bulldog. In a short time, the two men had forged a tight friendship, even if their massive egos ensured a healthy competitiveness between them.

Chloe, on the other hand, had continued in her psychiatric role at Blackwater and when she wasn't working she was usually flicking through wedding magazines and making preparations for their nuptials in the coming year. She had insisted fervently that Harker stay away from any such planning until the day in question, which was more than fine by him although he was fairly sure it had far more to do with her being a control freak than wanting to surprise him, as she had so far maintained.

As for Harker, the revelation of his own father's membership of the Templars had gripped him since learning of it and, apart from his busy schedule at the University, these were the thoughts that now preoccupied him. The documentation provided by Brulet concerning his father had been a revelation but had left him with as many questions as answers. For it transpired Liam Harker had indeed been inducted into the Templars and been granted the position of Jarl, which held not only considerable authority within the organisation but also entailed one of the most fascinating roles. Only a single individual could hold that position at any one time and it charged the recipient with 'determining any and all threats to the Templars and to civilisation at large'. That was the high-sounding brief but in practice it meant scouring the planet for any truths, legends or historical facts that might cause concern for humankind as a whole.

At first glance it seemed somewhat farcical but as Harker delved deeper into the records, it became apparent that it was a truly serious assignment. The position of Jarl had been initially formed soon after the Templars' divergence from the Catholic Church some centuries ago. In a world of unknowns, and when the exploration of reality was still in its infancy, the concept of witchcraft, monsters and everything else supernatural was still a very real thing. Today those ideas were still engrained in all earthly cultures in the form of legend and folklore, but in days gone by they had been seen as a genuine phys-ical threat to everyone and something which had to be addressed. Accordingly the Jarl was sworn to seek out and reveal the dark truths of the world, either to be dismissed as fantasy or to confirm and remove any genuine threats thus discovered. The historical records Harker had read so far were beyond captivating, including witches' covens, satanic societies, and even tales of defeating monsters. The last were taken by Harker with a pinch of salt but, in truth, who knew what animals and creatures might have still existed back then. In areas of the world untouched by man for millions of years, who could know what unique species had slipped through the noose of evolutionary extinction to remain in small groups until contact with humans was made. The obvious examples to Harker had been the English legend of St George fighting a dragon and Perseus confronting the sea serpent Cetus of mythology. It seemed extremely unlikely that dragons ever actually existed but who could know for sure, and perhaps there was some truth to such fables that had lasted until this very day.

Harker's father had been the last 'Jarl' in a line of hundreds, which at first had seemed an extremely high number but, upon reading of their dangerous exploits and given the nature of the job, it made sense. Spending your career chasing after everything and anything dangerous was not really conducive to one's health.

By the time Liam Harker had taken over in the twentieth century, most of these real or imagined dangers had been consigned to history or mythology, and the position had focused more on the dangers human beings posed, whether from cults, secret societies or even warmongering nations. Whatever the threats, his father had undoubtedly seen plenty of action in his time as Jarl, and the vaults' historical records attested to this in detail.

What was less clear, however, rested on the fact that his father had not been 'born into' the Templars and, even though Brulet considered Harker a Templar by blood, it wasn't clear why he had not been inducted earlier. Brulet had explained that, due to the nature of his father's work in dealing with various nefarious groups the latter had decided to keep young Harker removed for his own protection – and Brulet had decided to respect this. Furthermore, the Templar Grand Master had been considerably vague upon the question of how Harker senior had actually joined the Order in the first place or why the position of Jarl had been left vacant for over twenty years beforehand. Harker had not forced these questions because he was now totally concentrated on Brulet bestowing on him the honour of becoming the new Jarl. Besides which, with ready access to all the records and information pertaining to this area of the Templars' activities, he had no doubt he would discover the details for himself in due course.

For the time being, and especially with the complete annihilation of the Magi, the horizon looked clear and Harker had decided to allow Carter – with a little help from Doggie – to get to grips with everything contained in the vaults before stepping fully into his new role.

He also had ongoing commitments at Cambridge, and had spent the last three months putting his work in order before leaving his teaching role there for good. This departure from his academic career was difficult to make but the new position within the Templars seemed just too good an opportunity to pass up. He would now have access to aspects of human history and archaeological discoveries that no one else on the planet even knew existed let alone were able to get their hands on.

Doggie had been unusually understanding about his decision, which probably had something to do with his own new honorary membership of the Templars. For the Dean loved nothing more than being right in the middle of things, be it as host at a fundraiser or just engagement in the inner workings of the University. It was also this ensuing goodwill that made Doggie campaign for Harker being appointed a permanent member of the University's board of trustees, which meant he would always retain ties with the academic institution he loved so very much.

With all that said, however, there was still a very important question – perhaps the most important one – which was yet to be fully explained. And that was what the hell was the role, or the point, of a Jarl in this day and age? The last time he had seen Brulet himself was at Mont St-Michel during the celebration party, and since then his main point of contact had been with Carter. As Harker ran this through his head, he realised how little he actually knew when it came to 'Jarling' – if that was the right term for it. For now, he was focusing only on getting his affairs in order at the University and subsequently he was about to gain access to a hitherto unrevealed library of unwritten history and artefacts more impressive than any of the top museums and private collections in the world had to offer.

As Harker now caught up with his friends, they were already commandeering a table and chairs outside the reception building. Letting his recent thoughts fade, he couldn't help but release an excited chuckle. 'Not bad for a wee boy from Belfast.'

'Beer, Alex?' Carter yelled as he placed his paint gun down on a spare plastic seat and rubbed his hands together.

'I thought you normally abstained during the day?' Harker teased.

'I have, but beer is not a proper drink... Whisky's a drink. Besides...' Carter subtly pulled open his jacket to reveal the glinting badge that Brulet had presented him with. '…I may be able to get a discount if I flash this thing.'

'For God's sake why are you still wearing that?' Doggie exclaimed, dropping into his adjacent seat with a thud.

'Because, Dean Lercher,' Carter replied unashamedly while tapping the metal shield, 'it *means* something.'

'Yes, it does David, it means you're an idiot.'

Carter let go of his jacket and dismissed the insult with a wave of his hand. 'Chloe, would you allow me to buy you a drink?'

'Thank you, David, that sounds lovely,' Chloe replied, and with a wink at Harker she took Carter's arm and they both began walking towards the reception building, and the small corner bar inside it.

'Do me a favour would you, Alex?' Doggie asked, settling into his chair and enjoying this chance to relax his aching muscles, 'I left my wallet in the car. Be a good fellow and get it, would you? You'll find it in the glove compartment.'

He was already throwing his keys in Harker's direction before receiving an answer.

'Yes, your majesty.' Harker caught the keys and began to stroll towards the car park on the other side of the building, whilst Doggie called out to him again.

'You really are my best servant. Now hurry before I become impatient.'

Harker didn't even bother to reply.

The distance to the car park was no more than several minutes' walk and, on reaching it, Harker could have spent a few seconds scanning the entire car park in search of Doggie's Maroon S4 Volvo. But instead he made a beeline for the main entrance and sure enough, squeezed tightly between a filthy blue Mini Cooper and a silver

Peugeot 205 stood the vehicle he was looking for. Harker knew that the Dean had an uncanny knack of always getting himself the most convenient space in any car park. For a while he had surmised that his friend enjoyed better luck than most, but he had eventually discovered that Doggie made it a rule to always arrive at an engagement at least one hour before he was due, therefore ensuring the best place. Whether a result of OCD or just severe egocentricity, Harker wasn't sure, but who the hell hangs around somewhere for an hour beforehand just to secure bragging rights for gaining the prime parking position. And, furthermore, who anyway has the time to spare? Dean Tom Lercher, that's who.

Harker unlocked and opened the passenger door, reaching straight for the glove compartment. He found the thin black leather wallet immediately and scooped it out in one hand, then slammed the car door shut and made sure it was locked.

A voice called out from behind and Harker turned around to confront a young man in his thirties, with short-cropped black hair and wearing a blue cashmere pullover and a pair of tanned chinos.

'Excuse me?'

The man extended his hand and thrust a £10 note towards him. 'It was lying on the ground, and I thought it might be yours.'

Harker offered a shake of his head. 'No, not mine, but I'm sure you can hand it in at reception.'

The man smiled and then, with a nod, he pointed to somewhere directly behind Harker. 'How about that?'

Harker instinctively looked behind him and, as he did so, the man snatched Doggie's wallet from his hand and took off at a run towards the car park's front entrance.

'Hey.' Harker yelled, immediately bursting into a sprint after him. *Cheeky bastard* were the words that rattled in his head as he sped like a maniac. Besides this being bang out of order he himself would never hear the last of it from Doggie if he allowed the fellow to get away.

The wallet snatcher was far slower than his athletic form suggested and Harker was already catching him up by the time they reached the entrance. The thief continued around the corner and disappeared from sight for a moment and, pursuing him, Harker was met with a sight that brought him abruptly to a halt.

Catching his breath was the thief, standing next to another man, dressed in a grey suit and tie, who held out a Metropolitan Police badge towards Harker. 'I'm Detective John Owens; could we have a word, sir?' he asked politely before slipping the badge back into his inside jacket pocket.

Harker's hands dropped loosely to his sides and, before he could ask what the hell was going on, the thief threw him Doggie's wallet and then flashed his own detective's badge, clipped onto his belt and previously concealed under his pullover.

'Is it normal for detectives to rob members of the public?' Harker asked them, still taken aback by the bizarre charade.

'No, it's not, sir,' Detective Owens replied. 'We'd planned to come in and fetch you but, when we saw you in the car park, we decided a ruse was preferable. Pure luck on the timing, though.'

Harker was still looking doubtful at the detective's explanation, which was noticed by the other officer right away.

'We figured the last thing you'd want is to be taken away in a police car right in front of all your students, wouldn't you agree?'

Harker glanced over at the unmarked black BMW 530d parked next to them, and then back to the detectives. 'It's not exactly recognisable as one, is it?'

'That's true, sir, but we'd have had to enter the building and start flashing our badges, and that would have resulted in the same predicament.'

To Harker this was a sound explanation, but that was about all. 'OK, then, what can I do for you?'

'Actually, it's what we can do for you, sir. We're here to give you a lift, as there's someone who wants a word with you.'

The answer had Harker frowning and he glanced back and forth between them, with understandable mistrust. 'That's extremely vague, Detective.'

'I'm afraid it is, sir, but it's of the upmost importance, and I assure you we'll have you back here within the hour.'

Harker eyed the two men suspiciously, which was picked up immediately by Owens who now leant closer towards him. 'We have a serious situation developing sir, and it's one that the top brass believe you can help with.'

The officer looked sincere but it did little to shake off any of Harker's scepticism. 'And what would that be?'

'I'm not at liberty to say I'm afraid,' the detective continued politely, 'and you have every right to refuse, but I can tell you it's extremely important.'

For a few seconds Harker stood silently contemplating his response and then he nodded his head. 'OK, I'll bite, but can I at least change?' he asked, and pointing down at his paintball-stained camouflage trousers. 'And also let my friends know?'

'Afraid not, sir, as time is of the essence,' the detective replied. 'But my colleague here can let your party know that you'll be back soon, and who you're with... discreetly of course.'

Chloe would be a bit put out over him simply disappearing for an hour – but, seeing as this was official police business, she could hardly take it out on him, could she? Of course, she could and she undoubtedly would, but this matter sounded important. 'Yes, please. Be sure to let them know I'll be back within the hour, or my fiancée is going to throw a total wobbler.'

'A wobbler, sir? Not sure I know what you mean.'

To be fair it was more of a northern saying, so Harker wasn't wholly surprised by the man's ignorance. 'It's when someone gets so furious that they literally shake and wobble in anger. I suppose you could also say throw a shaker, but that wouldn't make any better sense now, would it?'

Neither man said a word, but just stared at him blankly.

'Just forget it,' Harker said in despair, and he tossed Doggie's wallet to the detective who had snatched it earlier, 'The owner is Tom Lercher, so tell him my travel plans, will you. He'll pass it all on.'

Detective Owens opened the BMW's back door and Harker slid inside, waiting for the officer to occupy the driving seat. Within minutes they were speeding along the A20 and heading north towards the nation's capital. Harker slowly became aware of a bulge in his camouflage outfit trouser pocket and it only then dawned on him that he still had the key to Doggie's Volvo.

Still it didn't really matter. He'd be back within the hour.

Chapter 3

The slanting glass dome of London's City Hall sparkled from across the river Thames as the black BMW 530d pulled up along Tower Wharf towards the red-striped barrier and the security guard manning it.

'Ever visited the Tower of London?' asked the driver, Detective Owens, as he wound down the side window to display his badge.

'A few times but never this way,' Harker replied, smiling back at the tourists now taking an interest in the only vehicle on the pedestrian walkway that ran parallel to the Tower walls. When he first realised where they were heading, he'd felt a jolt of concern, because he had presumed, given his current escort, that a police station would be their end destination. This goal was far more puzzling, though, and no matter how many times he asked, the good detective remained tight-lipped about who had demanded this meeting.

'Only deliveries or VIPs are allowed through this gate,' the detective now informed him as a guard inspected his badge and, with a nod, began to raise the barrier. 'So those tourists probably think you're royalty.'

As the BMW drove slowly through the stone archway, Harker couldn't help raising a hand to acknowledge the curious onlookers with a regal wave. It was a tad childish of course, but he couldn't help himself, and besides it would give them an interesting story to tell.

'I wouldn't get too cocky, sir. We're parking up just here.' Detective Owens remarked with a smirk.

Their car came to a smooth halt just beyond the entrance and, as more inquisitive gazes were drawn towards it, Harker gingerly lowered his hand and smiled uncomfortably. The detective then turned in his seat to face him. 'Your meeting is in the White Tower, right over there, just make your way inside the front entrance and someone will meet you, sir.' he said, clearly enjoying how uncomfortable Harker was now looking.

'Thank you, Detective,' his passenger replied, before he pushed open the car door and stepped out into the waiting crowd of tourists.

'I'll be here, sir, and don't be shy.' Owens called out, just as Harker slammed the door shut and turned to momentarily address his 'subjects'.

'Hello,' he began politely, as several smartphones snapped pictures of him. 'Great to see you all and thanks for coming.'

By now the onlookers were cottoning on to the fact that the man before them was wearing a stained camouflage paintballing outfit and therefore probably no one special, so the crowd began to disperse, allowing Harker the opportunity to slip off in the direction of his meeting.

Built by William the Conqueror in the early 1080s, the White Tower was gradually extended in the following centuries and became known simply as the 'Tower of London'. Initially constructed as a military strongpoint, over the following years it became a symbol of fear for Londoners and a warning to behave unless they wished to become a guest within its cells. Famous residents imprisoned or executed there included Guy Fawkes, Queen Anne Boleyn, and in the twentieth century it was even home for a time to the Nazi Deputy Fuhrer, Rudolf Hess.

Originally built from creamy-coloured Caen stone mined in France, the Tower symbolised the monarch's absolute power over his – or – her citizens, although these days you were far more likely to enjoy a good meal and trinkets from the gift shop than decapitation and a trip to the morgue.

Harker approached the White Tower's old-style, raised wooden walkway and made his way up to the main entrance, stopping at the top to take in the view of the Shard building across the way, its tip peaking over the top of the castle wall. With so many historical locations to see in the capital, this was a must, and Tower Bridge located next to it only added to the splendour, drawing millions of visitors from around the world each year.

He enjoyed one final glance at this magnificent skyline and then, with his hands snugly jammed into his boiler suit pockets, headed inside to meet his mysterious contact, whoever it might be.

The first room he entered was a testament to all things feudal, lined with cabinets displaying every suit of armour possible. It was truly a feast for the eyes of anyone wishing to learn more about English history or to get a few snap-shots to show friends and family back home. For Harker, though, this was something he had seen many times before and his only concern now – except for the meeting itself – was that it had taken forty-five minutes just to get here. So much for being returned within the hour!

He scanned the room, eyes darting amongst the crowds of people all scoping out the exhibits, and immediately clocked the only person not taking an interest in these displays but instead staring directly at him. This was an older man with white hair, a full beard and wearing a navy suit, red tie and a dark purple shirt – which surely meant that he was either colour blind or completely lacking in dress sense. Harker was about to offer an exploratory wave, to confirm if his instinct was correct, but the other man beat him to it and strode directly over with a serious look on his face.

'Alex Harker?' he asked in a quiet voice.

'Yes,' Harker replied.

'Follow me,' the man gestured and then did an about-face and began heading for the other end of the room. Harker followed close on his heels. From here a narrow wooden staircase led up to the first floor, then into a large function room with wooden pillars from floor to ceiling breaking up the length of the room. It contained four tables, each seating a number of well-dressed guests who appeared to be beginning their dessert course and as his guide beckoned him to wait at the entrance, Harker suddenly felt extremely awkward. Perhaps this was a normal reaction: *I mean who wouldn't feel out of place*, he thought, *appearing in a camouflage boiler suit covered with pink paintball splatters at a clearly swanky luncheon*. The weird thing for him was that, despite sticking out like a sore thumb, no one batted an eyelid. Harker was still scanning the tables for any obvious reaction when he was approached by a young, blonde-haired woman maybe in her twenties, wearing a charcoal business suit.

'Professor Harker?' She greeted him. 'Apologies for our cloak and dagger approach. I hope it wasn't too much of an inconvenience?'

'Not at all,' Harker replied, momentarily allowing her attractiveness to distract him, 'although this seems an odd place to meet with a police representative.'

For a second the young woman looked perplexed, then her eyes opened wide as she realised the mistaken conclusion he had made. 'Oh, I don't work for the police,' she said firmly. 'The detectives that brought you here were just doing a favour for me and the organisation I represent. Allow me to introduce myself. My name is Stefani Mitchell, and Sebastian Brulet sends his regards.'

The mention of Brulet's name in such a way had become a sort of Templar password for Harker and, as the penny dropped, he noticed that every one of the guests had now turned to him as they offered warm and courteous nods before getting back to their meal.

Stefani offered her hand and Harker shook it lightly. 'Pleasure to meet you Stefani,' he replied, though somewhat perplexed by the nature of this Templar meeting. 'You could have just called, you know? And please call me Alex.'

'Of course, Alex. I'm sorry but it couldn't be helped.' She raised her hands slightly in an apologetic gesture. 'There's a private office at the back, so I think it would be best to discuss everything there.' Harker followed her towards a small office, where she courteously ushered him inside before closing the door behind them.

The room was exactly what she had suggested: a straightforward office with several work tables, desktop PCs and a white marker board at the far end.

This was the first time Harker had felt truly at ease since getting in Detective Owens's unmarked police car. 'So they are all Knights Templars outside?' Harker asked, indicating to the dozen or so guests still enjoying their dessert.

'That's correct, Alex. We're all friends here.'

This confirmation had Harker nodding his head. 'Then perhaps you can tell me what is so important that I couldn't even get changed first?' He gazed down at his messy attire. 'Don't get me wrong, Stefani. If the Templars need me, then I'm here, but this meeting does seem to have been a bit rushed.'

'You're right but I'm afraid time is of the essence. Allow me to bring you up to speed.'

She made her way over to the farthest table, where she pointed to the nearest chair. 'Please, take a seat.'

Harker tugged at the leg of his boiler suit that had been riding up around his groin and dutifully sat down. This paintballing outfit was proving bloody uncomfortable.

'We were due to meet once you officially took on your duties as Jarl but due to unforeseen circumstances, that timetable needs to be brought forward. I was allocated to be – and still am your guide whilst you settle into your new position. Remember, we've not had a Jarl since your father died over twenty-five years ago, so a lot of this is new to me too.'

The fact that Harker's guide was clearly as unfamiliar as he was regarding the workings of his new job should have been worrying. In fact he couldn't help feeling glad that he wasn't the only one unsure what this newly resurrected position would entail.

'Well, that makes two of us then, so please go ahead.'

Stefani offered him a friendly smile, then took a seat at the work desk opposite. 'Last night news reached me of a double murder that took place on the outskirts of Turin, Italy. A young boy and his mother were viciously killed in circumstances that can only be described as… bizarre.' She opened the drawer next to her and pulled out an iPad, which she placed on the desktop next to her, then extracted a brown A4 envelope which she passed over to Harker. 'I must warn you, these images are extremely unpleasant.'

The warning only served to stoke up Harker's interest and he carefully reached inside the envelope to retrieve a series of colour photographs, the first of which had him turning away in disgust.

'I did warn you,' Stefani said as he now returned his attention to the offending image. 'And I'm afraid they don't get any easier.'

The first showed a naked woman propped up in a wooden chair with her legs splayed wide and her arms hanging by her sides. The deep, wide cuts across her body were too numerous to count but the nature of them suggested someone had slashed away at her in a frenzy, and had done so with such force that white ribs could be seen through the thick wounds in her chest. This alone would have forced Harker to look away but it was the damage to her neck and head that ultimately caused his most visceral reaction. The woman's entire head appeared to have been ripped off, leaving flaps of bloodied skin dangling from the neckline, but most disturbing of all was what had been deposited in its place. A young boy's decapitated head had been placed on top of the woman's severed neck, and his motionless blue eyes appeared to have been specially positioned so that they stared directly up towards the ceiling. 'Positioned' was the word because the head lolled forward at an angle, so this left Harker wondering how it did not fall off its perch. This gruesome question was answered when he noticed a small section of brown wood between the neck and the head, suggesting a stick or a broom handle had been used to fix the foreign appendage in place.

'Jesus, that's horrific.' Harker came close to choking on his words. 'Why are you showing me this?'

It wasn't an unreasonable question and Stefani responded by plucking the top photograph from Harker's hands to reveal the one underneath, which was as equally shocking. A decapitated body, also naked, lay sprawled on a bed and judging by its size – along with other more telling features – it was that of a young boy. More stomach-churning still was the water bowl located on a side table next to the wall, containing the head of a woman with long dark hair, her eyes staring forwards blankly. This presumably had belonged to the body from the first picture.

'I need your opinion,' Stefani continued and her strange request met with a perplexed look form Harker.

'My opinion?' he replied, still clearly revolted by the pictures. 'My opinion is that they're both dead!'

Had the circumstance depicted not been so appalling, his comment might have been considered comical and, without saying a word Stefani removed the photo to reveal the one underneath.

This third image showed just a wall and, because he could see the dangling wrist of the decapitated woman at its edge, he realised it must have been taken in the same room of horrors. A message had been scrawled onto the same wall, with red lines running downwards from each of the letters where the blood had dripped.

'Your opinion of that?' Stefani repeated, as Harker began to study and then identify the words.

'Well, I would say it's written in what's known as vulgar Latin,' Harker informed her as he focused on the words themselves rather than the sickening 'ink' that had been used. 'It's the common Latin once used by soldiers or working people of the Roman Empire rather than emperors or the scholars of the time.'

Harker ran a finger across the photo, translating as he went. 'You are I and I am you. When he is myth and we are reality. This grand deception will be repaid in blood.'

Harker dropped the photo into his lap and stared over at Stefani with a frown.

'Do you know what it means?' she insisted, biting her lower lip anxiously.

'It's fairly cryptic and evidently by someone with an axe to grind, but it doesn't ring any bells with me… Why? Who wrote it?'

If Stefani was disappointed with his answer, she didn't show it, but instead reached over and pulled away the photo from his lap to reveal the last in the set. 'Him.'

Harker looked down apprehensively with one eye closed, expecting to find another ghastly image, but instead it was a pleasant headshot of a smiling, grey-haired man and, so he relaxed and gave his full attention to it. 'He doesn't look that crazy,' Harker remarked, 'considering the damage he's done to his victims.'

Stefani now picked up the iPad from her work surface and passed it over to him, then switched it on and tapped on a film file.

'I've already watched it several times, which is more than enough for me.'

Her comment was ominous and, as Harker peered down at the revolving loading symbol, he narrowed his eyes in preparation for what might appear next.

As the clip began to roll it was difficult to make out any surroundings. The camera work was very shaky but, as it progressed, Harker soon realised it was the interior of a car.

'The police responded to a complaint about noise,' Stefani explained, pointing to the tablet. 'This was taken on a chest camera belonging to one of the responding officers.'

The vehicle suddenly came to a screeching halt outside a quaint-looking cottage, whereupon the cameraman got out of the car and swiftly made his way up the path, even as another officer joined him. The footage remained shaky but now showed one of the policemen taking the lead, and he was just metres from the front entrance when the door slowly creaked open. Both officers came to an abrupt halt and stood staring into the pitch-dark. 'Police,' a voice called out. 'Show yourself.'

All in a blur someone leapt through the opening and slammed hard into the lead officer, knocking the man to ground under a flurry of punches. Almost immediately screaming could be heard, and the cameraman's hands could be seen frenziedly struggling to pull the mystery assailant from his partner. It suddenly became apparent that the attacker had his jaws clamped around the officer's throat and even as he was grappled away, he took a thick chunk of the policeman's neck with him – before he spat it out and then, with a single punch, knocked the cameraman backwards onto the ground. The maniac next turned his full attention to the cameraman, as the wounded officer clung to his throat wound with both hands; at this point Harker got his first view proper view of this violent freak. A white, bubbling froth spewed from the man's lips, mingled with blood that appeared black in the evening light, and he now let out a deafening shriek before pouncing towards the cameraman.

Two shots rang out, one catching the frenzied man directly in the left side of his forehead and he dropped to the ground in a heap even as the cameraman got to his feet, breathing heavily, with his raised hand holding a gun which was now in view. The footage then came to a stop, showing the motionless body of the attacker lying face up, mouth wide open and eyes glassily void of life.

'Bloody hell,' Harker muttered, shocked by the violent footage, before taking another glance at the photo of a smiling gentleman in his lap and then focusing back on the screen. The fellow looked ravaged but it was definitely him, and Harker quickly placed the tablet onto the desktop, as if the very holding of it made him feel uncomfortable. 'Who is he?'

Stefani reached over to pick up the tablet and tap her fingers on the screen. 'Not who, but what.'

She passed it back with a news article now displayed, which Harker took a few seconds to scan through.

'Father John Davies,' Harker registered in surprise, and he passed the tablet back to her, 'He was a priest?'

'Yes, one whose training was called upon by the Vatican for specialised cases of possession.'

This explanation had Harker shifting in his chair. 'Father Davies was an exorcist acting for the church?'

Stefani nodded her head slowly. 'And he was attending an exorcism when all this took place. The boy had been afflicted for over a month and therefore, with Vatican approval, Father Davies was to perform the exorcism that night—' she motioned to the bloody photos Harker had studied earlier, '—and this was the result.'

A silence fell over them as Harker struggled with the very idea of possession and exorcism. He had never put much faith in the apparent causes, choosing to believe that it was the human mind that instigated such events rather than any 'supernatural' force exerting its will.

'Tell me, Alex, do you believe in possession?'

Stefani's question was asked in all seriousness and Harker treated it as such.

'Honestly, I don't know.'

His answer received a relieved smile from her. 'Good, because I feel the same way, and it's essential to have an open mind while going forward.'

Harker felt a chill run through him at her use of the word 'forward'. 'What do you mean, going forward?'

She got to her feet and placed herself in front of him, and Harker detected a pep talk of some kind was about to be delivered. 'I don't know what happened to Father Davies, Alex, but I can tell you what definitely did take place. A priest of the Catholic Church – and with its authority to perform an exorcism – simply murdered and mutilated a young boy and his mother in a way that even some of the worst serial killers would consider too messy. I should also mention that a friend of the Templars within the Vatican has asked that we look into this, because in twenty-four hours this story hits the media and I can't even imagine what it might do to the Church. A sanctioned exorcism that turned into a bloodbath?'

Stefani's main priority seemed a little off course to Harker and he couldn't help but think it an odd stance to take, considering the grisly nature of the deaths. He knew the Knights Templar had unofficial connections with the Vatican and indeed they had always taken to protecting it, but given the loss of two innocent lives, then surely they would be more troubled about the whys and not so much regarding who was going to take the fall. 'Why twenty-four hours?' he asked, choosing to overlook Stefani's rather cold stance on the matter – for now at least.

'Because, considering the implications of Vatican involvement in an incident so terrible, the police captain, – who is a practising Catholic, I might add – has, although continuing to investigate further, offered generously not to release anything to the media until the autopsy has been completed, which allows us twenty-four hours for you to find out what exactly is going on.'

'Me!' Harker felt a further chill run through him. 'What can I do?'

Stefani regarded him unsympathetically. 'The Templar role of Jarl was created specifically for this type of situation… to discover the truth, and protect people from it if necessary.'

Outwardly Harker remained calm and collected, but inside he was feeling increasingly twitchy. When he'd accepted the position of Jarl, he had essentially believed it was simply to go through and re-examine every item and artefact the Templars held in their possession. To be a curator like Carter only… only a head curator. This was quickly turning into something far more hands-on than he had anticipated. His experiences over the past few years with the Templars had certainly forced him to strengthen his character both in body and mind but dealing with a double murder! This, whatever 'this' was, seemed well beyond his skill set, after all, he was an archaeology professor, a scholar; not Hercule Poirot.

As Stefani continued to stare at him waiting for an answer, Harker found himself pondering on the responsibility he had taken when accepting the position of Jarl.

Of course having something like this dropped in his lap had never even crossed his mind but he couldn't just say no. It was a serious position and what would it say about him if he refused the first job handed to him?

'OK,' he replied, 'what is it you need me to do?'

Stefani let out a sigh of relief, then reached over and squeezed his arm. 'I can't tell you how glad I am to hear that, Alex. And if you are going to look into this, it's important that I be completely up front with you. I know I'm seeming to be more emotional about this than a Templar should, especially one who's going to be guiding you in your new role, but what no one else knows – including Grand Master Brulet – is that...' Her words trailed off and then her shoulders stiffened and a look of strength returned to her. 'John Davies is... was my adoptive father.'

This news came as a total shock to Harker but it still did explain why she had seemed so emotionally charged through the entire meeting. Adoption amongst priests was rare but in certain cases it was allowed after special consent from the Vatican had been obtained and evidently this was one of them. 'God, I'm sorry. I didn't realise.'

Stefani raised a hand towards him and clearly trying to maintain her composure. 'Sebastian, the Templar High Council... no one knows about these murders except us two and it has to stay that way.'

'Why?' Harker asked, perplexed by the notion of keeping it hush-hush when the Templars were meant to be a family: brothers and sisters who would help each other out at a moment's notice.

'I don't mean to sound condescending, Alex, but you're relatively new to the Order and, even though you categorically deserve to be here there are some things you have to remember. The Templars are a force for good and always have been. They are decent, self-giving and pragmatic, but they are also highly religious and devoted to their beliefs. If my father lost his mind for some reason, and as a result did those terrible things, then that is one thing. But, Alex,' Stefani paused as if the words were physically difficult to expel from her mouth, 'if my father was truly possessed by some supernatural force, a real-life demonic force, then I need to know first. It will have been the only time in Catholic history that an exorcist has become possessed by the very spirit he was seeking to exorcise. And it will have been my father, my line that allowed it to happen.'

Harker finally began to understand where she was coming from and, after a few seconds of frankly needless contemplation, he nodded in agreement once more. 'OK, Stefani, you and me. But once we discover the facts, we go immediately to Sebastian and the Council, agreed?'

As if galvanised by his offer, she nodded enthusiastically.

'But I want to bring in David Carter,' Harker insisted. 'I trust him and he has access to any Templar information I may need to source. OK?'

Stefani continued nodding even as Harker got out of his seat and placed Father Davies's smiling photo back down beside the others.

'I owe you, Alex Harker, and it's a debt I will repay,' she replied, pulling out her mobile phone. 'Give me a few minutes and I'll get a jet organised for you and also anything else you might need.'

Harker watched the young Templar woman head out of the room, leaving him alone, which gave him a moment to reflect on what he had just undertaken. In all his time on earth, he had never had anything to do with a case of possession, but he felt happy to help a Templar in need. Besides, truly awful as these murders had been, it would probably turn out that the priest had suffered some kind of major mental breakdown and, once that fact was established, he could fly home and together they would explain the appalling tragedy that had befallen Stefani's father.

It was with this comforting logic that Harker convinced himself. But as he glanced down at the horrendous series of photos, he felt those butterflies begin to twitch again in his stomach.

It had to be the result of a man simply losing his mind, and nothing otherworldly… didn't it?

Chapter 4

'That's creepy,' Detective Russo declared with a look of distaste. 'And he's a priest, you say?'

'Well, he was,' Harker replied, taking a few steps further into the living room. 'And it is creepy, yes.'

The small apartment was less of a living space and more of a tribute to all things avian, with its walls covered by framed pictures of birds of all species. This wasn't particularly odd, though perhaps a bit eccentric, but the hordes of stuffed animals littering the surfaces of tables and chairs did give pause for thought. Every bird Harker was aware of appeared to be represented. These included an American eagle, wings spread wide, hanging by a wire from the ceiling, while to his left a bright pink flamingo watched him as he studied the lifeless menagerie before him. The unpleasant atmosphere was compounded further by the lack of outside light which was being defused by the apartment's stained yellow windows, causing the shadows to shift from one moment to the next and giving the impression of movement from the otherwise motionless stuffed animals.

'I imagine Father Davies had an interest in taxidermy,' Harker suggested, reaching over to a motionless stuffed black raven perched on a wooden coffee table and tapping it on the head.

'I would say *obsession*,' Russo replied, electing to remain in the doorway. 'An unpleasant one, too.'

After parting company with Stefani back at the Tower of London, Harker had headed straight back to his home in Cambridge, care of Detective Owens, for a quick change and there to pick up his passport. The officer had initially appeared happy to provide a taxi service but had seemed visibly upset at Harker's request that he be allowed time to take a quick shower. Following possibly the quickest wash in his life, Harker had then been whisked away at high speed to Cambridge airport where, as promised by Stefani, a twin-engine Cessna Citation X jet was waiting for him on the tarmac. During the drive there, Harker had made a single call to Chloe, who at first had been furious for him 'dumping her' but, once his situation was explained, her mood had lightened... slightly. Sadly, this accommodating reaction was not shared by Doggie who, after grabbing the phone from Chloe, had literally screamed down the receiver and demanded to know where the hell his car keys were. After a quick apology, and a promise that Chloe would drive him to their house, where the keys were now waiting for him on the side table in the hall, the Dean had angrily hung up on him. This darkening mood was intensified further, by Harker himself this time, when he was informed by the pilot that Stefani would not be joining him and that he would be making this trip alone. He had called her straight away with the intention of throwing a few choice words at her, but had been unable to get through, which wound him up even more.

After sitting for most of the flight in a complete grump, he had come to the conclusion that Stefani had not wanted to draw any undue attention to herself by disappearing hurriedly from the Templar meeting at the Tower, which he had to admit seemed annoyingly reasonable. Whatever her rationale though, he felt like he'd been screwed over. But by the time he arrived at Rome international airport his blood had cooled, and being met by Detective Andrea Russo had helped immensely. The detective of the Rome's *Polizia di Stato* immediately introduced himself as 'a friend', and had driven them both straight to Father Davies's residence. The small apartment was within a stone's throw of the city's famous Spanish Steps linking the Bourbon Spanish embassy at the bottom to the Trinità dei Monti church at the top, and therefore the exterior of the place was impressive. The location was considered prime real estate – as pretty much everywhere in Rome was – and, with the Vatican just over a mile away across the river Tiber, it was a striking home for a mere Vatican priest.

The journey was made with little conversation and it became clear that Russo neither knew exactly why Harker was here in Italy or what he was looking for, and the man seemed happy to keep it that way – as was Harker. 'I was asked to drive you to this address, and I will help in any way I can,' the detective had merely offered, 'but the less I know about it the better.'

The cloak and dagger approach was only to be expected when it came to the Templars and, besides which, until Harker knew what was going on, he had no wish to drag the questionable idea of demoniac possession into the conversation.

'So, what is it you're looking for, Professor?' Russo finally asked, as he continued to hover in the doorway.

'Honestly, I'm not sure.' Harker replied, giving a mystified smile. 'Maybe I should have a look around.'

Harker's clueless response had the detective also smiling. 'OK, how is it you say... "knock yourself out"?'

In spite of Russo's offer of help, the man really didn't seem like he wanted to be here, and to be fair neither did Harker. But this was a way to prove his position of Jarl was justified and to that end he would do whatever it took to separate the wheat from the chaff – or rather the ectoplasm from the demoniac presence. He congratulated himself on thinking up such a bad joke and began navigating his way past the miserable-looking multitude of stuffed birds, who appeared to glare at their uninvited guest accusingly, and then on towards the rear end of the apartment, which opened up into a hallway with three rooms leading off it. The corridor was a mess, with nasty lime-green wallpaper peeling off at all angles and stacks of browning newspapers lined the skirting boards, giving it the look of a storage shed rather than a homely dwelling.

Harker entered the first room to his left, where immediately an unpleasant odour had him wrinkling his nose. The small kitchen was basic, with an ancient white, rusting fridge and a four-ringed stove that looked even older, its appearance not helped by it being covered in congealed grease. The grey linoleum floor tiles were clouded with age and a stained ceramic sink filled with unwashed plates protruded from the opposite wall. Either Father Davies had questionable domestic-hygiene issues or the priest had not been back home in a while.

Harker made his way over to the sink to find the source of the stench, which immediately made him feel queasy. Wedged between a couple of dirty dishes was a half-eaten ham sandwich that, at first glance, appeared to be moving, but upon closer inspection this was due to the maggots wriggling about on top of it. The sight only convinced him that no further investigation of the kitchen was needed.

The second room on the left was thankfully less offensive, with a neatly made single bed and an Ikea set of plywood drawers containing a meagre collection of trousers and T-shirts. At one corner was an en-suite bathroom which was cleaner than the kitchen and, with little else to check, Harker made his way back into the hallway and over to the final room whose door remained shut. He reached down to turn the cracked white plastic handle and poked his head inside.

If the smell of the kitchen had been unpleasant, what assaulted his nose now was downright offensive, and he recoiled back into the hallway with a hand over his mouth. It absolutely stank and Harker pulled out a white handkerchief from his jacket pocket and muffled his nose and mouth with it. The room was pitch black with seemingly no windows and, although it was impossible to make anything out clearly, he had the strangest sense he was being watched. He actually felt the hairs on the back of his neck stand up and this caused him to pull away from the open doorway and step to one side of it, out of view of anyone who might be lurking inside. The problem with instinctive feeling is that it is a process of evolution, a natural warning system that tends to favour caution above anything else, and if allowed it can override one's common and practical senses. Realising this, Harker now forced himself towards the open doorway, to peer inside with extreme wariness.

He was confronted by a wall of blackness at first but, as he slowly scanned the interior of the room, his eyes began to acclimatise to the dark and various shapes began to take form. He could now make out the edges of something, and maybe also a circular object on the floor, but no more than that. However as he continued to scan the room, his focus settled upon something that caused him to freeze and his blood ran cold. A pair of eyes stared back directly into his, with the light from the hallway just catching its pupils in nothing more than a temporary glint of light.

Harker abruptly pulled his head away from the doorway. 'Detective,' he shouted loudly, raising his fists to defend himself, while Russo came running along the hallway to join him.

'There's someone inside,' Harker informed him in nothing more than a whisper and the Detective, with no further persuasion needed, pulled the gun from his side holster and aimed it inside whilst taking cover at one side of the door.

'Police,' Russo announced gruffly. 'Come out with your hands up… and slowly.'

There was no sign of movement inside and, after a few seconds, he gestured to Harker with a flick of his chin. 'Reach for the light switch.'

It was a simple enough request but Harker found himself flexing his fingers nervously till, after an encouraging look from Russo he finally reached inside and slid his open palm across the inside wall until he felt the switch. With a nod to the detective, he flipped it downwards.

The room was instantly bathed in light from the single light bulb dangling from the ceiling and the sight of a shrouded individual standing before them had every muscle in Harker's body tensing. Even the well-trained Detective Russo was putting extra pressure on his trigger finger at first.

'What the hell is that?' Russo exclaimed, pulling his gun back to a resting position.

The unblinking glazed eyes of a bull stared back at them as flies began to zip around its head, having been disturbed by the light source now shining above them. Harker's first thought was that it was a man standing there in a mask, with a dark shroud wrapped around his shoulders which fell all the way to the floor, covering his feet, but a closer inspection dispelled that notion. Shreds of rotting meat hung from the neck where the head had been severed, and a gap in the shroud below the neckline revealed a section of the black metal candelabra that held it in place. The set-up reminded Harker of the terrible photos he had seen earlier that day of a woman's decapitated head impaled on a broomstick, and he wondered if this particular piece of artwork had been created as practice for the worse atrocity Father Davies would commit later on.

'That's pleasant,' Russo commented drily as he and Harker made their way on into the room and nearer to the revolting flesh sculpture on display. 'Your Father Davies was quite the budding artist.'

The bull's long blackened tongue lolled off to one side and Harker now examined the shiny ornaments surrounding the base of the candelabra, placed in a circle around it. A gold-coloured dish filled with coagulated gore sat directly beneath the head as if to catch the blood like a stale offering that no one in their right mind would ever want. Surrounding the gruesome effigy, burnt-out candles amid decaying bunches of flowers littered the floor, and a stained metal sickle protruded from the bull's neck. Judging by the blood smearing its surface the same implement had been used in dispatching the poor beast.

Neither man said a word as they approached this bizarre spectacle, with the foul smell of decay growing ever stronger. As Harker investigated closer, he noticed what looked like a black smudge on the bull's left cheek, so he craned his head around to one side and began to focus in on the mark while keeping as much distance as possible. Gradually a shape began to take form. At first, he thought it was a cross but, as he examined it closer, it became clear that this wasn't a smudge but a symbol – one that he knew well.

'It's a swastika,' he exclaimed, moving closer, 'and it appears to have been put there with a branding iron.'

Russo looked confused as he moved to Harker's side, inspecting the mark for himself. 'A swastika? What, like this is a Nazi bull?'

It sounded a dumb question but Harker could tell the detective wasn't joking.

'Not necessarily Nazi,' he replied, standing himself back from his inspection, 'The swastika itself was originally a sacred symbol used in many religions, Buddhism to name just one. It was only when the Nazis adopted it that it came to mean something altogether different in the eyes of the world.'

Russo was now looking particularly confused. 'You said the tenant here was a priest... was he a Buddhist priest?'

The question was going off on completely the wrong tangent, but it did still give Harker pause for thought.

'No, he wasn't a Buddhist but, that said, I'm not sure he was a Catholic either.'

'Well whatever he was, I need to call this in.' Russo took one last look at the bull's head, exhaled a large sigh and headed out of the room, and leaving Harker alone with his thoughts.

Exorcisms, bull's heads, swastikas? It was baffling, Harker decided, attempting to get his head around something clearly completely out of his reach for now. Following this gruesome discovery, what on earth was he going to tell Stefani? '*Hey, Stefani, checked out your father's place and you'll never guess… not only was he the first exorcist ever to become possessed but he also saw himself as prodigy of Damien Hirst.*'

As Harker contemplated how best to tell Stefani that her father was already nuts before undertaking the exorcism, a thudding sound began coming from the other room. 'Russo,' he called out but heard no reply, so he moved swiftly away from the bull's head and back to the menagerie of death in the living room, as the thudding continued. 'Russo, are you all alri…' Harker's words trailed off as he turned the corner to see Russo standing there upright and shaking. His first thought was the detective was choking, because the man was gripping at his throat with both hands. But as he swayed to one side, Harker caught a glint of steel laced around his neck, and then a hand connected to it and he froze.

Standing directly behind him, a hooded figure was pulling tighter on the wire garrotte as droplets of blood began to seep onto the detective's shirt collar. Russo's eyes were beginning to bulge due to the pressure around his neck.

'No,' Harker yelled and, as he launched himself forwards with arms outstretched, Russo was thrust towards him and slammed into Harker, who sank to the floor under the weight even as the hooded man, garrotte still in his hand, ran for the front door, sending stuffed birds flying in his wake.

Russo was now blue in the face and still clutching at his neck, but he managed a few words as Harker supported him under his arms. 'I'm OK,' he puffed finally, struggling to catch his breath. 'It didn't go deep.'

This was all Harker needed to hear and he rolled the larger man onto his side as carefully as he could, then jumped to his feet and sprinted towards the apartment's entrance. The front door was still wide open, and as Harker leapt outside into the stairwell, he could hear the scuffling of shoes on the level below. Without further thought, he raced down the two flights of stairs and towards the entrance leading out on to the street. He reached the last flight just in time to catch a glimpse of the hooded man's legs disappearing through the main door; a sense of urgency made him leap the last ten steps and he dived out the main entrance, almost breaking his ankle in the process.

The street was busy and though pain shot through his foot, he kept on moving. Up ahead of him the hooded man was already bounding along the street in a full sprint towards the Fontana della Barcaccia situated at the foot of the famed Spanish Steps. Harker knew the area pretty well but, with so many people milling outside, it wouldn't be hard to get lost amongst the crowds. As the hooded escapee started to pull away, Harker began shouting in Italian, 'Rapist! Stop the rapist!'

In almost any city in the world if a person shouts 'Stop that man' or 'Stop the thief', most people will not intervene, or if they do it's too late, but if a person shouts 'rapist' then almost always everyone piles in immediately and it was with this logic that Harker continued to yell at the top of his voice. Within seconds, heads within the crowd were darting back and forth and, as Harker barraged his way past the throng, he glimpsed his target's bobbing black hood in the distance, getting further away. With so many people it was impossible for any have-a-go-hero to tell who the 'rapist' was and instead people began to look towards at Harker with aggressive intent. As the hooded man put even more distance between them, Harker came close to giving up, his ankle now throbbing.

And then it happened.

The hooded man looked back for just a moment and, in doing so, tripped on something. What it was Harker couldn't tell, but the man went flying face first down onto the street and disappeared from sight. With renewed vigour Harker ploughed ahead and he reached the same spot just as the hooded man was still scrambling to his feet, whereupon Harker slammed into him with the full momentum of his body, sending them both sprawling to the ground and ending up in a heap right next to the fountain.

Harker was the first to get back to his feet but his ankle buckled underneath him and, before he could recover his balance, the hooded man leapt at him and propelled them both over the low boundary wall and into the main trough of the fountain. Harker landed face down and before he could pull himself up he felt a tremendous weight pushing down on his back to keep him below the surface. After that short but energetic chase, Harker already needed another breath of air and the panic of possibly drowning now fuelled him as he managed to flip on to his back and raise his head up to gasp for oxygen.

Above him his assailant allowed him no quarter, but instead grabbed him by his lapels and thrust him back underneath the surface, while some sort of unintelligible mumbling issued from the man's lips.

Back beneath the surface again, Harker stared with blurred vision and fought wildly against the rippling image of a hooded head hovering above him. The crazy thing was that the water itself was barely six inches deep, but this was all that was needed and digging his fingers hard into the man's forearms had absolutely no effect. Harker's lungs were now burning and then, as his strength began to weaken, the pressure around his neck suddenly eased, enabling him to propel himself upwards and suck in one of the most gratifying mouthfuls of air he had ever taken in his life.

Coughing and choking he still managed to look over and glimpse his hooded attacker sprinting off until he melted into the crowd, and out of sight.

His ankle aching painfully, Harker dragged himself shakily to his feet only to see a large man in an NYU sweatshirt moving rapidly towards him. He put up a hand and was about to say 'Thanks, but I'm OK,' when a voice from the crowd called out, 'He's a rapist. Stop him!'

Harker felt a solid punch catch him in the side of his head, then everything went black even before he hit the pavement.

Chapter 5

The woman's thick and matted dreadlocks slapped against her dark-black skin as she jerked her head backwards and raised her hands high above her head. 'And with dis truth you are free. No longer can the bonds of subservience bind you and no longer can those who seek to control your lives exert any influence.' The preacher's strong Jamaican accent meant certain words were shortened and, although not rare within the Catholic world, her very accent offered an exotic and vibrant feel to the sermon being delivered. 'You are now protected by the shield of your faith in me and in God, and if anyone has not felt the touch of this truth and enlightenment, let themselves be heard now or forever hold their peace.'

The small congregation maintained a respectful silence, with eyes wide open and still focused upon the silver cross the preacher stood next to. Numbering only six, this mesmerised group would have looked insignificant in any other setting but in such a small church, containing a couple of benches, the assembly seemed fitting. For this place of worship was nothing short of a hole in the wall and in the city of Rome, where basilicas – each with a rich history – reigned supreme, it was not exactly a focus for pilgrimage or tourism. The most impressive thing about the tiny church in fact was the beautiful stained-glass window behind the altar, stretching up to the ceiling, and it appeared to radiate a light from within it attesting to the fine craftsmanship of centuries before and now lighting up the preacher in a dazzling glow as she waited for a response, with her arms still raised.

A few seconds passed without any interruption, so the woman lowered her hands and a proud smile began to form across her bright pink lipstick-covered mouth. 'It is good to see dat your faith in me is unwavering, and is a reward dat shall be reaped back upon you tenfold for you are now my hands, my fingers and must know I will always be your body, your base, your strength.'

The shrilling of a mobile phone now began to echo around the sanctuary, and the preacher turned and scowled at the item responsible which lay on a simple wooden chair standing next to the altar. 'My apologies,' she said with an embarrassed chuckle. 'Even I myself am not without my failings.'

The congregation however, appeared unconcerned by this interruption and remained silent as the preacher strode over to the device and picked it up. 'One moment, please,' she addressed her flock, then tapped the green *accept* button and placed the phone to her ear. 'Yes?'

'Hope I'm not disturbing you?' a man with a heavy Italian accent began politely.

'I was in the middle of something.' She replied, glancing back at her audience who remained patient and motionless despite the interruption. 'But for you I always have time.'

'Good,' the voice replied in a more resolute tone, 'because I require your services, and time is of the essence. Are you still in Rome?'

'Dat I am,' she replied in barely more than a whisper, not wanting to be overheard. 'I was just finishing up with some recent converts to the flock, but this session will be ending shortly.'

'Ahh,' the man commented gleefully, 'there is no stronger zeal than that of a convert. I shall therefore await your call.'

The line went dead and the ping indicating a text message had her checking it. Then she reached underneath her white garb and slipped the phone into a trouser pocket. 'I'm afraid we have to cut today's service short,' she announced apologetically, making her way over the front pew and the man seated closest to her, 'but know I will be with you wherever you go.' She now patted his shoulder firmly, causing the attendee's head to slump to one side. His inflamed eyes continued to stare blankly ahead as blood trickled into them from where his eyelids had been sliced away. '*Always.*'

She turned her attention now to the rest of the congregation, who also remained motionless, and gazed upon each of their bloody faces and then down to the severed eyelids that had been deposited in each of their laps.

'I appreciate a captive audience,' she declared and began pulling off the white priest's garb and over her head. She then wrapped it up neatly before dropping it on the lifeless body of a man laid out flat on the pew behind. 'Thank you for the loan, Father, but I have no more need this.'

With a clicking sound from one the side of her mouth, the strange woman made her way to the chapel's entrance as the dead priest continued staring towards the ceiling, his eyes as wide as the others and his severed eyelids placed like medals across his top pocket.

'So, it begins,' She announced loudly, then unlocked the door and calmly made her way out into the bustling streets of Rome.

Chapter 6

'Professor, wake up,' Detective Russo growled before administering a hard slap across Harker's face. 'Are you with me?' His hand was already poised for another firm blow when Harker's eyes flickered open and he grabbed hold of Russo's forearm.

'Enough with the slapping.' he demanded weakly and, as his blurred vison became more focused, he began to look around him to get his bearings. He had been pulled out of the fountain and was now propped awkwardly up against its stone rim. 'What happened?'

'You got punched out by that guy,' Russo said indignantly, pointing over to a beefy-looking fellow wearing a NYU sweatshirt, who now raised his hands up apologetically.

'My mistake,' The man said in a heavy Floridian accent.

Harker gave an understanding wave and then suddenly everything came back to him. 'The one in the hood?'

'Don't worry, he's in custody. He ran straight into a couple of patrolmen at the top of the street,' Russo informed him with a satisfied smile. 'And he would have got away too, but the fool panicked and pulled a knife.'

'What happened then?'

'One of the officers wasn't as lucky as me,' Russo replied, pulling down his collar to reveal a thin welt cut running around his neck where the garrotte had dug in.

'He took a stab wound to the chest but he should make it.'

'Jesus,' Harker exclaimed, studying Russo's injury, 'you OK?'

'Fine, it didn't go deep enough but it would have if you'd not appeared when you did.'

The detective pushed his collar back up, and then hauled Harker to his feet, water running off his clothes and splattering onto the street as he did so. 'That man over there who punched you out, he thought he was stopping a rapist. Not a bad tactic, so shame it didn't work.'

'It was all I could think of,' Harker replied, now brushing down his sodden garments and becoming ever more aware of the large crowd surrounding them with interest. 'Where is he?'

'In the back of a police van over there.' Russo pointed over to a white transit van parked at the side of the road, the word 'Polizia' painted across its side. 'I thought you might want to have a word with him before he's taken to a holding cell, but we need to be quick. Attempted murder of a police officer is a serious offence, whichever way you cut it.'

Russo began pushing his way through the curious crowd and towards the van, with Harker, dripping wet, close by his side. 'You put up one hell of a fight. He could have drowned you.'

'Maybe.' The remark had Harker already shaking his head. 'I was about to pass out when he just let go. I think something must have scared him off.'

This received a knowing look from Russo. 'That would have been our helpful tourist. Lucky for you I reached you when I did, because he was about to punch the hell out of you.'

Harker could feel his ribs ache with every step, and he rubbed his chest where the big man had pummelled him. 'Yeah, really lucky,' he replied with an air of sarcasm.

Russo managed a vague smile. 'Bruises will heal, Professor, but I myself am going to have a permanent scar.' He pointed to his neckline. 'Now, why don't we both say hello to the man of the moment?'

Russo grasped the police van's back door and flipped it open so, for the first time, Harker got a good look at the man who had nearly drowned him.

He could not have been more than eighteen, with short mousy hair and a pathetic attempt at a beard which could only be described as 'bum fluff'. The offender looked anything but concerned about his predicament, offering them both a glare before returning to his navel gazing, while Russo and Harker joined him inside the tight confines of the vehicle. The teenager's hands were handcuffed to the seats on either side of him and, apart from a bruise developing on his left cheek, probably courtesy of the arresting officer, he looked none the worse for wear.

Harker took the seat opposite him, as Russo closed the door behind them and then sat down alongside. The only light now came from the rear doors, two porthole windows.

'Before we really start I need to get something out of the way,' Russo declared forcefully and, without warning, administered a heavy punch to the boy's already bruised cheek, sending him reeling sideways against the neighbouring seat.

'There's no need for that,' Harker protested, placing his arm defensively in front of the handcuffed youth.

'This little shit just stabbed a fellow police officer, so he's lucky I don't break his kneecaps.'

Russo's reaction was understandable but Harker wasn't about to let this go any further. He shifted his position and leant forwards so that he was partially positioned between the two men.

'Do you speak English?' Harker asked, but the boy gave no reaction. Then '*Parli italiano?*'

The teenager glanced briefly at Russo, then he returned to face Harker and offered a slow nod. 'Who are you?' Harker asked, using his best Roman inflection.

The prisoner remained silent for a few moments, then he uttered with a quiet, 'It doesn't matter who I am.'

'Considering you just tried to drown me, I'd say it does.'

The boy smiled at that remark before he slumped back into his seat. 'If I wanted you dead, you'd be dead just like that.' He held up his hands as far as his restraints would allow and snapped a thumb and finger together in a show of defiance.

Behind him Russo reached over and, before Harker could stop him, the detective gave the youth a hard smack across the cheek. 'And I could kill you even easier than that.'

Harker was about protest once more but the slap – or the threat of continuing punishment – appeared to settle the younger man.

'I am your wake-up call. I am the gun at the starting line.'

He spoke the words quietly, attempting to sound tougher than he really felt as do many teenagers, but Harker detected a sincerity in his response. There was no attitude in his tone per se but rather the suggestion that, whatever the boy was alluding to, he believed it wholeheartedly.

'What's your association with Father Davies?' Harker asked next, deliberately sounding more aggressive as Russo stared menacingly over his shoulder.

'He was on a journey,' the youngster replied with a wry smile. 'As am I… and, now, as are you.'

Harker sat back against the interior wall of the van and scrutinised the lad in front of him. Given his apparent youth, he was most definitely above his years in terms of maturity, for there was a confidence in his eyes and his demeanour had strength not built on testosterone but rather experience, and so Harker decided to treat this cryptic answer with the seriousness he felt it deserved.

'Do you know where Father Davies is now?' Harker asked, even though he well knew that at this moment the priest was probably lying in a refrigeration locker at the city morgue.

'Yes, he took a wrong turn and the path laid down for us has no room for detours.'

'And what path is that?'

'The only path that matters,' the boy offered sternly. 'That which leads to the kingdom.'

'And which kingdom would that be?' Harker replied, becoming impatient with this evasive back-and-forth.

'That is for you yourself to decide… and I hope you make the right choice.'

Russo was now visibly chomping at the bit. 'Enough with the bullshit, kid. I took philosophy 101, too. What goes up must come down. That which lives must eventually die. Stop talking crap and get to the point.'

He began to lean closer to the youth belligerently, and Harker gave him a restraining nudge. 'Are you referring to one of the two kingdoms?' he guessed.

The boy offered no response but instead turned his eyes to the floor of the van as Harker continued.

'The kingdom of Heaven and the kingdom of Hell.'

'You have no idea, do you?' The boy continued staring downwards. 'Just plucking at straws, trying to make connections that exist only in your mind.' He let out a deep laugh and shook his head condescendingly. 'His domain has been here since the dawn of time, but only now does he choose to visit it.'

The cryptic line of thought now began to make some sense to Harker, if only in a theological sense, and he immediately attempted to play into the boy's whimsical fantasies. 'You're talking about the arrival of the Antichrist, aren't you, and his kingdom is earth?'

The boy looked up with incredulity in his eyes and he let out a dismissive chuckle. 'His arrival occurred a long time ago, Professor, and I don't think you're going to make it.'

This mention of Harker's academic title and the puzzling nonsense Russo was hearing was as much as the detective could take as he pushed Harker aside and grabbed the boy by the lapels of his hoody. 'Enough of this movie talk, you little bastard. I want to know why Father Davies keeps a rotting animal head in his house, and I want to know what you were doing there. Not many teenage boys carry a garrotte on them and somehow you know he's a professor.' Russo gave a quick nod in Harker's direction. 'So you were waiting for us… why?'

'A test,' the boy replied in a nonchalant manner. 'A test you two idiots failed.'

This insult was the final straw for Russo and he was already raising his fist in the air, ready to strike, when the van doors swung open to reveal a man wearing the familiar black uniform and red-striped trousers of a Carabinieri officer's uniform. 'That's enough Detective. I allowed you a few minutes but I have orders to take him into custody,' the policeman stated firmly, 'and the less bruises found on him the better.'

At first it seemed like Russo was about to tell the junior officer to get lost, but then his clenched fist relaxed and he turned back to face the boy who was now smiling and looking as happy as a lamb. 'This conversation isn't over,' the detective hissed.

The teenager looked unfazed by this passive threat. 'Oh, I think it is, Detective Russo.'

Russo ignored this indication of the boy's obvious awareness of his identity and exited the van, followed by Harker.

'Good luck, Professor,' the boy called out and, just before the van doors were slammed shut, he shot off one last piece of advice, 'and choose wisely.'

'Freaky little bastard,' Russo spat out after they had put a few metres between themselves and the vehicle. 'You don't buy into all that crap of his, do you?'

'What… about the Antichrist?'

'What else?'

'Not really,' Harker replied as behind them the Carabinieri officer locked the van doors and started making his way over towards them, 'but from my experience I've found that keeping an open mind is crucial. The devil being in the detail and all that.'

Harker's play on words was ignored by Russo, who instead turned his attention to the policeman.

'I told you not to strike him,' the officer grumbled, clearly upset at Russo's technique of persuasion.

'It was only a little slap.'

'It doesn't matter. I'm the one who has to deliver him to the station and if he's all beaten up, they'll want an explanation.'

Russo looked unconvinced by such reasoning. 'That boy just tried to kill one of us. Trust me, they won't care so long as he's alive.'

The officer nodded, agreeably, although still unhappy, then he reached into his pocket and produced a folded piece of A5 card. 'I found this on him,' he said and thrust it into Russo's hand. 'Now, if you'll excuse me, I have a prisoner to drop off.'

'*Grazie*, Benito.' Russo said, brandishing the piece of card in his hand. 'Dinner next week with the family?'

Without a reply, Benito climbed in the driver's side and started up the van before briefly sticking his head out the window. 'And you're paying,' he declared at which he began driving off down the street, navigating through the pedestrians with sirens blaring.

'Family?' Harker asked as the van turned a corner and out of sight.

'He's my cousin,' Russo replied. 'Good man but he worries too much.' Now turning his attention to the card still in his hand, he unfolded it and held it visible between them both. 'What do have here, then?'

The card was marked on one side only and the message was handwritten with a fountain pen.

7 p.m.
Baths of Caracalla
Usual attire

'You think that means tonight?' Harker enquired, but already assuming the answer.

'I've no idea,' Russo replied before checking the other side in case he had missed something at first glance.

'I know the baths mentioned. Can you take me there?' Harker was now looking back towards Father Davies's apartment block and trying to remember where they had parked.

'Hold on, Professor, I think you've done enough investigating for now, don't you?'

The comment had Harker looking bewildered. 'We haven't discovered anything so far, except that the youngster who tried to kill us both has serious mental issues, and that Father Davies's extracurricular activities include butchery and animal sculpturing.'

'We actually know a lot more than that. He knew that you were a professor and clearly he was expecting us.'

'That's true,' Harker replied unfazed, 'but it leaves us with more questions than answers, doesn't it?'

'What do you mean "us"?' Russo's highly authoritative tone caught Harker by surprise.

'I thought you'd offered to help me in any way you could.'

'That's true, Professor, but the attempted murder of a police officer changes the landscape a bit.'

Harker rested his hands on his hips and turned away momentarily, as he got to grips with controlling the frustration attempting to claw its way out of his mouth. 'Are you religious, Detective?'

Russo offered a dry smile, leaning in towards him surreptitiously. 'I wouldn't be helping out the Templars, in clear breach of my official position in the Polizia di Stato, if I wasn't.'

'Good, then perhaps it's time I told you why I was asked to come here in the first place.'

Russo's silence in response only confirmed to Harker that the detective was willing to listen and so after a slight hesitation, he began to explain. 'OK, now bear with me, because this is all going to sound a little… strange.'

Chapter 7

Officer Benito Romano brought the police van to a screeching halt within just metres of a body lying directly across the road before him. It was impossible to tell if it was male or female as it wore a dark red leather overcoat with the lapels pulled up concealing the head.

He leapt out of his vehicle without delay, but he slowed down as he cautiously reached touching distance. He knelt down and placed a hand on the fallen body's shoulder, then delicately pulled it towards him, just an inch or so at a time, not wanting to cause further damage if bones were broken.

The light weight of the figure became a dead give-away and Romano soon realised what it was. Tugging it towards him until face side up, he let out a disgruntled sigh. The face of a shop mannequin smiled at him, its eyes wide in excitement, and Romano instinctively began inspecting the buildings on either side of the road. There was no one in sight, which was hardly surprising given the back streets he had chosen to take him back to Police headquarters, and he scanned the closed shop-fronts attentively until he spotted a dress shop with its front window smashed in. Two remaining mannequins greeted him with the same inane smile as their fallen colleague. Either Benito had come around the corner just in time to panic some low-level robbers into abandoning their loot in the middle of the street or a bunch of kids were at that very moment desperately trying to stifle their giggles at having watched him fall for such a stupid prank.

Romano picked up the mannequin and placed it back inside the shop's front window, broken glass crunching underneath his shoes. He himself had played a few jokes in his time but breaking and entering was not one of them. What was wrong with that age-old stunt of depositing dog crap in a paper bag and then setting light to it outside someone's house, only to have them emerge and stamp the flames out, providing for a hilarious finale. Now *that* was funny.

Romano made a final check of the other shop windows, hoping to catch a glimpse of a couple of sniggering street urchins but he saw none and so made his way back to the van and opened the driver's door. He could report the incident once his prisoner was safely behind bars and, although it had been a waste of his time, it would at least be an amusing anecdote to tell the others in his squad.

He was still considering whether it might make him look like an idiot when something solid slammed into the back of his shoulder, sending him crashing to the ground in an unconscious heap.

A woman loomed over Romano with the handle end of twelve-inch machete aimed in his direction and with a flick of her head she tossed back one of the long black dreadlocks that had fallen across her face. 'Go to sleep, little babylon,' she said mockingly in a thick Jamaican accent, then bent down to unclip the key-ring from the officer's belt. 'I 'ope you don't wake up for your own sake.'

She made her way back to the rear of the police van, then fingered though the keys before settling on the smallest one and inserting it in the keyhole. With a click she undid the lock and promptly swung open the twin doors, shedding daylight on the teenager handcuffed to a metal bench inside.

At first he looked terrified at the sight of a dark-skinned woman with dangling dreadlocks brandishing a machete but as she smiled, so did he and he leant his head back against the van's interior wall in relief. 'I knew you'd come for me,' he said in perfect English though with a heavy Roman accent.

'Dat be true, brother,' the woman replied, not shifting from her position at the open door, 'but you slipped up. You weren't supposed to be caught, were you?'

'They know nothing.' The boy shifted apprehensively in his seat and he raised his hands upwards pleadingly, as far as the handcuffs would allow. 'They're clueless. There's no need to change the timeline or the plan.'

His words had the woman nodding in agreement. 'Dat true, dat true,' she agreed, pulling the ring of keys from the door and dangling them in front of her, 'but we must always abide by our doctrine.'

The woman placed the keys on the van's floor and used her black T-shirt to rub away any fingerprints on them and then she raised the shiny machete towards the boy who was now focused solely on its glinting tip. 'And that is?' He gulped as a thin bead of sweat began to form on his brow.

'All debts must be repaid.'

Chapter 8

'You'll never get in there,' Russo declared as he and Harker watched the latest guest arriving at the main entrance to the Baths of Caracalla. The security guard scrutinised the invitation which the man had handed to him, then with a gracious nod he swung open the metal gate and allowed him to pass inside.

'How many have arrived so far? Over twenty?' Harker surmised, as he poked his head around the temporary metal fencing surrounding the adjoining car park. 'The guard over there seems to only be interested in one thing, and that's an invitation.' Harker brandished the piece of card they had retrieved form the young boy earlier. 'And I'm on the guest list.'

The detective shrugged his shoulders despondently. 'While all I need to do is show my ID and we're in, simple as that.'

Harker was already shaking his head at this idea. 'No, I need to find out what's going on here and if we waltz in there flashing your badge, they are likely to clam up.'

They both turned away as another car pulled into the dusty car park and two more men wearing black-tie got out and made their way over to the waiting guard. 'OK, wish me luck,' Harker said and, with a reassuring pat on the back from Russo, he strolled through the entrance and headed towards the guard who was still in the process of admitting the latest guests.

With the invitation already clutched in his hand, Harker tried to look as relaxed as possible, even if his stomach was beginning to rumble nervously. The worst thing that could happen now was to be refused entry and if that was to happen, then he'd come back with Russo and do the whole police badge thing. But if it was that simple, why did he feel so apprehensive? *Oh, I don't know*, he thought *maybe because someone tried to drown you earlier and your nerves are still shot to shit?* This seemed the likely cause, but as Harker reached the navy-suited guard he could not shake the feeling that something was extremely wrong here.

'Lovely evening,' Harker said with a smile, holding the invitation out before him in the same manner as the guests preceding him.

The guard gazed down at the invitation and then promptly whisked it from Harker's fingers. 'You are aware it's a black-tie event, sir,' he said on taking note of Harker's jacket and the slacks that still showed signs of dampness from his earlier encounter with the fountain.

'Don't ask. It's a long story,' Harker replied, managing to retain an air of superiority. 'But I could not miss this evening's event for anything, so here I am.'

The guard maintained his judgemental stare and then, with eyebrow raised, he examined the invitation card and passed it back. 'Follow the illuminated path to the main bath house, where your additional attire may be picked up at the entrance.'

Harker's ears pricked up at the mention of 'additional attire' because, except for perhaps an eccentric-looking top hat, what could anyone possibly add to black-tie.

68

'Thank you,' he replied and began making his way slowly along the path with flaming torches set on either side.

In its heyday the baths were considered the pinnacle of Roman ingenuity, and they could accommodate a staggering sixteen hundred people at one time in a number of hot, cold and steam rooms, as well as fifty-metre, Olympic-sized swimming pool. Built by two Emperors, Septimius Severus and his son Caracalla, the facilities were free and open to all citizens of Rome. The complex itself was so huge that a single extension aqueduct was constructed to provide enough water, which was then heated via underground coal and wood burners. An impressive feat even by today's standards, it must have been a sight to behold back in the day. Of course, after a couple of millennia of neglect and weathering, all that stood now were the walls but at thirty metres high they still commanded respect, and as the sun set over them this made for a spectacular setting.

Harker followed the torch-lined path all the way to the base of one of the massive walls where, from a small arched opening, a short man, no taller than five foot, wearing a distinct red and gold hooded cloak approached him. With long white hair tied in a ponytail, he would have fit in perfectly at a wizards' convention and Harker had to suppress the urge to look surprised by this little fellow's odd appearance.

'Can I help you sir?'

The man's voice was unusually shrill with a high-pitched squeak that could have made even a professional castrator proud.

'I'm here for this evening's events,' Harker declared with a ring of entitlement in his voice, passing over the invitation. 'Forgive my attire but it could not be helped.'

The odd little man looked him up and down after inspecting the invitation and cast a look of distain at Harker's clothing, which seemed rich considering his own bizarre get-up. He finally offered a nod and then directed an arm towards the open archway. 'Please, follow me.'

The sky overhead now beginning to darken, Harker was led through the ruins, room by room, until they reached a small alcove in one of the limestone walls, where a metal clothes stand had been placed. It was an odd to see this piece of modern equipment set here against the back-drop of such ancient architecture, but Harker remained silent as the little man selected a coat hanger holding an identical robe to the one he himself was wearing.

'You are the last to arrive,' the little man said, just managing to wrap the garment caringly around Harker's shoulders and, with a hop, flipping the hood up to conceal the newcomer's face. 'They are waiting for you,' he announced and that statement produced a pang of alarm in Harker. But, as he was guided into the adjoining room his nerves immediately settled. In the middle of the large unroofed space burned a small fire that had been built on the grass and around it stood more than thirty people, all in exactly the same hooded robes as he wore. With so many people present it was reasonable to assume that not every face would have been recognised by the diminutive guide, and Harker's hood afforded enough anonymity for him to observe without being rumbled as an outsider.

He made his way closer towards the fire and took a place amongst them, but seemingly not one of these people even registered his presence. Instead all seemed to be mesmerised by the fire there in their midst.

'Welcome,' called out a loud and joyous voice, and all hoods, including Harker turned to a gap in the farthest wall, where a man dressed in a white tunic and black trousers addressed them with hands high in the air. He was six-foot tall, completely bald, and with his thin, black goatee and manically happy smile, there was about him a whiff of Ming the Merciless from the famous comic strip *Flash Gordon*. Without another word and still with no verbal reaction from the people assembled, the man made his way towards the fire, stopped suddenly at a piece of broken rock about a foot in height which protruded from the earth, then stepped up onto it.

'This night your dedication is rewarded and you will become far more than you were,' he proclaimed. 'Now find your equals.'

They don't hang around, Harker concluded as all the hooded individuals now began moving about one another, checking each other's sleeves and, as he stood there bewildered as to what he had now stumbled into, he noticed a symbol embroidered onto the left arm of his robe in yellow cotton. It was a simple V, the Roman numeral for the number five and he watched as pairs of attendees with identical numbers began to link arms with one another – until everyone there had a partner except himself. It was at this point Harker felt a gentle tap on his shoulder.

He whirled around to face a robed figure holding up his right arm, which also had the 'V' symbol sewn into the sleeve. Even through the hood made identification impossible, it was obvious by the size of the figure's hands that this was a male.

The man slipped his arm under Harker's and began to lead him over towards the others, who were already lining up in a series of two rows of ten people in each. Even though every fibre of his being was telling him to run for it, Harker remained compliant as his partner pulled him into position at the end of the first row.

'Now each of you address your brother, and administer the bonds of strength,' ordered Ming the Merciless, with that same smile still resolutely emblazoned on his face. 'For through this act you may step into a new realm and let light shine over you for all eternity.'

Harker's new-found 'brother' took him by the hand and with his own other hand produced a thin strip of tanned leather string which he proceeded to wrap around both their wrists, as the other robed figures all did likewise.

To say that Harker felt uncomfortable at this moment would have been a mammoth understatement and as the bald-headed cartoon-strip lookalike began to speak again, he found himself desperately trying to figure out what the hell was going on. The hoods, the fire, the ancient setting... it was all reminiscent of pagan worship, maybe even Devil worship, but it wasn't a ritual he was familiar with – or wanted to be familiar with, for that matter.

'Now pray with me, brothers.' Ming continued, whereupon all the hoods lowered their heads to the ground as he began mumbling something unintelligible with his eyes closed.

This mumbling lasted for well over a minute and all the while Harker kept his head bowed along with all the others, until finally Ming looked up and gazed out upon them all, then spoke aloud once more.

'It is below the glowing stars that you enter a new stage of your existence and, by the power God has placed in me, I now pronounce you joined in union and forever more in holy matrimony.'

'What!' Harker exclaimed loudly enough that every hood in both rows instantly turned their attention towards him. But if Ming had heard anything, he didn't show it, and instead wrapped up the ceremony as quickly as it had begun.

'Congratulations, my nymphs. Go forth and rejoice now until next we meet.'

Harker was still reeling from the implications of what was just said as all the hoods – without saying a word and including his 'partner' – went off into the dark bowels of the baths' ruins leaving him on his own in a state of complete and utter bewilderment. *What the hell just happened?* he wondered.

Then, after a few seconds of stunned silence, a voice called out to him. 'It is finished.'

Harker turned around to see the same little fellow who had met him at the entrance.

'May I have the robe please.' Then without pause, he made his way around behind him and gently tugged the garment off him before folding it neatly. 'Please now follow me.' And Harker was led out through the entrance and back onto the path beyond, still lined with flickering torches. 'Have a pleasant evening,' he said, with a courteous bow, then headed back amid the shadowy ruins until he was out of sight.

Harker's head was spinning and he stood motionless in a confused daze, feeling like he'd just been mugged even though nothing was taken. It was clearly a ritual but unlike anything he had ever seen or even heard of.

'Professor.'

Harker spun around to see Detective Russo making his way up the pathway towards him and looking highly suspicious. 'That was quick,' he pointed out, looking surprised. 'I saw people leaving by car out the front, so I flashed my badge and came in here to find you. Are you OK? What happened?'

Harker still felt shell-shocked as he ran a hand through his hair and exhaled a long deep breath. 'I'm not sure exactly,' he glanced back at the ruins in confusion. 'But I think I just got married.'

Russo stared at him blankly. 'Uhh, congratulations?' He followed this up with an uncertain smile.

'Thanks,' Harker said doubtfully, 'but I think it was to another bloke!'

Chapter 9

'What kind of question is that?' Stefani yelled, forcing Harker to hold the iPhone away from his ear with a wince.

'A reasonable question,' he explained, as Russo rode the curb momentarily while just missing a pedestrian by inches, 'considering what we found in his apartment.'

The line went quiet and, after a few seconds, Harker began to answer his own question. 'Stefani, I know that whatever's happening here is not your fault, but since arriving in Rome I've discovered the only resident in your father's apartment was the head of a decapitated bull, then I myself was almost drowned by a man who an hour ago was found chopped up into pieces in the back of a police van…' Harker glanced over at Russo who was still looking frankly relieved at the news that his cousin had not been hurt during the incident. 'And I just became a male bride.'

Harker let his last words hang in the air for a moment and then, with continued silence from Stefani he repeated the question. 'So all I'm asking is, are you sure your father was a priest? And how well do you know him? What age were you adopted at? I left the UK with that part still being pretty sketchy.'

As Harker waited for an answer – any answer – Russo swerved again sharply, just missing an old man with a carrier bag carrier of shopping, who flicked the bird sign as they flew by. For a trained officer of the law, Russo was a bloody awful driver.

'Take it easy, Detective.' Harker scowled with one hand covering the mobile's receiver. 'I'd like to get there in one piece!'

Russo shot him a dirty glance of the type that said, 'If you don't like it then get out and walk.' He had seemed on edge ever since receiving a call informing him his cousin Benito Romano had been found unconscious and that the butchered carcass of the teen suspect lay scattered in the back of Benito's police van. The detective had since decided that his job acting as Harker's guide was over, and the sooner he dropped him off at the airport and headed back to Police headquarters the better.

'Can you hear me, Stefani?' Harker almost yelled.

'I can hear you Alex,' Stefani replied calmly, 'I've known him all my life and for the record I was adopted by him from an orphanage in Venice, as a baby. How do you think I got initiated into the Order of the Templars in the first place? You don't just apply.'

Up until that moment Harker had not even considered that Father Davies might have been a Templar, and now all these bizarre events seemed even stranger. 'He was actually a Templar?'

'Yes, since birth.' She sounded angry at his questioning but he ignored it.

'Why didn't you tell me that in the first place?'

'My father was recently shot at by the police after committing two horrific murders, Alex. Forgive me for leaving out some of my detailed family history.'

She was sounding increasingly furious and it was now that Harker decided to subdue his tone. 'Well, it makes sense that you'd want to keep all this below the Templars' radar – at least for the time being.' It was one thing for a family member to be involved in something so heinous, but an actual member of the Knights Templar – that was far more complicated and potentially damaging. 'Does anything I've just told you make any sense? I'm trying to make a connection here. Was there something he might have been involved in that was Templar-related?'

There was another short silence and Harker was about to begin demanding why the hell she was dragging him into all this without briefing him fully, when Stefani came back on the line in a far more measured tone.

'My father was one of only a handful of Templars who actively serve as a member of the Catholic Church. His position was what we call a "guardian": a Templar who participates wholly in his role as a Catholic priest but watches over the Church as a protector. He was never involved in anything other than that, and certainly not in the type of things you're speaking of.'

Harker had never heard the term 'guardian' before but it made sense that the Templars would have such a position. 'OK, if we put aside for one moment the supernatural elements surrounding his demise,' – and that was a pretty big *if*, Harker thought – 'could he have become embroiled in something while carrying out his guardian's duties?'

'Yes, it's possible,' Stefani replied, now sounding more collected in her thoughts, 'though he would have contacted us with any information that suggested even the slightest threat to the Catholic Church. But...'

There was a pause and Harker leapt upon it immediately. 'But what?'

'After you left, I did some checking into my father's phone records, and for the two days prior to his death he made a number of calls to a certain address in Greece. In fact it was the last number my father called before attending the, uh… the, exorcism.'

Harker could understand her hesitation, given what had happened, and considering the occult nature of such events he would have been twitchy on the subject himself. 'Who was it?'

'The curator at the Acropolis Museum in Athens.'

'OK, I'll take the jet there right now.' Harker replied without hesitation, but Stefani was already interrupting his generous offer to intervene.

'No, Alex, you've already done enough. I was just booking a flight there myself when you called.'

'Why? Use a Templar jet – it'll be a lot quicker.'

'I'd love to, but you yourself are using the only jet we could spare… without drawing any further attention. And, until I find out more, I still want to keep this between us.'

It seemed bordering on insanity not to get the rest of the Templar organisation behind them at this point, even if Harker understood her motives. What had set this whole thing in motion was unsettling enough but the whole business was getting stranger by the moment. 'I'll meet you there, then. We can look into this together.'

'I appreciate it, Alex, but if Sebastian Brulet knew I had already put you in harm's way – and not informed them – he would be unhappy to put it mildly.'

'No,' Harker insisted, determined now to see this through to the end. 'And, anyway, they would have to reveal everything to the Templars eventually. It's like you said, Stefani, I'm the official Jarl to the Templars, and so it's my duty. I'll see you at the museum itself.'

The ensuing pause seemed to go on for ages, then finally she came back on the line. 'Thank you, Alex. I'll let you know what time I'm due to arrive, and where we can meet up. After that, whether this leads to a dead end or not, I promise we'll bring everyone in on it.'

'Sounds good,' Harker agreed, glad to know that, whatever results the trip yielded, he would once again have the full force of the Templars at his back. 'See you soon.'

The line went dead and, just as Harker began tapping another number into his mobile, Russo gave him a heavy slap on his shoulder.

'Well, what did she say?'

'Would you just focus on the road,' Harker demanded while pointing in front of them, as Russo just managed to miss the traffic warden placing a yellow ticket on the windscreen of a rusty old green Citroen.

'Don't worry,' Russo replied dismissively, continuing to accelerate along the narrow city thoroughfare in the direction of the airport, 'he would never be missed.'

Russo was now smiling and, although still glancing between Harker and the tight road ahead, at least he now had both hands on the steering wheel. 'It looks like you're in luck, Detective. You are about to get shot of me.'

'Get shot of you?' Russo was looking offended. 'I never had any intention of shooting you!'

'I mean you're about to get rid of me. Just get me to the airport and your chaperoning is over.'

If such reassurance was meant to settle the man it most certainly did not, and Russo instead looked insulted. 'I'm happy to take you wherever you need to go. That's not the issue. You just chose one hell of a day to do it, that's all.

Murder attempt on a cop, dead suspect, cousin knocked unconscious – it's been a bad day.'

Harker had already returned his attention back to the phone and the number he was dialling. 'And it's all much appreciated, but shortly I will be one less thing you have to worry about.'

Russo managed a gruff snort and focused back on his driving as Harker waited for his call to be answered.

'David, it's Alex. I need your help. Where are you?'

David Carter's husky voice growled back over the receiver, sounding less concerned than annoyed. 'Where the hell have you been? You really pissed off Doggie, you know, taking his car keys. Poor old boy had a dinner appointment in London which he missed, thanks to you. He's not a happy bunny.'

'He'll survive, David...'

Before Harker could finish his sentence, Carter was already laughing out loud. 'It's been very funny actually. He was really getting his knickers in a twist on the trip back, whingeing and whining. Highly amusing.'

'Trip? Where are you?' Harker asked, having assumed they were still in the UK.

'We're back at the vault in Mont St-Michel. Doggie is with me. I think that, after being left high and dry, he wanted to feel important so he came along too. I was going to butter him up at first – you know, at least get him smiling – but then I thought what the hell so... you know how much he detests sugar? Well, when he wasn't looking I dumped four spoonfuls in his coffee. I think he has a cold because the fool almost finished it before noticing. He went absolutely ballistic. He is such a drama queen.'

'He's a diabetic, David!' Harker yelled.

'He's fine,' Carter replied casually. 'True, he was a bit twitchy at first and he did go a light shade of yellow but, like I said he's fine… now.'

Maybe because Carter himself had spent so many years not looking after himself and experiencing what could have been described by many as slow suicide through the use of alcohol, the man had developed a complete lack of sympathy for other people with issues or problems. Akin to a reformed smoker who then turns into a pain-in-the-arse advocate of all things pure, it was like he had personally reeled himself back from the edge of despair – and death – in his own life and so this badge of distinction, of bettering himself, somehow put him on a higher plain. Especially when it came to Doggie.

'OK,' Harker groused, not wanting to get into a shouting match. 'I need you to do some checking for me on satanic cults. I'm going to send you over a list and, from your own knowledge, or using Google, I need you to check if there are any specific references to them recorded in the Templar vaults.'

'Absolutely. But why, what's going on?'

'I'm not sure. In fact I have no idea.'

'No change there, Alex, but at least you're consistent.'

Carter sounded in an even more spritely mood than usual; perhaps he was enjoying a sugar rush of his own.

'Take a look at the list I'm sending and see if you can make any connections, any at all. No matter how much of a stretch.'

'Send it over and I'll take a look,' Carter replied, suddenly sounding more professional. 'If there's a connection, I'll find it.'

'Good and thanks. I'll be in touch,' Up ahead Harker could make out the entrance to Rome International airport which Russo was speeding ever faster towards. 'Oh and, David, don't give him any more sugar… please.'

Chapter 10

'There was no need to kill the boy, Michael,' the red-haired man exclaimed scathingly, slamming his fist down on the table. 'He'd done everything that was asked of him, and you know it.'

Michael Donitz sat seemingly unperturbed as he brushed a speck of black fluff from his white Charles Tyrwhitt dress shirt and then examined his fingernails. 'What I know, Marco, is that the young lad had a simple job not to get caught, and he managed to screw it up completely.'

In his late thirties and solidly built but of short stature, Marco Lombardi looked like he belonged more in a boxing ring rather than as a partner in a law firm, what with a crooked nose and a thick horizontal scar underneath his right eye. 'The boy was trained for this kind of situation, and we could have got him out safely if we had wanted to.'

Donitz wagged a finger from his seat across the table. 'It wasn't my choice, Marco, but had it been mine to make, I would have made the same call. Such complications are like threads and it only takes some nosy official to pull one hard enough to put us all in danger.'

Donitz's analogy did little to quash the younger man's anger. 'If wasn't you, then who?'

'Who do you think!'

Lombardi's eyes began to widen anxiously. 'I didn't think he was getting involved at this early stage.'

Donitz now looked astonished. 'Not get involved? It's all by his design, for Christ's sake.'

'No, I just thought—'

'You thought nothing. You never do, Marco; that's always been your problem.'

Donitz got up from his chair, paced over to the large single window and stared out onto the sprawling city below. 'Everything we have done, everything we have given up, everything we possess, including this legal firm, is because of him and our oath, and you're now having issues over one teenage boy. What the hell is the matter with you?' He remained at the window but turned his head to one side. 'I do wonder, Marco, is your commitment waning?'

'Never!' Lombardi hurried over to within a foot of him, shaking his head furiously. 'How could you even think that?'

'I'm not saying I do, Marco, but if *he* does… Well, you know what lies at the end of that road, don't you?'

Lombardi sucked in a long breath before clearing his throat and attempting to reclaim his composure. 'I'm sorry. I meant nothing by it but dutiful concern. I just think that boy could have been a great asset to us in years to come. So who carried it out?'

'The Red Death,' Donitz replied coldly. 'She's now in charge of this project of ours, unless he sees fit to alter that.'

Lombardi said nothing and simply offered a solemn nod as Donitz tore himself away from the beautiful view outside the window and retrieved his black Armani jacket from the back of the chair.

'He's called a meeting in the pit – for all of us.' He slipped the jacket on.

'What for?' Lombardi asked, looking highly suspicious.

'I presume he wants to update us on how his grand plan is progressing.'

Lombardi thought about this reply for a second and then, with his teeth clenched, he softly grasped Donitz's forearm. 'I'm now having doubts about this and can't help but wonder if this is the right course of action. If it doesn't result in the right outcome, years of work could be wiped out in the blink of an eye. No one has any idea we even exist and, until the time is right, it needs to stay that way.'

Donitz looked openly shocked at his associate's admission. He wrenched his arm away quickly and stuck a thick finger in Lombardi's face. 'You're beginning to worry me, Marco,' he said indignantly. 'The things we've already done! It's too late for second thoughts.' Donitz then dropped his finger and headed over to the office door. 'You have to ask yourself, Marco,' he continued, turning back momentarily with one hand resting on the door handle, 'what scares you more? That this "endeavour" fails... or that you fail him?'

Chapter 11

Harker made his way up the last flight of stone steps to the plateau on which the Parthenon sat and turned to take in the view. It was already well past midnight but, given all the lights glittering across Athens, it could have been mistaken for a city just gearing up for the evening's activities rather than bedtime. His jet had landed at Athens International Airport and, after a surprisingly brief trip into the city he had made his way up to the rocky outcrop of the Acropolis which rose in the very centre of the capital and offered a glorious sight of the sprawling cityscape below. Stefani had originally planned their encounter at the Acropolis Museum, just a stone's throw away, but had subsequently sent a text changing it. And, although she had not offered any reason, Harker was glad she had done so. He rarely visited this famed city and certainly not at this time of night, when access to the Acropolis was denied to the general public. Clearly Stefani had some pull with the authorities and, as he leant back against one of the towering columns of the mighty temple, he allowed himself to relax and just enjoy the experience.

Originally built as a shrine for the Greek goddess Athena and completed in 432BC, the Parthenon was considered a wonder of the ancient world and even today it stood as a symbol for the birthplace of Western democracy and civilisation. The roof may have fallen in long ago and the only remaining structures to survive over two thousand years were its impressive pillars, surrounding the original temple. As Harker gazed down across the ancient city, he could imagine how impressive the edifice must have looked back in its heyday. High above the city, like a beacon of human triumph the sight must have elicited in its citizens the same feelings of marvel and awe that the pyramids of Giza aroused amongst ancient Egyptians.

'That view never gets old, does it?' a voice spoke up from behind him and Harker turned to see Stefani leaning against the next pillar along.

'How could it?' he replied, slowly making his way over to her. 'Especially at this time of night.'

Stefani gave an approving smile. 'Being a Templar definitely has its perks. Especially when it comes to gaining access.'

Harker considered offering her a handshake but thought better of it as the young female Templar remained propped against the pillar with both hands firmly in her pockets.

'I lived here in Athens for a couple of years when I was younger,' she said, continuing to enjoy the view. 'It's funny but you'd be astonished at how many people actually born here have never bothered to make the short trip up to where we're standing.'

'It's always the way when you live in a city of historical wonders,' Harker replied. 'For tourists they are the attractions not to miss, but to the citizens living and working there they simply provide a stunning backdrop. I lived in London for years and in all that time I never once made a trip to see Buckingham Palace or Big Ben. They seemed just part of the landscape.'

Stefani continued smiling and then pulled herself away from viewing the stunning panorama and gave Harker her full attention. 'I know we were originally going to meet at the museum, but Mr Anastas – the curator – got caught up, so I thought why not enjoy the sights while we wait for him.'

'No complaints here,' Harker replied, beginning to register how distant and preoccupied she looked. 'Apart from the obvious, are you OK?'

'I'm fine,' she said firmly, a sense of purpose returning to her. 'But after we spoke, I delved a bit deeper into my father's past on the flight over and found out some things that were... troubling.'

'Well they can't be any more troubling than what I experienced in Rome. I got married, for God's sake. Try me.'

Stefani hesitated for a moment and then finally pulled her hands out of her pockets and rubbed them together apprehensively. 'After you questioned my father's position within the Church, I called a friend at the Vatican. I wasn't looking for anything nefarious, just to discover if he was given any new roles, or maybe even a change of parish – anything really.'

'What did they say?'

'They told me he hasn't been an officiating priest for over three years!'

This news came as a shock and Harker winced in confusion. 'How's that even possible? Wouldn't the Templars have realised?'

Stefani was already nodding. 'Yes, we would have known, which is why it makes even less sense, but apparently he handed in his collar, despite much pressure from the Church to try and convince him to change his mind.'

'Why?'

'My contact was a bit cagey but his official reason for leaving was due to a crisis in his faith and because he had fallen in love.'

'With who?' Harker asked astonished, thinking the man had been pretty long in the tooth to allow such notions to overcome a lifelong belief.

'I don't know,' she replied and with a frustrated sigh, 'but obviously he did.'

The idea that Father Davies – or rather Mr Davies as of now – would not have told his own daughter seemed perplexing to Harker. Perhaps he felt ashamed of something, like his disgusting hobby of dead animal posing discovered back at his apartment, but Harker could see the young Templar woman was still reeling from their news, and so he decided to tread carefully with his next question. 'You had no idea – not even an inkling?'

'No, nothing. I mean, over the past few years I had not seen him as much as I would have liked to, given all the troubles the Templars have experienced recently but I still visited him a couple of times a year including monthly phone calls, and he never mentioned a thing.'

Part of what Harker was now being told actually came as a relief because, after the unpleasant scene her father had left behind in his own apartment, it meant at least there was now no direct embarrassment to the Church. But that the Templars themselves had no idea meant only one of two things. Either they'd had the wool pulled over their eyes, or more worrying still, someone within the organisation had in fact known and deliberately covered it up. It was a disturbing thought and even though Harker had complete faith in Brulet, and those that guided the

Templars, what if there was someone working on the inside and more importantly – why?

He cast the unsettling question to one side, for the moment, and now turned his attention to the reason they were here. 'Did you mention any of this to the curator we're going to meet – this Mr Anastas?'

'No, I only confirmed that he once knew my father, and that I needed to meet with him as soon as possible. I wanted to gauge his reaction face to face concerning everything else.'

'That's smart… makes sense,' Harker replied. 'So how did you persuade him to meet us so late at night, and at the museum, which I know is always closed at this time?'

Stefani's worried expression evaporated and she glared at him amusingly. 'That bit was easy,' she replied and then checked her watch, 'why don't we stroll down there now? He should be arriving soon.'

Without actually answering his question, Stefani turned and headed for the winding path leading down to the Acropolis Museum below.

'Well?' Harker called after her, and then quickly caught up. 'Why exactly was it so easy?'

She continued to smile. 'Oh, once you meet him, you'll understand.'

Chapter 12

'Professor Alex Harker in the flesh, as I live and breathe. I cannot tell you what an honour this is.'

Adonis Anastas skipped merrily towards Harker and excitedly flung his thick hairy arms around him before administering a powerful hug. 'What an absolute treat it is to meet you. A real treat!'

He was a bear of a man standing at least six-foot-tall and with the chubby, yet solid, frame of a wrestler from the 1980s. With wavy black hair gathered in a ponytail, wearing brown slacks and a red striped shirt with sleeves rolled up to his beefy elbows, the man would have been a daunting sight if not for his friendly manner. The latter was something that to Harker was actually more unsettling than the man's size.

'I want to say it's a pleasure to meet you but... have we already met?' Harker asked, as Anastas released his lung-crushing hug.

'Not until now but I have been following your career closely these past few years, and the discoveries you have made during that time have been marvellous. You are truly a credit to us all.'

Since joining up with the Templars and thus gaining access to all their artefacts, hidden away and protected in its various vaults around the world, Harker had indeed 'discovered' many lost historical treasures including the gold death mask of Julius Caesar. Initially he'd felt a bit of a con-merchant because his only real triumph had been in convincing Sebastian Brulet to let him bring these artefacts out into the light of day, but on reflection his view had somewhat changed. Firstly, there was no way he could ever reveal how these items had ended up in his possession, because he could never betray the oath he had taken as a Templar and, secondly, without him the world would not have ever got to know about them. After some reflection he concluded it was nothing more than a necessary white lie which allowed everyone to now enjoy these previously hidden artefacts, so he felt justified in doing so. Besides, he was committed to keeping his most interesting discovery ever being revealed to the public – and that was the continuing existence of the Templar Order itself.

'And, Miss Mitchell, it is so good to finally meet you too.' Mr Anastas exchanged the constricting hug that Harker had received for a polite and gentle kiss on the back of her hand. 'I hope your father is well?'

With the police thus far holding back the details of the exorcism, it was no surprise that Mr Anastas had no knowledge of Stefani's father now being deceased, but still she froze slightly before smiling back at him.

'Thank you for asking,' she replied, while not responding to his question. However the polite brush-off was completely missed by Anastas who now turned his attention back to Harker as he thrust out his arm towards the building's entrance.

'Welcome to my museum,' he said proudly with eyes full of enthusiasm. 'Please come inside.'

With Stefani arching her eyebrows comically at Harker due to their host's obvious excitement, the three of them headed inside to find an impressive interior with the lighting already turned on.

With a total square footage of fourteen thousand square feet, the edifice was less museum and more of a tribute to the Acropolis of Athens itself. Containing over four thousand objects of historical significance, displayed over four floors, the foundations had been laid directly on top of Roman and Byzantine ruins. The museum was constructed on thick white stone pillars that acted as stilts laid carefully in between the ancient ruins. Outside the front entrance an enormous opening had been cut into the walkway itself, allowing visitors to lean over the plate-glass railings and wonder at the exposed remains of an ancient city that, although long forgotten by time, was today flaunted proudly by modern Greeks as a link to their distant past that should never again be lost.

The debris of crumbling walls was also a major feature and, leading up to the ground-floor gallery, the glass panelled flooring allowed visitors to see the whole extent of the ancient ruins as they proceeded.

'This place always reminds me of an airport terminal,' Stefani remarked in a whisper as they made their way across the gallery floor towards the main steps.

Harker shot her an unamused look. 'Philistine.' he replied quietly, so the excited Mr Anastas could not hear. The museum, to his mind, was one of the most beautifully simplistic showcases in the world, and designed to be just that. There were no hedonistic statues placed outside, bearing down on every visitor as they entered, but instead the basic rectangular-shaped building represented that perfection of angles ancient Greece was known for. The arrangement of exhibits inside was simple by design and deliberately intended to focus the attention of the millions of tourists arriving every year onto the wonderful collection of objects themselves. If anyone wanted to be bowled over in awe by some gigantic man-made structure then all he had to do was check out the towering Acropolis itself.

'My office is on the first floor,' Anastas explained, now sounding coolly professional, 'but I would love to give you a tour of the museum before we get down to business.'

'I'm afraid not, Adonis,' Stefani replied politely, 'as we're on an extremely tight schedule.'

Anastas came to an abrupt halt at the top of the stairs and turned to face them with a wholeheartedly disappointed look.

Harker felt obliged to step in. 'But if you're willing to give me the full tour at another time, I'd be honoured.' This suggestion perked the curator up instantly. 'I've been here before and my favourite area is without doubt the glass gallery of the Parthenon on the third floor. The frieze encircling the inner walls is exquisite.'

Anastas was now beaming at Harker's knowledge of the museum and he began to nod ecstatically. 'The honour would be mine, Professor.'

'Please, Adonis, call me Alex.'

The pleasantry worked a charm and Anastas was now gesturing them up towards a side door with a black sign reading 'Offices' in white lettering. 'Come inside.' With that he swung the door open and ushered them both through.

It was a thoroughly modern workspace with new grey carpeting and white walls adorned with photographs of the museum's exterior on one side, while on the other several large windows allowed a view of the illuminated Acropolis set high above them on the plateau.

'What a view,' Harker remarked, taking this opportunity to enjoy the vista, though Stefani appeared far more interested in an expensive-looking glossy, wooden work desk supporting a transparent Perspex display case holding a gold-leaf laurel with a red sticky label on it reading '*restoration*'.

'It's good to see the EU spending their budget wisely for a change,' she chuckled.

'Isn't it?' Anastas replied. 'For how can you expect to build a new future in Europe if you don't protect the past... In fact, Alex,' he strode over to the display cabinet, 'allow me to show you this as I think you'll appreciate it.'

Now curious, Harker joined him as Anastas donned a pair of purple velvet gloves that had been lying on the desk top before gently opening the display case and tenderly retrieving the gold-leaf laurel in his careful grip.

'This was discovered only very recently and although it's not been confirmed, and maybe never will be, we believe this laurel crown to be of Roman origin. Whoever it was made for, judging by the quality of gold used, and the impressive craftsmanship, he was a highly important figure within the hierarchy of Rome.'

Anastas seemed to be glowing with pride over the item, and he then raised it up and gently laid it on top of Harker's head. 'Just think, Alex,' he continued excitedly while keeping both hands hovering around the gold wreath protectively, 'this could have been worn by Augustus Caesar himself.'

The man's enthusiasm was infectious and Harker could not stop an excited smile crossing his lips. It was exactly this kind of moment that had made him fall in love with archaeology and to become someone who felt exactly the same way as Anastas clearly did. 'A real treat.'

'I pronounce you King Alex Harker, servant of the heavens and he who rules it.' Anastas declared with all the giddy silliness of a child, and Harker glanced over at Stefani who played along, by offering him a mildly condescending bow.

'I appreciate the generosity of your time, Adonis, but we really are on a tight schedule,' she chided. 'Perhaps you two boys can continue this during your next visit?'

Harker's smile disappeared and now both men looked a tad embarrassed. Anastas swiftly took the wreath back into his velvet-gloved hands and placed it securely back in its display.

'You're right, Stefani.' Harker admitted. 'But, Adonis, I would love to spend a day with you in the near future, and please let me know eventually what you discover about that beautiful piece of work, would you?'

'Give me your telephone number before you go and you have my word on that,' he replied. 'So, Miss Mitchell, it's down to business now. What is it that I can help you with?'

Stefani glanced over at Harker who merely tilted his head towards her, expressing a non-verbal wish for her to go first. She cleared her throat and began, 'Adonis, there is something that you may not be aware of, and in part it's the reason I'm here.'

It was obvious that he could sense negative undertones and he now began to look on in earnest. 'Then, please, tell me. Would you like to take a seat?'

'No, thank you,' she replied and with renewed resolve she began to explain. 'Did you know that my father quit his priesthood?'

Anastas looked unsurprised. 'Yes, I did – some years ago now.'

'OK,' she continued, giving no hint that for her this discovery was recent news. 'Well, yesterday… no a couple of days ago now,' she corrected after glancing down at her watch, 'he died.'

The shock on Anastas's face seemed genuine and he moved closer to her and took her hand. 'Oh, Stefani, I am so sorry… How did it happen?'

'He was shot by the police.'

'What? Surely not, for he was one of the gentlest people I ever knew.'

'I know. It's come as a great shock to us all.'

'Why?' Anastas continued to look perplexed. 'How?'

She was now becoming noticeably agitated and it was at this point Harker decided to enter the conversation. 'The circumstances are slightly murky but it would appear that Father Davies had been in the process of performing an exorcism and whilst doing so he became possessed himself.'

The moment Harker mentioned the word 'exorcism', Anastas's eyes began to widen and he pulled his hand away from Stefani's. His expression was not so much one of bewilderment but of realisation. 'What happened?'

There was no easy way to explain, so Harker just said it. 'He murdered and… mutilated the apparently possessed boy, along with the child's mother and then was shot dead by an arriving police officer.'

Anastas's breathing began to quicken and he pretty much *staggered* back to one of the nearby desks and slumped against it. 'It can't be,' he muttered, his lips quivering with every syllable, then looked uneasily towards the desk positioned at the far end of the room.

'Adonis, I know that he contacted you just before it happened,' Stefani interrupted as Anastas continued to stare over at that same desk. 'What did he say? What is it you know?'

It seemed like an eternity before he turned back to face them, but now his complexion had grown pale and sweat was forming on his brow. 'You didn't realise that he had left the Church, did you?'

The man's question was directed towards Stefani, and she stiffened awkwardly before shaking her head. 'I just found out a few hours ago.'

'Then you don't know what he's been doing, do you?'

She said nothing, but once again shook her head slowly.

'I first met your father about five years ago at a charity dinner in Rome held for underprivileged children. The museum was part of a programme that allowed such children from all over the EU to visit Italy and Greece, to experience different cultures etc. It was the usual type of EU project aimed at trying to create a unified European identity. Your father and I got talking and I discovered he had a fascination with Greek mythology. Anyway we got on very well, so I invited him here to the museum and our friendship began to take off from there. We got in touch with each other a couple of times a year, then one day he just turned up and told me how he'd quit the church and wanted to follow another path.'

'Did he explain why?' Harker asked.

'Not in so many words. It clearly wasn't something he felt comfortable talking about but I always got the impression he had experienced – or maybe realised – something that was incompatible with his role within the Church. What I did notice, though, was that he became fascinated with the concept of good and evil, not just in a spiritual sense but rather in a real physical, tangible way. It was quite odd, really, but I believed he was only trying to figure out what lay beyond religion – and reality itself.'

'Reality?' Stefani was now looking as confused as Harker.

Anastas took a deep breath and glanced over again at the same desk. Harker was about to ask why when the man began to explain further. 'It was as if he had come to believe that religion was not so much the final say but rather the outer layer of truths that lay beneath, and he had to know what those truths where. That's the best way I can put it because he didn't ramble on, as it were… but it was as if he had developed all these ideas that he believed were linked somehow and it was like he was trying to connect the dots. It was about this time that he started making trips to Egypt, Lebanon, Iraq and even the Republic of Congo in central Africa – going there twice if I remember. Then a month ago he turned up and told me this story that had me thinking he should maybe see a mental-health professional.'

'I could have helped with that,' Harker said with sincerity – then wishing he hadn't as Stefani now stared over at him.

'How do you figure that?' she asked sharply.

'My fiancée works with the criminally insane…' Harker let the explanation tail off and he glanced towards her gingerly. 'Not that your father was actually like that but… Sorry, I didn't mean…'

'It's OK. I know what you meant.' Stefani replied with no trace of bitterness. 'Please, Adonis, continue.'

Anastas was now also looking sheepish and he scratched the back of his head whilst looking uncomfortable. 'Your father told me that he had discovered the truth of life and what it meant, and that there were two kingdoms overshadowing ours but that history and all religions had got it all wrong. All topsy-turvy, as he put it. I suggested that his "two kingdoms" were the obvious – Heaven and Hell – but he became extremely agitated when I mentioned it and insisted that was exactly the same mistake religion had always made.'

'I met a young man earlier who also talked about the two kingdoms,' Harker intervened. 'Of course that was before he was murdered, and after he had tried to drown me.'

'Was murdered!' Anastas exclaimed in nothing short of a yell.

'It's a long story, Adonis,' Stefani said wanting the conversation to keep moving forward instead of getting caught up on following another tangent.

Anastas gawped silently at Harker for a few more seconds, then he continued with his strange story. 'OK, so he told me that deep in the jungles of the Congo he had found something that allowed him "the price of admission" to the one who revealed to him the truth of the real world and the actual nature of our reality.'

This whole conversation was becoming a little bit funky for Harker's taste, but on the other side of the room Stefani was staring diligently at the curator with a look of total fascination.

'What did he find and who was the one?' she asked, her mouth hanging open slightly in anticipation.

Anastas let slip a small gulp and he motioned towards his desk. 'What he found is locked securely in my desk drawer, and the one he claimed to have met was… well, he said he met the Devil… in person.'

Chapter 13

'Look, Stefani, I know I'm being a little bit blunt given that you just lost your father, but someone needs to be the voice of sanity here.' Harker was almost shouting at the top of his lungs.

Anastas began waving his hands defiantly. 'Hold on there, Professor. Don't forget that you came to me looking for answers. If anyone's being the voice of reason here, it's me. I was doing just fine until you turned up, getting all crazy.'

'Crazy! You're the one telling us that Stefani's father met with the Devil,' Harker yelled back. 'And what happened to you calling me Alex and saying what a treat it is to have me here?'

'That was before you called me a… what did you say? A whack job! How dare you insult me in my own place of work.' A dark rosy flush had now returned to Anastas's cheeks and he was still showing no sign of calming down.

'I didn't call you a whack job, you fool. I said that what you're saying is completely whacky, and that's not what a daughter who just lost her parent needs to hear.'

Anastas's temper finally began to cool on realising the mistake he had made, and Harker grasped this opportunity to return his attention back to Stefani.

'Please, listen to me for a moment, Stefani. What seems more likely? That your father managed to conjure up the

Devil, who bestowed upon him the secrets of life, or that sadly he had developed serious mental problems, travelled into the African jungle and, hey who knows, maybe he got stoned on some of the local peyote and had a crazy psychedelic trip.'

'Enough, both of you,' Stefani snapped, and then she pointed over to the desk that Anastas had seemed fixated on earlier. 'You said my father gave you something?'

Anastas glanced over at it too, and nodded. 'That is correct, and he asked me to keep it safe for him.'

'And are you aware it's now glowing?'

From Harker's perspective, directly underneath the ceiling light, it was difficult to tell if that was true and so he reached over to the light switch next to him, clicked it off and finally saw what the others in the room had already noticed.

From in between the cracks in the desk, could be seen a dark red light pulsating on and off, on and off, like an emergency light.

'What's causing that?' Harker asked as both he and Stefani cautiously moved closer.

'It did the same thing just after receiving your father's last call.' Anastas explained, gesturing towards the strange anomaly that was spreading red flashes of light across the white walls all around them.

'What is it?' Stefani asked as all three of them now stood around the desk.

'Take a look for yourself,' he replied and pulling a key from his pocket and then slowly unlocking the drawer which he then tugged open, bathing all three of them in the same flashing red. The object revealed was around five inches long, oval in shape and transparent as if it was made of quartz or crystal. Its ends were perfectly smoothed and rounded and the red light from it seemed only to be pulsing from the surface itself. The truly strange thing was that inside the object were small dots of light that zipped back and forth, like after someone sneezes heavily and upon reopening their eyes finds numerous little fizzing specks crossing their line of vision. It was a strange thing indeed.

'It's beautiful,' Stefani gasped and she raised her hand towards the object, but Anastas grabbed her wrist.

'Be careful. It's got some unusual properties,' he warned, then slowly moved her hand closer to it with her index finger still outstretched.

A thin blue electrical charge leapt out from the object and connected with Stefani's fingertip, and she pulled it away in fright.

'Don't worry, it doesn't hurt,' Anastas declared firmly, and Harker now moved his own hand towards it. Once again, a thin blue line of flickering electricity leapt up towards the tip of his finger and, despite the urge to pull away, he held it there as it licked the end of his finger like an electric bolt from a tesla coil. But instead of feeling pain, Harker felt no more than a tickling sensation.

Feeling more confident now, he moved his hand even closer and the blue charge now separated into two bolts, one still concentrated on his finger and the other one moving across his open palm. 'That's amazing,' he said, transfixed by the sight. Then the bolts suddenly disappeared and the pulsating red light cut out completely, plunging them into darkness.

'What happened?' Stefani asked as she watched the silhouette of Anastas making his way to the light switch on the wall to click it back on. The ceiling lights again burst into life and Harker and Stefani found themselves staring at each other blankly.

Anastas returned and stood beside them. 'Like I said, it did exactly the same thing soon after the last call I received from your father, and it stayed on only for a few minutes – exactly as it did just now.'

'What's its purpose?' Harker asked, clenching his fist shut, then opening it as the tingling began to disperse.

'I have no idea, but take a look at this.'

Anastas picked up the object itself and turned it over to reveal a cluster of engravings on its surface, running in a circle around one single larger symbol. The outermost circle was made up of identical symbols with which Harker was becoming ever more familiar, and he ran his finger around them.

'Swastikas,' he decided, counting them in a whisper. 'Fifteen of them circling around this other one in the middle but I don't recognise it.'

The central symbol was simple in its design and consisted of just two circles overlapping each other like a Venn diagram producing an oval where they crossed and inside that sat a six-pointed star which had been etched directly in the centre.

'That's a pentagram – the symbol of Satanism,' Stefani suggested, as Harker studied the strange object closer.

'No, it's not, since a pentagram has five points,' Harker corrected, 'and this star has six points. It's the star of David, the symbol for man.'

'Exactly,' Anastas said, now offering the object to Harker. 'Here, take it.'

At first Harker pulled away from the weird artefact being presented, then he blew caution to the wind and took it from Anastas's hand. The object was light but it crackled under the touch, as if a light electric charge fizzed across its surface, and he even laughed at the tickling feeling on the palm of his hand.

'Why didn't you tell us about this as soon as we arrived?' Stefani asked, with her eyes still fixed on it.

'Because it belonged to your father and you'd only just told me that he passed away. It was strictly his business,' Anastas replied, 'but whatever that thing is you're now welcome to it.'

This offer drew Harker's attention straight away and he looked at their host with surprise. 'You don't really think this is somehow evil, do you? You're an archaeologist after all, supposedly a man of science and reason.'

'That may be so but, given that thing's back-story and the fact that it pulsated in just the same way before her father went... crazy, I'm happy to leave it as a mystery, thank you very much.'

Harker was dumbfounded at this response. He didn't believe for a second that the artefact was in any way devil-related, but it was certainly worth further investigation.

'Why do you think it started glowing again just then?' Stefani asked, seemingly more curious than annoyed at her father having been just called crazy.

'Maybe it's a signal that it's time for you both to leave and take that blessed thing with you,' Anastas replied politely, still obviously extremely wary of the item. 'Consider it now yours in the spirit of our newly established relationship, Alex.' He thrust his hand forward and offered it to Harker. 'I somehow have a feeling that this is the beginning of a great friendship.'

A loud smashing sound erupted behind them and Anastas's whole body went rigid before he looked down at a small patch of blood that had suddenly appeared in the middle of his chest, soon spreading outwards like red ink spilled on blotting paper.

Harker spun around to see a hole in the window surrounded by cracks. 'Get down,' he yelled just before he leapt over and pulled Stefani to the ground, even as another bullet struck Anastas in exactly in the same spot and this time dropped him to the floor in a heap.

'Anastas!' Stefani yelled but got no response from the curator's glazed eyes which stared up at her as he remained motionless.

A burst of automatic gunfire now strafed across the windows sending glass shattering all around them. They lay huddled together until it finally stopped as suddenly as it had begun. Before Harker knew what was going on, Stefani had crawled across the broken glass, making minimal sound, then stood up to lean against the edge of the window. She reached inside her leather jacket and produced a black Walther P99 compact handgun, which she held up to one corner of the frame. 'Get over here,' she hissed quietly, and Harker carefully made his own way over the jagged shards of glass on all fours and reached her just as she poked her head quickly around the window's edge to steal a peek.

A second barrage shattered the frame and sent a thick chunk of plasterboard hurtling across the room. Stefani pushed Harker along with herself, backwards towards the doorway as further bullet holes exploded along the wall towards them. Without needing further prompting, Harker flung open the office door and the two of them threw themselves onto the cold marble-tiled floor outside as the final shot ricocheted off the wall and embedded itself deep in an ancient statue of a beautiful woman with braided hair.

'Jesus,' Harker gasped before checking the transparent object he was holding had not been damaged in the jolt. Once satisfied it was still in perfect condition, he dropped it into his jacket pocket for safe keeping. 'Why didn't you shoot back?'

'What's the point?' Stefani replied coolly, getting to her feet. 'That was a Herstal FN SCAR machine-gun, full metal jacket, serious hardware, and besides I'd rather they didn't know I have a weapon… yet.'

The Templars trained their members well, so this should not have come as a surprise. 'Have you got a spare by any chance?'

'Sorry, just the one,' she replied and Harker began rummaging through his pockets for anything he could use, before finally settling upon the only thing he found.

'It's better than nothing,' he whispered as he held up a steel-nib fountain pen.

His proposed weapon was met with a dry smile from Stefani, who shook her head and reached down to her ankle to unstrap a black, three-inch, boot knife that she slid over to him across the shiny floor. 'Now, *that's* better than nothing.'

With a thankful nod Harker picked it up and held it close to his chest as the sound of breaking glass could be heard from somewhere on the gallery level below.

'Front door,' Stefani whispered and she quietly moved over beside him and placed her finger to his lips. 'I'm heading over there.' She pointed to a small overhang where the first floor overlooked the staircase below. 'You stay here and when our mystery guest comes into view, I'll take the shot.'

In only about forty-five seconds the seemingly sweet young Stefani Mitchell had transformed into a highly skilled Templar operative and, as he clutched at his teeny three-inch boot knife, Harker was glad of that. The only blade he had any familiarity with was the type used to eat dinner with.

He nodded and watched as, with a light step, she made her way across to the overhang, then rested her gun on the railing waiting for Anastas's killer to appear. Meanwhile Harker hugged the two-foot-high partition next to the same statue of an Athenian woman that had taken the ricochet bullet, positioned at the head of the gallery staircase.

Thirty seconds had passed since the sound of the front doors being bashed in and from Harker's angle it was impossible to see anything below. After another thirty, and with still no further noise, his curiosity began to get the better of him. On his haunches he leant past the statue and very slowly craned his head around the topmost edge of the stairway.

The metal muzzle of a Herstal FN SCAR machine-gun gently pressed against his skull as the black-skinned woman with thick dreadlocks holding it smiled down at him, her pearly white teeth glinting from one of the stair lights.

'Ello there, pretty,' she rasped in a Jamaican accent, 'got something there for me, 'ave you?'

The woman clearly had Harker cold but he was already tightening his grip on the knife in his right hand, obscured from her view by the stairway partition. His muscles already tensing, he prepared to lunge. There was no way he could get to her before she unloaded at least one shot into his face, but if she wanted the artefact, would she really not want the chance to interrogate him as to its whereabouts? It seemed more likely that she would use the gun to try and knock him out and that delay might give him a chance to attack her – or give Stefani a chance to take a shot. *That's a point*, he thought to himself as the woman dug the muzzle harder into his temple, *where the hell was Stefani?*

His unspoken query was answered in the form of a gunshot that struck the assassin directly in the back. She toppled backwards and landed, face up and sprawling half-way down the wide staircase, with her machine gun noisily rattling down the steps and ending up on the tiles of the galley floor below.

'I warned you to stay where you were!' Stefani shouted in annoyance, and she began to make her way towards him. Harker was about to offer his apologies when he spotted something moving in the lower corner of his vision. He snapped his head towards it only to see the assassin already pulling herself to her feet, with the swiftness and speed of nothing less than a cheetah. Without hesitation he lurched for the statue next to him and slammed against it with all his strength.

The stone statue tumbled down hard onto the concrete steps and, even though it landed in front of the woman, under its own weight, it cracked into two halves and the smaller one smashed against her chest, slamming her hard against the stairwell wall so that she went down for a second time. The collision knocked her out cold and she slid down the steps like an unstable sledge, until the rubble now lying at the base of them finally brought her to a complete stop.

'That was foolish,' Stefani growled at him and she snatched the knife off him then made her way down to the body to check for a pulse, before securing the SCAR machine-gun by flicking it to one side with her boot.

'She's still alive… as she's wearing a Kevlar vest,' Stefani explained, then she did something that Harker had not been led to expect from a Templar. She stood over the unconscious figure and aimed her Walther P99 directly at the woman's forehead.

'NO,' Harker yelled, running down the steps to her level. 'You can't kill her in cold blood!'

'Nine times out of ten you'd be right, as it's not established protocol,' Stefani replied, still aiming her gun downwards, 'but this isn't a normal situation is it, Alex?' She now turned to him, her face glowing with sweat. 'Just look at the hardware she had. She's a trained killer and we're on our own here, no one to back us up.'

From the look in Stefani's eye Harker could tell she was absolutely serious and he gently placed his hand on her wrist and pushed it downwards until the weapon was aimed at the gallery floor. 'Then it's time we did get ourselves some back-up, isn't it?'

Stefani's face began to soften and she nodded agreement before placing her Walther back in its jacket holster. She then picked up the SCAR. 'We need to dispose of this safely,' she declared, shaking it lightly and, with a final scowl at the unconscious woman at her feet, she began to head towards the museum entrance with Harker following close behind.

'I'll call Sebastian and let him know what's been going on,' Stefani decided as they reached the main doors, which had been smashed in probably with the butt of the assassin's SCAR, and made their way out past the broken frames. 'We'll wait outside here until a clean-up crew arrives, and they can secure that woman and liaise with the police. In an unofficial manner, of course.'

Harker was well aware of the term 'clean-up crew' and although it sounded like something the Mafia would utilise, it actually referred to a Templar associate – or member – within the local police force who would become involved in whatever capacity was needed. In this case it would mean ensuring that the murderer of poor Adonis Anastas back there would be taken into custody and prosecuted. 'Shouldn't we wait to make sure she doesn't wake up and abscond?'

'I'd love to but there's a good chance the police are already on their way, after all those gunshots, and we can't be found here when they arrive.'

That made sense and it was clearly the right call but Harker couldn't shrug off the gnawing feeling of guilt in his stomach at just leaving Anastas lying dead on the floor of his own office. He now came to a stop at the glass barrier outside and looked down into the ruins of ancient Athenian buildings below. At least the curator had managed to pass on the artefact now sitting snugly in Harker's jacket pocket and although it provided little consolation, he vowed right there and then to find out what the hell the item was – and why the late Father Davies had coveted it so much.

'Come on.' Stefani yelled back at him as she began dialling into her Samsung smartphone. 'No time for dawdling.'

Harker was aware she had been through a lot of stress in the past couple of days, but so had he and this kind of teacher-speaking-to-pupil mode was beginning to grate. He took one last look at the ruins below, and was about to follow when something hard slammed into his back, flipping him over the railings and about ten feet down into the ruins below, with a painful thump. He was already thanking his lucky stars, for once not getting winded and landing in a small space with no ruins protruding up from the ground, when a shadowy figure landed beside him feet first and right side up. A plume of dust erupted in all directions and Harker looked over to see the same dreadlocked assassin glaring at him furiously, her eyelids narrowed in anger.

'You ain't getting away that easily, little man,' she mocked aggressively. 'I want what's mine.'

Despite the hard knock to his body, for some reason Harker was more offended that she had called him a little man, because he was certainly taller than she was!

The woman closed the two-metre gap between them in less than a second and hurled herself upon him, but Harker managed to raise his left leg squarely into her chest and flung her backwards violently, sending her skidding all the way back to her starting point.

'Not so small now, you crazy wench,' he managed.

The insult clearly bit as the assassin screamed in outrage and charged him ferociously, but stopped dead in her tracks as two shots from somewhere above dug into the ground between them.

'If you move another inch, I'll shoot you where you stand,' Stefani bawled down at her, the SCAR resting on the railing above so it was aimed directly at the assassin's head. 'It's your choice.'

All three of them remained frozen like the statues in the museum as the assassin mulled over her next move. It was only when the sound of police sirens closing in on the museum made Stefani glance back towards the road that the killer made her move. With speed she dove off to one side and into the shadows of the ruins, and thus out of Stefani's line of sight. A shaft of light from above now separated them, and she stared at Harker with menace as he got to his feet.

'Dat doesn't belong to you boy,' she growled, pointing to the bulge in Harker's jacket pocket. 'Dis ain't over... not by a long shot.'

With that, the dreadlocked woman disappeared into the ruins beneath the museum, and Harker watched until her blurring silhouette melted into the darkness and out of sight.

'Alex, we have to go now,' Stefani yelled from high above. 'There's some stairs over to your right.'

Harker scanned the gloom of the area he was being directed to and caught a shimmer of metal. Within seconds he had reached them and hurtled up to find Stefani disposing of the SCAR. She ejected its magazine, and after cleaning the trigger handle for any prints, she placed the weapon right in the centre of the entrance for the police to find on their arrival.

'This way,' she urged, her breathing heavy as the sound of sirens became close enough for the red–and–blue flashing lights to be seen reflecting off the Museum sign at the top of the steps leading into the main courtyard. Sprinting in tandem, they hurried down one side of the building and into an adjoining parking lot. Then, once they had reached the main road, both of them slowed to a relaxed saunter as another two police cars, sirens blazing, flew past them heading in the direction of the Museum.

'You good?' Stefani asked, sounding barely out of breath.

'Fine – and you?' Harker replied, struggling to maintain his cool due to lack of oxygen.

'I'll call Sebastian... but first we need to find somewhere we can talk.'

'Agreed.'

'Is that… thing in one piece?' she asked, glancing at his jacket pocket.

'Yep, but I still have no idea what it is.'

'Neither do I, but we will soon.'

'You can bet on that.' Harker agreed and, although still rocked by Anastas's sudden death and their narrow escape, he felt a growing confidence. 'Whoever or whatever is behind all this is going to get a rude awakening by the time I'm done,' he added grimly.

A grateful smile appeared on her lips. 'You know that in this modern age it's not really a Jarl's job to go chasing after trained killers?'

Harker smiled and a look of sheer determination descended upon him. 'Well today it is.'

Chapter 14

The night air was chilly as the small group of hooded figures made their way along a muddy path and up into the torch-lit cave entrance while the silver light from a full moon shone down upon them. Not a word was spoken as they negotiated the uneven stone surface in single file before moving ever deeper into the gloomy tunnel beyond. The only light came from small metal oil lamps that hung from the rocky ceiling, which all tinkled in the light breeze attempting to snuff out their blue flames.

The pathway itself was no more than twenty metres in length but, the further in the figures penetrated, the thicker the air became and sniffling sounds echoed off the stone walls as they approached a dim glow of light at the passageway's end before stepping into the considerable void beyond.

The cavern was oblong in shape with curved corners at both ends, and a smooth stone surface due to water erosion over the decades, with a ceiling over fifteen metres high. It proved more than capacious enough to house these latest arrivals now joining the small gathering already inside.

Marco Lombardi pulled back his black flannel hood and took a seat at the long rectangular dining table running almost the entire length of the cavern, before immediately taking a sip from the shiny metal goblet already placed in front of him. The sweet, velvety tasting honey-mead slipped down his throat with ease and then, with a shaky hand, he placed the goblet back on the table.

'Cold or just nervous?' Michael Donitz asked with a machiavellian smile as he sat down next to him on the bench.

'Please. It's chilly tonight,' Marco protested but swiftly withdrew his unsteady hand and placed it on his lap and out of sight.

Donitz only nodded, and took a sip of his own drink as Lombardi gazed down the table at the other men present and was met with smiles from some, while others continued talking amongst themselves. Everyone looked so relaxed that it imbued Lombardi with a sense of calm, but that quickly evaporated as a scraping sound began to echo through the cavern.

The oil lamps suspended from the ceiling began to flicker as a strong draught swept along the table and suddenly, at its far end something began to emerge from the rock floor, eliciting an eerie hush from all those present. Slowly the silhouette of a robed and hooded figure rose upwards until finally a form six foot tall stood before them.

They rapidly got to their feet in unison even as the figure stretched out its arms with its palms raised to the ceiling.

'Welcome, my sons.'

The voice was male and extremely low and it seemed, impossibly, to come from all directions at once. As those present remained silent, the robed figure took his place at the head of the table, where he slammed a gloved hand down onto its surface three times in succession. On the third stroke they all dutifully sat down, still none of them saying a word.

Only then did he speak. 'Thank you for meeting me here at such short notice. Your patience is, as always, appreciated.' It was said with courtesy but in an almost playful tone. 'You will be glad to hear that we are progressing nicely, and exactly as I foretold.'

His audience remained silent and heads began to bow in grateful acknowledgment – but then they abruptly froze as the hooded individual raised a finger straight in the air.

'But! There is something I need to address first, something unsettling.' The last word was spoken with a hiss and all the attendees glanced back and forth at one another uneasily. 'Our way of life – who we are, our very essence – is grounded on the very earth and rock of this reality. It is a reality we have sought to change and soon we will achieve just that.' The hooded speaker slowly pushed his chair back and stood up. 'But our strength and sense of purpose is only as strong as the bonds that link us, because without that, our foundation, our rock, begins to crack and crumble.'

The heads were all now nodding again as he began to slowly move down the left side of the dining table and behind the seated attendees, sliding his hand across each of their backs in turn. 'And in one of you I sense doubts regarding the path we have chosen to follow.'

Marco Lombardi began looking exceedingly uncomfortable and he shifted in his seat as Donitz glanced at him with a devious smile.

'But redemption is always possible for anyone as long as he recognises his own shortcomings, and in doing so may be retrieved from the depths of despair and returned to the fold by means of my loving embrace.'

The hooded figure came to a halt behind Lombardi and rested both gloved hands on the man's shoulders, which were now visibly trembling. 'Marco, is it true?'

Lombardi turned his head and stared up into the black depths of the hood. Then, with a tear in his eye, he offered a slow nod. 'It is true that doubts have entered my mind, Father, but I still remain loyal and therefore true to you and our cause.'

The hooded one said nothing and instead he moved back towards his own chair and raised his hand outwards. 'Your rebirth awaits,' he finally declared.

Donitz instantly grabbed Lombardi and pulled him to his feet, then dragged the quivering fellow towards one end of the dining table, as the hooded man sat back down and clicked his fingers.

Behind him a section of the cavern wall slid aside, revealing an adjoining room which was empty except for a plain, red stone sarcophagus with two horns sticking out from the top end, resting flat on four wooden plinths. On either side of the bulky casket stood a robed guard. They both had shaven heads and waited with wicker baskets at their feet.

By this point Lombardi was nothing more than a sobbing wreck as Donitz dragged him right up close, still smiling excitedly and the two robed men slid the heavy sarcophagus lid to one side.

'Please, Father, I have sinned but forgive me. I have always remained true to you and will ever do so.'

Donitz now appeared even more thrilled with his role as he began to shove Lombardi down inside the casket. But then he paused as the hooded one began to speak again, his back still facing them.

'Doubt is a shameful failing my son, and forgiveness will set you free. But lying can never be tolerated.'

Lombardi's tears began dry up and he now resisted Donitz, who continued to hold him firmly. 'But I have never lied to you, Father.'

The hooded man calmly swivelled round in his chair and began to stare in their direction. 'No, you haven't... but *you* have, Michael.'

One of the robed guards suddenly grabbed Donitz tightly around the neck from behind and slipped a cloth gag around his mouth while the other one pulled their new prisoner's hands behind him and slapped on a pair of handcuffs. Meanwhile Lombardi was released and he dropped to the floor.

Donitz now looked terrified and, although unable to speak due to the tight gag, he began to shake his head in frantic denial of the accusation.

'When you first had suspicions of Marco's doubt you never told me, did you?' The hooded one growled as the two guards restraining Donitz picked him up and thrust him into the sarcophagus, feet first. 'Instead you kept it to yourself – until I found out through other means, and that, my son, can never be forgiven.'

The two robed guards now pushed the sarcophagus lid back into place so that Donitz's muffled screams became only just audible. Then they picked up the wicker baskets and awaited their next instruction.

'Come to me, my son,' the hooded one ordered, standing up.

Lombardi rushed over and clasped both arms firmly around him. 'Thank you, Father, for your infinitely wise judgment,' Lombardi sobbed as fresh tears welled.

He gently pushed Lombardi away and placed both hands on his shoulders. 'Such flattery is most unbecoming to you, Marco.' He then clicked his fingers and one of the robed guards reached over and slid back a metal cover so that Donitz's face became visible. They then raised one of the baskets and directed it towards the narrow opening.

From the gloom inside the basket something small stirred, followed by another and then another until reaching its edge, something poked into the light. Something which caused the imprisoned Donitz to scream in terror.

The pincers of the shiny black emperor scorpion clicked together just before it dropped into the sarcophagus and onto Michael Donitz's face. There it immediately administered a sting to his left cheek, causing him to convulse in pain within his small prison. Another scorpion now appeared at the basket's rim but, before it could leap down, both the robed guards tipped their wicker containers forward, simultaneously shedding dozens of these small stinging beasts right on top of the man's face.

With the screaming getting louder and more frenzied, the slot on the sarcophagus cover was slid shut so his yells of agony and fear became muffled.

The man addressed as 'Father' now turned his attention back to Lombardi, wiping away his tears with a gloved hand. 'Now re-join the others, but know this: your doubts must be addressed. You need no rebirth, but instead a show of faith must be given.'

Lombardi stole a glance at the sarcophagus, which was now rocking back and forth in desperation and he shuddered. 'I will prove my faith, Father. I now make you that promise.'

'Good.' Father gestured Lombardi back to his seat. To his left, another small portion of the cave wall slid away, and a man in a black suit emerged, holding a silver platter with a glazed suckling pig resting on top. 'Now let us eat, my sons, and discuss our plans further.'

Chapter 15

'Sebastian Brulet sends his regards,' Stefani said as she climbed up the flip stairs and into the cabin of the Cessna Citation X jet, 'and you'll be happy to know he didn't seem as pissed off as he could have been.'

Harker slouched back in his seat and let out a light sigh. 'Good. That's one less thing we have to worry about.'

They had caught a taxi straight away and had been holed up inside the jet for the past few hours, in case a quick getaway was required. There had been no news reports as yet concerning the murder of Adonis Anastas, but Harker wanted to be in the air before it received national coverage.

Stefani reeled in the steps and then closed the door behind her, just as one of the pilots poked his head around the cloth drape dividing the cockpit. 'Do we have a destination?' he asked in a Scottish accent.

'We do,' Stefani replied and handed the captain a note. 'Would you please file a flight plan, as we'll need to leave shortly.'

She took the seat opposite Harker and stared at him as he continued his examination of the strange artefact retrieved from the museum. 'It means a lot to you what he thinks, doesn't it?'

'Who… Sebastian?' he replied, continuing to rub his fingers across the undeciphered engravings, clearly deep in thought as to its origins.

'Yes, I mean Grand Master Brulet.'

'If you're insinuating he's like a father figure to me, you'd be wrong.'

Stefani gave an amused chuckle. 'You have to admit it does sometimes seem like that.'

Harker placed the artefact on the table between them and stared at her knowingly. 'When I first met Sebastian he was more of a mystery to me than anything else, and because of the unique way I entered the Templar organisation it makes my relationship with him different from most others – such as yourself.'

This explanation was given with a sliver of sarcasm and Stefani now adopted Harker's relaxed demeanour by slouching back into her own seat and placing both hands behind her head. 'Do tell.'

Harker was now enjoying the uncaring, too-cool-for-school body language Stefani was giving off and he too placed his hands behind his head and upped the ante by stretching his muscles with a satisfied groan. 'Almost all Templars are inducted from a young age, correct?'

Stefani continued to smile, offering a slow nod of her head.

'Well, to an impressionable child the Grand Master must seem like a giant of a man – the head of a family, if you will – and along with his distinctive appearance and those cross-shaped pupils of his, it would be hard not to hold him in a certain, perhaps mystical, reverence.'

'Now that is true,' she replied and was also clearly enjoying this moment of play after those heart-pounding moments back at the museum, 'When I was first introduced to Sebastian, I was only six and my father said that he found me in an orphanage and that I showed promise. I will admit, initially, that I found him frankly terrifying, but the conversation we then had put me at ease right away.'

'Oh, what exactly did he say to such a fragile, young slip of a girl?' Harker replied, trying not to chuckle over his blatant teasing of her.

'He joked that, although he might have the appearance of a wizard, his spell-making abilities were zero and if he possessed a wizard's name it would be "Snotbags", because the only thing he could conjure up these days was a snotty cold.'

This comment had Harker laughing out loud. 'He does have a way of putting one at ease, doesn't he?'

'He certainly does,' Stefani replied, but now looking serious. 'You're right when you suggest I held him in the upmost esteem from the get-go – and I still do. So, then, Alex Harker, how is it that our views of him differ?'

Harker definitely detected a spot of flirtation materialising between them and he now made a conscious decision to curb down the tone, slowly. 'As I said, at first Sebastian was more of a mystery to be uncovered but, as I delved deeper into your world, it developed into more of a tight friendship than anything else, and one on an equal footing.'

'We all know about your delving deeper into our world,' she replied more seriously. 'Your adventures are quickly becoming the stuff of Templar lore, since every major recent event has found you at its centre, Alex Harker, and there are many who see your arrival as a gift from heaven itself.'

'Well, I do possess a magnetic personality,' he joked, unconsciously dipping back into flirt mode. 'And I seem to attract some pretty unexpected occurrences, so that's no surprise.'

'Then you should also know that there are others who believe you were sent to us directly from the gates of hell.'

This last remark caused any feelings of self-esteem to evaporate immediately, and Harker lowered his hands to his lap. 'Well,' he cleared his throat, 'you can't have one without the other can you?'

'Very well put,' Stefani replied. 'Truth is that if the majority did not subscribe to the former assessment, you would never have been accorded the title of Jarl. But you'll be glad to know I happen to be one of those also.'

As he gazed across at this attractive young woman with a sparkle in her eye, an image of Chloe materialised in Harker's mind, wearing an expression that said one thing and one thing only: 'Grow up, Alex'. With that mental warning, he now turned to the matters at hand. 'So what exactly did Sebastian say?'

It was obvious she sensed the change in him and she too snapped her full attention back to business. 'He said that he's glad that we're safe but that we should have informed him first before taking off on our own, and he agreed with me that we should continue investigating this rabbit hole to see where it leads.'

'Just like that?'

'Just like that. But he now wants me to take our latest acquisition,' she pointed to the crystal artefact lying on the table between them, 'to be examined by someone in-house.'

'Fair enough.' Harker replied, realising it was the right thing to do because so far he was at a loss regarding its purpose. 'And how about me?'

'We found out that the boy who died during my father's exorcism was previously being treated by one Dr Marceau, who made a visit to the residence just hours before… well, you know what. The police have already interviewed him, but Sebastian thinks it's worth another – less formal – visit to find out what he might know, if anything.'

Harker suddenly felt as if he had just been benched and Stefani noticed the change immediately.

'You're not getting side-lined, Alex, believe me, and if you want to switch places with me and drop off the object yourself, I'm happy to take a punt with the doctor instead.'

It was a generous offer and Harker took a moment to consider this but then he shook his head and passed the artefact over to her. 'I just don't like dropping out in the middle of an…'

He paused and it was Stefani who finished the sentence for him. 'An adventure. That is what you were about to say, wasn't it?'

'Something like that, yes' he replied, now feeling rather childish.

'Only you would call chasing devil-worshippers and getting shot at an adventure but don't worry, Professor Harker, your reputation for being in the thick of it remains safe. You've had more adventures in the past few years than most of us have experienced in a lifetime.'

'Hey, it was you who called them adventures, not me.' He got to his feet as she shot him a friendly smile. 'Who's going to look at that thing, anyway?'

'Not sure yet, but I promise you we will find out exactly what it does and then keep you in the loop.'

'Thanks.' He then placed a hand around her wrist and pointed down at the artefact's markings. 'And tell whoever examines this that I think these two circles must represent the two kingdoms your father spoke about, and here where they intersect with the star of David, that's us – it represents Earth or something.'

'Go on,' Stefani urged, and looking extremely curious.

'I'm not really sure but what if these two circles represent *other* places... I don't know, something like other realities, or perhaps the image really does signify heaven and hell, despite your father's thoughts on the matter, and how existence is caught between the two.'

'And this surrounding circle of little swastikas?'

'To the Hindus the swastika was the sign of good fortune – a power symbol which was also the emblem of Ganesh, the god of good luck.'

'That doesn't sound too bad.'

'I know, but in Janism it denotes the four possible places of rebirth: the animal or plant Kingdom, Earth itself, the spirit world or hell.'

'That sounds less good,' Stefani replied. 'Sounds like deep stuff altogether.'

'Most religious symbols are.' He now let go of her hand and pulled away.

'I'll let them know that,' she said, and then reached over to the door hatch and swung it back open, pausing as the steps unfolded down onto the tarmac outside. 'I almost forgot to say: use this phone from now on and no other. Sebastian's orders.' She passed him a brand new iPhone X. 'There's a worry that if that assassin found us once, it's quite possible she could track either of us via our mobiles. So why take the chance?'

Harker was in complete agreement. 'Never turn down a brand-new phone,' he remarked, and he flicked it on and downloaded all his contacts via Bluetooth in matter of seconds. Once that was completed, he passed his old phone over to Stefani who placed it into her pocket.

'Have you got all your information backed up at home?' she asked.

'Not a problem,' he replied, 'I can reload it when I return to Cambridge.'

'Good, then I'll have this one recycled. And, Alex,' she leant towards him and delivered a soft kiss on his cheek, 'thank you for helping me out with all this on just a whim. It means a great deal. It really does.' She pulled away and turned to the open hatch. 'Give me a call after you've spoken with the doctor.'

It was a nice gesture on her part and Harker offered her a wave in response, but then he called out after her as she descended the steps and began making her way towards a waiting black SUV. 'Where am I actually going?' he yelled as the jet's engines whirred into life.

'Paris,' she shouted back. 'Dr Marceau was renting a room in Turin but his main residence is in Paris. I'll send you the address and set up an account for you to charge the taxi to.'

Harker watched her climb into the back of SUV and then he waited until her vehicle began to pull away before closing the hatch door and taking his seat just as the jet started to roll forward towards the main taxiway. 'Paris,' he said out loud, feeling more than happy with the destination. 'The city of light and love.' There were worse places to go even if he would be travelling there alone.

As he settled back further into his seat and watched the lights of the airport pass by, he increasingly began to feel good. Of course what he really wanted was to know what those weird rituals back in Rome were about, what the object they had found was used for, but most of all why that insane, dreadlocked Jamaican woman had been so dead set on acquiring it.

Harker took a deep breath, closed his eyes and let himself enjoy the low hum of the jet's engines. He had done his job and, although unfinished, the Templars now had everything in hand and his trip to the doctor's would no doubt prove a cakewalk, because the police would have already squeezed the man for any information he might have.

It was with these thoughts that he now began to drift off to sleep and yet, even though he was feeling totally at peace, something began pecking away deep in the pit of his stomach. It was the last words the assassin had spoken to him back at the museum. 'This ain't over boy... not by a long shot.'

Chapter 16

David Carter held the three cubes of sugar in his fingers hovering over the top of the steaming mug of Earl Grey tea with a mischievous smile. Better not, he decided and dropped them back into the white Silver Spoon-brand box. Dean Lercher had proved a complete pain in the arse since arriving back at the Templar vault tucked away deep within the granite rock of Mont St-Michel. Carter couldn't tell if it was his own little joke in spiking his friend's tea on the flight over or whether the man was still furious at having his car keys taken by Alex, but either way he continued to blow up at any chance offered to him.

'Is that my tea?' Doggie asked, appearing around the corner of the nearest walkway.

'Certainly is,' Carter replied, nudging the hot beverage towards him, 'completely free of sugar, as promised.'

Doggie picked up the mug and sniffed it warily. 'Mmmm,' he grunted and then took a sip.

'So, did you find anything?'

'Not really,' Doggie replied, placing the mug back down onto the lacquered Cherrywood desk that Carter was sitting at, 'although I did find a reference to an exorcism that went wrong – horribly wrong in much the same way as this Father Davies's.'

'Really?'

'Yes, there's a record of a similar occurrence back in the sixteenth century when a Catholic priest performed an exorcism on a young girl in France, and soon afterwards he himself became possessed.'

This titbit of information piqued Carter's interest right away. 'What happened?'

'The report was rather lax in detail but essentially the girl never recovered from her ordeal and was burned as a witch.'

'Charming.' Carter grimaced at the thought of such a horrendous death, 'And the priest?'

'Doesn't say, except that he disappeared into the night, still foaming at the mouth.'

'Sounds like rabies.'

'Impossible to say but I'm going to keep looking. Perhaps there's another entry somewhere which records the poor man's fate.' Doggie picked his mug of tea back up, then stopped himself from taking another sip. 'There's definitely no sugar in this?'

Carter looked insulted by the accusation. 'Hey, what kind of person do you think I am? I promised you, didn't I, and besides can you taste any sugar?'

Doggie continued to stare at him mistrustfully. 'No, but I do have a cold.'

'Such a doubting Thomas.'

'Well, my name actually is Tom,' Doggie said before finally taking a sip. 'So, did you find anything?'

'I did, but it's more on the satanic side of things.' Carter began and pulling towards him a large leather-bound book, its cover cracked from age and with a thick, frayed binding. 'It's remarkable how much information the Templars recorded over the centuries,' he said and as if marvelling at the thought. 'It will take a lifetime to go through it all.'

'Just the facts, David, if you please. Just the facts,' Doggie replied dismissively and took another sip.

As Carter began heaving open the thick outer cover, his iPhone suddenly began to vibrate on the table beneath him. 'Number not recognised so it has to be Alex. He's the only one except yourself that has my number at the moment,' he informed Doggie, picking up the mobile.

'Well, then, "Billy no mates", tell him he stills owes me for that car keys debacle.'

'Yeah, yeah,' Carter groaned as he slid the green answer button across with his finger. 'Alex, is that you? How's it going at your end?'

'Yes, it's me and so far it's not your average trip abroad.' Harker was only just audible over the poor connection, 'I'm on a plane to Paris to do some fact checking... Can you hear me OK?'

The reception was awful and Carter pulled the mobile from his ear and pressed the speaker symbol. 'Just about. You're now on loudspeaker and I've got Doggie here with me. So, you're coming to our neck of the woods, then?'

'Only a couple of hundred miles away yes, but I can still feel Tom's eyes burning into the back of my head even from here, so can I first offer, once again, my apologies for the keys, Tom.' This received little more than a silent shrug from the Dean, 'OK, with that out of the way, tell me, what did you find out?'

'The list you sent me was a bit vague but I did uncover a lot of information on satanic rituals such as the ones you described, including one pertaining to your own personal marriage ceremony.'

'Alex got married!' Doggie exclaimed with a look of astonishment.

'Yeah,' Carter chuckled, 'to another man.'

'Really, Alex, I didn't know your bread was buttered on that side!' Doggie joked but still looking surprised. 'Does Chloe know?'

'Ha, ha, Tom, it wasn't like that.'

'Huh, shame,' Doggie replied before expelling a loud chortle. 'You'd have made an excellent bride.'

'I appreciate that, Tom, but can we now get to what you've found out please?'

'Of course,' Carter said and he began to flick through the old book before settling on a single page with a green cardboard bookmark protruding from it. 'There's an entry here pertaining to a ceremony called "the joining of the light", but there was nothing satanic about it. It was a Druidic ritual, for men only, that signified self-dedication to the gods or perhaps to the earth itself – that part's a bit unclear, I'm afraid. What's interesting, though, is that one of the symbols used was a swastika, which really stands out because I can't find any other connection between Druids and that sign elsewhere. Furthermore, there was another ritual linked to it, but I've not yet managed to unearth it.'

'Thanks David. Can you keep looking then, and there's something else I need you to look for.' Harker was now almost shouting to be heard above the static. 'See if it's linked to any objects or specific runes.'

'Objects? Such as?' Doggie wanted to get involved in the conversation.

'Like an oval crystal that pulsates with red light.'

Harker's description had Carter and Doggie staring at each other blankly.

'I've never come across anything like that, Alex,' Carter finally replied, frankly dumbfounded.

'I'm going to send you a picture of this thing. It's really weird, emitting a red light, and has swastikas and other such markings engraved in to it. I've never seen anything quite like it.'

'OK,' Carter was looking puzzled, 'send it over and I'll see what I can come up with but, for the record, I have never even heard about a runestone displaying those kinds of properties – or anything even close. It sounds like something from *Close Encounters of the Third Kind* or something.'

'Tell me about it,' Harker replied, as the line began to worsen. 'Just see what you can find... and, David, I'm sending you two numbers. One is the mobile I'll be using from now on, and the other is for Stefani Mitchell.'

'Ahhh, that lady Templar you told me about?'

'Yes, we've gone our separate ways for the time being, but I want you to bring her up to speed with anything you do find as well, OK.'

'Leave it with me,' Doggie declared firmly and he raised his left eyebrow as if to lay down his authority in this matter, but the gesture was met instead with an embarrassed shaking of Carter's head.

'Don't worry Alex, we'll keep her in the loop,' Carter assured.

'Thanks, I'll be in tou—'

The line abruptly cut out and Doggie began to head back down the walkway without saying a word.

'Hey, Tom,' Carter called out after him and the Dean stopped and swivelled on his heel to face him. 'Don't forget who's in charge here,' Carter continued as he opened up his jacket and pointed to the shiny metal badge that Brulet had bestowed upon him.

Doggie stared at the trinket for a few seconds without any expression, then he slowly began to clap. 'Yes David, you have a little badge. Good for you.' He gave a sarcastic smile then turned around a full 180 degrees and continued striding till he had disappeared down one of the walkways.

Carter huffed loudly, then he grasped the badge, opened up the work-desk drawer and dropped it inside. He next took a sip of his tea and let out a disgruntled sigh.

'Twat!'

Chapter 17

Due to a strong tailwind, the flight to Paris had been quicker than expected and Harker had slept the whole way, just waking up in time to see the sun rise as they touched down at Charles de Gaulle Airport on the outskirts of that beautiful city. A short taxi ride later and he asked to be dropped off a quarter of a mile from the address that Stefani had texted him. Initially he had intended to be driven right up to the door but when he realised where it was, he couldn't deny himself the chance to take some time to enjoy his present surroundings. Located on Avenue de New York and at the edge of the Seine river, the house had a perfect view of the Eiffel Tower, which soared high above the skyline on the other side. Whatever kind of practitioner this Dr Marceau was, he got well paid for it because the house prices here must have been astronomical.

With his hands in his pockets, Harker strolled up to the front door and gazed up at the fine stone façade of the Haussmann-style building. Built in six storeys, the second floor was known as 'Noble' because in the days before elevators it allowed the wealthy owners easy access to the grandest rooms. Of course in the modern era it didn't matter and, as Harker inspected the apartment buzzers, he found Dr Marceau's nameplate linked to that on the third floor. Not quite 'Noble' but still impressive. He pressed it and waited patiently, enjoying the sight of two young lovers passing him by, who clung together so tightly that he doubted even a crowbar could prise them apart.

'*Oui?*' a voice crackled over the intercom, and Harker dutifully reverted to French.

'Dr Marceau?'

'Yes.'

'Mr name is Alex Harker and I was hoping to speak with you.'

'Who?'

'Alex Harker. I was an acquaintance of the late Father Davies.'

There was a pause and then the intercom clicked on again.

'I've already spoken to the police. I've told them all there is to tell.'

The man sounded cautious but this was no surprise to Harker. 'I'm not with the police, Doctor, I'm a professor at Cambridge University and a close friend of Father Davies's daughter. It was she who asked me to speak with you – if you have the time?'

The respectful pleasantry had the intended effect and the door lock now buzzed open.

'Very well, please come up.'

The lobby was dark inside and, after noting the elevator's 'out of order' sign, Harker, with a groan, climbed the black stone steps to reach the third floor, where he found a chubby man in his fifties about six-foot-tall, wearing a beige cashmere jumper, brown corduroy trousers and sporting a peculiar pair of red horn-rimmed reading glasses and standing in the apartment's doorway. Dr Marceau said nothing as Harker approached but he protectively closed the door halfway.

'You've nothing to fear from me Dr,' Harker reassured, with both palms raised in a gesture of peace. 'I only want to talk to you, if that's OK?'

Dr Marceau gave Harker a careful look up and down and, seemingly convinced his guest was not someone to be worried about, he beckoned him closer. 'Then you'd better come in, Professor.'

The door had now been opened fully and Harker offered a polite nod before entering, whereupon Marceau closed the door behind him and clicked a couple of thick brass locks, one underneath the other. Whoever this was, he was definitely a man who considered his security of paramount concern.

'After you.' His host pointed along the bare-wood flooring of the hallway. 'We can talk in there.'

The living room was as charming as the building's exterior and, although somewhat sparse in furniture, it boasted a wealthy, aristocratic vibe that said 'I'm wealthy but have no need to show it'. Off to Harker's left a light-green double sofa stood behind a cracked marble coffee table, with a tub chair on the opposite side, and at the far end of the room hung a large mirror above a white, stone fireplace, its reflection giving greater depth to the room. Off to the right an open doorway led into what looked like a narrow dining room with a thin table surrounded by black leather doughnut bar stools. Either the doctor did very little entertaining or he didn't mind his guests being extremely uncomfortable whilst eating.

'Have a seat.' Dr Marceau gestured and Harker took the far end of the sofa, as his host took the black leather tub chair. 'Now, what is it I can do for you, Professor Harker?'

Despite the cordial words Dr Marceau looked intensely uncomfortable and Harker immediately set about trying to put the man at ease.

'As I said, Dr Marceau, I was asked by Father Davies's daughter, Stefani Mitchell, to speak with you in the hope you could spread some light on his...' Harker paused as he tried to find the appropriate words, '...untimely and macabre demise.'

'Well, that is one way to put it, I suppose, but perhaps gruesome, or even ghoulish is a better way.'

'Quite,' Harker replied, glad to see the doctor was prepared to be upfront concerning the unpleasant business. 'She learned that you were there tending to the boy shortly before he and his mother were killed.'

'That is correct. I was treating the boy for paranoid schizophrenia, as I informed the police.'

'Really? Because we were told that Father Davies believed the boy to be possessed.'

The very mention of possession had Dr Marceau squinting and shaking his head dismissively. 'Rubbish, the boy had a mental disorder, and it was Father Davies who managed over time to convince the child's mother to accept otherwise. Davies should have been ashamed of himself for taking advantage of a vulnerable single parent like that.'

'So you knew Father Davies then, before the murders?'

Marceau's eyelids dipped so that it was clear to Harker that, even though the doctor had let slip his familiarity with the priest, he had certainly not wanted to.

'Our paths had crossed from time to time, yes.'

'How so?'

'I saw him at the mother's residence a few times when dispensing my medical duties, but we were never friends.'

He was now becoming visibly agitated and began to rub at the forefinger of his left hand and Harker now became convinced that, despite the good doctor's evasive response, the man was chomping at the bit to get something off his chest.

He leant forward and eyed his host closely.

'Doctor, I recently came into ownership of an item that Father Davies had apparently given to a friend for safe keeping. This item is rather unique and the man holding onto it was subsequently murdered because of it.'

Marceau said nothing but his eyes began to widen and he rubbed his forefinger ever harder as Harker continued.

'I also went to visit his house but was greeted by a grotesque sculpture of a slaughtered bull, before some young man attempted to drown me. That same fellow was found chopped up into pieces in the back of a police van soon after, and later on I myself witnessed a satanic ritual of some sort – one that he was supposed to attend. Would you have any thoughts on the matter?'

A thin film of perspiration had now appeared across Dr Marceau's temples and, although he had stopped rubbing at his finger his breathing was getting quicker and he inhaled deeply, then slowly released a sigh.

'Do you still have that object?' Dr Marceau asked blankly.

'Not on me but, yes, I do.'

Marceau sat back in his tub chair, letting his arms droop over the sides as his shoulders sagged. 'You know you're on a dangerous path, Professor?'

'That I'm aware of,' Harker replied, leaning in closer as one would do to tell a secret. 'The real question is,' he said in little more than a whisper, 'what do *you* know?'

As Harker watched the man's expression begin to glaze over, he realised that the one to talk next would be the loser. Like during an interrogation, where silence itself is one of the most powerful weapons available, he remained silent as outside the droning of a bus passing by did nothing to relieve the intensity of the moment.

Nearly an entire minute thus went by, and Harker was almost about to put the same question again, when Marceau's lips opened very slightly and he quietly murmured, as if having to force the words from his mouth, 'Come with me.'

The doctor stood up and made his way into the adjacent dining room, followed closely by his visitor. He then stopped at a closed door, produced a silver-coloured Yale key from his pocket and slid it into the lock. 'Don't judge me until I've had a chance to explain,' Marceau continued, waiting for Harker to nod in agreement before turning the key and walking inside and flicking on the light.

The aroma of burnt joss sticks hung in the air and, even though they stank, that was the only pleasant thing about the room. It was about half the size of the living room and every square inch of wall space was covered with framed photographs, drawings and newspaper cuttings relating to God knows what. Four plywood bookshelves held what must have been a few hundred titles, ranging from Dante's *Inferno* to works concerning human biology and particle psychics. At the far end, underneath a blacked-out window, a thick beechwood writing desk held on its surface a pile of papers and journals, along with three small shrunken heads; the eyes and mouths sewn shut and acting as paperweights.

Harker had seen shrunken heads once before at Oxford's Pitt Rivers museum and, although ugly little things, they weren't exactly something for which he would judge someone badly, but as he gazed downwards he realised what Dr Marceau had been referring to. Taking up the entire width of the floor was a pentagram carved into the floorboards, embellished with the satanic image of a goat's head whose horns, ears and chin comprised the five points.

'Please allow me to explain.' Marceau stated quickly, as Harker stared at him in surprise and contempt. 'The pentagram on the floor is just for research. It's not what you think.'

'No, what I'm thinking is far worse,' Harker stated flatly, staying close to the doorway. 'What kind of doctor are you anyway?'

'I'm not Doctor Death, if that's what you're suggesting.'

Marceau headed over to the desk, opened a drawer and pulled out a picture frame. 'All this stuff is research, nothing more,' he explained and passed it over to Harker. 'Father Davies and I were working on it together.'

Harker warily took the frame from Marceau's outstretched hand and glanced down at it, but all the time keeping the creepy fellow in his line of sight. The frame contained a colour photograph of Father Davies and Dr Marceau both wearing shorts, matching blue T-shirts and each with a heavy backpack on his shoulders. The two men were smiling and behind them lay a vast expanse of thick forest wilderness stretching out as far as the eye could see.

'That's us in the Republic of Congo during our last trip there,' Marceau said with pride before retrieving the frame.

'Let me guess, that's where you met the Devil and his strange glowing orbs.' Harker said sarcastically, beginning to feel queasy from the sheer stuffiness of the room.

'No, it wasn't like that at all.'

'Then what was it like?' Harker erupted, now having reached his limit. So far he had been drowned, shot at and even got married, and he did not intend to finish it all off with having to sit through a presentation of this nutty doctor's holiday snaps.

'You said you would allow me to explain, so let me.'

Harker rubbed at his forehead, then nodded, as Marceau now trailed a finger across the row of books sitting on one of the shelves.

'Since the time mankind was first able to pass on stories from one generation to another, either orally or through drawings, the concept of good and evil has always existed – or to use modern language, heaven and hell.'

'OK.' Harker gave a sigh. 'I'm listening, but could you start at the beginning. Because I'm struggling to get on board here, if you know what I mean?'

'Understood,' Marceau agreed, appearing glad just to have the opportunity to tell someone about what he at least believed he had discovered. 'I have always had a fascination with the occult,' he began.

'You're not kidding,' Harker said, looking down at the pentagram at his feet.

'Yes, yes, yes. Well, I first met Father Davies at a lecture on the very nature of heaven and hell, on the concept of good and evil. Father Davies had just given up his position in the Church, and was now looking for answers to this very issue. It was this very subject, I discovered later on, that encouraged him to leave the Church in the first place. So we met by chance and then began researching the subject together: what were the origins of these concepts before religion, before society, even before any real culture had taken hold. Back when modern humans had barely begun to spread out from Africa.'

Marceau pulled a slim book out with its red cover, flicked it open to the right page and then passed it over to Harker.

'We heard about a tribe still living deep in the Congo which had been completely isolated since... well, forever. From what we can gather none of the members ever left Africa or even the Congo.'

Marceau pointed next to a black and white photograph in the book of some tribesmen dancing in a group, with the words Mbuti inscribed above it.

'I've heard of them before,' Harker remarked. 'They rarely grow above five feet tall and are also known under the umbrella term "pygmies". They live somewhere in the northern Congo – the lturi forest I think.'

Harker's display of knowledge earned a smile from Marceau, and he continued with enthusiasm. 'We found tales from the 1600s relating to the Mbuti stating they originated from another core tribe that remained still unaccounted for... until we discovered it.'

Marceau looked thrilled and, even though the idea of lost tribes was certainly interesting to Harker, it was not really at the top of his priority list at the moment. He remained quiet, listening attentively.

'Some off the stories we heard were just so intriguing that we decided to travel there and it wasn't until our third trip that all our research, bribery and hard work paid off – because we *found* them.' Marceau licked his lips and took the book back from Harker, returning it to the shelf. 'This tribe don't even have a name, for they refer to themselves only by a series of sounds or calls and, Professor, they have never left the Congo since the dawn of modern humans. And it was the *why* which turned out to be the interesting part.'

He reached for the top shelf now and pulled out an A4 cardboard envelope, from which he tipped out a number of photographs into Harker's hands. 'It took almost a month for them just to allow us near their camp, but after another three we were well enough accepted to be allowed access to their most important and sacred sites – like here.'

Marceau selected one of the photographs and Harker began to examine it. At first it looked like just another cave painting but as he examined it more closely it began to dawn on him that there was nothing familiar about this image all. It showed a group of humans gazing up towards a sky portraying white clouds and the orange glow of the sun in the corner. The image had used the natural curvature of the bumps in the wall it was painted on to produce an almost 3D image. And although that in itself was not unique, what Harker now saw in the depiction was.

For in the sky directly above the group of people there was a large black hole, like a gap torn into space, while inside dark wispy shapes appeared to be approaching from within it.

'They tell tales of something they refer to as the "happening",' Marceau said, sounding more excited with every word he spoke. 'We took a small chip from the cave painting itself and carbon dating couldn't even date it because it must be older than fifty thousand years old, which is as far back as carbon dating can go.'

'Are you sure?' Harker asked with surprise because, as far as he knew, the oldest cave painting ever found was thought to be about forty thousand years old.

'No doubt,' Marceau crowed and he turned his attention back to the picture of the ominous cave painting and tapped at the image of a large black hole in the sky. 'The events of this particular day were passed down in an oral tradition to five of the tribe in each generation, in case one should die suddenly, and what they eventually described to us was chilling.'

Harker picked up the book and began to examine the photograph in detail as Marceau revealed more of what he had discovered.

'This event they called "the Happening" was like a collision of realities when a rip in the sky opened up and a dark force descended upon the earth and became trapped, only to wander the confines of the planet causing great pain and misery wherever it went. This force could inhabit and enslave the minds of man… but then something occurred, not recorded, and that same dark force was banished to the peripheries of the world… until now.'

Harker now stared at the doctor with a look of deep concern. 'Dr Marceau, you seem like a nice man but I have to suggest you're not just wacky… but maybe clinically insane because what you're saying is just—'

'I am *not*. So listen, and listen up good,' Marceau replied defiantly. 'Mathematicians and physicists now believe that our universe is just one of many alternate realities, each with its own laws of physics completely different from our own. So everything Father Davies and I discovered leads me to believe that this "happening" the tribe described… well, maybe it was real. But, instead of something spiritual, it was actually another reality that collided with ours and left these beings – demons, spirits, whatever you want to call them stranded on our planet. Over thousands of years, stories of these same spirits have inhabited every culture on the planet and eventually when Catholicism rose to prominence, those very tangible notions were repackaged as the Devil and his army of demon spirits. A spiritual set of ideas was therefore based on a very real occurrence. The Bible is littered with stories or analogies that show us certain truths about us as human beings and our history, so why couldn't the same thing have happened with those beings that eventually got rebranded as the Devil and the kingdom of Hell?'

Harker closed his eyes momentarily and stifled a laugh but it was not one born from humour but rather frustration, because this tale was just too much to swallow. 'So let me get this straight. You think that spirit-like beings from an alternate universe got stranded here during some cosmic event, in a colliding of realties creating… what? A doorway to this world? And they've been stuck here ever since, causing mayhem?'

Dr Marceau eyed him now with a look of complete conviction. 'Well, I wouldn't put it exactly like that but essentially… yes.'

'And how about the pulsating artefact, where did you find those things?'

'That for me became the game changer,' Marceau replied and roaring along without even a hint of hesitation. 'We found it in the possession of the same tribe. It had been protected and passed down through countless generations, along with stories of their arrival, since the dawn of time as they themselves explained. I don't know if the artefact arrived on Earth at the same time as the "demons",' Marceau said wiggling his fingers in up the air, 'but apparently these objects are the only things that can send them back, or destroy them… who knows. But the pair of us made a big mistake.'

Harker didn't know how much of this stuff arose solely as the result of Dr Marceau's obviously troubled mind but he did realise where the story was going. 'You stole the artefact, didn't you?'

Marceau looked guilty as charged, and nodded his head ashamedly. 'At the time we thought such a monumentally important item needed above all to be protected, but now I see we were unfathomably wrong. There are people, servants to these things that want it badly, because it is these spirits' only weakness, and the very reason the tribe kept the artefact hidden for thousands of years.' He looked in complete awe of the idea. 'For all that time, these people stayed hidden away in the darkest most primordial spot on planet Earth, just so as to keep this artefact concealed and thus stop it falling into the hands of those that might seek to use it for their own twisted aims. And, in a matter of only months, we two managed to screw everything up royally.'

'Woah, woah, there Doctor,' Harker gasped and barely keeping up with Marceau's ramblings, 'What the hell are you talking about? What people? What servants?'

'Yes, of course, I'm jumping ahead; I tend to do that.' Marceau said fretfully, only just registering Harker's confusion of his tall tale. 'Once we got back from the Congo someone, one of these people I mentioned, turned up on Father Davies's doorstep, asking questions. She was aware of the artefact's existence and knew we had stolen it. Crazier still, she and her partners were convinced it signalled the arrival of the Antichrist, if you can believe that. Of course that's just total rubbish. The Devil,

Antichrist, spirits – whatever you want to call them, have always been here. Biding their time until things were just right.'

'Oh, right, because dimension-jumping beings seem plausible to you but the Antichrist is just plain crazy,' Harker replied with a shake of his head. 'And what exactly is the reason they were biding their time?'

'To use your jargon, to open the gates of Hell or, to use my own wording, to open a link between realities.'

It was clear that Marceau felt like he was on shaky ground in this part of his explanation, which was ironic considering the tall story so far, but he immediately sought to sum it all up for Harker. 'I don't know... maybe they want to bring all their brethren into our universe and claim it for their own. Or maybe they just want to go back to their universe. All I know is that these things are as real as you or I and so I believe it was they who possessed Father Davies and caused him to do the things he did. He was controlled by the very hand of the so-called Devil himself.'

Harker watched his host nervously fidgeting with his fingers and he realised that, even though he himself was wholly unconvinced by the man's truly nutty explanation, it was something that Marceau believed without question. It would be plainly wrong to play on the doctor's delusions but perhaps there were some truths wrapped up amidst this whopper of a tale. 'There's a woman I ran into back in Athens who seemed dead set on getting her hands on the missing artefact. So dead set that she killed the man Father Davies had entrusted it to.'

The very mention of this had Marceau gulping, and the blood began to drain from his face. 'Was she a black woman with dreadlocks?'

'That's the one,' Harker replied in surprise, 'with a thick Jamaican accent.'

The man's teeth began to chatter slightly and his eyes darted back and forth as he pondered. 'There's a group I belong to which I think you should meet.'

'A group? Who exactly?' Harker asked apprehensively, finding that his host's panicky demeanour was beginning to rub off on him.

Marceau was already tapping a number into his phone as he replied. 'A group set up a long time ago to act as guardians for just this reason.'

As the doctor waited for the phone to reply, Harker found his head spinning from all this craziness and he couldn't help thinking that this group might have been more appropriately a mental health support group than the supposed guardians of Marceau's dimension theory.

'This group... er, they don't sit around in a circle and perhaps indulge in some kind of medication, or maybe herbal remedies, do they?'

'Oh, shut up, you condescending idiot,' Marceau snarled as his call was now answered. 'It's Gérald. We have to meet... I know, but it's serious. I'm here with someone who knows where the stone is and I think the Red Death does as well.'

'The Red Death!' Harker mouthed in alarm but Marceau ignored his concern with a grimace and instead concentrated on his phone call.

'He calls himself Professor Alex Harker... Bring him with me? Are you sure? Very well, we'll see you there in one hour on the dot.' Marceau hung up and slipped the phone back into his pocket. 'You're in luck as they'll meet with us, but listen here, Professor – if that's truly your identity – I'll have no more of your contempt, do you hear me?'

Marceau's demand was made with total and absolute seriousness and, even though Harker wanted nothing more than to just grab a taxi and subsequently drop the good doctor off at the nearest mental health clinic for some well-needed R&R, he instead decided to give this man the benefit of the doubt. He steadied himself and offered a compliant nod of his head.

'Good,' Marceau said, with his beady eyes bulging behind those thick-lensed horn-rim glasses of his. 'Because if you want to live past today, you'll now do everything I tell you and without question, understand? Everything I say from here on in must be treated with complete and unwavering seriousness. You have found yourself in the midst of a war, Professor Harker, where even the slightest mistake can lead to certain doom.' He said this in a raised voice that was now quivering with a rage. 'Now tell me… How do you feel about hot buttered toasted teacakes?'

Chapter 18

'Told you they were good,' Marceau said with a satisfied smile as he wolfed another generous portion of buttered teacake into his mouth and chomped away happily. 'Better than in the UK, that's for sure.'

Harker glanced down at his own untouched plate of teacakes and also managed a smile. 'Honestly, I wouldn't know. I'm not a fan.'

Marceau shrugged his shoulders. 'Your loss.'

The short five-minute walk to Cafe Ribe brasserie had been uneventful and Harker had since been counting down the minutes until the meeting Marceau had organised for them both earlier. The small cafe was surprisingly quiet for the time of day but for any customer it seemed a perfect place to watch the world go by. For Harker on the other hand it was rapidly becoming torture. In all the time they had been seated here the doctor had seemed unwilling to explain who was due or why this meeting was necessary. Even though he believed it possible that the recent murders and also the death of his friend Father Davies may have caused a nervous breakdown in Marceau, his sheer curiosity had convinced him to at the very least, give the fellow an hour.

Harker glanced down at his watch to check the time. 'Well, that's an hour gone.' he declared, getting to his feet. 'Dr Marceau, I'm very sorry to have troubled you but I really must be going now.' He picked up his own untouched teacakes and placed it on the doctor's now empty plate. 'Please have mine and I must bid you adieu, sir.'

At first Marceau looked rather shocked but seconds later his expression changed and a smug smile appeared on his face as behind them the bell on the door chimed. Before Harker had time to turn around, he felt a hand rest lightly on his shoulder.

'You must be Professor Harker?' a voice inquired in English with a resolutely thick French accent.

Harker turned around to find himself looking into the face of a man in his sixties with a short white beard, steel-framed reading glasses and the kindly expression one would expect from a lifelong friend.

'Thank you for meeting with us,' the newcomer continued.

Harker glanced over the man's shoulder to see two more people with equally affable expressions. One was a younger man with a clean-shaven face, short light-blond hair and wearing a smart suit with a tan mackintosh draped over his forearm, and the other a woman in her mid-twenties with short black hair. She wore a colourful summer frock with distinctive purple and red zigzag patterns, and carried a slender dark-brown Louis Vuitton satchel clasped in one hand.

'It's nice to meet you… I think,' Harker replied, slightly taken aback because he had decided all of twenty minutes earlier that no one was likely to show up.

'I apologise for the wait but this meeting was so last-minute,' the bearded man explained politely. 'My name is Henri Berger and with me here are Pierre Beaumont and Monique Couture.'

Harker dispensed with any handshakes and offered a nod of his head to each of the new arrivals in turn. 'Forgive me for looking shocked but I wasn't expecting you to actually turn up.'

'Don't worry,' Henri continued to smile, 'we were just as surprised when we got the call an hour ago. Hi, Gérald.'

Marceau pushed his plate to one side, stood up and shook the older man's hand. 'As surprised as I was when Professor Harker arrived on my doorstep.'

There was an awkward moment of silence before Pierre gave a wave to the proprietor of the cafe and the man immediately headed away from his post behind the counter and disappeared through a door marked 'Staff Only.'

'Let's find somewhere private to talk, shall we?' Henri proposed and, with himself and Monique taking the lead, they headed towards and through the same door the owner had used only moments earlier. Harker was still unsure where all this actually was heading but his instincts told him he was in no immediate danger and, despite not knowing of what this group stood for, he was happy to tug on the string and see where it might lead him.

Beyond the door Harker found himself in tight proximity with the others in a small pantry full of restaurant stock, from large retail tubs of granulated coffee to packets of croissants and an assortment of other patisserie items, all packed neatly on rows of shelves. The owner stood furthest in and, with a smile from Henri, he slipped his fingers into a small crevice at the base of the wall and gave a gentle tug. The wall swung backwards with the sound of air pressure being released as the small hydraulic hinges compressed until it lay flat against the adjoining wall, thus revealing what lay behind it.

Set into the plaster partition was a heavy-looking steel door with chipped green paint and rusting edges and, as Marceau shot Harker a wink, Henri and Monique both produced long black, tarnished keys such as one might associate with an old-fashioned safe.

At this point the proprietor slid past them and headed back towards the kitchen, closing the pantry door behind him. Henri and Monique inserted their keys in two small holes on opposite sides of the metal door, then they glanced at one another and began to count down in unison.

'Three, two, one.'

Both keys turned simultaneously and, with a click, the entire metal door swung inwards to expose a dark entrance-way. Harker felt a gust of stale air rush past him as Henri reached inside and flicked a switch.

Ahead of them, the grilled covered work lights lining the wall began to turn on one after the other, and Harker watched as they gradually lit up a long passageway with each fresh bulb illuminating it further, eventually showing its full length.

The entire passageway, heading downwards on a shallow incline, was over one hundred metres in length, before it curved off to the left and continued for who knew how much further. Harker was now coaxed forward along with the rest of the group and stepped onto a small platform which offered him his first complete view of what this chamber was all about. The passageway contained a set of small metal tracks running straight down its centre, and at the edge of the platform itself, a pair of mini train carts sat waiting for them though they looked more suited to hauling coal out of mines than offering passengers a ride.

'What is this place?' Harker hissed as behind him Pierre pushed the heavy metal door back in place.

'Abandoned military tunnels,' Monique explained, and motioning him towards the open-top carts that Henri and Marceau were already climbing into. 'Built before and during the last war. They run for miles underneath Paris,' she explained with a certain pride, 'connecting to exits all over the city, although almost all of them were boarded up long ago.'

'But not this one,' Pierre said and, with a gentle shove, he pushed Harker into the back seat of the second cart and sat down next to him. 'This particular one has a far darker history to it.'

With everyone now seated, Henri pushed a small green button on the dashboard and with a lurch the two carts began to set off down the track until reaching a top speed of around fifteen miles an hour, which was maintained as the glowing wall lights zipped past them.

'The Nazis made use of this one during the occupation, and then expanded it to serve as a travel hub for high-ranking government officials,' Henri explained as the carts approached the bend up ahead. 'It was meant to be a secure way of transporting the fascist elite through the city without fear of being assassinated.'

'Fear of the Resistance, no doubt?' Marceau interjected, looking rather proud of that thought.

'Quite,' Henri replied, 'but like many structures the Nazis built using slave labour, they were never finished or even used, as you can now see.'

Harker saw exactly what he meant as the cart finally turned the corner and the tunnel suddenly opened up into an impressive station point, bearing a striking resemblance to a London tube platform except it was only half finished. Another track ran parallel to theirs and led off down another dark tunnel while on the other side, dark grey tiles ran alongside only half of the platform, allowing cracked concrete and strips of rebar to show underneath. Cobwebs hung from the wire mesh covering drop-down cylindrical lampshades above them, and large numerals had been sprayed in sequence directly onto the walls, each with that familiar metal eagle emblem next to it, which the German army was known for.

'It was supposed to be linked to the main Paris railway so that Hitler's personal train could make full use of it but, given that the Fuhrer visited the city only once and insisted he travel by car, work stopped on the project and it subsequently became irrelevant.' Monique smiled at Harker's look of intrigue as the cart reached the end of the platform and entered another lit-up tunnel. 'Fascinating, isn't it?'

It then rumbled over its electrified tracks for another thirty seconds before it came to a stop at the last illuminated wall light, next to a small metal platform similar to the one right back at the entrance.

'Everybody off,' Henri instructed.

Harker exited the cart and offered to assist Marceau, whose podgy stomach was getting in the way of him standing up, but his helping hand was batted away. Henri and Pierre meanwhile took up position at a grey metal door with added strips of steel bolted across it for extra strength. They again both produced long keys and inserted them in the locks on either side of the door.

'It takes all three of us, each with a key, to gain access to this place.' Henri explained.

'As it should be,' Pierre added then they both turned their keys at exactly the same time and swung the door backwards.

'You don't have a key, then?' Harker asked Marceau with a hint of sarcasm, but the doctor didn't look put out.

'Oh, I do have a key, but it doesn't open doors,' he said ominously.

As Harker was led inside, he felt the first pang of concern arise in his chest and he very slowly clenched his fists just in case they might soon be needed.

The interior was pitch-black but, to Harker's relief, the air smelt far cleaner, He watched with growing apprehension as Henri reached up towards something dangling above him and, with a small tug, the overhead lighting flickered on.

If Harker had been having misgivings about taking this trip into the bowels of Paris, they were immediately dispelled by what he saw. And, as Marceau closed the door behind them, he stepped forward and took in his new surroundings.

The room was large, about half the size of an Olympic-sized swimming pool, with smooth concrete walls and the height of a two-storey house. The ceiling was supported by two thick concrete pillars positioned halfway along each wall. Directly in front of him was a long granite table facing the rest of the room and thirteen stone chairs set around it, six each on facing sides and a single one at the head. The far end of the room looked like the chancel end of a church, with a magnificent carved arch rising above a white limestone altar with two wide marble steps leading up to it, while behind stood sculptures of three haloed saints gazing down on a box about half a metre by half a metre which was crafted of yellow amber panelling.

'What is this place?' Harker asked as he now took note of the beautiful paintings hanging on the walls, seemingly displaying the images of a range of saints from St Peter through to John Pope Paul II, and above the altar itself two stunning oil paintings of the Virgin Mary hung beneath one of Jesus Christ himself.

'We're currently almost directly underneath the northern leg of the Eiffel Tower. The Gestapo used this as a place to torture and kill anyone they deemed to be an enemy of the state, and it remained very much a secret until the US army discovered it soon after the liberation of Paris. Goes without saying therefore, it was a place few ever got to talk about,' Henri explained solemnly.

'Charming history it has,' Harker said with a wince. 'I'm surprised it wasn't demolished.' His comment was made with no malice and he stepped forwards to the granite table as Pierre now began to speak.

'We've been aware of you for a while now, Alex, but it was only in the last few days that you truly came to our attention, with particular interest. Your uncovering of the location of the blessed candle has been timely to say the least, but many of us – as I do – believe that fate has played a hand in it.'

'I told him the truth,' Marceau insisted and looking offended, 'but he thinks I'm crazy.'

This received a warm smile from the others and Henri moved closer to Harker, clasping his hands together piously. 'I'm afraid Gérald's interpretation of events is a bit more colourful and elaborate than our own. Father Davies and he were able to track down the original blessed candle that I believe is now in your possession and perhaps its origins are as exactly as Gérald claims, but I'm afraid our own involvement and knowledge comes from a far more recent period in history.'

Marceau continued to look offended and Henri sought to soothe his friend's irritation. 'But it's no less worthy and there's truth in it I'm sure... on some level. Please allow me to now show you something that might offer some perspective.'

'That would be nice,' Harker replied. 'I'm guessing the glowing oval rock we found is this blessed candle you're referring to?'

Henri merely smiled then he and the others began to make their way towards the altar at the other side of the room. 'Let us show you.'

With Marceau close behind, Harker followed them past the granite table towards the altar and up the marble steps rising behind it, to the yellow amber box, where-upon they all came to a halt.

'St Paul, St Peter and St John,' Harker decided, pointing out individually the three sculptures facing the amber box from each side.

'That is correct, for who else could we ask to watch over such an important item,' Pierre replied, crossing his hands respectfully, and then glancing up to the image of Christ gazing down on them. 'After him of course.'

That comment drew a smile from Harker who now began to examine the unique-looking box positioned in the alcove beyond the altar. All sides of it were constructed of a light amber resin, almost honey-like in colour which was interrupted by darker shades and textures just below the surface, making it impossible to see clearly inside. There was no latch or lock on it that he could make out, but at one side two gold hinges revealed which way the box would open.

'We four belong to the order of Tharmis, and our associates have protected what lies within this box for centuries. Until very recently our role was simply one of vigilance, but as of today it becomes one of war.'

Henri then reached over and gently pulled back the amber panel at the front and although he was still mystified as to what it all meant, Harker now understood how he himself was connected. There in the middle of the box an oval crystal stone perched on top of a red velvet cloth, but that's where any similarities ended. For this stone was not transparent but instead a dark red colour and with no engravings so far as he could tell. There was no light emanating from it either but whoever had created this one must surely have created its sister.

Although the others all gazed at it in reverence, it had little effect on Harker and he shot Henri a blank look. 'Sorry to burst your bubble but, like I told Gérald and as you know, I've already seen one of these.'

Everyone else but Henri looked shocked by Harker's seeming indifference, and the older man lifted the stone from its resting place and held it up with both hands.

'But do you actually know what it is?'

'Unless it's some piece of alien technology that opens portals to a parallel universe then no,' Harker replied. He glanced back towards Marceau, who was tutting away unhappily at the lack of respect their guest was showing. 'What I do know is that Father Davies had secured the other one before he went – frankly – batshit crazy, and there are other people out there who are prepared to kill for it.'

Harker was getting close to the end of his tether and apart from the impressive room he found himself in – and it *was* impressive – so far nothing he had seen was anything to be astonished by.

'If you don't believe I'm telling you the truth, then perhaps you will take more seriously those others that do believe,' Henri said coldly. 'I believe you've already met the Red Death… long dreadlocks, brutal disposition and a heart as cold as ice.'

Finally, here was something Harker could take rationally. 'Yes, we've already met. She killed an acquaintance of mine and tried to kill me.'

'Trying to get hold of the candle, no doubt.'

'As a matter of fact, yes.' Harker replied, now keen to know more about her. 'Who is she?'

'Well, as you now know, she's come to be known as "the Red Death" due to her unsavoury willingness to leave everyone she meets in a bloody mess, but her real name is Avi.' Henri replied, and it was clear he was encouraged to find Harker was at least listening to this part with interest.

'Avi?'

'Yes, Avi Legrundy. But where she comes from I have no idea,' he glanced over at Marceau, 'unless you believe Gérald's theory. That woman first appeared on our radar a few weeks ago when she paid a rather unpleasant visit to Gérald while looking for information on the candle in Father Davies's possession. Suffice to say she left an impression.'

'She left more than that,' Marceau interjected now rolling up his sleeve to reveal a deep scar on his forearm in the shape of a swastika. 'She told me this was a sign of good luck… but for her, not me.'

'That same symbol was left on the boy Father Davies killed,' Harker said grimly. 'And it was also on the other candle, but there were fifteen swastikas instead of just one.'

'That we didn't know, but it goes without saying that she obviously likes to mark her prey,' Pierre contributed, patting Marceau reassuringly on the back.

'Why she uses this mark I don't know,' Henri continued, 'but it confirms her relationship to the candle in some way or another.'

Seeing the mark disfiguring Marceau's arm had brought a certain reality into the discussion, and Harker's mind became flooded with questions. Could he really even contemplate that this Avi Legrundy was possessed by a demon – or was a demon herself!

Henri now held the stone out in front of him where it began to glow bright red, as he fixed Harker with an empathetic stare. 'It's a lot to take in, I know, but I need to justify to you the importance of this blessed candle because in less than twenty-four hours, the lives of over four billion people will be snuffed out otherwise, from the face of this earth… and that is just the beginning.'

Chapter 19

'The Order of Tharmis was formed back in the late eighteenth century, with protection as its primary goal,' Henri
explained before passing the glowing 'blessed candle' over
to Pierre, who clasped it protectively between both arms,
'However, our mandate has changed much since its initial
inception.'

'Mandate for what?' Harker demanded, becoming
frustrated with the way his host seemed to skirt his way
around a subject and it was an irritation Henri himself
immediately sensed.

'My apologies, Alex, but I'm just not sure how much
you already know. Allow me therefore to start at the
beginning. Let's sit down.'

As they headed back to the granite table near the
doorway, the man's voice deepened as he began to
explain. 'Have you ever heard of the three days of Darkness?'

'The prophecy, or the plague of Egypt?' Harker replied,
knowing both stories well.

'The prophecy, but both are related.'

It was only after a pause that Harker realised he wanted
him to recount the story himself. 'OK, well, the prophecy
was first told by the Blessed Anna Maria Taigi back in the
1800s. It was said that, at the end of time, the world would
be consumed by three days of darkness, during which

Satan's horde of demon generals would devour most of the earth's population. The stars would be blotted out and all light banished from the planet, and the only beacons that would protect the faithful would be blessed candles whose illumination would keep those who were deemed worthy alive.'

Harker glanced over at Pierre and the glowing stone he held in his hands before continuing, 'It was a prophecy echoed by many over the centuries and it's supposed to be the same as the ninth plague of Egypt that Moses brought down on that ancient superpower to negotiate the release of the Israelites.'

'Very good,' Henri replied as they both sat down at the table. 'Your knowledge on the subject seems sound.'

'Not really,' Harker replied. 'Every child in Sunday school has heard of the plague and the three days of Darkness.'

'True. But I've no doubt that is where the teaching ends and yet there was far more to it than just that.' He shuffled about upon his stone seat, clearly settling in to divulge something further. 'There was also a lesser known Vatican official, Cardinal Vicci whose prophetic vision revealed to him that the "blessed candles" were not, as many thought, church candles blessed by a priest, but actually, tangible artefacts forged by God Himself and given to the Israelites to ward off future plagues.'

'Never heard of him.' Harker replied, feeling his patience being pushed to the limit now.

'You wouldn't have since it's not common knowledge,' Henri replied. 'But what he saw was that these plagues would not be the same as bestowed on Moses from heaven, but would be created and unleashed by the fallen angel himself.'

'The Devil!' Harker exclaimed, taking all this with the pinch of salt it clearly deserved.

'Yes, the prince of darkness himself, who would turn the plague against God's children as a final act of scorn against the beings he detests so much.'

'OK and, with respect, so what? It's just a story, and there are many of them out there.'

'It's more than just a story,' Henri replied as he placed his elbow on the table and leant in closer. 'The Cardinal's vision also included a location for where the blessed candle could be found – and so it was.'

With a wave of his hand Pierre now approached and placed the still glowing red rock on the table before them, resting the item in a small concave dimple carved into its surface.

'Does the Ethiopian Orthodox Tewahedo Church mean anything to you.'

Harker recognised the name and with that came a glimmer of what the man was getting at. 'You're talking about the Ark of the Covenant, aren't you?' he asked, incredulously.

Michael gave a slow nod but with his expression blank. 'Yes, the place believed to be one of a handful of places where the Ark still resides until this day.'

The Ark of the Covenant had always inspired a strange fascination in the people's minds due to the films and popular culture surrounding it. But, although this piqued his curiosity, he was a long way yet from finding this whopper of a tale credible. 'Are you telling me that the Cardinal's vision led him to the Ark of the Covenant, and inside it he found this?' He pointed sceptically at the glowing rock. 'This blessed candle!'

'I'm not saying it held only the candles, for it without doubt carried the Ten Commandments, but haven't you ever wondered why every description or illustration made of the Ark always has rays of light emanating from it?' He persisted. Michael continued in his efforts to convince whilst ignoring Harker's look of total disbelief at what he was being told. The older man rubbed a finger along the candle's surface and nodded. 'It's not simply something I believe, Alex. It's something I know to be true.'

Harker gave a clearly resigned sigh. 'Why?'

'Because I have seen it with my own eyes,' Henri replied with the utmost sincerity. 'But allow me to explain before I get to that.'

'That would be good.' Harker declared and although intrigued by his new friend's story, nonetheless highly sceptical.

Without pause Henri dived into his explanation, all the while his eyes barely blinking. 'When the Cardinal received his vision, it did indeed lead him to the location of the Ark – in Ethiopia, just as he had been told. Inside it he found the blessed candle that sits before you now. But his vision did not just bless him with a location but also a warning that the Devil would unleash his army of demons upon the world during three days of darkness, and that this candle would not only repel the satanic onslaught but also have the power to stop it from ever happening in the first place. He brought this same candle back to the Vatican but, rather than see it as a protector, the then pope and his council saw it as the work of the Devil, and Cardinal Vicci was eventually excommunicated and banished from the Church for his apparent deviance and deception. Then the Church took his written prophecy and locked it away but, before they could do likewise with the candle he absconded with it and formed a secret protectorate that could keep it safely hidden until such time as it was needed.'

'The order of Tharmis.' Harker suggested, noticing how Marceau and the others were now circling the table – like knowledge-hungry children – all wanting to hear their favourite story.

'Correct. It has been over two hundred years since the order was created and during all that time we, as those before us, have kept the blessed candle safe. Until now.'

Harker rubbed his forehead with both hands and sucked in deeply as the group watched him like Hawks, waiting for his reaction. 'OK, let's just put aside for a moment what you're telling me and instead answer me two simple questions. Firstly, if this is the blessed candle, then what is the other one I found? And, secondly, what has any of this got to do with Father Davies?'

Henri once more dived into further explanation with vigour. 'Our meeting with Father Davies was no coincidence, Alex, as we sought him out because he was the only one who had access.'

'To what?'

'To Cardinal Vicci's original Prophecy which is locked away in one of the securest places on earth… the secret Vatican archives. It is still there, after centuries, unacknowledged by the Church who deem it nonsense, but at the same time they keep it carefully under lock and key. Father Davies was not an exorcist, as you may have been led to believe, but an advisor to the Congregation for the Doctrine of the Faith.'

'That's the part of the Vatican responsible for promulgating and defending all Catholic doctrine,' Harker volunteered, knowing it well because he still had friends there.

'And safeguarding against heresy in the old days, like the time of the Spanish inquisition.'

'Indeed, the oldest section of the Roman Curia. Due to his position he was able to gain access to Cardinal Vicci's original Prophecy and what he read caused a complete loss of his faith, so in turn he joined us.'

This revelation came as real shock to Harker because he already knew that Father Davies had lost his faith, but to put it all down to simply the reading of a prophecy was truly bizarre. 'So what did it say?'

For the first time Henri looked genuinely distressed. 'That's the whole point; he wouldn't tell us. But whatever it said, led to him discovering the second blessed candle, which until then we had no idea even existed.'

'If he didn't actually tell you anything, then why do you think his "possession" and subsequent death were in any way related to the prophecy?'

'Because of this,' Monique replied and she stepped over to the edge of the table, where she clicked a switch on its underside.

Embedded in the surface, a small LED bulb lit up and focused directly at the glowing red stone, and in doing so projected an image onto the white wall opposite. At first it was blurry but she then manoeuvred the stone gently in its support groove until the image became clearer.

It consisted of symbols and, as Harker leaned closer to the wall and squinted, he began to recognise them as letters. 'It's Aramaic,' he confirmed, 'the language of the Israelites.'

'Yes, we know that,' Pierre sounded impatient, 'but it's what it reads that's important.'

Harker ran through the translation in his head and then read it out aloud. 'You are I and I am you. When he is myth and we are reality. This grand deception will be repaid in blood.'

The message struck a chord with Harker even before he had finished reading it. 'I've seen this before although it was written in vulgar Latin last time. It's also the same thing Father Davies wrote in blood after murdering that boy and his mother.'

'Exactly,' Marceau replied, 'and apart from it being the same message as found on this blessed candle, we have absolutely no idea what it means!'

Monique switched the LED light off and Harker turned back to face them all, full of interest. 'Did Father Davies ever see this image?'

'No. never,' Pierre replied. 'We showed him the candle, indeed, but never revealed the sacred inscription it contained.'

This was puzzling to Harker, but another possibility came to mind. 'Is it feasible that the other stone – candle – carried the same inscription?'

'We don't know because we never got to see it,' Pierre responded, 'but we have assumed it to be the warning.'

'What kind of warning?' Harker asked, now becoming increasing enthralled by what he was learning.

'The prophecy stated that there would be a warning just before the three days of darkness commenced, and that it would thus give those that knew of it time to prepare.'

'Are you telling me that after two centuries, the Order of Tharmis hasn't been able to find out what the entire prophecy is!'

Harker's comment sounded like a recrimination, which in truth it was, and had Henri already shaking his head. 'Alex, this Order was created primarily to protect the blessed candle, and that is exactly what we have done.

And the closest we have ever come to seeing the Cardinal's written document was via Father Davies, who is not only dead but appears to have learned more about all of this in a short time than we, as you so kindly remind us, have discovered in two centuries. Furthermore we appear now to be on the precipice of the prophecy coming true, yet we've only recently found out that there are two candles… and we don't even know how to use them! In others words, we're at a total loss.'

Harker surveyed the worried faces around him and whatever the reality of this situation and no matter if he felt bad for them, he couldn't help but detect a strong whiff of sheer incompetence. 'I don't believe in kicking someone when they're down but… well, you're not a very effective Order, are you?'

Given the reaction Harker received, one would have thought he had just insulted their beloved mothers. Some were clearly fuming and Marceau slammed his fist down on the table.

'I knew this was a bad idea,' the doctor raged. 'Not only doesn't he believe us but he's just taking the proverbial.'

Pierre and Monique nodded their heads in complete agreement yet there was one person who remained calm and collected.

'I don't blame you Alex,' Henri said calmly. 'It is indeed a rather fantastical tale and maybe every one of us is inclined to be a doubting Thomas, when all is said and done. But, given what you have seen, can you honestly deny me that something very strange is going on here?'

'On that we can certainly agree, but to take the next step of accepting this prophecy of yours is another matter entirely,' Harker replied as politely as he could.

Instead of Henri looking frustrated by this response, he looked determined as he got to his feet and picked up 'the blessed candle', which was still glowing red. 'Then perhaps it is high time you saw the truth with your own eyes.'

Henri gestured Harker to his feet and, with his finger, pointed him to move a few metres away from the table, then extended the red candle towards him as the others – including a now more composed Marceau – flanked him on either side. 'Not every person sees the same thing but what you do see will constitute the truth and only the truth.'

Monique gently grasped Harker by the wrist and pulled it upwards towards the glowing candle. Even though he resisted initially, a reassuring look from her persuaded him to relax and he edged his hand closer and closer until his fingertips grazed the surface. An odd tingling sensation began to resonate through his muscles before slowly spreading up his hand and then through into his wrist while in his line of vision the small specks of dust in the air began to multiply. They grew in number until it seemed like spitting raindrops were very slowly falling from above and on down past him to the floor, but so slowly that they appeared to have little or no mass. Before his eyes the room, and Marceau's face, began to warp and melt like candle wax… and all the colours began to mingle into a bubbling mass… and then everything went black.

At first Harker felt a terrifying loss of control but the darkness that enveloped him then began to subside, and now he could hear the rhythmic beating of his heart lightly thumping and, despite what was happening, he felt completely at ease. His mind and his thoughts were still acute and clear but he had neither the wish nor desire to think about anything. Instead he gazed into the darkness as somewhere off in the distance a pinprick of light began to appear. It was small at first but began to grow in size, pulsating with each expansion, and as it did so Harker felt a cosy warmth embrace him like an invisible blanket. And the only thought that came to mind was how content he felt at this very moment.

The light was soon a spherical ball getting ever larger, then suddenly he felt himself propelled towards it at an unimaginable speed and, with a sudden flash, he was surrounded by brilliant white light. It was not painful to his eyes and, as he gazed into it, small pixel-like dots began to form randomly and began creating little clumps that now grew as others joined them. Within what seemed like only seconds a picture formed before him like a television screen, but one as clear as if peering through a glass window and out onto the world beyond. Then he began to move towards it slowly, until he had passed beyond the threshold of the screen itself.

It took a few moments for him to register, then a sense of panic shot through his body as he realised what he was looking at – and where he was looking at it from. The continent of Europe lay squarely below him as he hung above the earth in a starlit sky, and he watched as white storm clouds slowly swirled in spirals across the top layers of the earth's atmosphere.

Is this real? was his only thought as the sun began to peek above the earth's curvature, appearing in a brilliant display of golden rays which cast themselves first across Greece and then up and over the terrains of Italy, France and finally Great Britain. Harker could feel himself breathing but, given that he was hanging in the vacuum of space, it made absolutely no sense. But the logic of it, or lack thereof, didn't bother him. In fact he felt completely calm as off to his left, the illuminated surface of the moon shone brightly before beginning to disappear over the far side of the planet.

Suddenly something began to change and at first he couldn't identify what it was, but then he began to see the stars gathered around him fizzle out in quick succession, until the heavens were now nothing more than a black void. And then, wham, he was diving face first towards the planet with great speed, and he could feel the wind rushing past him although his eyes remained clear and not watering, until he plunged through the layer of white clouds and was getting ever closer to the ground. He was over Italy, then closer, and next over the Swiss Alps and down into northern France, and he caught a sight of the English Channel rushing towards him, and at this point he closed his eyes with his heart pounding in his ears.

The sensation of falling stopped as abruptly as it had begun and he cautiously started to open his eyes, expecting something terrible, but instead found himself standing in the middle of Cambridge city. On the horizon he could make out the familiar towers of the university and all around him were people, none of whom he recognised, all frozen in different poses as if someone had pressed a pause button on reality itself. And he felt suddenly compelled to reach down and touch the concrete pavement beneath him. As he pulled his hand back away, he noticed small pieces of gravel and soil sticking to his palm and he rubbed at this with his fingers, feeling the sharp corners of each stone. It was all so real, but it couldn't be.

Harker tried to remember where he had been before arriving in this place, but his memory just wasn't there and, as he attempted to focus his mind, he looked up and saw, only a few metres away, a woman wearing a bright yellow dress, standing motionless. Her blonde hair was frozen in the process of being flicked back, and each strand hung in the air unnaturally, like in a still photograph. It was now then Harker became aware of the expression on her face, for it was a look of absolute terror. And, although at first he thought she was looking directly at him, it soon became evident that she was staring at something over his shoulder.

Harker did a 180-degree turn and what he saw had him recoiling in shock. As he leapt backwards he tripped and ended face up on the ground, both his hands raised up to his face protectively.

The being before him was colossal, about the size of an elephant, with two flaming arms as thick as tree trunks flung forwards in a grabbing motion, but frozen in time the same as was everyone else. Thick horns protruded from each side of its head and yellow cat's eyes the size of saucers beamed menacingly at the woman standing behind him, while thick threads of saliva oozed from the corners of its huge mouth to dangle like white nylon shoestrings.

Behind this monstrosity hovered numerous dark spots whose shadowy cores were not penetrated by the sunlight, as if they absorbed any light immediately around them. They possessed something of a human form in terms of shape and size, but with no identifying marks that Harker could recognise as he got to his feet and scanned the surrounding area further. People were frozen in the midst of fleeing in a panic, and then the clouds overhead began to turn blood-red and up high the sun quickly turned black as if in eclipse, but completing the transformation within seconds. The air became filled with scarlet-red light as if one was looking through a coloured filter, and in places it morphed in intensity as the clouds continued to roll forward, changing the colour spectrum of the landscape as it did so.

The air in Harker's lungs felt hot and he coughed in irritation as all around him the world began to shift, slowly at first like an organ-grinder building up momentum, with people beginning to move in slow motion at first and then faster and faster, until a critical mass clearly was reached and everything returned to normal speed, revealing the true chaos playing out around him. The woman in the yellow dress was now screaming at the top of her lungs as the titan of a monster lumbered past him and slammed hard into her, before ripping her in half at the waist with its massive hands. The sounds of further screams filled the air as the dark shadows now flew past him towards hordes of shrieking people all scrambling to escape.

The sickening noises of pain and despair were blood-curdling, and as they continued Harker saw a bright white light on the horizon which shot a broad stream of light upwards into the sky and everyone – including the brutish monster – now fell still with all attention focused solely on that beam.

Almost immediately the same white light exploded with a deafening boom, then it expanded outwards in all directions, overshadowing everything in its path as its nearer edges raced towards Harker. When it hit him, the impact was like the shock wave of a bomb blast, then everything went black.

'Alex?' a voice called out from the darkness. 'Can you hear me… Alex?'

Harker's eyes flickered open and he instinctively wrestled against the hands holding him down.

'Alex, you're safe,' the voice spoke again, and Harker looked up to see Henri staring down on him as he lay outstretched on the floor, with Pierre and Monique gripping his shoulders on either side.

'What happened?' Harker muttered, and the question was directed at himself rather than anyone else.

'Take it easy,' Henri continued, pulling him up into a sitting position with the help of the others. 'You're just disorientated. It's quite normal.'

'There's nothing normal about it,' Harker coughed, his mouth dry, and he stumbled to his feet and instinctively pushed away their helping hands. 'What was that thing?'

'Not so crazy now, hey?' Marceau remarked sarcastically, sitting back against the granite table with his arms folded.

'Not now.' Henri waved a dismissive hand towards the doctor. 'The blessed candle offers each person an insight, but only once, Alex... I hope yours was worthwhile.'

Harker's brain felt fried and cumbersome but his balance was strong and he stood up stoutly, beginning to go over in his mind what he had just witnessed, as if to convince himself he had seen it at all.

'What did you actually see?' Henri probed quietly, trying not to sound pushy.

'I'm not sure... but a vision of anarchy and destruction,' Harker replied, still trying to regain some clear focus. 'My home town of Cambridge totally laid waste by... something.'

'It didn't possess horns, did it?' Marceau asked. When Harker shot him an unsettled look, the man gave a brief shrug of his shoulders. 'Welcome to my world.'

Harker remained silent as images of his experience continued to run though his mind like a film reel, each fresh one causing him to shudder involuntarily.

'It sounds as if you just came face to face with a demon, Alex – one of the Devil's generals,' Henri explained and the others began to nod. 'I'm afraid we've all seen them and it's just the beginning of what those three days of darkness will have to offer. The word terrifying doesn't do it justice.'

Harker's normally rational mind was in turmoil by this point, because this was altogether just too 'out there' to fathom. But he couldn't deny to himself what he had seen, and it was as real as anything he had ever experienced. 'There was a white light emanating from an explosion,' he stuttered, 'but it wasn't like a bomb, or anything like that. The only way I can describe it is as if it was banishing or cleansing the horrors I had been witnessing.'

He was, to himself, sounding crazier with every word he uttered, but Henri glanced over at Pierre with a look of encouragement, and he in turn moved to Harker's side. 'From what we've been able to discern over the years, the blessed candle offers us a glimpse of what could be – like a list of future possibilities – but in all our experience it has only showed us the worst-case scenarios of destruction that the prophecy will bring to bear. But none has ever seen a positive outcome like the one you describe – except one other.'

Pierre didn't need to utter the name because Harker already knew. 'Father Davies?'

'Yes,' Pierre continued. 'In his vision he described a bright light that laid waste to all the evil surrounding him.'

'And how would we do that?' Harker asked and now fully giving in to the bizarre nature of what this all meant.

'We don't know how, but he did,' Pierre explained and now looking nervous.

'Because he was able to read the whole of the Cardinal's document.' Harker concluded and rubbing the top of his skull which was now aching painfully.

'We believe that not only did the Prophecy document infer the events accompanying the darkness,' Henri added, 'but also how to prevent it.'

As Harker looked at the weary looking faces before him, a gaping hole in their story suddenly became obvious. 'You said that the Cardinal initiated the Order of Tharmis, correct?'

Henri offered another nod as the others followed suit.

'Then why didn't he tell anyone what the entire Prophecy revealed?'

If Henri was rattled by this inconsistency, he didn't show it and he smiled sadly. 'Because he was murdered the very same day he set up the Order, and before he could tell anyone. All the Order had to go on was the candle you've just touched, their own disturbing visions, and partial knowledge of the prophecy itself… We have therefore only half of the knowledge needed to stop the disastrous events soon to befall this world.' A look of hardened determination formed on his face. 'We need you to get hold of the Prophecy held inside the Vatican's secret archives, because without it we are lost.'

'And we need the second blessed candle you have in your possession as well,' Marceau added.

At this request Harker expelled a loud sigh before he laughed out loud, this exacerbating the pain in his head. 'Why on earth do you think I can get hold of the Prophecy? You said it yourself, the archives are one of the most secure places on the planet.'

Henri looked undeterred by his incredulous response. 'Because we know who you are, Alex. We know you yourself are member of an Order, one that has impressive ties to the Vatican.'

Even though he had not mentioned the Templars by name, he evidently did know something, and Harker now remained silent as the older man persisted with his pitch.

'I won't lie to you because we are short on time; any mistrust generated at this point will not benefit either of us. We don't know who or what your Order actually is but we have reliable sources confirming that they are a powerful group with many connections. We have our own higher-up contacts as well, you know.'

They were clearly plucking at straws and Harker knew it but, with what he had just seen and everything else that had happened in the last few days, he decided there and then it was in everyone's best interests to dig a little deeper, so long as the anonymity of the Templars was preserved. 'I may have some contacts at the Vatican that could help but it's not that difficult to gain access these days. Why haven't you tried before? Researchers, scholars, they can usually get in by making a simple request.'

'It's not the regular archive we need to get in to,' Henri explained, getting a confused look from Harker because, as far as he knew, the secret archive was the only one at the Vatican.

'Not sure I know what you're getting at, Henri,' he said, and it was now Pierre who took over.

'There's a section of the archive that has never been acknowledged: a place that stores only the most sensitive pieces of Catholic doctrine or artefacts. That's where the Darkness Prophecy is stored, and it was to there that Father Davies gained access.'

Harker was stunned by the disclosure. 'If there is one, I haven't heard about it and, anyway, what could be more secure than the archives themselves? Why would you need a vault within a vault?'

'Because there are things that even the head of Christendom would not want even his most loyal devotees to see. Perhaps the type of thing that might lead to a complete loss of faith in the Church, just as Father Davies suddenly lost his.'

Even though to Harker this had 'conspiracy theory' blazed across it in red neon lights he couldn't deny that something supremely weird was going on. And given his recent 'vision', he had a distinct feeling there was a lot of truth in what he was now being told. How much, though, was anyone's guess. 'What are you asking me to do, exactly?'

Henri paused, stroking his beard, and then gazed towards him grimly. 'We want you to break into the archives and steal the Darkness Prophecy.'

Chapter 20

Bishop Leonardo Grochea sat patiently in the waiting room situated on the top floor of the palace of the Holy Office, tapping his fingers rhythmically on the varnished surface of the desk next to him. Located at the southern boundary of Vatican City, the building housed the Curia Congregation for the Doctrine of the Faith. Considered by many as the guard dog of Christianity, Grochea had always considered himself immensely fortunate to work in such an important division of the Church, but this was the first time he had felt so concerned about their role.

This modest building held vast swathes of Catholic history within its walls and although working here by day, he felt ever more like a stranger as he tussled with the difficult issues which had brought him to the Prefect Archbishop's office in the first place. With the news of Father Davies's unspeakable actions plastered across the morning's papers, he could only guess where it would all lead in the minds of the public. Father Davies had been a respected colleague for some years before his abdication from the clergy and, even though Grochea had not been very close to the man, his departure seemed a loss felt by all. That failure, however, was nothing but a minuscule blip in comparison to the ex-priest's brutal murder of a woman and her teenage son. Never in Grochea's lifetime had a man of the Church committed such a terrible crime as these murders and subsequent desecration of the bodies, and it still made him sick to his stomach. Even those who had known Father Davies only from a distance were shocked that such a mild-mannered man could turn into little more than a vicious beast.

As for the exorcism and possession elements of the incident, well, that was what Grochea was here for and he only hoped the archbishop shared his concerns and therefore agreed with the solutions he was about to offer. Coupled with the horrendous and senseless killing of three local bishops and their congregations the day before, it had produced a dark cloud of despair hanging over all those who worked at the Vatican, as well as in the wider community beyond. These were dark days indeed.

At the end of the room two white double doors opened inwards and Archbishop Angelo Federar strode through and made his way over to the waiting bishop, who rose swiftly to his feet and met him halfway.

'I apologise for your long wait, Leonardo, but I suppose you've seen the morning papers?'

'I have. It's been an awful shock,' the bishop replied, sounding genuinely subdued by the news. 'And that's the reason I'm here.'

Federar looked immediately troubled, a frown appearing on his brow. 'You'd better come in then.'

With a nod from Grochea, the two men walked briskly over into the archbishop's office, with Federar closing the doors gently behind them.

'Please, have a seat,' Federar insisted and dutifully Grochea sat down on a red satin court chair as the archbishop made his way back around to the other side of his desk. This room was not as lavish as some other offices in the Vatican but its shiny wood panelled-doors and the classic grey plaster provided a humble décor that suited the archbishop's personality to a T.

Federar sat himself down in the green leather armchair positioned behind the desk, below a picture of the current pope, sitting back into it comfortably and placing his hands in his lap. 'So what can I do for you, Leonardo, on a day of such awful news?'

Grochea squirmed a little in his seat, not because it was uncomfortable but because what he was about to say was unlikely to receive a warm reception. 'I know your recent feelings on the subject but, given what has just happened, I need to ask if you would reconsider your decision to keep the Prophecy strictly off limits.'

Federar looked unimpressed and his mouth curved downwards like a bulldog's. 'And which Prophecy would that be?'

The archbishop's spurious attempt to play dumb only emboldened Grochea's resolve, and he sat right up in his chair defiantly. 'Did you read what Father Davies wrote on the wall in the blood of the woman and child he butchered?'

Federar's expression changed not one iota but his nostrils did inflame somewhat, which was a tell-tale-sign for those who knew him that he was either unimpressed or annoyed. 'I did read the report but hardly think it has any tangible bearing on what we're discussing here.'

'No tangible bearing!' Grochea exclaimed, raising his eyebrow. 'I admit I've not read it myself but I have it on good authority that those are the exact words used in the Prophecy, are they not?'

Archbishop Federar opened his mouth in surprise and he began to slowly bob his head. 'Oh, you mean the three days of Darkness Prophecy?'

'Yes, that one,' Grochea replied, giving him an unimpressed stare.

'I'm not sure how or what you've heard, Leonardo, but, that aside, I don't think it really qualifies as being relevant – besides which it isn't even recognised officially by the Holy See.'

'Right, Angelo, and that's why it's hidden away so securely?'

Federar's nostrils flared again, but after a few moments his shoulders sagged and he slumped forward and ditched his formal demeanour. 'Few people in this office have ever seen that scrap of paper...'

'Father Davies did, though,' Grochea interrupted, doubling down against the archbishop's intransigence on the subject.

'That's my point, Leonardo. The poor man lost his mind and reverted to writing about the very thing that consumed him... Tragic? Absolutely, but to think it in some way gives credence to justifying any aspect of that prophecy is just lazy thinking. And that aside, you – or anyone else – should not even be aware of what it says.'

'That's immaterial now,' Grochea replied, looking undeterred as he remained sitting stiffly in his chair. 'And maybe you're right. But if there is even a sliver of truth in it, then it is in everyone's interests to at least allow others to conduct a proper examination of the document.'

Federar looked like a man who had just been battered over the head with a truth he was not quite ready to accept yet and, although he said nothing, he now looked po-faced and his nostrils went into overdrive.

'I understand why it's been kept hidden all these years,' Grochea continued sympathetically, deliberately adopting a yielding tone of voice, 'but should both of us choose to stick our heads in the sand when so much is at stake? Would you, at the very least, allow me access to it, or at the very most speak with his Holiness on the matter?'

Federar considered this proposal and then, after a few thoughtful moments, his expression began to soften and he sat back again in his chair. 'Very well, Leonardo, I will speak with the pontiff this evening.'

Grochea was already out of his own seat and resting both hands on the archbishop's grand cherry-wood desk. 'Thank you. It's all I ask.'

Federar offered him an obliging nod, then he wiped his open palm down one side of his face, the frustration he felt obvious. 'Anything else?'

'No, thank you. Now, if you will excuse me, I have things to attend to.'

'Of course,' Federar said, in truth just wanting this man to leave his office. 'And please refrain from discussing this business with anyone else – for the time being.'

'I will, Angelo. I know how difficult this is for you,' Grochea replied, with a complete understanding of the bind the archbishop was in. 'It will probably amount to nothing.'

That comment had Federar suddenly looking nervous. 'I hope so, Leonardo, because if you're wrong… then God help us all.'

Chapter 21

'Burgle the Vatican's secret archive? Are you crazy!'

Stefani's voice was so loud that Harker had to pull the phone away from his ear, and even Marceau jerked his head back as they continued to walk briskly down New York Avenue on their way towards his apartment.

'No one's going to burgle anything,' Harker assured her, placing his hand over the receiver for fear that people passing by would hear the suggestion. 'I have a friend over at the Vatican who might be able to help.'

'I thought your friends over that neck of the woods were few and far between these days,' she replied, still sounding more than doubtful.

'I still have some but whether they'll be sympathetic is another thing entirely. All the same I have to try.'

There was a brief silence, then Harker could have sworn he heard a deep sigh from the other end of the line.

'And you're absolutely sure this vision of yours was real?'

'As sure as I am talking to you now, Stefani,' he replied resolutely, even though he knew how irrational it all sounded. 'Something very real is going on here and it all seems to revolve around the Vatican archives.'

There was yet another pause until she came back on the line, but this time sounding more confident of his plan.

'Very well, Alex, it's your call. I'll take a flight to Rome asap, and meet you there.'

'Thank you.' He took some comfort in her willingness to believe him, 'Do you still have the stone?'

'I have someone looking at your "blessed candle" right now. He's tried shining a light through it, but there's no message such as the one you described.'

'OK. It was worth a try,' Harker said, disappointed by her answer. 'In the meantime I'm going to call Sebastian and get his approval.'

'No, I'll call him. It would be better coming from me.'

'Fair enough,' Harker replied, quite glad that he would not have to mention his supernatural vision to the Grand Master, because even he himself was having a hard time accepting what he had seen. The experience could only be described as paranormal, and that was something he felt personally uncomfortable with. 'Dr Marceau wants to pick up a few things from his apartment and then we'll head straight for the airport.'

'Is it wise to bring him along, Alex? We don't really know anything about him.'

Harker glanced over at Marceau, who was clearly attempting to hear the discussion, his eyes screwed up in concentration. 'I know enough and, besides, even though his friends are at a loss, they seem to know far more of what's going on than we do.'

'Your choice,' she said, sounding unconvinced. 'I'll see you at the Vatican. Have a safe trip.'

The line abruptly went dead and Harker slipped the phone back into his inside jacket pocket. 'She'll meet us there,' he announced.

'Good, good,' Marceau said enthusiastically, as they approached his apartment door, 'The more the merrier – and the sooner we get to Rome the better.'

They had left soon after Henri had dropped the bombshell regarding the Prophecy's location, along with explicit instructions that they keep the Order updated as to what progress they were making. Harker had been wary of the suggestion he bring Dr Marceau along with him but, given what he had witnessed after touching the blessed candle, he figured he now needed all the help he could get. The vision had truly affected his whole being, like one would react after some serious event when you replay the shocking incident over and over in your head, scavenging through every detail. That experience was like nothing he had ever known and had he not seen it with his own eyes, he would have thought it as crazy as Marceau's own account of dimension-jumping beings opening portals in space. Indeed it still sounded barmy to Harker but, given his recent personal encounter with a ten-foot-tall behemoth running rampant through the streets of Cambridge, he found himself far more open now to other possibilities, no matter how wacky.

'Should only take me a few minutes to get some provisions,' Marceau advised as he opened the front door and began climbing the stairs to his apartment, 'and most importantly of course, my passport.'

'Passport! We're only going to Rome,' Harker declared sounding irritated at this time-wasting.

'Now, now, Professor. You never know where we'll end up and being unprepared is the sign of an unworthy soul.'

Harker didn't even bother with a reply. Since leaving the Order's secret hideaway, Marceau had become increasingly excited at the prospect of actually seeing the Prophecy document in the flesh, and Harker wondered how long the man had waited for this moment. 'How long have you actually belonged to the Order of Tharmis?'

'Not until quite recently,' Marceau replied as they reached his floor and pulled out his key to unlock the apartment door. 'Father Davies inducted me less than a month ago but, as you can see, it's been something of a rapid education since then.'

Suddenly the Doctor's differing interpretation of the prophecy began to make more sense. 'So that's why your analysis of the candles differs so much,' Harker suggested as the doctor took off through the living room and in to his bedroom.

'It's all a question of how you determine the truth, Professor,' Marceau replied, as Harker turned to the window and took in a breathtaking view of the Eiffel Tower just across the river. 'Henri and his lot were taught their belief, but I had to discover the truth for myself... with a lot of help from Father Davies, of course.'

'How much help?'

'Pretty much all of it.'

This reply set off alarm bells and Harker pulled away from the beautiful view and turned his attention to the empty doorway of the room Marceau had disappeared into. 'That African tribe you mentioned earlier, where you found the second blessed candle... you didn't make that trip there yourself, did you?'

There was no response, and then a sheepish-looking Dr Marceau poked his head around the doorway. 'Not exactly.'

'How, not exactly?' Harker quizzed, sensing that an omission was about to be forthcoming.

'I did accompany Father Davies on one of his trips to the Congo – to do some aid work – but he made his remarkable discovery during a solo trip.'

Harker's look of suspicion had Marceau gingerly making his way into full view, until he stopped a few feet outside the doorway. 'After Father Davies saw the Prophecy for himself, and the Order made contact with him, he brought me up to speed and so I fibbed a little so I would be accepted by them.'

'Why?' Harker asked, somewhat bemused.

'Because he didn't know who the Order were at first and, although we had speculated about what the Prophecy might mean, well… strength in numbers and all that. Simply put, he didn't want to deal with all this on his own, and initially I was the only one who knew about his discovery of the blessed candle, and so he brought me in on it.'

It seemed reasonable to Harker that Father Davies might want someone by his side whom he could trust and confide in when surrounded by a secretive Order he knew little about. But something else niggled him. 'So how did you become involved with the possessed boy who died, then?'

'Oh, that was on Father Davies's account. The mother had approached him with the belief that her son was possessed, and it was the Father who requested me to give my expert opinion before he went ahead with an exorcism. That's where we disagreed,' Marceau replied, puffing out his chest at the mention of his services being needed. 'I myself believed the boy to be schizophrenic… but after what happened I freely admit I was wrong. Whatever had taken hold of that boy's mind subsequently took hold of Father Davies too.' Marceau now looked deeply sad.

'After the writing on the wall, and its precise match to what we had seen within the blessed candle, it became impossible to reach any other conclusion. Which is why it is so imperative for us to find out what the original Prophecy says.'

The plethora of discrepancies in Marceau's logic was as beguiling as his dimension-portal theory, but before Harker could bombard him with questions, the doctor raised his head up magnanimously. 'Whichever idea you choose to believe in, Professor, whether astrological or religious, you should nevertheless believe this. Those demons are very real and if we don't find a way of stopping it, that vision you saw will come to pass. The absolute truth is to be found in a saying that I'm sure you will be familiar with: that the greatest trick the Devil has managed to contrive is to convince humankind that he doesn't exist.'

'No words, 'ave ever been truer,' declared a husky voice loudly from behind them.

Harker glanced instantly over at the hallway to see Avi Legrundy – the Red Death – standing calmly in the doorway with a machete in one hand and holding some-thing else he could not make out in the other. She raised that hand and pointed the mystery item at Harker, where-upon something like two thin, glinting bolts of lightning flew out from her fingertips and struck him directly in the chest.

The pain was intense and he immediately began to shake as his hands clenched and unclenched uncontrol-lably. The woman then administered a second pulse of electricity from the taser gun she held, which propelled Harker convulsing to the ground. 'You 'ave something that don't belong to you, you little thieves,' she rasped, moving closer towards Marceau, all the while keeping her finger pressed firmly on the taser's trigger. 'And all debts must be paid in full.'

Chapter 22

Harker's eyelids twitched painfully as he opened them fully and began to make out his surroundings through blurry vision. His ears prickled with the sound of static as a bright square light began to take shape, until he was able to recognise clearly the television set which had been placed directly in front of him. He was still in Dr Marceau's living room, although it was dark now due to the heavy curtains pulled across the windows. As his faculties gradually returned to him, he gazed at the TV screen, his eyes wincing as they adjusted to its brightness. The news story now playing was a CNN report and the red banner running along the bottom read 'Seven dead in church massacre,' while above it a reporter was in full flow.

'Authorities are still withholding the details of events that transpired today within this simple Roman church, but eyewitnesses have confirmed that seven people in all, including the priest, were not only murdered but then mutilated after death, leaving a horrifying sight for the cleaner who discovered them. This was the second massacre within a city church, during the last twenty-four hours, and Vatican officials have yet to comment

on the deaths, where the victims in each
case included a Catholic priest along with his
entire congregation.'

'It wasn't no mutilation. I only cut their eyelids off,'
protested a familiar voice with a heavy Jamaican accent.
Harker flicked his head up towards the source and spotted
the shadowy figure of Avi Legrundy standing right behind
the television screen. 'It was an awakening for all and them
dat were blind can now see.'

Harker felt a cold shiver run through him when the
remorseless killer offered a wide grin, allowing her teeth
to glint in what little light there was. As he attempted to
move, he became aware that his body was restrained by
a rope wrapped around him, securing him to one of the
wood dining chairs he had noticed in the kitchen earlier.

'Who are you?' he croaked, his throat dry and his lips
sticking together.

'Dat's not important,' she replied and reaching over
from behind the TV to press the mute button at the base
of the screen. 'But *he* knows who I am.'

Harker craned his neck over to the right, in the direction of her pointing finger to see Marceau in the same
predicament as himself, tied to a chair, with the exception
that a cloth gag had been stuffed into his mouth.

'I gave him a love tap the first time we spoke.' Legrundy
now pointing to the scarred swastika on Marceau's
forearm, 'But the conversation was pretty sparse.' she
added coldly, moving over to her victim who was now
shaking all over, 'that time anyway.'

At first glance the gag appeared to be made of some
red material but, as Marceau pulled his head back fearfully
on Legrundy's approach, Harker could now see its white

edges and it became clear the crimson originated from another source.

She pulled the blood-soaked cloth from Marceau's lips to reveal a painful-looking jagged stump where his tongue had been. 'He's a noisy one,' she continued with a smile as a nauseating gurgling sound emanated from Marceau's twitching mouth and blood began to trickle from the corners. 'The human tongue is a beefy organ, so it took me a few attempts to cut it all the way through.'

Harker could not help but notice the glinting of her fingernails as she wiggled them right in front of him, and the glinting of their razor-sharp tips made him flinch. These nails weren't acrylic, but instead sharpened metal, and with them she now retrieved something from her pocket and dropped it into Harker's lap. It made him want to throw up.

With Marceau's severed tongue resting limply in the crease of his trousers, Harker instinctively jerked his pelvis upwards sending the nasty offering tumbling to the floor. Legrundy meanwhile jammed the rag back into the doctor's mouth and turned her attention back to Harker.

'Where's the candle?' she demanded menacingly, lightly brushing those razor-sharp metal nails against Harker's cheek. 'It is time to give back what don't belong to you.'

Apart from the obvious disadvantage of being tied to a chair at the mercy of a woman with knives in place of fingers who had a genuine love for the art of butchery, Harker found himself in a real bind. Only two choices were available to him at this moment. Admit he didn't have it any more and risk becoming disposable to this maniac, or lie and say he didn't actually have it on him but knew how to obtain it. Both responses were likely to elicit a dire outcome – not unlike the one which had befallen the still gurgling Marceau – but with no other options Harker chose the better of the bad ones he had. 'I don't have it on me, but it's somewhere safe.'

Without warning she rammed a steel-tipped forefinger into his shoulder, its tip being so sharp that it sliced through his jacket and buried its full length into the muscle.

'You can do better than that.' she growled, and Harker grunted in agony as she rotated her finger this way and that. He could even hear a muffled scratching as metal scraped against the bone, inflicting maximum pain for such a small wound.

'It's the truth,' He hissed through gritted teeth as the throbbing in his shoulder increased tenfold. 'I don't have it… but I'll tell you where it is, if you let us go.'

He gestured towards Marceau whose widened eyes blinked in agreement, a fresh trickle of blood dribbling from one side of his mouth. But this request already had Legrundy looking doubtful. She administered one more twist of her forefinger, then withdrew it and gave him a hard slap across the face.

'If you yourself don't 'ave it, den dat woman you were with does,' she snarled. She now took a step towards Marceau and pressed those sharp fingernails against his throat. 'As for you, Doctor, you're just dead weight now.'

With a swift flick of her wrist she sliced through Marceau's windpipe and sent a spurt of blood splattering across the TV screen, which acted like a filter in bathing areas of the room in a dark red light.

'No!' Harker yelled as he wrestled against his bonds.

Marceau's eyelashes fluttered uncontrollably and his whole body twitched, while glistening blood pumped out of his throat, each jet less powerful than the last, until his struggling faded and his body became still.

'You didn't have to do that,' Harker yelled, still fighting against his own restraints.

Legrundy looked unmoved, and gave Marceau a hard slap on top of his head, then made her way into the centre of the living room. 'Of course I did. He is no use to me now,' she mocked, before bending down to rummage through a container whose edges Harker could only just make out in the gloom. 'And neither are you.'

The ominous sound of some unknown metal object clanking against the side of the container immediately quelled Harker's anger, because whatever it was, it didn't sound good. Instead he now began to consider his options and any ploy that would gain him some extra time.

'Why did you kill all those innocent churchgoers?' he asked calmly, nodding towards the TV screen, as the sound of her rummaging continued. 'Why choose such easy targets for someone with your skills?' The sound of rummaging now stopped, before Legrundy stood back up and approached him, resting her steel nails on top of the TV and double-tapping upon its the surface.

'They may have been easy to overcome physically, but their minds were far more dangerous.' she stated before making an odd clicking sound with her mouth. 'They were thieves, nothing more.'

'Thieves?'

'Yes, thieves,' she continued and, much to Harker's relief, seeming to be genuinely engaged by his question. 'Through their practice of a fake religion, a stolen doctrine that has blinded the world with lies since its inception. They were little more than lambs to the slaughter but devotion to such false practice was nothing short of heresy.'

'Heresy! They were worshipping their own God inside a church. That doesn't sound much like heresy to me.'

Legrundy scowled at him and, whether deliberately or unconsciously, began to rake her fingernails along the top of the TV leaving thin jagged scratches across its surface. 'It depends who you have faith in, for Christianity is nothing but a usurper and a thieving, crooked lie. But don't worry, like all things that 'ave a beginning, they also 'ave an end, and that time has now come.'

It was a strange reply from someone Harker believed to be a Satanist, because you had to believe in one so as to believe in the other. 'To me that seems an odd stance for a devil worshipper?'

A wide grin spread across her lips and she began to stare at him dubiously. 'Depends on your definition of the Devil don't it? For someone who's about to meet his maker, you got a lot of questions, don't you?'

Clearly she knew Harker was attempting to postpone his fate but the killer seemed intrigued by his question. 'From de time of the Persians to the gluttony of de Roman Empire and beyond, we have endured, little man. Long before the bandits that you call "de faithful" stole our creed and ravaged it of truth, we have existed. And as it was back then, so it shall be again.'

The pomposity of her statement left Harker's mind awash with confusion as she retreated into the shadows and picked something up which she raised to her chest, then walked forward so he could see it. 'Enough talk.'

The red petrol can she showed him produced such a feeling of dread in Harker that his body froze, leaving him completely at a loss for words. The thought of being burnt alive was about as terrifying as anything he could imagine and hearing Legrundy shake the can so the liquid sloshed around inside it only added to his panic. Having one's throat slit suddenly seemed like a luxury, but one that he would not be afforded.

'That's right, Professor,' she said, unscrewing the cap and taking a sniff, 'you're about to burn along with everything else in dis apartment, and you can consider that a preparation for your eternity in hell.'

She began by dousing the sofa, then quickly moved on to the curtains. Harker silently looked on, as the acrid smell of fuel pervaded the air, stinging his nostrils.

'Dose two candles represent more than you can ever know,' she announced flatly and remarkably calmly considering she was now preparing to roast him alive. 'They mean different things to different people. To Dr Marceau dey represented a gateway to another dimension.' She gave a condescending shake of her head even as another slosh of petrol was splashed over the fireplace. 'To others dey are vessels containing ancient spirits, to be worshipped above all else. Some even reckon dey embody the creation of the universe itself.'

At that moment, even though he had asked the question, Harker could not give a damn what those candles were. The thought of being burned alive was all that preoccupied his mind and, even though he was desperately wondering how the hell he was going to get out of this in one piece, his only option was to keep this conversation going until the moment seemed right. 'So what exactly do they mean to you?'

Legrundy shook the last drops of petrol against the far doorway and then threw the empty can down on the floor. 'Salvation, brother, and the end of the beginning,' she concluded and, pulling a shiny brass Zippo from her back pocket, headed back towards him. 'In all there are only two candles dat have been lost to us since the dawn of creation and some believe that, when they are reunited again, dey will offer the world a truth that has been lost since from long ago.'

Her explanation seemed just as ambiguous as Marceau's theory but to Harker none of this mattered. He steadied himself and leant forward in his chair, appearing to seek clearer answers than the ones being given. 'And what do you believe?'

Legrundy flipped open the Zippo and flicked her thumb across the flint wheel, causing a spark to light its wick. 'I believe that this is the day you die, brother – and not too soon neither.'

With that she threw the lighter back towards the fire-place and flames immediately burst upwards, before a rolling wave of blue spread across the floor, then shot up the curtain and in turn lit up half the sofa. With yellow flames already licking at the ceiling behind her, Legrundy raised both arms high above her head and began to bellow a deep chant that Harker couldn't interpret. It could have been words or just a collection of hollers, but it lasted only a few seconds before she gazed down at him, with flickering gold flames reflecting in her eyes, and shouted above the crackling of the blaze consuming a meal of wood and fabric. 'Goodbye, Professor.'

With flames rising up less than a metre away from her feet, she gave a booming laugh which could be heard even above the roaring of the fire. But, as she took a moment to relish her ravenous creation, Harker was already preparing for his escape. For all the care she had taken in binding him to the chair, she had made one crucial error and it was one that Harker now used to his full advantage. Because, even though the rope was tight around his chest, Legrundy had omitted to bind his legs.

Harker lurched forward onto his feet and, even as she continued to laugh, slammed himself shoulder first into her sternum, sending the psychopath flying backwards into the yellow wall of flame with a high-pitched screech. Harker himself came to a stop, face down, just inches from the blaze. Even as he rolled backwards to put some distance between himself and the escalating inferno, he could feel the intense heat threatening to scorch his flesh. Struggling onto his knees, he rested his chin on Marceau's limp thigh to steady himself, then hoisted himself further to his feet.

He was still stumbling to maintain his balance when something shifted in the corner of his eye, and he turned to see Legrundy come hurtling through the flames towards him. The collision sent him crashing onto his back, the force of it mercifully snapping the delicate join of the dining chair and allowing his bonds to loosen.

Her dreadlocks ablaze like pirate torches, Legrundy slapped frenziedly at the flames as she tried to put them out. Her back burned blue where the shirt had absorbed some petrol and the killer twisted and turned as she desperately attempted to put out the flame now searing her skin. Amazingly, and no doubt proving her mental toughness, she didn't make a sound, but managed to shoot Harker a vicious glance as flames licked her cheeks before she ran off to the back bedroom. The sound of smashing glass could be heard as she hurled herself through one of the windows and landed somewhere below.

Harker staggered back onto his feet as noxious fumes swirled around him. He considered for a moment attempting to drag Marceau's body out with him but, on realising that it would be impossible due to the quickly thickening smoke, he staggered into the hallway and then out through the front door. Behind him a loud explosion erupted from somewhere in the living room which sent him tumbling amidst a ball of hot smoke onto the third-floor landing, its momentum carrying him as far as the flight of stairs, where he tripped and then stumbled down them.

Harker couldn't tell if he then passed out momentarily or if he was merely stunned after whacking his head during the fall but, dizzy and gasping for air, he lurched downwards from one step to the next, with the air getting cleaner, until he reached the main entrance door, which he pulled open before collapsing in a heap on the pavement outside.

Up above him, thick black smoke poured out of the windows of Marceau's apartment as, like a godsend, two random female passers-by gently slid their hands under his arms and began to haul him off to one side. Coughing and spluttering, his ears were ringing and, even though everything sounded fuzzy, he could hear one of the women offering him reassurances in a Parisian accent, as the other pulled out her mobile after helping lower him gently onto the curb.

'You need water,' one rescuer said, before heading off to find some while the other continued making a call, presumably to the fire department. With their attention distracted, Harker seized the opportunity to stand up and take off down a dark side road behind him. Still spluttering and wheezing he reached the far end and flagged down a passing taxi that, by good fortune, was just passing by.

'Airport,' he managed, with a cough. 'Triple fare if you can get me there quickly.'

Even though the driver looked surprised at his ruffled appearance and the stench of smoke, he nodded and simply took off. There obviously wasn't a driver in the city who hadn't seen something ten times worse than this and the offer of a triple fare meant that few questions would be asked.

Ordinarily, if ever involved in such a situation, Harker would not have abandoned the scene. But, given there was nothing he could now do for Marceau, and a debrief by the police would only lead to wasting valuable time he didn't have, he felt it was the right call. He pulled out his phone and tapped on the mirror app before gazing at himself in the screen. Apart from a few black smoke smudges on his cheek he looked remarkably presentable, all things considered, and as he dropped the iPhone in his lap he looked up to find a wet-wipe being offered to him by the driver.

'You OK?' the driver asked with a smile.

Harker took the offering and nodded. 'Had a spot of car trouble,' he replied, wiping his face with the damp tissue.

'I'll say,' was all the driver said, turning his attention back to the road as he speeded up, evidently keen to make his extra money.

Did Legrundy make it or was her plunge from that third-floor bedroom window a death sentence? It was impossible to know but if she was still alive there were two things Harker could be sure of. *One*, the blessed candles held more significance than Harker could possibly have fathomed initially, and after seeing her murder Marceau with such ease, the psychotic killer would stop at nothing to acquire them. And, *two*, if their paths ever crossed again, he would be toast. For real this time.

Chapter 23

'Enough!' yelled Marco Lombardi, slamming his fist down so hard on the light-wood dining table that a red apple dislodged itself from the central fruit bowl and rolled to the edge and onto the floor. 'There is a traitor amongst us and no one leaves here until that person is found.'

The four other people seated around the table appeared in stark contrast to the dilapidated kitchen itself, its walls disfigured by flaking white paint and sporting a stove and scuffed metal basin that, judging by the rust, had not been used in a very long time. For each of them wore brand-name clothing, from striped business suits to blue Armani jackets, and in the middle sat a woman with neatly braided black hair, her business suit and skirt hugging her body so snugly that it looked as if she had literally been poured into it. All those present were now looking shocked by his accusation and the sound of shoes nervously scraping the leaves strewn on the concrete floor could be heard clearly as Lombardi continued his rant.

'Somebody here is trying to ruin our plans and Father is furious. He says someone has been in contact with the Red Death issuing conflicting orders.'

Even though all present appeared indignant at the claim, it was the woman who was eyeing Lombardi with particular scorn.

'No one at this table has – or ever would – consider thwarting Father's wishes, Marco,' she snapped back. 'Our confidence in his plans is as unwavering as it has always been, and to think that anyone would dare put their own life at risk is pure idiocy. We agreed to this path a long time ago and besides, she's gone dark and no one can get in contact with her until it's all over. You know that.'

'Well someone has and Father's convinced of it,' Lombardi snapped, now breathing heavily as the others continued to shift in their seats.

'Well, if there is anyone who deserves greater scrutiny, then it's you.' the woman replied with a menacing smirk.

Lombardi's stare hardened and he glared back at her with contempt, his jaw muscles visibly tensing. 'Now is not the time for games, Sofia,' he snarled. 'We are not children any more.'

'Then stop acting like one,' Sofia growled. 'We all know that Father mistrusts you and if he does believe someone is trying to cause problems then perhaps he wanted to see your reaction by bringing it up with you. I'd be watching your own back before trying to place blame on any of us.'

The room fell silent as the others now fixed their attention on Lombardi. He remained stiff and defiant, watching as Sofia confidently settled back in her seat and concluded her outspoken rebuttal: 'You wouldn't want to end up like poor Donitz, would you?'

The mere mention of that name instilled a chill in the others, and she placed a palm on the worn and cracked plastic table and tapped it warningly. 'They say he's still alive and you can hear him whimpering inside that death casket of his. Emperor Scorpions are large and their stings are painful, yet weak. I wonder, Marco, how long you would last?'

The thought had Lombardi visibly rattled and a gulp rose in his throat. 'Do you honestly think I would open myself up to Father's wrath after so many years of loyalty? After all, when the Red Death returns to us, when this is over, she'll simply reveal who gave her the new commands.'

Sofia waved her hand at him contemptuously and shook her head. 'Stop calling her that ridiculous name, you're making her sound like a comic-book character. She's a trusted part of this family, and her name is Avi Legrundy.'

'She's more than that; that woman's a believer, and her nickname is more than justified. She has caused more pain, death and misery than all of us here combined, and she has never failed whilst serving us.'

'Well it appears she is being tricked into serving someone else's will at the moment,' one of the others interjected bluntly, and Lombardi now seized upon that statement.

'Precisely. So if she's not serving one of us, then who?'

The question drew a slew of blank expressions. 'Someone is trying to disrupt what will happen here in less than twenty-four hours, and that cannot be permitted. With his return to us tonight, the house of our Lord will be restored, and with it the beginning of a new chapter for the world we have all been working towards for decades. Our belief in what we are trying to achieve is undeniable, so I ask you all again: whose faith could have waned to such a degree that they would even attempt to turn one of our own against us?'

The small group then began to eye one another with suspicion, and even Sofia started to look unsettled as Lombardi resumed his seat and watched them debate amongst themselves.

'Let us suppose for a moment that you are right,' Sofia said finally, again tapping her palm on the table top. 'There are only a few of us who know the whole plan and even fewer bold enough to go against Father's wishes. If it is not one of us here, then it has to be one of the others.'

'Which should make it that much easier to expose them, shouldn't it?' Marco suggested smugly.

After thinking about it for a moment, Sofia then stood up and made her way over to the door behind them. 'I'll start making enquires,' she affirmed flatly, clearly unhappy to even consider such a betrayal. 'And I suggest the rest of you all do the same.'

Without even a word the other three men rose to their feet and followed her out the door, leaving Lombardi alone in the derelict kitchen. As the door closed shut behind them, he took a moment to survey the surrounding mess. *So much history*, he thought before allowing himself a moment to reflect on the trials, tribulations and tragedies that had been forced upon him – upon them all – and it angered him to the very core. A lifetime spent, toiling away and building up towards this moment, which was his by right, just to have Father tear it from his grasp and thrust him to one side like some plaything no longer needed or wanted. That was the true treachery here, and he had no intention of letting it reach its finale.

Lombardi retrieved the mobile phone from his inside pocket and began to tap away at it, before placing it to his ear. 'Avi, what the hell is going on? Father knows someone's been in contact with you.'

Avi Legrundy flicked a badly seared dreadlock from her forehead with one hand before pressing an adhesive bandage to her blistered cheek while she held the mobile in her other.

'Dat's impossible. I've not spoken to anyone and you alone are the only one who has my number.'

'That may be so Avi, but he knows you're being given orders on his behalf.'

There was a moment of silence as Legrundy mulled over the problem and she licked her scorched lips thought-fully. 'Then you better find someone to blame it on, hadn't you?'

'Very well.' Lombardi replied, now sounding less agitated. 'And how goes our plan?'

'There were complications,' she replied, barely wincing as she patted another bandage over the deep and painful looking burn mark running down the full length of her left arm. 'But I know where he's planning to go next.'

'What complications?' Lombardi's voice cracked due to poor reception.

'Nuthin I cannot handle.'

'Good, because we're quickly running out of time.'

'I understand, Marco. I won't be letting us down.'

There was a short silence as Lombardi cleared his throat and then he continued in a low, deep voice, not wanting to be overheard by anyone nosing around nearby. 'You do still believe in what we're doing don't you?'

'I do, brother, on that you can be certain.'

'Good, because by this time tomorrow you and I will stand at the precipice of a new dawn and Father will be consigned to where he belongs. The depths of hell itself.'

The reception was now getting worse still as Lombardi gave his final wishes. 'Just make sure Stefani Mitchell and

Alex Harker are dead and that you retrieve what does not belong to them. And, Avi… make sure the professor suffers, would you please.'

Legrundy gazed down at her swollen, scalded arm and gritted her teeth. 'That you can count on.'

Chapter 24

'Rome? I thought you were in Paris,' Carter replied, sounding surprised at his location.

'I was but I then had to backtrack,' Harker informed him, as he received his change from the taxi driver and exited the cab. 'I'm paying a visit to the Vatican.'

'Really.' Carter's response came off sounding a bit aloof, 'I don't mean to appear negative, Alex, but you're not exactly tops with them at the moment, are you?'

Carter's cutting observation had Harker biting the inside of his cheek in anger, and he came to a halt as crowds of tourists flowed around him. 'Why does everyone keep saying that?' he demanded, genuinely irked by the assumption that somehow the Vatican had it in for him.

'Well, I don't know. Maybe because you got involved in the loss of a pope. And then let's not forget the time St Peter's Basilica was half destroyed.'

'None of which was my fault,' Harker barked, frankly tired of the bad reputation he kept attracting. 'And if not for me it would have been a hell of a lot worse.'

'I know that, Alex. You've done more for the Catholic Church than they can ever know, but you have to admit their perception of you is not particularly stellar, is it?' Carter was trying to sound as sympathetic as he could. 'Do you still have any friends there?'

'Yes, I have a few,' snapped Harker, then he took a deep breath and tried to calm himself, realising that blowing up was not going to help at all. He also had a cracking headache. 'Now I need you to focus, David. Is that too much to ask?'

'Fine, Fine. No need for you to get stroppy. What can I do?'

Harker ignored the criticism and continued walking again. 'I need any information you can discover on an old Catholic prophecy known as "the three days of Darkness".'

'Now, that I know,' Carter replied with excitement in his voice. 'End of the world, plagues and legions of demons… It's pretty dark stuff, Alex – if you'll excuse the pun.'

Harker did just that and ploughed on into explaining what he needed. 'See if there's a connection of any kind you can make… and also those glowing rocks I told you about, well, there's two of them and I've seen them both. If I believe what I was told, then they're the blessed candles referred to in the "three days" prophecy.' He considered mentioning his vision but then abandoned the idea because he had no wish to set Carter off on elaborating about supernatural mysteries of this sort. His friend's love of all things conspiratorial was familiar to all who knew him and he would undoubtedly find a way to tie it all in with the Kennedy assassination and aliens, given half the chance.

'Well, smack my bottom and call me Frank,' Carter exclaimed, plainly gobsmacked by what he was being told.

'What! Who's Frank?'

'It's just a saying, Alex.'

'No, it's not,' Harker replied, not sure he knew exactly what Carter was talking about but now deciding it was best to just ignore it. 'I need you to check a name for me – one Avi Legrundy. Can you see if the Templars have anything on file; ask around if necessary and see what you come up with.'

'Avi Legrundy? Doesn't sound familiar but—'

'I know, David. Which is why I need you to do some digging. Is Doggie still with you?'

'He's around somewhere, planning his trip back to Cambridge. I'm meeting him for lunch. Do you want me to ask him to put his plans on hold?'

With Carter now on the case, there was little reason for Doggie to hang around and, besides, there was something Harker needed him to do. 'No, don't. He's got a lot on his plate back at the university but could you ask him to do me a favour. Could he call Chloe for me and say I'm fine and I'll be back home in a couple of days.'

'Why not call her yourself?'

Nothing ever made it past Chloe. As well as being a top psychologist, she had an almost creepy sixth sense like a lie detector. If he spoke to her, she'd realise in an instant that something was going on. 'She'd know something was up and I don't want her to worry, is all. Just tell her the Templar business came to nothing and so I offered to do some university work here in Rome.'

'OK,' Carter replied doubtfully, 'but you do know she won't buy that.'

'Just do it, please. No one can spin a tale like Doggie. Now I have to go, David, but get back to me if you find anything, will you?'

'Will do… and, Alex, do try not to destroy any more of the Vatican will you, please.'

'David, go fuc…' Harker yelled gruffly, but the line went dead before he could finish and, as he looked up at the humble building of the Palace of the Holy Faith, he heard someone calling out his name.

He looked over to see Stefani striding towards him before she gave him a generous hug around the shoulders.

'Are you OK? You look like you've been through the mill,' she remarked, pulling back a bit to note the smoke stains on his jacket. 'What happened to you? Apart from the whole vision thing of course.'

There was a playful tone in her tone of voice but it evaporated rapidly as Harker began to explain what had taken place back in Paris. 'I had another run-in with that psychopath we encountered back in Athens. Oh, and her real name is Avi Legrundy. She killed Dr Marceau and I only just escaped being burnt alive when she set his apartment on fire.'

'Oh, my God. That's terrible,' was all Stefani could say but the look of shock and loss said it all.

'It was awful, Stefani, I haven't even had the heart to tell the Order yet.' Harker said, feeling a real sense of loss for the poor doctor but now putting on a brave face given everything else they were facing. 'Did you speak with Sebastian?'

She placed her hands on her hips and offered a deep sigh, still reeling from the news of Dr Marceau's brutal demise. 'We have his blessing to try to gain access to the archives, but he was adamant we do it on our own. He said the Templars could not afford to be linked in any way to trying to access Church doctrines.'

'Understandable,' he replied, knowing it was a delicate matter, but still he reckoned Brulet would have reached out to one of his contacts within the Church for some help. It seemed the Grand Master was testing Harker's metal to see if his new position as Jarl was truly warranted.

'He wants you to call him, though, when we've tried our hand here.' Stefani added, 'So what now?'

'Now we must make sure that Dr Marceau didn't die in vain,' Harker replied, making his way up a short incline to the grey, eighteen-foot, double doors of the Palace of the Holy Faith. The building was unique because, although considered an internal part of Vatican City, it was actually built upon land that belonged to the Italian government. Its curved archway, recessed doorways and windows on four floors, with the lowest clad in stone while the upper three were painted in yellow, gave a unique feeling to the building. The front façade was designed by many fine architects, most famously Michelangelo, setting this building apart from the others found in this hub of Catholicism.

Harker raised his fist and banged hard upon the door, then waited. In the days of ISIS and international terrorism there was usually a military presence at the Palace, which stood on the southern edge of Vatican City, but clearly not today. While Harker waited he gazed off in the direction of St Peter's Square and the many-pillared Colonnades surrounding it, and he felt sad to see the yellow tarpaulin barriers barring visitors a glimpse of the destruction that had occurred there a year and a half ago. Rebuilding of the area was now nearing completion and, although both the square and the basilica were being restored to their original specifications, it was reported on the news channels that additional structures were being erected to commemorate the great loss of life, including the Pope himself, that had taken place during the tragedy. It was a feeling of loss and guilt about the whole incident that overwhelmed Harker as finally the right-side door swung open.

'How can I help you?' inquired a man with short-cropped black hair wearing a short-sleeved white shirt, as behind him two Swiss Guardsmen flanking the entrance checked out Harker from the corners of their eyes.

'We're here to see Archbishop Federar,' Harker announced, suppressing any feeling of inadequacy he felt about how well-groomed the man looked compared to his own smutty appearance.

'Is he expecting you?'

'No,' Harker replied, 'but I'm a friend of his and was hoping he could spare me five minutes.'

The doorman looked very unsure and shook his head. 'I'm afraid he has no spare time currently, but if you would like to phone and make an appointment, I'm sure he could accommodate you.'

Harker could tell this man was not for budging but he pressed on regardless as there was too much at stake. 'I know this seems unorthodox but if you would just be so kind as to mention my name to the archbishop, I would be eternally grateful.'

The doorman thought about this for a second before answering, all the while taking note of Harker's less than presentable appearance. 'And your name is?'

'Professor Alex Harker from Cambridge University, and this is my colleague, Stefani Mitchell, daughter of the late Father Davies.'

The mention of Father Davies produced an immediate effect and the doorman's eyes were now full of inquisitiveness. He glanced beyond them both to the road behind, then to his left, and without further pause invited them both inside. 'Please come in and I will see if the archbishop can give you any of his time.'

With a grateful nod Harker allowed Stefani to enter first, then he strode past the two pontifical guards, who closed the door behind them as they headed on into the main foyer. The interior of the Palace was as beautiful as he had expected, with a high ceiling decorated with frescos. Numerous works of art adorned the white walls and he could not help but briefly admire them. Meanwhile the doorman picked up a phone from the reception desk and began a call.

Stefani seemed less captivated by her surroundings, though, and by the time the doorman returned Harker had worked out why. For him it was a rare treat to see inside this treasure house, but for her it was just a further reminder that not only her father was dead but, given the reaction to his name at the door, it was something at the forefront of everyone's minds.

'Archbishop Federar would be most happy to receive you,' the doorman announced with a smile. 'We will now take the elevator up to his office.'

Unfortunately the elevator was the point where the grandeur of the building stopped and, after a short ride in a modern, and by comparison very dull conveyance, they were both led to a waiting room. But before they even had time to sit down, the doors opened and Archbishop Federar himself appeared with a look of real pleasure on his face.

'Alex, what a surprise,' he began, clasping Harker's hand warmly. 'What has it been four... no, five years?'

'Too long, Angelo,' Harker replied, just grateful the archbishop was happy to see him, given recent happenings. They were hardly old and dear friends but he had first met this man when he was still only a priest and whilst Harker himself was training at the Vatican. Since then the two of them had remained in touch, but only about once a year and by e-mail. It was now as the archbishop turned to greet Stefani, that Harker realised it hadn't been he who had secured this invitation inside but rather his female companion.

'Miss?'

'Mitchell, Stefani Mitchell,' Stefani replied before also shaking the hand of the archbishop who noticeably took far longer over it than he had with Harker.

'Miss Mitchell I, we, are so sorry for your loss. Your father was a wonderfully good man and we were all truly shocked by the events leading to his death. Please accept our sincerest condolences.'

'Thank you,' Stefani replied, seemingly pleased with the genuine affection being offered.

'You won't remember but we met many years ago when you were just a toddler and soon after the Vatican granted permission for your father to adopt you. I see you chose not to keep your natural hair colour.'

Harker could have sworn she blushed, perhaps more out of embarrassment than anything else.

'I never liked that red,' she replied, stroking one of her locks. 'Blonde is definitely more my colour.'

'Both suited you equally, young lady, but it is a treat to see you again after so many years, though I must confess I wish it could have been under different circumstances.' Federar pointed to the window overlooking the street they had just been standing in. 'Later this afternoon I am due to give a press conference out there regarding your late father's demise. Most unfortunate.'

It was partially because Harker felt as if he had been jettisoned from the conversation that he now did his best to make himself heard. 'That seems unusual, Angelo, since Stefani's father resigned his priesthood years ago.'

His comment had Federar nodding in agreement. 'Yes, but given the nature of what happened and the media's preoccupation with all things morbid, his Holiness the Pope himself suggested that we be as transparent as possible regarding Father Davies's connection to the Church.'

'What's the point of trying to defuse a bomb once it's gone off, that kind of a thing?' Harker replied, now understanding what was going on. Damage control, basically, and it was the sensible thing to do.

'Something like that, yes,' Federar replied flatly. 'An acute awareness of the intricacies of how the world works has always been your gift, Alex. Now, please come into my office and tell me why you've both arrived together on my doorstep at this most unhappy time.'

As they followed the archbishop inside, Harker managed to lean close to Stefani and whisper out of earshot, 'I didn't know you were really a redhead.'

'Yep, I was once a ginger,' she whispered back as they took their seats. 'There's a lot about me you don't know.'

'So please tell me what I can do for you,' Federar requested as he sat down behind his desk. He watched his two visitors look at each other briefly before Harker began to speak.

'Firstly, Angelo, we want to thank you for meeting us at such short notice.' With the comment Carter had made earlier still preying on his mind, he added, 'I know my name and reputation inside the Vatican isn't as high as I would like it to be…'

Federar sat up straighter in his seat and wagged a finger in Harker's direction. 'That's not true, Alex. There may indeed be some confusion and even concern about your actions over the past few years, but before we get started allow me set the record straight. You still have many friends within the Church, myself included, and despite some of our more vocal and energetic brothers who unfortunately equate you with some type of modern plague, I assure you those are in very much a minority. The ones that know you are aware that your intentions have been – and I don't doubt always will be – pure and good.'

Federar settled back comfortably having made his point and, although it was not as bad as Harker had expected, it could have done with some improvement, especially the plague part, but it did allow for the perfect segue. 'Thank you, Angelo. That means a lot to me and I don't want to take up any more of your time than necessary, but you mentioned plagues?'

Federar did not shift in his seat but his eyes betrayed him when they opened wider, like those of a rabbit caught in the headlights.

Harker continued, 'Stefani and I have been attempting to make sense of her father's death except it's led us deep down a rabbit hole that we never expected.'

'Extremely deep down,' Stefani added.

'Tell me, Angelo, are you familiar with the "three days of Darkness"?'

By the way Federar's shoulders suddenly slumped and his eyelids drooped, anyone would have thought he man was going into cardiac arrest. An uncomfortable silence descended upon them all until the archbishop's lips began to curl in anger. 'I was wrong. You *are* a plague.'

'Now, Angelo...' was all Harker managed before Federar swiped the air with his hand and turned his attention to Stefani.

'I apologise for my lack of patience, Miss Mitchell, but Alex's obsession with all things conspiratorial is well known within the walls of Vatican City and incredibly frustrating.'

'That's not fair and before we go any further you should be aware that we already know about the unacknowledged secure section of the secret archives – the vault within a vault,' Harker interjected, drawing Federar's attention quickly back to him. 'And also the Prophecy that, although not recognised officially by the Holy See, is nonetheless kept there under lock and key.'

Federar said nothing but he did not look happy.

'We also know that it was the reason Father Davies lost his faith and how the prophecy refers to "the blessed candles", and what you might not know is that... we found them.'

'What!' Federar exploded, now appearing to be in complete shock.

'Yes, Angelo, they're very real, and I've seen them with my own eyes. The words inscribed within them reflect precisely those written in blood by Father Davies, on the wall of the house where he murdered the mother and son. The same words, I believe, he first saw in a document buried deep in the Vatican's most secret archives.'

That mention of murder had started Federar shuddering and he seemed to zone out as his eyes became glassy and unresponsive. Frankly he looked like someone who had just received the worst possible news imaginable.

'You have been busy, Alex,' was all he managed to say in little more than a whisper, whereupon his gaze fell to the floor for a few moments, before he looked up again with some fresh resolve in his eyes. 'Let me be up front with you when I say that were it not for Miss Mitchell's presence here, I would not be telling you what I am about to say. But it is the least I can do for a family member whose loss has so much been speculated on. Besides, considering what you already know, it may be you two who can best help me.'

Harker looked surprised at this. The Vatican needed help from him? *In your face, Carter!* he mused as the archbishop explained further.

Federar let out a muffled sigh and then his lips trembled as he prepared to say something that he evidently found most unpalatable. 'You're correct about there being a sealed section of the Vatican archive. It was created just before the beginning of the Second World War, and for obvious reasons. There was need for a highly secure area where documents, doctrines and artefacts could be kept hidden, due to their highly sensitive nature as regards to both the Catholic faith as well as humanity itself. And before you speculate further, *no* we don't keep alien bodies down there… or anything like that.'

The very mention of aliens had both Harker and Stefani leaning forward in anticipation, but as Federar vigorously shook his head they settled back.

'Your father, Miss Mitchell, was an advisor to us here at the Congregation for the Doctrine of the Holy Faith of which, as you know, I am the Prefect. He became convinced that "the three days of Darkness" prophecy was soon coming to pass, so he believed it was imperative that he be allowed to see the original kept within the archives.'

'How did he know it was there in the first place?' Harker asked.

'He professed to have experienced a vison wherein St Peter himself disclosed its location and warned that the fate of humankind rested upon his revelation of it. I can't say if this vision was real but, as a result, he was more than persistent and he even convinced two other bishops serving within this office not only of its existence but the necessity for an examination of the document as being crucial to the planet's survival.'

'Is the existence of this special archive widely known?' Stefani seemed riveted by the archbishop's disclosure.

'There have always been rumours since it was first assembled, but that is not what convinced me eventually to allow him admission. There are only two people allowed access to the area at any one time – his Holiness the Pope and the Prefect of this Office – and only we knew what items were kept within it. There was no other way your father could have known it even existed unless some heavenly intervention had granted him knowledge of it.'

The archbishop was now on a roll but Harker couldn't help but interrupt to ask a question now top of his list. 'Why were only two people permitted?'

'Because,' Federar replied with a deep frown, 'contained down there are things that might possibly cause even a man of the greatest faith to… question his beliefs.'

The response seemed incredible and Harker now realised how not only honest, but trusting the archbishop was being, and he watched with respect as Federar continued.

'Without the pontiff's approval I allowed Father Davies to examine the original Prophecy in the company of two others, so that a shared perspective could be maintained.'

'You didn't even tell the Pope!' Harker gasped, surprised by this omission.

'It's a decision I have wrestled with ever since but at the time I wanted his Holiness to be spared any embarrassment and I planned to inform him if they found anything of worth... which they did not.'

This retelling of events had Federar growing paler and both Harker and Stefani remained respectfully quiet as he paused to prepare himself for what was obviously the hardest part of his story.

'They examined and discussed it thoroughly over the next few weeks, and at the end of it all no conclusion was reached except that the Prophecy explained how the blessed candles were indeed the only means to prevent the total spread of darkness during this terrible time. The archive was then closed, and it was shortly after that Father Davies suffered a complete collapse of his faith. He was irreconcilable and, as you know, he left the Church to follow another path in life. With the exception of his loss to us, life here moved on as normal... that is until a few days ago when he... Well, you already know what.' Federar glanced over at Stefani sympathetically. 'But what you might not be aware of is that, since then, two bishops have been brutally murdered, along with their entire congregations, in the most terrible ways.'

Harker thought back to those news reports playing on the TV as Legrundy had slit Dr Marceau's throat open. 'And they were the two advisors who had examined the Prophecy along with Father Davies?'

'Yes,' Federar replied miserably. 'And it happened just as the prophecy said it would, just before the three days of darkness would begin.'

Even with all Harker had seen, even after his vision, it was only after the archbishop's latest disclosure that he finally began to accept the real possibilities and consequences of what he had learned over the previous few days. 'Then we need to see it,' he demanded with more force than might be justified, 'and we need to see it now. Both of us.'

Federar stared back at his visitors with the look of a beaten man and slowly he began to nod his head. 'But only that one document and nothing else. And if you can make sense of it, Alex Harker, you are a better man than I am.'

Chapter 25

Harker poked his head into the cold and unwelcoming grey corridor stretching before him, as Archbishop Federar closed shut the palm-print ID panel located on the other side of the now open elevator.

'And you and the pontiff himself are the only people aware of this place?' Harker asked, glancing back at Federar.

'That is correct, Alex. But without the required palm ID it won't take you anywhere.' He patted the scanner plate.

'Very secure,' Stefani added as she followed the archbishop, heading past Harker and out into the narrow corridor.

'Catholicism may be thousands of years old but when it comes to security we use only the most up-to-date technology.' Federar motioned for them to both follow him as he proceeded down the narrow passage.

'And the most secretive,' Harker remarked, referring to the place where they had accessed the elevator only minutes earlier.

When Federar had ushered them both into the back room of his office, Harker had expected to encounter a couple of pontifical guards who would escort them outside and as far away from the archbishop as possible. Instead Federar had pulled back a large oil painting of himself on metal runners, to reveal the door of an elevator. With the simple pressing of his palm against a dark glass-tile palm-scanning plate, the door had slid open. Once they had gathered inside, he repeated the procedure and the elevator had begun to descend about ten metres or so.

'I never realised the Vatican went for all this James Bond stuff! Where's Q?' Harker inquired but, even though said in apprehensive jest, Federar did not find it amusing.

'Please show some respect, Alex. This is the most highly secured area in the entire Vatican City, and for good reason too.'

'Frankly, Archbishop, I'm surprised this section wasn't incorporated within the secret archives' building itself.' Stefani pointed out as she followed him down along the corridor.

Federar did not venture an answer until they reached a matte-black metal wall at the corridor's end, where-upon he raised his open palm and placed it on a scanning plate cut into the frame. 'The secrets we hold here are only intended for the very few, as you can see from the security,' he said, motioning to a green strip of light that moved down from the top to the bottom of his hand before confirming his hand print with the one recorded in its storage banks. 'And if anyone did search for it, then this is the last place they would look.'

Harker watched the door slide down into a narrow cavity within the floor, now allowing them access to the secret vault.

'Also the palace above us is actually built on Italian soil, and we are now about twenty metres from the Vatican border, albeit underground, so if this place was by some miracle ever broken into, the Vatican would technically be afforded some deniability as to the charge of hiding these items from the world at large.'

'That seems pretty thin reasoning,' Harker noted, though unsure if his analysis was foolish or showed total genius.

'Perhaps yes, but it's still better than if they were found wrapped up among the Pope's personal effects within the Vatican's secret archive itself.'

The doorway had revealed a further few metres of corridor before a ninety-degree turn-off to the right. With Federar again taking the lead, the three of them proceeded ahead and then around the corner, one after another.

'Now that's indeed a secret archive,' Harker announced as, next to him, Stefani let out a light gasp, while Federar forced himself to smile at his two visitors because even the idea of showing them this place was as unsettling as anything he could have imagined.

'Welcome,' Federar languidly raised his arm and gestured ahead, 'to the most clandestine location in the entire Catholic world.'

The room in front of them extended for over fifty metres, cut directly into the bare rock and illuminated by glowing uplighters that at first glance suggested a large wine cellar with support pillars of grey granite positioned in rows to create a grid comprising four passages. Each passage was connected to the other by walkways, allowing easy access to any corner of the archive, no matter where you were positioned. On either side of these walkways large containers were attached to the pillars and whilst some of these were transparent containers, others were covered by wire-mesh screens, and above all of them were buzzing units connected to a central system regulating the air temperature.

'I never thought there could be so many items considered to be of danger to the Church's integrity,' said Harker inquisitively, and he began to head further into the archive. But he was stopped before completing more than a single footstep by Federar's outstretched arm.

'Do not for even a moment imagine that this storage facility is packed with such perilous objects,' Federar replied sternly. 'The things actually stored here take up less than twenty-five percent of the available space.'

'But what a twenty-five percent that is, I'll bet,' Harker said, speculating on what amazing artefacts could be concealed down here.

Stefani, however, was looking mystified.

'Then why all the extra space?' she asked, noticing how much of the area was indeed empty.

'I think I could make a guess at that,' Harker answered, remembering gossip he had heard whilst training at the Vatican decades earlier. 'I remember stories about further storage facilities that no one ever got to see. This place was originally excavated to hold the entire Vatican archives during the Second World War, wasn't it?' Harker suggested with an intrigued smile. 'To stop anything falling into the hands of the Axis powers, should they decide to ransack the Vatican itself.'

'That is correct, it was a safety measure for that real possibility in the context of that time.' Federar moved over to the first row and approached an illuminated cabinet secured to a granite pillar by heavy duty iron bolts. 'Hitler was trying to get his grubby little hands on literally anything with religious connotations. By the time this place was built, he had already acquired the Spear of

Destiny and had sent Himmler and the SS off in search of the Holy Grail.' He let out a small sigh. 'Thank the Lord he never found it… but let us focus now on what you're both here to see.'

With Stefani at his side, Harker approached the cabinet, too, and looked down at a single sheet of notebook-sized paper. Just then he couldn't help but marvel at how such an insignificant piece of scrap could have such an impact on so many, including the Order of Tharmis which had evolved itself around it.

'What's kept in there?' Stefani was pointing to the cabinet adjacent, housing an aged book with cracked leather binding, but Federar immediately moved himself between the display and her line of sight.

'Nothing that concerns you, young lady.'

Harker tried to catch a glimpse of whatever had aroused Stefani's curiosity, but in view of the archbishop's protective stance and the no-nonsense expression, he withdrew and concentrated instead on what they had come here to see. *Shame*, he thought, because he would wager there were far more intriguing things to get sight of, given the very nature of this archive.

As Harker craned his head closer to the sheet of paper, he noticed that its edges were discoloured and brown, undoubtedly due to its age, but the writing it contained was in modern Latin, and far removed therefore from the Aramaic script he had seen projected by the Blessed Candle. Harker had initially considered revealing to the archbishop the existence of the Order of Tharmis, but he had second thoughts on such disclosure until at least he had taken a better look at the document for himself.

'Can you get it out?' he asked hopefully.

Even though Federar had decided to allow them access here into this highly secretive place, his hand hesitated nevertheless above the cabinet.

'It won't take long, Angelo,' Harker urged and with his uncertainty evaporating, the archbishop nodded and raised the lid of the cabinet.

'If this place is so secretive how on earth did you manage to get it fitted out with all this high-tech security stuff?' Stefani asked, gesturing back towards the security door with its palm ID scanner. 'It must have taken a few people to install all this.'

Federar kept the cabinet lid raised and gently pulled out the document. 'The professionals who excavated this place during the 1940s passed away a while back, and as for the security measures, they were carried out in a single day by just one engineer.' He clutched the document tightly in his fingers. 'The man in question agreed to be blindfolded and driven randomly around the city before I myself led him down here to complete the work. Once finished, he was again blindfolded and then driven back to his offices by a roundabout route. He had no idea where he had been, so our secrecy was ensured.'

'Having signed a non-disclosure agreement as well, no doubt,' Harker ventured.

Federar smiled and nodded. 'Just to be sure.'

He continued to grasp the item protectively and it wasn't until Harker stretched out his hand that Federar reluctantly passed it over, allowing a first real look at this troublesome document.

The lighting, although low, was still bright enough for him to scan the lettering, which Harker began to read slowly out loud, line by line.

'"What I write is the truth regarding of what is to come, and from the sacred lips of St Peter himself. It was no dream or whimsical fantasy but a revelation bestowed upon me so that I might release it to the world and offer a hope that has been decreed by the will of God himself. For unto me was revealed a moving image of that which will come to pass, and by this divine disclosure we may stave off that which Lucifer wishes to see come to pass. When the world is ripe and bursting at the seams with disbelief and avarice, the demon generals and the vile hoardes will see fit to firstly take possession of those in power and then reclaim their prize of hell on earth and return our world to the darkness from where it was born. I saw devastation predicated on a scale that few could even imagine, and during those vile days only the Blessed Candles might keep the rotting stench of the Devil's breath from enveloping even the most devout and worthy. These same words I now write will precede three days of Darkness sent to shred all God's children, no matter what their faith, and at that darkness's end even those saved by the blessed candles' holy light will be doomed to serve their beastly masters until the end of time.'"

Harker then turned over the document and what he saw on the reverse caused him to feel a lump in his throat.

'"*You are I and I am you. When he is myth and we are reality. This grand deception will be repaid in blood.*"'

'That's what my father wrote,' Stefani said, as these last words left Harker's mouth, and he now thought back to what the late Dr Marceau had told him and he whispered. '"The greatest trick the Devil has managed to contrive is to convince humankind that he doesn't exist.'"

'What?' Federar said loudly.

'"When he is myth and we are reality,"' Harker pointed to the sentence. 'How many now consider the Devil merely a myth?'

Harker flipped the document over again and began to read it for a second time, but had only got half-way through it when he heard an odd noise coming from behind him. It sounded like heavy breathing that was becoming rapider with each passing second. He glanced over at Stefani whose stare was fixed upon something behind him, and Harker slowly turned to find the arch-bishop staring down towards the ground with his shoulders quivering as that heavy breathing turned into a high-pitched cry.

'Angelo,' Harker called out lightly, resting his hand in the man's shoulder, 'none of this is your fault.' For he had hazarded a guess at why the archbishop seemed suddenly so overcome with emotion. 'For what it's worth you were right because, as far as I can see, this prophecy doesn't offer us anything new.'

'Doesn't it?' Federar replied, continuing to weep with increasing intensity.

This was an odd reaction from the man but, given the deaths surrounding this scrap of paper and Harker mentioning people's loss of belief in the Devil's existence, then perhaps the archbishop saw it as a personal failure in his role of maintaining the Church's doctrine and belief system. That was, after all, his main role as head of the Congregation. 'Whatever's going on here then, I can say with all honesty that you are neither responsible for nor connected with the recent deaths, or those in Rome's churches yesterday, or Father Davies's. You have no reason to feel guilty.'

The weeping subsided and, as Harker decided to divulge the existence of Avi Legrundy and how she was the one killing church congregations, Federar began to shake his head whilst still continuing with his navel gazing.

'It's not guilt that I'm feeling.'

Harker glanced over at Stefani who responded with a sympathetic shrug. 'Then what is it?' he asked, not knowing whether he should hug this man or give him a wake-up slap.

'It's the feeling… no the urge,' Federar continued and taking in a deep breath, 'that makes me want to kill you.'

The archbishop flipped his head up violently, flicking frothy saliva into the air as he did so, and then clasped both hands around Harker's throat with such force that his knuckles turned white. His eyes were now bloodshot and his facial muscles spasmed with such ferocity, and so awkwardly, that the prelate was barely recognisable. In fact he looked like another, unrecognisable person. 'I want to kill you both,' he snarled.

The whole performance caught Stefani by complete surprise and, as Harker wrestled with the man's ever-tightening grip, it took her more than a second to react so that by the time she landed a heavy kick to Federar's side, Harker's face had already turned a deep red.

Her blow sent the archbishop sprawling to the floor with such force that he slid along the shiny stone surface a few feet, while Harker coughed and gasped to recover his breath.

'Archbishop!' Stefani yelled as Federar leapt to his feet and plunged headfirst towards them, snarling again as white froth spewed from his mouth, like an animal afflicted with rabies.

Even though he was still catching his breath, Harker managed to propel himself forward, slamming hard into Federar's chest and sending him careering back against one of the displays, where his hand smashed through the glass with a tinkle. Harker was on him immediately but even as he reached him, he caught sight of the large shard of glass now gripped in Federar's fist. He flung out both hands in time to grab the archbishop's wrist and the two men fell to the floor in a desperate struggle to get control of the razor-sharp weapon.

Federar wasn't just like a man possessed, he *was* a man possessed, and even though the twitching muscles made his face almost unrecognisable, it was the man's supernatural strength that forced Harker onto his back. He now struggled for dear life as the shard bore down towards him, until it was only inches away from his neck.

'Angelo, stop,' Harker hissed under the archbishop's weight, but his appeal for sanity only encouraged Federar to thrust even harder. He screamed wildly as saliva spilled from his mouth, just missing Harker's face and dripping onto the floor below. With the assailant's weight becoming too much to resist, Harker instead slammed a knee straight into the archbishop's groin and sent the man yelping to the floor beside him. In the frenzy he fortunately let go of the glass shard which smashed into pieces on the hard stonework of the floor.

Harker had already risen to his knees and was ready to pounce when a fist came out of nowhere and slammed into Federar's face. Harker looked up to see Stefani now offering him the same hand, which he grabbed to help haul himself to his feet. Although the blow was not enough to knock Federar out, it had left him temporarily dazed. So, after grabbing the document off the table and with no other plan, Harker took the one option seemingly left open to them.

'Run.' he yelled, as he grabbed Stefani by the arm and pulled her along with him. Such protection seemed a bit silly really considering it was she who had just saved him.

Within seconds they reached the elevator where Harker felt his heart sink as he scrambled to find the button. Then he realised the palm ID panel offered them the only route of access. 'Shit,' he shouted in frustration as the scuffling of footsteps somewhere back inside the archive began to get louder.

'I've got an idea,' was all Harker could manage before Federar burst through the entrance, his arms flailing and his mouth wide open like some crazed meth-head. He had launched himself along the short passageway in the blink of an eye and crashed into Harker's waiting shoulder. With all his weight Harker slammed the archbishop against the wall, then pushed him forward and slipped one arm around his neck before jamming one of Federar's arms up behind his back.

Stefani instinctively knew what Harker was up to and she secured Federar's free arm with both hands and as he desperately attempted to twist out of the choke hold, together they edged him step by step towards the elevator.

'Now!' Harker yelled, whereupon Stefani thrust Federar's palm up against the ID scanner and held it in place, and maintaining his grip, Harker used all his weight to keep the archbishop in position.

The green scan light descended the length of the plate and straight away the elevator doors slid open.

'There's another one inside,' Stefani called above the man's intensifying screaming.

'I know, so he's coming with us.' Harker yelled back and then, with the choke hold still in place, he raised a foot and pushed it firmly into the back of Federar's knee, sending him forward and into the elevator, with Stefani pulling his hand ever closer to the ID scanner located inside it.

Trying to subdue anyone is hard enough but dealing with a possessed madman within the tight confines of an elevator was near impossible. However, as Harker tightened his choke hold and Stefani dodged Federar's snapping teeth as he attempted to bite her, they managed to slap his open palm onto the scanner. Within seconds the elevator doors closed again and as the ascent began with Harker applying a brutal chokehold to the Prefect of the Holy See and Stefani struggling to restrain his arms, it became suddenly hard for either of them to imagine how this could end well.

'Once the doors open, we throw Angelo back into the elevator while we make a dash for the front entrance?' Harker suggested, as Federar continued to resist them with every ounce of his strength.

'You know we could go to jail for this, Alex,' Stefani yelled over the commotion.

'Really, Stefani!' Harker yelled back sarcastically. 'Somehow that never crossed my mind.'

'I'm just saying, is all.'

She was right of course at this point but what else could they do? Call the Pontifical guard and explain that their boss had apparently become possessed, and had tried to take a bite out of each of them. *Oh, and by the way, would you mind calling a taxi for us since we're in a bit of a rush.*

'OK, we'll tie him to his chair and then get out of this place… When his own staff find him, they can take it from there.'

Harker's mild suggestion had Stefani looking horrified and, without warning she pulled her fist back as far as the confined space would allow and then landed a punch directly across Federar's cheek, knocking him out cold.

'I am not tying up the Prefect of the Holy See to his chair and just leaving him.'

It was now Harker who looked shocked. 'Oh, right, but breaking his nose and knocking him unconscious is a reasonable alternative!'

'It's the lesser of two evils. We'll leave him back in his office and when his staff find him, they can take charge and get him to a hospital.' She gazed down at Federar, who was now at least still. 'This is so bad.'

Harker, who was still catching his breath nodded in agreement. 'It is. And it could get a whole lot worse, too.'

Chapter 26

'Tom!' David Carter called out, as he navigated the cobblestone road on Mont Saint-Michel as quickly as his rather ample frame would allow. Built on a granite rock just off the shore of Brittany in northern France this was one of the most impressive sights overlooked by regular tourists. Looking more like the castle from the Disney logo than an ancient monastic community, it was considered one of the most uniquely beautiful locations in all of Christendom. Tidal fluctuations meant that access from the mainland to this rocky island was only possible at certain times of the day, which – amongst other advantages – had made it the perfect location for the Templars to house their most secret vault, hidden deep inside the rock itself. But it also meant steep streets leading up to the abbey at the rock's summit, and this was a fact that irked Carter every time he had to clamber up there... which as it had turned out was quite a lot.

'Ahh, David,' Dean Thomas Lercher replied, with a relaxed wave and taking another nibble of his salmon sandwich, 'come to see me off, have you?'

The tiny cafe was a perfect place to relax and watch the passing tourists, although it was clear by Doggie's expression that he could have done so without being interrupted by Carter, who now arrived with a reddening face, lightly sweating.

'You know, David, the more times you traverse these streets, the less sweat you appear to produce. Now that you're a permanent fixture here, you will be ready to run a marathon in no time.'

'I'll try to keep that in mind.' Carter replied with a forced smile as, attempting to control his heavy breathing, he sat down next to him. 'I've been all the way down to the car park and back up again, trying to find you. I wish you'd keep your mobile turned on.'

Doggie shook his head. 'In actual fact I'm on university holiday time and, as such, yearn to be spared from any annoying business calls.'

'Bloody teachers,' Carter muttered under his breath. 'Look, Alex wants a favour from you.'

'Where is he?'

'Should be in Rome by now,' Carter replied before snatching a bit of Doggie's quartered sandwich and guzzling it down. 'Sorry but I'll need sustenance if I'm going to train for that marathon.'

'Then buy your own sustenance next time, will you?' Doggie said, pulling his plate closer to him. 'What's the favour?'

'He hoped you wouldn't mind letting Chloe know he's OK and that he'll be away for a few more days, on university business.'

'Passing the buck?' Doggie let rip a short burst of laughter. 'She always knows when something's up. He's such a chicken.'

'He really is,' Carter replied in complete agreement. 'But, to be fair, he appears to be in the thick of it, so would you mind?'

'Of course, not a problem. I'm sure I can come up with some reasonable story.' Doggie flicked some offending breadcrumbs from his tweed jacket. 'You know, David, I feel so lucky to be involved with this whole Templar thing. On one hand it really makes me feel like I'm part of history itself... In the know.'

'But?' Carter was finally recovering his breath.

'But, on the other hand, it is so incredibly frustrating that I can't tell anyone about it,' Doggie replied with his eyebrows rising upwards. 'Anyone important, at any rate.'

Carter offered an understanding nod. 'I know what you mean but you can always discuss it with me.'

Doggie's eyebrows lowered and his eyes dulled. 'Like I said, anyone *important*. Now, did it help with Avi Legrundy?'

Carter looked dumbfounded and his eyes began to squint. 'Did what help?'

This clueless response had Doggie lightly slap his own face in disappointment. 'The information I dropped on your desk... about Avi Legrundy. Her name was in the vault's inventory. No actual files but her name crops up a few times.'

Carter's eyes widened and his cheeks began to flush with anger. 'Why didn't you tell me?'

'I did,' Doggie replied firmly, not about to take any crap from his colleague. 'You never listen, David, you damn cloth-ears. Pay attention, man. There's a separate storage room, on the second floor of the vault, containing a few dozen boxes of files and logbooks. The inventory included the name Avi Legrundy, pertaining to those files.'

Carter now looked embarrassed.

'Did you actually check the inventory logs?'

'I didn't even know there was a second floor,' Carter replied. 'All my time so far has been taken up with the artefacts side of things. I've not had time to reach the logs yet.'

'Then perhaps that time has come.' Doggie rose from his seat and pointed his finger in the direction of the vault's entrance, located on the top plateau of the Mont. 'Allow me, therefore, to be of some use before I leave.'

Within a few minutes, and after a lot of heavy panting from Carter, they made it into the Abbey's storage room, then accessed the concealed elevator via the palm-print ID. A few more minutes passed and they were back in the bowels of the Mont itself, with Doggie leading the way down a zigzag of steps and onto the second floor.

'I can't believe you didn't know there was a second floor!' Doggie exclaimed, relishing his colleague's naivety.

'I was joshing with you, Tom,' Carter replied as, with wide eyes, he took in the sight of the second floor for the first time. 'I just haven't had a chance to explore it yet.'

The second-floor vault was almost identical to the upper level, with numerous walkways allowing access to multiple shelves on either side and each filled with case after case of Templar antiquities collected since the group's inception. The only difference was that some of them were huge and, although all were still contained within those familiar pressurised cases to protect from the damaging effects of air and temperature, they were clearly constructed to house the Templars' larger items.

'Here it is,' Doggie announced, halting outside a white door with the number '2D' inscribed on it in black paint and a silver aluminium handle protruding from it which he now grasped firmly and twisted. 'Take a look at this.'

As the door swung open, some strip lighting above automatically turned on and Carter found himself staring at what amounted to a glorious hodgepodge of items that looked already packed and waiting for a removal truck to take them away. On the nearest shelf were rows of journals with dates printed on their spines in gold lettering, like an encyclopaedia collection, while varnished wooden boxes sealed shut with yellow tape were piled up in the middle of the small room. Leaning to one side were much larger items wrapped tightly in Saran wrap which concealed any clear view of what they might be.

'I haven't had a poke around yet but the logbooks definitely indicate this room as containing information regarding Avi Legrundy.'

Carter made his way further into the room and up to the boxes stacked neatly in the centre. 'What did the records say?'

'That's the odd thing,' Doggie replied. 'Just her name and the storage number, 2D, which is surprising given how detailed the records are for everything else stored here.' He moved over to the first journal on the shelf top and tapped it with his index finger. 'Simply stored or hidden away out of sight; I wonder which.'

Carter offered a grunt of curiosity and then reached into the first box to pick at the yellow tape, before pulling it away and crumpling it into a sticky ball which he dropped on the floor. 'Let's take a look then, shall we.' He carefully pulled open the lid, which swung back on brass hinges to come to rest in an upward position. He began to inquisitively rummage through the contents, and within seconds found something of interest. He now pulled out a small clothbound diary and flipped open the front cover. The pages within were handwritten in black biro and, before he even had a chance to read all the way through the first line, his eye was caught by a familiar name printed neatly in the top right corner: 'Liam Harker.'

Doggie now leant closer to read the name for himself. 'That's Alex's father… which means these must be his personal effects.'

Carter said nothing more but began to read through the entire page as Doggie turned his attention instead to the large wrapped-up object leaning against the facing wall. He began to rip off the silver plastic packaging and in no time at all had stripped the whole lot off. He then took a step back to examine a large slab of oval-shaped white marble, measuring over a metre in height and almost twice that in length.

'This thing must weigh a tonne,' Doggie stammered, which caught Carter's attention. He placed the diary back in the box and made his way over to take a look for himself.

The marble slab had a single image carved into its surface and, given the visible erosion, it was without doubt extremely old. But even at first glance Carter knew what it was and, more importantly still, what it represented. At the centre was a man, with a long cape flowing behind him, kneeling on an animal with his left hand muzzling its mouth. In his right hand he held a dagger which had been plunged into the creature's shoulder. To Carter, though, the important thing was not the man which the relief clearly centred upon but rather the animal. It was a horned bull that appeared to be in muffled agony as the man knelt on its back, forcing it down to the ground. A long narrow serpent was slithering up its spine, while underneath it a dog bit at its ankle whilst a large scorpion attacked the beast's genitals with sharp-looking pincers. Above, from opposite corners the sun and the moon shone down on this violent image, and over to one side a long beaked raven watched eagerly from the branch of a tree, at the dagger being plunged into the bull's neck.

An uncomfortable feeling began forming in Carter's stomach and, even though he wasn't exactly sure why, he now realised what they were up against – and what this Avi Legrundy represented.

'I know what this image means,' he said softly, and Doggie nodded silently in agreement because he too knew what they were looking at and he uttered just a single word.

'Mithras.'

Chapter 27

'Just relax and try not to look so nervous,' Harker quietly urged as he and Stefani made their way off the twelve-seater shuttle bus and out onto the tarmac of Ciampino airport, just south of Rome. 'We haven't done anything wrong.'

'Of course we haven't,' she replied sarcastically but with a bemused expression. 'Just like we haven't assaulted Archbishop Federar back at his holy palace, and neither have we left him propped him up in a chair in a state of unconsciousness.'

'Only after the man went totally crazy,' Harker offered as they both continued swiftly towards the Cessna Citation X waiting for them with its cabin door already wide open.

'He wasn't crazy, Alex. He was possessed, just like my father. And we're going to burn for this, you know?'

Stefani had seemed unusually shaken by the ruckus back at Vatican City, and she wasn't the only one. Harker was only too aware of the seriousness of what essentially amounted to inflicting GBH on a high-ranking Vatican official – and just as importantly, an old friend. Also the idea that Archbishop Federar had become possessed was hard enough to digest but that it happened so quickly and with almost no warning was just as disturbing. 'Look, I don't know how but we'll make this right, I promise.

And for the moment no one has any idea what really happened.'

'How on earth can you be sure of that?' she gasped just as they reached the jet and she paused with one foot resting on the first step.

'Because, if they did, then we wouldn't be getting onto this aeroplane, would we? So let's not hang around here any longer.'

It was a reasonable suggestion and Stefani gave a slow nod, before Harker pushed her up the stairs and into the cabin, where they found one of the pilots waiting patiently for them.

'Destination sir?' he inquired, and as Stefani took her seat, Harker was already gesturing the man towards the cockpit.

'Anywhere but here. Just get us airborne and out of Italian airspace as soon as possible.'

'Like, is that it?' The pilot raised his eyebrows. 'Very well, take a seat and we'll get going.'

Until that moment it had not occurred to Harker whether the crew were Templar associates or just hired professionals but, given the man's response, it was clear that they were the former, and he was glad of it. For most people, alarms bells would have gone off the moment they were instructed to get out of the country ASAP.

'What the hell are we going to do?' Stefani asked as Harker sat down next to her. 'This whole business has become a totally confusing nightmare. I myself don't even know what we're doing.'

She was right, of course, and he knew it. What had started as simply an enquiry into the death of Stefani's father had now morphed into a tangled mesh of murder, conspiracy theories, prophecies, and satanic worship.

Then add to this mix those glowing artefacts capable of delivering visions, and the whole thing seemed no more than a chaotic mess.

'What the hell is going on?' Stefani continued loudly and because Harker was just about to say the same thing, he began to laugh out loud.

'I'm not sure I've an answer for you, as my brain is buzzing with confusion,' Harker replied, then shook his head in despair because he had been feeling somewhat removed from reality ever since he experienced that vision. It was like his mind was no longer firing on all cylinders and as if he had lost – or gained – something. 'If there was any such thing as a mind enema, I'd be all for taking a triple dose.'

The idea of such an imagined medication had Stefani looking wide-eyed, and Harker raised his eyebrows wistfully. 'That's not a real thing, is it?'

'Of course not,' Stefani scolded. 'But, you're right, we need to clear our heads now and figure out exactly where we're at.'

'OK,' he replied, also wanting to get things straight in his own mind. 'This whole series of events – your father's death, the Blessed Candles and the group seeking them – they all revolve around the three days of Darkness prophecy which,' he paused and scratched his neck in irritation, 'if I hadn't seen that vision I would be hard pressed to believe. But with that still in mind, I've come to genuinely believe that something unearthly is going on, so it all has to be taken seriously. And the members of the Order of Tharmis are convinced that this prophecy will come to pass within the coming hours.'

Harker gently pulled out of his pocket the scrap of paper they had stolen from the Vatican's secret archive and placed it on the table in front of them. 'They also believe that this here is not only the solution to stopping an apocalyptic tragedy, but contains instructions on how to stop it from beginning at all. But, apart from corroborating that those currently holding religious power will become consumed by Satan's minions – which as we saw with Archbishop Federar, is definitely true to its word – there's nothing else written in there which helps us one bit.'

He picked up the scrap of paper and began to reading it yet again, and was only a few sentences into it when he noticed something odd being illuminated by one of the cabin's floor lights alongside him. At the very edge of the note appeared to be shadows or a discolouring and, as Harker scrutinised those closer, he made something out. They were symbols... no letters, tiny letters which lined the edge of the page like a dull grey watermark, and were easy to miss. He raised the note towards the brighter overhead lights and the closer he moved it, the clearer the miniscule lettering became.

'What is it?' Stefani asked, peering more closely at the note.

'Something added in invisible ink.'

'That's impossible. They didn't have invisible ink two hundred years ago.'

'Of course they did,' Harker replied, glancing at her momentarily. 'They used a mixture of lemon juice and water, but there's no way it would have gone unnoticed by anyone examining it thoroughly.'

He ran his index finger along the hidden message, with squinting eyes. '*Ospedale del Santo*... Orphanage of the Saint. I've not heard of it.' He turned back to face Stefani, who now looked as if she had just seen a ghost.

She said nothing at first and Harker was about to ask what the problem was, when her lips began to quiver. 'I have.'

'What is it?' He asked, placing the scrap of paper down on the desk in front of them.

'It's the orphanage where I grew up. It's in Venice.'

The coincidence was incredible to Harker. 'Could your father have written it?'

'I suppose that's possible, but you heard the archbishop, there were multiple people working on it at one time, so it would have been hard to get away with.' Stefani's eyes began to widen. 'But if not, then Cardinal Vicci wrote it over two hundred years ago.'

They both sat in stunned silence as the jet's engines roared and began to gather in speed, until finally they felt the aircraft lift off its wheels and begin its ascent into the sky.

'Do you believe in fate?' Stefani asked him in a voice just audible above the engines.

Harker remained silent as the two stared at each other unblinkingly, then just as he was about to reply the phone began to vibrate in his pocket and broke the eerie moment between them. He pulled it out and swiped the answer bar to one side. 'Hello.'

'Alex,' Carter began and he was interrupted immediately by Harker.

'Hold on, David, I'm putting you on speakerphone,' he explained, tapping the appropriate icon on his touch screen. 'OK, go ahead now. I'm here with Stefani; please tell us you have something.' Harker sounded practically desperate but that was immediately swept away by the excitement in Carter's voice.

'Oh, I have something all right and you're not going to believe it.'

Harker shot Stefani a look of anticipation as Carter began to unload information in haste, as was his usual style when extremely excited.

'We've been looking in the wrong direction all this time. They're not Satanists, and neither is Avi Legrundy,' Carter explained eagerly. 'The bull's head you found at Father Davies's apartment, the ceremony you got caught up in in Rome, those weren't satanic rituals… they were rites of passage.'

If Harker had hoped his friend was about to clear things up, he was now sorely disappointed and was already shaking his head in confusion. 'What are you talking about?'

'That group you've been encountering, they're not devil worshippers… they're followers of Mithras!'

The very word had Harker's mouth dropping open in bewilderment. 'That's impossible, David.'

'I know, I know, but just hear me out,' Carter replied with defiance in his tone, 'Tom found a reference to Avi Legrundy in the Templar archives and we discovered a storage area full of stuff. Now, I've not had time to go through it all, because there's just so much there, but what I have discovered is bloody fascinating – and your father was at the centre of it.'

The mention of his father had Harker shifting in his seat uncomfortably. Stefani was now leaning closer to the phone as Carter continued with his news.

'We were led to believe that the Magi were the Templar's biggest threat and adversary to date, but if your father's records are anything to go by, then they were just the half of it, Alex. The cult of Mithras posed just as big a threat, if not more.'

'Who are the Mithras?' Stefani asked, noticeably twitchy over her unfamiliarity of the subject, but Harker raised a hand in a bid to placate her.

'David, you're not making any sense. Sebastian has never mentioned any of this before.'

'And why would he? This stuff was all put to bed twenty-five years ago,' Carter replied and a deep frown appeared on Harker's forehead. 'From what I've read, this Mithras group were at war with the Templars for years and it was your father – as Templar Jarl – who was largely instrumental in shutting them down altogether. A lot of lives were lost, so it says in his journals, and Avi Legrundy was a major player. Until they were all wiped out… apparently.'

Harker remained silent, not knowing what to make of any of it, as Carter continued.

'This storeroom I mentioned is full of Mithraic artefacts that must go back to the days of ancient Rome. And, Alex, if I'm being honest, they seem to consist less of antiquities being stored and more likely trophies of some kind.'

'Trophies!' Harker looked troubled. 'How?'

'Well, I even found a sealed package containing some kind of ceremonial garb covered in bloodstains, which to anyone knowing their history is very similar to those described in Mithraic texts. Couple that with the fact that there is no mention of the Mithras cult in the Templars' vault database and, if it wasn't for the name you gave us, I doubt we'd have found it at all. Not any time soon, anyway.'

Carter's breathing was now sounding nervously inter-mittent and his tone hesitant. 'If I didn't know better, I would say that someone wanted their very existence hidden away, and as for all the stuff we found... well, it wasn't exactly hidden but it wasn't really out in plain sight either, if you know what I mean.'

Harker remained silent as he considered what all this meant. But, if he wanted a few moments to think it through, Stefani was not about to allow that.

'If someone doesn't tell me who the cult of Mithras are right now, then, my friends... there's going to be trouble!'

Harker looked over and noticed that apart, from gritted teeth and glaring expression, she also had one of her hands clenched in a fist, and he had no doubt she meant what she had just said. 'The followers of Mithras, or Mithraism, are one of the oldest cults on the planet. They are also one of the most mysterious, and even today we know very little about them. That particular cult was said to have originated in Persia, maybe a few thousand years BC and long before Christianity had been born. When Rome expanded its rule across the globe their legionaries brought it back with them, and it grew and spread throughout the empire, mainly amongst the less reputable classes, not among the elite, and of course it became embedded within the army and legions.'

'Nero was hardly middle-class.' Carter protested, keen to set the record straight.

'That's true,' Harker replied, keeping his attention on Stefani who still looked unimpressed. 'Emperor Nero was himself inducted into the cult of Mithraism and soon afterwards he set about imprisoning and murdering as many Christians as he could get his hands on, but most of the cult's followers were middle-of-the-road in social standing.'

Stefani's expression softened and her shoulders began to loosen up. 'Why?'

'Because the early Christian faith was in direct competition with that of Mithraism at the time and amidst much scholarly debate on the subject, there's an argument that many of the Mithras practices were literally absorbed by the early Church itself.'

'What!'

Harker was surprised at Stefani's lack of knowledge on this subject but, given what Carter had suggested earlier, perhaps it was not a topic that the Templars were encouraged to learn about. Perhaps it was even taboo. 'There were certain similarities still debated today but the devotees of that cult worshipped Mithras, the sun god, who was born from his mother, the rock of Earth, without the need of a father. Some say it's another take on the virgin birth. There are other similarities with their god being able to create water out of soil and an ability to walk upon it. Furthermore the date of his birth was 25th of December by our calendar, which perhaps is enough said.'

'And don't forget the banquets where they would eat food symbolising the body of Mithras himself, just like is done with wafers during communion.' Carter interjected so loudly that his voice crackled in the receiver.

'That's merely a matter of conjecture, David,' Harker replied before turning to whisper to Stefani, 'He loves a good conspiracy theory.'

'I heard that.' Carter's objected in a deep tone.

'Nevertheless, what has become regarded as the mystery of Mithraism arose because in the first century while Christianity was becoming ever more popular, all the cult's devotees disappeared into history. Some say they were overwhelmed by the Christians and forced to convert, while others say they were slaughtered by their highly pious rivals. But one thing is fact: they pretty much disappeared without trace except for their temples being discovered in almost every country in Europe that had once belonged to the Roman Empire. They were constructed underground with the one distinct similarity of decorative symbols – the god Mithras slaughtering a bull with his knife while a snake, a dog and a raven attack it and, even worse, a large scorpion attacking the victim's testicles.'

Harker winced at the thought but Stefani remained expressionless as he elaborated on the subject further. 'There are many that think the bull represented Jesus and the sacrifice as Mithras's wish to destroy his competitor. But that's only conjecture because no one knows for sure, and we likely never will.'

'Maybe so,' Carter still sounded stern, 'but if what we've found is anything to go by, the Mithraic cult never disappeared – it did so from public view only.'

The notion had Harker shaking his head, even though it might explain much of what he had witnessed over the past few days. 'David, I honestly doubt that such a once potent force could have survived in absolute secrecy for over two thousand years, and anyway, what has it got to do with an apocalyptic prophecy – and a Catholic prophecy at that?'

There was a short silence before Carter began speaking again in that same deeply serious tone. He was clearly getting excited by the mystery he had uncovered. 'I don't know, Alex, but if your father's journals are anything to go by, the Mithraic cult managed it and, given they were apparently suppressed by the Templars in recent years, they appear to have a habit of making a comeback again and again.'

'This all sounds crazy,' Stefani exploded, and completely unconvinced. 'I have been a Templar all my life and I've never heard anything about that or any kind of rivalry except with the Magi. They were always our only adversaries and, believe me, if these Mithras people had been such a threat, and as destructive as you claim, then there is no way it could have been kept such a secret. More importantly, the Templar high guard would never have kept such an important secret from their members.'

'Maybe you're right, Stefani,' Carter conceded while privately becoming even more convinced of the possibility, 'but everything I'm telling you derives directly from the words of Alex's father. Remember, he was the Jarl and this is exactly the type of thing he himself would have dealt with.'

This time there was no response from her and she gave Harker an uncertain look. Whatever the truth, they were unlikely to find a consensus amongst themselves, and Harker knew it, but that aside, his position of Jarl now began to take on a more potent significance to him. If the Mithras were truly behind all this, and as powerful as Carter believed them to be, then he was now not only at the front of the charge but would soon become the tip of the spearhead in opposing them.

The realisation had him gulping nervously and Harker immediately pushed the idea to the back of his mind, not quite ready to confront the realities that his accepted role might soon entail. 'Let's all just focus on where we're going next. David, there's an orphanage in Venice, Ospedale del Santo, that could tie into all this.' He glanced over at Stefani and found her already nodding in agreement. 'We're going to take a look and see if it's connected in any way.'

'An orphanage? How?' Carter now sounded extremely interested.

'Not sure yet but I'll let you know when I do. In the meantime, could you contact Sebastian and see if he can shed some light on all this stuff please; if anyone knows anything it will be him.'

'Will do,' Carter agreed. 'Oh, and Tom is on his way back to the UK right now and he promised to speak with Chloe, so all good there.'

'Thanks, David. Be sure to let me know the moment you hear from Sebastian.'

The call ended abruptly and Harker placed his iPhone on the table and settled back in his seat with a look of puzzlement. 'If these people do belong to the Mithras cult and, apart from it being amazing that it's survived for this long without being detected, we still know absolutely nothing about them.'

'What concerns me more is that if the Templars had dealings with them, then why doesn't anyone know about it?'

It was a concern that was not lost on Harker either, and frankly it was what worried him most. If Carter was correct about all this and his father had indeed been instrumental in it all, then why the hell had Sebastian never mentioned this? Was it because his father – and the Templars – had done something terrible? Something so dreadful that they had kept it from the younger initiates rising up in its ranks? It was a troubling thought and he was just about to raise it with Stefani, when his phone rang again.

'It's probably David again.' Then he noticed there was no name on the call tag. 'It's a video call,' he announced before he swiped the accept bar to one side, which illuminated the screen to display the face of a white-haired man with a fraught expression.

'Alex… can you see me?' Henri Berger offered a lacklustre smile.

'I can see you, Henri,' Harker replied, not certain if this man knew about the death of Dr Marceau. 'Are you OK?'

'Yes.' The caller offered a light nod. 'How did you get on?'

No, clearly he didn't know and Harker elected to keep it that way for the time being. 'Long story short, we managed to get hold of it and we're in the air at the moment.'

'Good. That's good,' Henri replied and with a genuine hint of relief. 'Have you managed to read it?'

'Yes… but it wasn't very helpful. Not in the way you may have hoped. But there's good news, too, because we just discov—'

'We've heard about Gérald Marceau. It's horrible,' the man interrupted, and Harker could tell from the look in his eyes that he was extremely upset about it. 'Were you present?'

'Sadly yes, and am sorry to say it wasn't pretty. It was the doing of the Red Death, and her real name is Avi Legrundy. She's as vicious as anyone I've ever met.'

The caller gave another slow nod of his head before he gazed back at Harker with a tear forming in his eye, due to him not blinking once since this call had begun. 'Yes… I know.'

A thin blade, held in a black hand, crept around Henri's throat like a steel serpent which slithered into place beneath the man's left ear. Then another hand pulled his head back, allowing a better view of the knife's owner.

Avi Legrundy flashed those white teeth of hers and grinned towards the camera, whilst revealing that the entire left side of her face was covered by a white bandage patch peppered with red stains.

'Hello, Alex,' Legrundy said and, as she pulled Henri back further, Harker could see the limp bodies of both Pierre and Monique lying on the floor, face down. 'I've been getting to know your friends.'

With the blade still held tightly at Henri's throat, Legrundy slowly peeled back the bandage to reveal a deep burn mark extending from her jaw up to one side of her forehead. Her burnt dreadlocks had been roughly hacked off and, after displaying the nasty wound, she pressed the bandage back in place. 'You owe me a debt, Alex, and I intend to collect.'

'Oh, my God,' Stefani gasped as she moved closer to the small screen and was immediately noticed by Legrundy.

'Stefani Mitchell. I'm glad you're there... Hold on.' With dull eyes Legrundy sliced the knife across Henri's neck and dropped him to the floor in a convulsing heap, before stepping over his twitching body and moving so close to the camera that her face filled the screen. 'It's a pleasure to see you again.'

'Jesus, you're sick,' Harker growled and, although feeling absolutely helpless, he wanted nothing more than to reach through the display and choke the life out of her.

'Sickness got nothing to do with it,' Legrundy answered with a smile that revealed how much she was enjoying his disgust, 'but getting this has *everything* to do with it.'

Legrundy reached somewhere out of sight and her hand reappeared holding the familiar red 'blessed candle' the Order had been protecting for centuries – until now. 'Your snivelling fat friend Marceau gave up his hiding place long before I cut his tongue out.'

'You've got nothing, Legrundy,' Stefani yelled. 'You may now have one of them but you'll never get the other.'

Legrundy shook her head and chuckled before again ducking out of view only to reappear, this time with the other 'blessed candle' they had retrieved back in Athens. 'You mean this one?'

Stefani's mouth dropped open and her look of complete surprise elicited a victorious grunt from the killer.

'You thought you were so clever in getting away from me at the Acropolis Museum dat it never occurred to you I might be following you?'

Stefani remained silent, frankly ashamed that she had made such an obvious mistake in not better covering their tracks.

'I trailed you to the airport, and then on to the nice man you gave this to for safekeeping.' She began juggling them both in her hands before drawing them close to her chest. 'I want you to know that he died pissing himself as he begged for his life.'

This goading insult proved too much for Stefani and she grabbed the phone from Harker's hands and began to rant at its screen. 'Wherever you go, I'll find you, Legrundy. I swear it.'

The Red Death looked unmoved by this outburst and once more moved closer to the screen. 'Swear it on what... your oath as a Templar?'

It was the first time, since crossing paths, that any knowledge of their both belonging to the Templars had been voiced, and it not only shocked Stefani but Harker as well.

He calmly took the phone back from her. 'You seem to know more about us than you've let on,' he said, now taking the opportunity to test out Carter's theory for himself. 'I thought we'd destroyed the pathetic cult of Mithras years ago.'

Legrundy's eyes widened in surprise but that chilling smile persisted. 'So now we both know who we are,' she replied, tilting her head forward. 'That's crucial if friendships are to flourish.'

This reply was bizarre and Harker now glared back at her with a steely look. 'There was no friendship to flourish in the first place, Legrundy, but I'm getting to know better what you are, and we'll be paying you a visit soon.'

This was of course just angry bravado on his part but, given he had just watched a new acquaintance callously murdered before his eyes, he wanted the killer to realise this wasn't the end, but just the beginning of any lengths the Templars would go to in order to get her.

'Oh, I know far more about you, Alex – which isn't saying much. You don't know *who* I am, you don't know what dat stupid note you managed to get is, and especially...' She raised the two blessed candles in to view momentarily... 'you don't have a clue what these are for, do you?'

Harker gulped in frustration because everything she said was absolutely true, and he couldn't help but now feel that she had been playing them both all along. 'It's not over yet,' he growled sternly but this only brought forth a deep laugh from her.

'Not over! You don't even know what it was to begin with.' Legrundy placed both the blessed candles down on the floor and pressed her face up towards the screen. 'In mere hours it ain't going to matter anyway because all that exists of your world will wither away and disappear, and then you will realise a truth that you never even understood in the first place.'

The assassin scowled at them, then reached towards the side of the screen and she repeated the ominous line that Father Davies had written in his own blood and which appeared in the Prophecy. '"You are I and I am you. When he is myth and we are reality. This grand deception will be repaid in blood." and I will always be one step ahead of you,' she hissed, clearly taunting him with knowing exactly what he had already managed to discover, before the screen went black.

'That bitch is dead,' Stefani now raged and she slammed her fist down on the table hard, as Harker slipped the phone slowly back in his pocket. At any other moment he would have tried to calm her, but in truth he was just as livid. The deaths this woman had on her hands amounted to nothing short of a bloodbath, but she was right in saying that she was always one step ahead even when it seemed they had left her scowling in the rear-view mirror.

'You couldn't have known,' he reassured Stefani, as her clenched fists continued thumping lightly on the table top.

'It's my job to know, Alex, and, as a result of my failure, someone else has died needlessly. And your contact, Henri… disgusting.'

'I myself am to blame for them, if anyone,' Harker said despondently. 'I led her straight to them. Marceau said so himself.'

'Maybe, but this Legrundy woman is a tracker, and a damn good one.'

'Same then goes for you,' he replied, still trying to soothe her anger.

But Stefani was already shaking her head. 'I've trained for this type of work all my life only to fail those poor people, the Templars – and myself.'

There was little Harker could say to that, but there was an unanswered question still niggling him, and possibly the reason for her increased anger. 'Who exactly was it you left the blessed candle with?' he asked, sensing that this lay at the true core of her feeling of guilt.

'He was a Templar associate – and not only a close friend of mine but of Sebastian's as well… It appears that David Carter was correct. The Templars know of them and they know us, but why the hell weren't we informed?'

This was probably the most important question to resolve at this point. 'I don't know,' he said before picking the note up off the table and waving it in front of her, 'but I'm willing to bet your father did… and mine too.'

This observation saw Stefani beginning to calm, and now she focused her gaze on the piece of paper being brandished in her direction.

'Perhaps destiny really is about to play its part.'

Chapter 28

God, I hate this place, thought Marco Lombardi as he perched on the uncomfortable plywood bench and waited like a good boy, as instructed. The large room was shabby and unkempt, with straw littering the floor and clumps of it swept up against the base of the wall, so it looked more like a stable than a meeting room. Hardly a fitting place for an animal to spend its time in, let alone that thing kept down there. How many years had it spent roaming its private underworld, its personal dominion, just waiting for the next soul to gorge upon?

Lombardi's lips curled at the thought and he rubbed his hands together as he pondered who would be next to face that inhuman beast. In all these years he had only ever caught a glimpse of it once, and he had to admit it had terrified him to the core. Yet that couldn't even begin to approach the dread that those who sought to face it must have felt. Anyway, that wasn't something to concern him because he wasn't looking to usurp Father, but only to change the direction of things to come. And given his faith in Avi Legrundy, that change would be coming soon enough.

In all these years he had never been able to get used to this place, and he yearned at every opportunity to return to the opulence of the city. Maybe he had become softened by a lavish lifestyle but, given all the hard work he had put in, it was something that he felt he thoroughly deserved. What was the point of creating such wealth and opportunity only to be force-fed this diet of antiquated rubbish from a bygone era he no longer even respected. How could Father expect him, of all people, to continue on a path that would ultimately lead to the misery of billions of others? Of course it was not the thought of this consequence that concerned him but rather that he had to waste his own time participating in it.

Lombardi again glanced around his dilapidated surroundings and shook his head disparagingly. With its cracked grey plaster walls and stuffy atmosphere the room looked less like an office and more like a storage room. *What a shithole.*

Just then the sound of the door opening had Lombardi snapping to attention. He stood up immediately as the tall, hooded figure of Father glided into the room and closed the door behind him. Only the lower portion of his mouth could be seen as the sagging hood covered the rest of his features.

'Forgive my tardiness, Marco, but I had things to attend to that could not have waited.'

Whether through respect or indoctrination, Lombardi gave a vigorous shake of the head. 'Not at all, Father. Thank you for seeing me.'

With a slow nod, Father placed a gloved hand on Lombardi's shoulder. 'This has been a long road for us, son, and I am aware that your patience and loyalty have been tested, but you will be rewarded with everything you deserve.'

Lombardi nodded gratefully and seized upon Father's words to begin his prepared speech. 'That means every-thing to me, but it is also why I asked for this meeting.'

Father remained silent and he stood back, with his hands clasped, and waited for the young man to explain himself.

'I believe I have discovered the person directing Avi Legrundy against us,' Lombardi said proudly, then paused for a reaction but, on getting none, continued with his revelation. 'I tracked several phone calls made to her by none other than Sofia, and it appears she is the one who has been trying to thwart your careful plans.'

'But why?' Father asked, sounding deeply unconvinced.

'Perhaps a lack of faith in what we are trying to achieve?'

There was an awkward pause before Father began to nod slowly. 'Her willingness to conform has always worried me, I have to admit, but I never thought she would go this far.'

Lombardi struggled to prevent a smile forming on his lips but nevertheless he succeeded and he now pushed ahead with his story. 'I was as shocked as you are now, to say the least, but I assure you I've told no one else of her treachery in regards to you and how you may wish to proceed.'

Father's hooded head swayed from side to side, and he folded his arms before turning away in apparent dismay. 'What do you think we should do then, Marco?'

This question caught Lombardi off guard, but he smiled graciously and was now totally taken aback by the deference he was being shown by his leader. 'Well, I think firstly Sofia must be confronted with the truth of her disloyalty, and then I would like to personally meet with Miss Legrundy and determine whether she was in any way involved with this betrayal or simply weak-minded and tricked into compliance.'

As Father mulled over the suggestion, Lombardi couldn't help but feel an enormous sense of satisfaction at his own cunning. Once the Red Death had got rid of Alex Harker, and that idiot sidekick of his, he could meet with Legrundy, take back the item she had retrieved from them, then deal with her in person, and in doing so tie up any loose ends connecting him to anything questionable. With that achieved he could finish off what had started and take his place at the head of the family. *Perfection itself, and a scapegoat offered*.

'Yes, Marco, that would be good,' Father replied, and turned his attention back to the younger man. 'But only if I had not already managed to contact Miss Legrundy myself.'

Lombardi's heart sank like a stone and his breathing grew shallow and erratic. 'You've spoken to her?'

'Yes, Marco, and what she had to say was really quite enlightening. She said that it was you that had been instructing her, purportedly on my behalf.'

'That's a lie,' Lombardi said defiantly, even though he was beginning to sweat and his voice starting to tremble nervously. 'Why would I do such a thing?'

Father grasped him by the shoulders and gave him a light shake. 'Did you really think you could so easily pit us against each other, Marco? Did you really think I hadn't noticed your loyalty ebbing away these past few months? Such a waste of talent.'

Father released him and turned to face the opposite wall. 'I was thinking of having you taught a lesson in the same way as poor old Donitz, but I believe you should have the chance to prove yourself once more and let *him* decide.'

Lombardi knew exactly what was being offered and he had no intention of taking it. He leapt towards the door and swung it open – whereupon he came to a dead stop at what he saw ahead. Sofia stood there in the doorway and glared at him menacingly, as seven of his brothers and sisters stood ranged behind her. 'All debts must be repaid, Marco, and betrayal is a difficult one to reimburse.'

With Sofia at the fore, the group poured into the room and wrestled Lombardi to the floor. He kicked and screamed wildly, but with little effect, so it was all over before it even really started. Within seconds they had overpowered him with ease.

'Consider yourself fortunate,' Sofia yelled over the commotion, then she swept away a small pile of hay alongside the far wall to reveal an old wooden trap-door set in the floor. Its surface was covered with carved symbols of scorpions, swastikas, snakes and beaked ravens, all of them surrounding a large bull's head with two thick horns protruding from it. 'Not many are given the chance to test their mettle and thus gain entry to the hallowed Kingdom of God. The true god.'

Lombardi was now sobbing uncontrollably as the trap-door was flung open. He was dragged towards it with his feet scraping against the wooden floorboards as he tried in vain to resist those pushing him ever closer towards that dark gap in the floor. The smell it emitted was truly awful and just as he attempted to scream for forgiveness, someone muzzled him with an open palm and in one swift thrust, he was dumped head first, through the trap-door and disappeared from sight somewhere down into that gloomy darkness.

The others now withdrew from the opening and Father approached with a hand in one of his robe pockets, from which he now produced a small knife with a leather-wrapped handle, and dropped it inside just as Sofia slammed the trap-door shut again.

'Let us pray for the brother lost to us, and hope he returns to us with a purified heart.'

The group gathered around the trap-door with clasped hands and began to murmur a prayer, even as somewhere beneath them, a deafening roar cut through the air with such power that its vibrations could be felt through the wood flooring itself.

That's when the screaming began.

Chapter 29

'Venice, the Queen of the Adriatic, the floating City, City of Canals. I want to take in the sights and all I can think about now is how I wish I'd brought my wellingtons,' Harker said gloomily, looking down at his black leather brogues that were nearly soaked through. 'Beautiful city, though.'

Stefani just about managed a smile as he moved away from the massive puddles alongside the Basilica overlooking the famous Piazza San Marco. 'It does experience some minor flooding from time to time, but you can't deny those views.'

Harker surveyed the sprawling L-shaped open space which constituted the principal public square in Venice; absolutely packed with tourists at this time of day. The Church's façade boasted enormous arches and marble walls adorned with mosaics, its main entrance attracted a constant crowd of tourists all putting up with those large puddles to gain access to the wonderful interior. He still found it hard to believe that this ancient city was being supported on nothing more than wooden posts, even if there were a million of them constantly sinking deeper into the mud year on year. This place was undoubtedly one of humanity's most impressive architectural triumphs.

'Do you remember much of this from your childhood? Harker asked, trying to engage with Stefani who had been uncharacteristically – though understandably – subdued on the flight over.'

'Hardly, Alex, I was barely one year old when I was adopted, and I never came back.'

The strain in her voice was obvious and Harker moved closer to her. 'So where's the orphanage?'

'Should be just around the corner if this map is correct,' Stefani replied studying it for a few more seconds before folding it up and slipping it into her leather jacket pocket. With sagging shoulders she made her way off the Piazza and down a side street running next to the Basilica. Harker followed in silence and, even though he sensed she wasn't in the mood to talk, he tried anyway, if for no other reason than simply to elicit a smile from those brooding lips.

'I haven't been here since I was eighteen,' he remarked as a group of tourists headed past them, their smartphones held up in front of them like weapons. 'Only spent one day before I had to get back.'

'Family visit, was it?'

'No, nothing like that. I was training at the Vatican and used a day off to come and see the sights.'

The remark seemed to puzzle her. 'Training for what?'

'To be a priest.'

This disclosure had her looking shocked and she stopped short as a further wave of tourists flowed past them. '*You* were a priest?'

'Yes… with the emphasis on *was*.' Harker replied and he felt as if she was judging him for some past crime.

'I never would have thought that.' She shook her head and continued walking, 'You're just so…'

'Rebellious? Defiant?' Harker offered, listing what he concluded some of his best qualities.

'No, I was going to say stubborn and slightly annoying.'

Harker's face dropped and he was starting to feel a bit annoyed, when she began to laugh, and he immediately relaxed. 'Very funny.'

'I just didn't know, that's all,' Stefani continued, suddenly appearing more upbeat. 'The famous archaeologist Alex Harker was a priest.'

'OK, now you're just taking the piss,' Harker said with a grin.

But Stefani looked serious. 'No, I mean it. You know how the Templars feel about you… well, a small number of us anyway.' She let out a laugh. 'OK, now I am taking the piss.'

'Enough.' Harker was glad to see that she now seemed in a better frame of mind than during the previous few hours. 'Now, where precisely is this place we're looking for?'

Stefani turned her gaze to the row of buildings lining one side of the narrow street and finally pointed to one of them: '340 Calle Canonico. That's it.'

On the corner leading off into another tiny side street stood a small restaurant with large bay windows. Inside were people eating, some of whom began staring out at them.

'Unless they now serve hungry passers-by as well as parentless kids, I'd say your orphanage was shut down a while back,' Harker observed.

Stefani pulled out the map again and examined it closely. 'This is definitely it,' she confirmed.

With a shrug Harker led the way inside to take a closer look. The interior was exactly what it seemed: a restaurant. And, after staring around for a few moments, Harker approached the blond-haired waitress in a black uniform who was sitting behind the small counter. 'Excuse me,' he began politely, in order to catch her attention. 'We're trying to find the Ospedale del Santo. I was given this address.'

The young woman swept back several loose strands of hair that had escaped her ponytail before she shook her head courteously. 'We're a restaurant.'

Harker persisted 'What was here before it became a restaurant?'

Already used to strange questions from sight-seeking tourists, she shook her head again. 'Sorry, I've only worked here for a few months; would you like a table?'

'Thank you but no,' Harker replied, as Stefani dodged a waiter carrying two bowls of spaghetti carbonara and a Diet Coke to a nearby table, 'it's the orphanage I was looking for.'

She raised her shoulders helplessly. 'Would you like to speak with the owner?'

Finally some headway, Harker thought, even if just grasping at straws. 'That would be perfect, thank you.'

The girl headed off down a narrow corridor leading to the rear and within a minute a heavy-set woman in her late fifties appeared. Sporting a bouffant hairstyle that only served to accentuate her ample frame, and dressed in a tan business jacket and skirt, with a necklace containing the largest set of fake pearls Harker had ever seen, the sight of her rapidly disproved the idea that all Italians were born with an inherent sense of fashion.

'Can I help you?' the woman asked in a strangely, high-pitched voice somewhat at odds with her generous frame.

'We're trying to get some information on the orphanage that used to be here. Maybe you can help us?'

Her eyes squinted slightly, not with any sense of defensiveness but rather an air of puzzlement. 'Why?'

Stefani gently stepped past Harker and right up to the counter. 'I was adopted from here as a baby, and my husband and I were putting together a family tree…' She patted her stomach which she was now forcing outwards to suggest a bump.

Without needing a prompt, Harker draped his arm around his supposed wife and nodded eagerly with a smile. 'Family history has become so important to us now little Edward is on the way.' He felt a pinch to his waist from Stefani indicating 'Don't overdo it'.

The proprietor remained blank-faced, then a wide smile emerged on her puffy lips. 'When you have children your life does take on a different meaning, doesn't it? I'd be happy to show you around the place, if you'd like.'

'That would be great,' Stefani enthused and, with a beckoning flick of the woman's hand they followed her beyond the counter and along the narrow corridor towards the far end of the building.

'I bought this place about twenty-five years ago, after the orphanage closed down.' The plump woman guided them on past the kitchen area and out into a small back-yard patio bordered on all sides by neighbouring build-ings. The surrounding walls supported trellises hung with a beautiful collection of passion vines in a refreshing mixture of purple and orange, while in the centre was a round wooden table and several chairs whose varnish had long lost its shine.

'There used to be some additional rooms here but we received special permission to take them down and build this seating area.' The woman proudly swept a hand over the attractive arrangement.

'It's lovely.' Harker nodded in approval.

She turned back to face them both. 'So what can I show you?'

At that moment Harker returned gratefully to their reason for being here. 'We were hoping to find out more about the orphanage's history. Why it closed, for instance?'

His question drew a look of wide-eyed surprise from the restaurant owner.

'You don't know, then?'

'Know what?' Stefani replied.

Signora Busetto began to look uncomfortable. 'I'm sorry, I assumed you knew – seeing as you were adopted from here.'

She was obviously curious at their lack of knowledge and so Stefani began to explain herself. 'I was adopted as a young baby and this is the first time I've been back. I honestly expected the orphanage to still be here.'

Signora Busetto looked sad that Stefani was going to be disappointed and she motioned for them both to take a seat. She followed suit, the wooden chair creaking underneath her plentiful weight. 'I'm sorry to be the one to tell you this but the orphanage was closed after a dreadful incident here some twenty-five years ago. I suppose it must have occurred shortly after you were adopted.'

'What exactly happened?' Harker demanded, as Stefani leant closer to the table.

'About twenty children between the ages of one and eight years old used to be cared for here at the Orphanage of the Saint, which back then was attached to the Basilica out on the main Piazza. It was overseen by a priest – I can't remember his name, I'm afraid – but by the early nineties orphanages had become all but extinct, so as such it had become a well-known institution in the city of Venice. Everyone knew of it.'

Signora Busetto paused and began to rub her hands together anxiously, her retelling of this story clearly troubling to her. 'One night the police responded to a reported disturbance right here, and what they found still haunts the memory of the locals who witnessed it.'

'What did they find?' Harker asked so impatiently that he was sharply nudged in the arm by Stefani.

'Let the lady finish.'

Signora Busetto appeared grateful for the pause, then she continued with a look of genuine sorrow on her face. 'They found the supervising priest mutilated, so the newspapers reported, and the body of one of the eldest children treated in much the same fashion. I don't know exactly what, but such terrible things had been done to both of them that the details weren't fully reported.'

'Oh my God, that's awful,' Harker mouthed, massaging his forehead vigorously, as the woman nodded slowly.

'I know. The things some people are capable of can be quite overwhelming – which is how the surrounding community reacted at the time.'

'What happened to those other children?' Stefani asked, and her expression remarkably hard given the nature of the atrocities they were learning about.

'They didn't find all the… body parts,' Signora Busetto replied cryptically, 'but I do know some remains were found at the bottom of the canal just a few streets over from here.'

'Jesus Christ,' Harker muttered sympathetically.

'I know, that's how the whole local community felt, and it is also the main reason we were allowed special permission to demolish those rooms of the building in which it actually took place and had this garden built in its place. It's also the reason my husband planted these passion vines surrounding us: to honour those poor little souls.'

There were few things in the world that Harker could not find some semblance of understanding for but when it came to the rape, abuse or murder of children his heart, like most people's, was turned to stone and the retribution of an eye for and eye seemed not just justified but a human duty. 'Did they catch anyone?'

She shook her head mournfully. 'There was an arrest but the fellow was released without charge and, although he was innocent, a stain like that doesn't easily wash off. I read somewhere later that he became a recluse and drank himself to death… but, apart from that, no one was ever apprehended.'

'How about the bodies of the other children? Were they ever recovered?' Stefani intervened, her voice quivering slightly.

'That's possibly the worst part of it,' replied Signora Busetto, who stopped fumbling with her hands and laid them out straight on the chair's arms. 'They were discovered several weeks later just a few miles from here, on the island of Poveglia. They had been drowned and were then piled up on one another like in some kind of sick monument. No shred of evidence regarding the killers was left behind except this "gross shrine to pure evil", as the newspapers put it. You don't forget a headline like that. They later placed a memorial up there as I remember.'

Stefani sat back in her seat and exhaled deeply. The other woman leant forward and tapped her warmly on the hand.

'I would therefore say you're extremely fortunate,' she gave a caring smile. 'If you hadn't been adopted when you were, I suppose you'd have ended up like the others.'

It was a disconcerting thought and, seeing how deeply it affected Stefani, Harker began to shift the conversation along. 'I've heard of this Poveglia island many times. It's got a grim history, hasn't it?'

Signora Busetto pulled back her hand and placed it in her lap where she began to fidget with her fingers. 'Every city in the world has its own dark past.'

'Why, what else happened there?' Stefani now sat straight up in her seat as if glad to be distracted from brooding on the lucky escape fate had afforded her.

'It was a quarantine station during an outbreak of plague back in the eighteenth century,' Harker explained, 'when thousands of the citizens were abandoned there to die and their bodies later burnt in an effort to control the epidemic.' He was well aware of the island's unpalatable history, which was well known. 'It then became a mental hospital in the 1920s but got shut down sometime in the '60s after they caught one of the doctors performing crude lobotomies and a number of other nasty goings on – in the name of medicine.'

'That's correct,' Signora Busetto confirmed, seeming more than happy to discuss such a morbid topic. 'The same doctor committed suicide by throwing himself from the top of the bell-tower after being tormented by the ghosts of those he defiled, so the story goes. Even today there's a saying amongst Venetians that when bad people die they don't wake up in hell but instead are imprisoned on that island for all eternity.'

Stefani looked up at her host with a grimace, to which the woman gave a dry smile. 'As I said dear, every city has its own dark history, and Venice is no exception.'

The gloomy atmosphere was suddenly broken, much to Harker's relief, when one of the waiters stuck his head out through the open kitchen door and called out to Signora Busetto.

'Martina, can you give us a hand. It's getting really busy up-front.'

Mrs Busetto waved a hand elegantly in the air. 'I'll be right there, Lorenzo,' she replied and heaved herself to her feet. 'If you want to have some lunch here, I would be happy to show you upstairs as well if you'd like. Not that you'd remember much as it's changed quite a bit since you were here last.'

Stefani stood up, shaking her head and Harker also rose to his feet. 'Thank you but I think we've seen enough,' she said bitterly and their hostess immediately noticed how sad she looked.

'I'm sorry, it's a horrible story, but I've lived with it for so many years that I may have become somewhat numb to it.'

'That's totally understandable,' Harker replied, before shaking her hand gratefully, 'At least we now know what happened.'

'Yes,' Stefani added quickly, 'at least we know.'

With a polite nod Signora Busetto headed back towards the kitchen, pausing at the doorway. 'I'll have some sandwiches made for you and waiting at the front desk. Consider it a parting gift, and if you take away anything from our conversation, let it be this. If fate had not smiled on you that day when you were adopted, you would not now be about to welcome your own child into this world, would you? That is surely something to be grateful for.'

She then disappeared into the kitchen, leaving them alone together in what had previously looked like a charming back patio but whose brightly coloured flowers now only seemed like a bizarre testament to the horrors that had taken place all those years ago.

'You OK?' he asked Stefani.

She looked up and gave him a brave look. 'I'm fine, just a bit taken aback really. Putting all that to one side now, if it's possible, I'm trying to understand *why* the message led us here?'

In his mind Harker already knew the answer but for some reason he felt that he should not launch straight into it. 'Well, if that message on the Prophecy was written by Cardinal Vicci a few centuries ago, then I'm still not sure what to make of it. But if it was your father who wrote it, then this place obviously had some significance that he wanted you to know about, or at least investigate.'

'And that would be…?'

He slipped his arm under hers and drew her towards the kitchen doorway.

'The island of Poveglia.'

Chapter 30

The outer edge of the twenty-five-foot launch knocked gently against the jetty with each following wave lapping up against it as Harker secured the mooring line to its post. The time required to rent a boat and then sail the short few miles to Poveglia Island had taken far longer than anticipated, and with only half an hour of sunlight left, the skies were beginning to darken.

The island was tiny – only a few hundred feet wide by three hundred feet long – and split in two by a narrow canal running directly through it. Its small extent, though, was rendered far more mysterious by the overgrown trees and bushes that covered its entire area in jungle-type vege-tation.

Harker heaved himself out onto the moss-covered jetty and offered a hand which was grasped keenly by Stefani, who then managed to exit the boat with far more grace than he had.

'So, this is the island of the dead,' Stefani remarked, catching a glimpse of the crumbling bell-tower just visible above the treeline. 'More like the island of the dilapidated.'

If it was meant as a joke Harker didn't laugh as he proceeded down to the end of the rotting dock to the gap where a clump of thick bushes had been pushed aside, no doubt by curious tourists wanting to add a scary element to their holiday snaps.

'I think we can get through here,' he decided, kicking a few fallen branches back from the opening. 'According to Signora Busetto, the plaque can be found near one of the main buildings.'

'After you,' Stefani suggested, gripping tightly the LED torchlight they had bought in view of the approaching twilight. 'Remind me why we're doing this again?' she added as Harker continued to wade through dense foliage.

'Because we don't have anywhere else to look,' he replied, slapping a giant mosquito that had landed on his neck. 'And, besides, why else would your father leave us a trail of crumbs leading to the orphanage… I mean to the restaurant.'

Stefani said nothing to that, herself now batting away the increasing hordes of flies gathering around them in their eagerness for a feast.

'I need to take a look at that commemorative plate left here for the lost children, and if it turns out to be a dead end, then we'll head back and…'

'And what?'

Harker came to a halt and turned back to face her, his expression blank. Because if this venture went nowhere, and with the prophecy taking place within possibly hours then what else exactly could they do? Who knew as yet where this was all leading? Discovering the existence of the mysterious cult of Mithras, and its worrying ties to the Templars, had been a shock to him and extremely worrying in its own right. And he still needed to work out exactly why this group of zealots sought to bring about such a world-changing catastrophe as the three days of Darkness. Deep in his gut the idea appeared nothing more than a fanciful legend or the foretelling of a disastrous event that, like so many before it, would culminate in absolutely nothing. That is until he took into consideration his own apocalyptic vison. The otherworldly, supernatural events he had witnessed in his head had completely obliterated the normal scepticism and doubt that came naturally to him, and so he couldn't shake off the nagging feeling that something really big was about to take place.

As Harker pushed ahead along the overgrown path and deeper into the island, something else began to tease at his thoughts. That strange symbol he had noticed on the first blessed candle began to assume heavier significance the more he considered it. Two overlapping circles surrounded by swastikas had suggested, to his mind, a representation of heaven and hell – two kingdoms of the religious realm with Earth shrouded by the presence of both – but with Carter's subsequent discovery of the Mithras cult they now demanded further examination.

'Those engravings on the blessed candle we discovered in Athens,' he began, just avoiding a small branch about to slap across his face as he moved forward, 'we assumed they represented heaven and hell, right?'

'Yes, why?' Stefani recoiled as the same offending branch caught her right across the forehead.

'But what if they represent the Mithras cult and the Catholic Church… two kingdoms fighting for the mind of humanity.'

She now appeared more concerned with a small scratch the branch had left her with than any philosophical discussion, and merely offered an uninterested murmur. 'There's one problem with that,' she added after a moment, 'If we take Dr Marceau's beliefs seriously then that same candle has been around since the dawn of time itself, and well before Mithraism was even dreamed up.'

It was a fair assumption but Harker was now allowing himself to think beyond the rational and practical, again as result of experiencing that vision deep in the foundations of the Eiffel Tower. 'What if destiny – fate – was a real and tangible thing?' he asked, somewhat rhetorically. 'What if there really is a guiding line constant through space and time which humans are unaware of, like a thread determining all events which a select number of people have the ability to tap into at some level.'

'What, like visions of the future?'

'Something like that, yes.'

The idea made her chuckle. 'I'd say that you'd been smoking something you maybe shouldn't have.'

He shot her a reproving look. 'I'm being serious here. What if a few people such as Nostradamus, were born with the ability to gain insight into this "thread"? A natural and biological capacity produced through evolution and mutation?'

Harker's thinking might seem pretty 'out there' but with a jolt of understanding, she realised what was causing it. 'That vision you had really did have an impact on you didn't it?' she suggested, and he offered a silent nod of the head.

'I haven't mentioned it but, ever since it happened, my head has seemed all over the place,' he then admitted, and he came to a halt as Stefani placed her palm on his back.

'You've been through a lot over the past few days,' she said sympathetically, before turning her attention to the clearing up ahead. 'I don't know exactly what to think right now, but I would say we found the right place for it.'

Harker gave her a puzzled glance, then he turned and looked forward again to see what had grabbed her attention. What he saw there made him smile.

About ten metres in front of them, and now visible amongst the bushes, stood a large white sign with thick black lettering. *Reparto Psichiatria.*

'Psychiatric Department,' he translated, 'sounds about right.' Then he shook his head. 'I wonder what the food's like?'

'Not too good, I'll bet. Let's take a look around, shall we?'

Just beyond the sign itself the vegetation fell away and they found themselves staring up at the long crumbling wall of a building whose roof had long since caved in. It ran along for some length and the entire bell tower could now be viewed clearly. Harker poked his head through a gap in the wall to find the interior exactly as one would expect of a place left to rot for decades.

In the room in front of him he could see that all the flooring was missing and a mixture of dirt and dead brown leaves were scattered everywhere. Bolted to the side wall, rusting metal bars extended outwards in racks above a single scuffed metal drain hole, and Harker recognised their use instantly. 'I've seen this set-up in books,' he said, pointing up to the metal rafters. 'When an inmate died, they would wash and drape the patient's mattress over these and then leave it there to dry out for the next occupant.'

'Very hygienic.' Stefani turned up her nose up at the thought.

'When these methods were in operation, health-and-safety wasn't even in the vernacular,' Harker responded with a grimace, before he made his way through the scruffy breach in the wall. 'The commemorative plaque should be somewhere up ahead.'

The building had been large and they had to carefully navigate their way through heaps of fragmented brickwork and past rotting chairs and rusting bedsprings. It wasn't just through fear of catching themselves on sharp bits of twisted metal but more because this whole place stood as a filthy and terrible memorial to the thousands who had died here. Whether that was from the plague or as a result of the torturous experiments conducted later, there was a genuinely ominous feel to it all that was not just the result of its noxious dereliction, because Harker couldn't shake off the impression that they were being watched.

'What a dump,' Stefani complained, carefully avoiding a partially melted black shower curtain draped across a foully stained mattress. 'Who owns this place now?'

'Private owner bought it years ago, I believe, and given its history it's hard to envisage why. I can't imagine building some sort of a hotel resort on an island known for nothing else than plague, death and torture.'

The sound of shuffling in the next room brought them both to a standstill and, after glancing at one another anxiously, they stepped forward gingerly and peered inside. Like all the others the room was a wreck, but empty at least. And as they made their way further along the central corridor running the length of the entire building, they began to hear further scraping noises coming from all around them.

'Just rats.' Harker suggested confidently, but it didn't stop him from quickening his pace. He sped on along the corridor with Stefani at his heels, not stopping until they had exited through the main entrance door and came out into a small open area, thankfully devoid of bushes, in the centre of the island.

'Case of the willies,' Harker remarked, looking slightly embarrassed at his display of nerves. 'Let's just find this plaque, shall we?'

Stefani nodded, herself also looking twitchy, and she was about to take her first step when she noticed something in the bushes up ahead. 'What's that?'

With the light around them getting dimmer by the minute, Harker focused in on the dark shape she was pointing towards. The covered object had no defining edges and, whilst craning his head for a better view, he took a few steps closer to the bushy thicket.

'Pass me the torch, would you?' he asked with hand outreached and Stefani obliged, clicking it on as she passed it over.

Its intense beam illuminated something solid but it was still impossible to discern exactly what, so Harker moved closer and then, once satisfied it at least was not something alive, he pushed his way further into the thick brush. Within a second he had barrelled his way to the other side, only to find himself in a cavity within the bushes which was covered completely overhead by the sprawling branches of the surrounding trees. This leafy ceiling was over four metres up, allowing Harker to stand upright while the hedge acted as walls for this forest hiding place.

'Alex,' Stefani called out from beyond the barrier, sounding concerned. 'What is it?'

He didn't reply but instead focused his attention on the structure before him, taking a moment to admire the simple yet effective cover the trees and bushes allowed it. The whole area had been excavated into the soil by a metre or so, over which a trail of thick wooden planks ran directly up to the mouth of an open cave.

'Come take a look.' he replied quietly and with the rustling of leaves being pushed aside Stefani joined him and herself stared at the oddity in surprise.

'What on earth?' Stefani gasped, appearing just as Harker dropped down into the trench and cautiously made his way towards the gloomy entrance.

'It's an entrance,' he replied, stating the obvious whilst shining his torch beam ahead, 'and there's a pathway inside.'

His curiosity was suddenly replaced with a dose of reality given that, for all he knew, a pack of wolves could be living inside this damn place. He came to an abrupt stop as Stefani jumped down the incline to join him. 'Look at that.' He aimed the torchlight up at the stone surface towards the symbols that had been carved into the dull, brown rock. 'Swastikas.'

There were fifteen in all, circling the symbol of two circles overlapping one another which Harker was now becoming all too familiar with. 'The two kingdoms,' he declared and gestured to the engraving. 'This is what your father was directing us to. It has to be.'

'So what does it mean?' she asked, eyeing the emblem carefully as Harker took a first step inside the rocky opening.

'It means we go inside.'

If Stefani had any misgivings about Harker's proposed course of action, she didn't have time to voice them, for he was already swiftly moving along the passageway. 'Alex…' was all she managed before, with a shrug, she followed his lead and headed in after him.

The interior of the passage was clammy as Harker used the torchlight to illuminate their way down the pitch-dark passage. The stone floor was moist and slippery where condensation had accumulated due to hot evening air against a cold rock surface, and he almost lost his balance whenever his leather-soled brogues fought to maintain their grip.

'I think I see something,' he whispered eventually, now slowing his pace as he approached an area where the passage appeared to open up into a larger space. 'Stay close.'

This last instruction was wholly unnecessary because the eerie atmosphere of this dank interior had her as close to his back as was humanly possible.

'What do you see?' she whispered.

'It's a room,' Harker replied after reaching the entrance. He then waved his torch around from side to side before coming to a rest on an object located at the far end of the room – one that provided as much encouragement as it did trepidation. 'We're definitely in the right place.'

Looking over his shoulder, Stefani squinted her eyes to inspect the object his torchlight had settled upon, and she was in total agreement, because there was only one thing it could mean.

The sculptured marble image of Mithras stared back at them in his flowing cape, as the bull he straddled succumbed to the dagger jammed deep into its shoulder, while a snake, dog and scorpion attacked the suffering beast's underbelly. The statue had none of the appearance of being thousands of years old but instead looked like something carved only recently.

As they made their way into the stone-walled room, neither of them said anything, and as Harker shone his torch on the large stone-slab dining table, lined with benches on either side, Stefani produced a lighter from her pocket and flicked it on.

'Hold it,' she said, moving over to a small oil lamp attached to the wall by a metal bracket. She lit the wick and soon a good portion of the room was illuminated in flickering light. 'There's another,' she noticed and slid past the benches to another wall lamp, which she also sparked into life.

Another two lamps and the interior of the cavern was bright enough for Harker to assess the area in its entirety, so he now turned off his torch.

The cavern was oblong shaped with curved corners at either end, and its smooth, stone surface curved upwards into a ceiling over five metres high, which was exactly what one would expect from a Mithras temple.

Only a year earlier, Harker had made a visit to the evacuated London Mithraeum in Walbrook, which had been restored and opened to the public. Considered the city's most important Roman discovery of the twentieth century, it had added greatly to what little knowledge existed on that ancient cult. And, as Harker looked around now, he realised that this supposedly lost historical heritage had never been lost at all.

'What exactly is this place?' Stefani asked, dropping the lighter back into her pocket while taking note of an impressive sculpture placed at the far end of the room and directly beyond the head of the table.

'This is a Mithraeum,' Harker explained, raising his hand towards a row of tiles running round the base of the ceiling, 'It's a Mithras temple and those figures up there show the initiation rites one went through to gain admittance and in order to progress within the cult. And that,' he was now pointing to the Mithras sculpture itself, 'that's their equivalent of the cross.'

Stefani made her way closer, but something else caught her eye. 'How about that?' She raised a finger towards a small adjoining room and what looked like a red, stone, person-shaped coffin resting on sturdy wooden supports. At one end of it two horns stuck out, one on either side, and Harker immediately went over to inspect it.

'It's not just an ordinary coffin,' he rubbed a hand across its smooth surface. 'It's a sarcophagus.'

Stefani looked puzzled as she joined him to inspect the stone box. 'I thought they were confined to the Egyptians?'

Harker looked up at her and smiled excitedly as his archaeological instincts sparked. 'Apparently not,' he replied – just as a large thud came from inside it, causing him to jump back a pace.

'There's someone inside there,' he said and, without pause, stepped back to the sarcophagus and ran his fingers along the edges until he found the line indicating the cover. 'Give me a hand,' he ordered and began to grasp hold of the heavy stone lid.

Stefani on the other hand, was far less enthusiastic and she wavered as he began to struggle against the lid's weight. 'Is this such a good idea? We don't know what's inside… It could be a rabid dog for all we know.'

The young Templar's caution was warranted but then there came another thud and now, after a demanding look from Harker, Stefani set about helping him by grasping the opposite side of the lid firmly.

'Damn, it's heavy,' Harker observed as he looked over towards her and began to count down: 'Three, two, one…'

With some strenuous huffing and puffing, Harker pushed at the lid as Stefani pulled, then in one fluid motion the lid slid back, with a tooth-grating noise as stone ground against stone, eventually revealing a six-inch gap.

With only the wall lamps in the main room for light it was near impossible to make out what was inside, but Harker could detect something moving. In fact there was quite a lot of movement and he could make out small hints of something shiny, so he pulled out his torch. He clicked it on and shone it directly through the gap, and what he saw there had every muscle in his body tensing as he let out a shocked gasp.

Michael Donitz's swollen blue face and bloodshot eyes stared up at him with a look of panic as a large emperor scorpion scurried across his face and disappeared down one side of his neck and out of sight. The sound of multiple other scuttling insect legs and clicking pincers was also audible and this noise was intensified by an echo due to the tight confines of the sarcophagus. Soon, more of the predatory arachnids appeared on the man's chest to investigate the source of light permeating their dark nest.

The sight was so hideous that Harker just stood there in shock as Donitz opened his mouth and a bulbous black tongue attempted to form a plea for help through bright-red, enflamed lips but he achieved nothing more than a few saliva-filled gurgles.

'We have to get him out,' Stefani cried, pulling desperately at the stone lid as Harker continued to stare motionless at the horrific sight, absolutely stunned by the look of complete pain the man was enduring. 'Alex, snap out of it!' she yelled, and this time Harker woke from his traumatised inertia, grabbed hold of the lid and began pushing it aside as the poor fellow continued his attempts to speak. He still couldn't make out what was emerging from the man's mouth, though he clearly wanted out of his box of torment. But as the stone cover began to shift further, Harker caught sight of some movement at the corner of his eye.

Two thick arms suddenly wrapped themselves around his chest, like a vice, and he twisted his head around just enough to see a hooded figure clinging to him, but with its face impossible to make out. At the same time Stefani was grabbed by a couple of similarly dressed figures, and one of them raised a small bone-handled blade to her throat.

Though she went rigid as the hunting knife tip was held to her jugular, Harker continued to struggle for a moment further, the thought of those scorpions crawling over his own body making him feel jittery. A few more seconds of resistance, followed by a sharp knee planted in the back, and he finally started calming down. With his composure restored, he turned his attention to the hoodie holding a knife.

'Don't harm her,' he warned angrily as Donitz himself endeavoured to slide the sarcophagus lid back further, but this pathetic attempt was foiled as a two more figures dressed in the same red and black hooded robes entered the small alcove and slammed their hands down on the lid. Harker was now hauled backwards to allow these two newcomers to slide the lid back in place, when a final gurgling squawk from Donitz became nothing more than a muffled yell from within.

'Look, this has to be some terrible mistake—' Harker began to protest as the person restraining him now gripped him firmly by the throat and then retrieved his iPhone before slipping it underneath his robe. He was then dragged back forcefully into the main room and hurled against the wall, before his handler stood back to stand alongside the others. It was clearly a useless plea and he was already opening his mouth to try again when the same hooded man who had been holding him waved a finger menacingly, then reached over to take the knife still being held at Stefani's throat – and threw it over to Harker who managed to catch it in one hand.

It was a perplexing move and he held the weapon out in front of him defensively. It was at this point the knife giver reached over to the wall and on one slab pressed a small tile which then sank back into the wall.

Before he could even guess what was happening, Harker felt the floor give way beneath him and he found himself hurtling downwards into the pitch dark below, coming to a stop as he slammed hard against the floor and almost snapping his ankle in the process. He gazed upwards to the open trap-door just in time to see one of the hooded figures staring down at him drop something in after him before the trap-door shut, plunging him now into complete darkness.

Clasping the knife tightly, Harker could feel his heart beat thumping in his ears even as he felt around in the darkness for whatever had been dropped in after him. He didn't even know if it was important but, as his escalating fear attempted to get the better of him, he continued to slide his hands all around the floor, feeling only gravel and soil. Eventually, close to losing hope, he chanced upon the object and thanked God for it, as he clasped it in his spare hand and turned it on.

When the torch erupted into light, he found himself staring directly into the face of a bull with thick horns. He yelled in shock and fell backwards, and away from it, only a few moments later to realise he was staring at a painted sculpture of the creature hanging on the opposite wall.

'Get a grip Harker,' he urged himself quietly and started mustering some semblance of self-control. He forced himself to his feet and began sweeping the torch-light around him, trying to figure out what this place was.

The first thing he noticed was that the walls were built with red brick and the floor wasn't rock or soil but rather grey linoleum covered in dust and, although scuffed and worn this space looked relatively modern compared to the rocky cavern above it. He was in a room with tattered bits of wallpaper hanging off its walls. What was more, it looked like old-style flock wallpaper adorned with a flower pattern of some kind. In fact the kind you'd associate with an Indian restaurant back in the Seventies. Apart from that, the room was empty. Harker flashed his torch-light over a small open doorway and, with his breathing now becoming steadier, despite the fact that internally he was close to freaking out, he ventured over and poked his head through the doorway. There was a musty old corridor beyond, with other doors leading off it, and he noticed small wall lamps illuminated further along, which at least gave him a visual sense of his surroundings. With the small hunting knife held out before him in one hand and the torch in his other, he began to slowly make his way towards the nearest open doorway, then on past it.

He peered around the corner and noticed yet more doorways and even a flight of stairs at the far end. It was at this point it dawned on him: this wasn't a basement or even the foundations of the buildings above. No this was a house. An underground house.

It was a bizarre realisation and as Harker stifled his disgust at the vile smell of something he honestly cared not to know about, a scuffling sound had him spinning around towards one of the open doorways. He flinched again as he found himself staring into the eyes of another bull's head, although this statue possessed the body of a man. He let out a jittery laugh at his own nervousness. The Mithras cult and their obsession with bull symbolism was just as strong obviously down here as it was above. He glared back at the painted sculpture and shook his head in relief. But no sooner had he done so than he now noticed something else that made every muscle in his body tense up. He gripped the small hunting knife and aimed his torch directly into the doorway, and that was when he spotted it. The bull's head was still staring forward, but its eyes were now fixed directly upon him.

And this was confirmed as they blinked slowly.

Harker recoiled as the black bull's head began to slowly turn towards him. Its deep-set eyes began glistening, then it planted one of its legs forwards and gradually it shifted its massive frame to face him directly. He noticed how its muscular hide was covered with scars and sores as its chest began heaving up and down.

'What the fu...' was all was all Harker managed as the monster raised its horns and emitted a bellowing growl.

And then he was running for his life.

Chapter 31

Another guttural roar thundered from somewhere behind him as Harker flung himself around the corner in such haste that he slammed painfully against the brick wall beyond. The creature in pursuit was like nothing he had ever seen before, and seemed extremely agile despite its bulky frame. Harker sped on along the dimly lit corridor as behind him the sound of heavy footsteps pounded on the tiled floor.

Within seconds he reached the staircase, then skidded down it, sending dust up from the floor in plumes as he descended deeper into whatever lay below, while above him the thudding of a large body colliding with a brick wall could be heard. Harker jumped the last few steps down into another corridor but tripped upon the impact of his injured ankle on the hard floor. But he recovered his balance by diving into a roll, using the momentum to get back on his feet. Unfortunately the hunting knife he was still holding got knocked from his hand, and went shooting off into the gloom with a clank.

With the thudding overhead now rapidly approaching the top of the stairs, Harker instinctively dived into the nearest doorway, praying that his knife had gone the same way. He then came to a complete stop in a dark, stuffy room.

As he scanned the floor for any sight of his weapon, he noticed that this room adjoined another similar one and was also lit by wall lamps allowing him a vague awareness of the extent of this lower level. Or at least the parts he could actually see.

Trying to catch his breath he desperately searched the floor, but couldn't spot it, and he began instead cursing quietly in frustration when he realised something had changed. The sound of heavy footsteps above him had stopped, and the conclusion he took from this was more unnerving still. Either that creature was waiting for him to come back up, or more likely it knew Harker was trapped down here and so was taking its time.

The latter surmise was confirmed when Harker heard the plodding of footsteps slowly approaching down the stairs, with each step creaking under the creature's massive weight.

What the hell was that thing? was the thought that was racing through his mind and he backed as quietly as possible towards the doorway leading into the next room. The monster's horned head was that of a black bull but set upon a man's body and, as crazy as this sounded, he could only think one thing. The Minotaur was a creature of Greek legend, half man, half bull, imprisoned at Knossos, on the island of Crete, in a maze that acted as its cell. There it hunted those unfortunate people being regularly sacrificed to it, and this time Harker himself was to be that sacrifice!

He moved stealthily into the next room and hugged the inner wall as the footsteps reached the bottom of the stairs, there coming to a halt so that a deafening silence fell upon the air. Harker focused solely on breathing quietly because of the irritating dust. He covered his mouth for fear of coughing but removed it immediately upon realising that the sound of his breathing was amplified within the fold of his hand.

This was insane. Here he was being chased by some psychotic mythical figure inside an underground building and not only had he lost his only defensive weapon through clumsiness but his leather shoes made it impossible to move without revealing his position. A feeling of renewed dread washed over him as the sound of footsteps started up again and began approaching down the corridor alongside the room he was hiding in.

On the wall opposite, a narrow crack ran all the way from top to bottom allowing murky yellow lamplight from the corridor beyond to seep through, but momentarily darkening as the thing moved past it and along to the doorway, just metres now from where Harker was crouching.

As the beast came into view, he now got his first proper sight of it and found himself tensing in terror as its features were revealed under the dim light of the flickering wall lamps. It stood close to seven feet tall but with those long horns protruding from its skull it must have cleared easily over eight. There was no visible neck, and the bull's head, endowed with a protruding black snout, rested upon muscular shoulders attached to thick arms that would have made a professional wrestler jealous. The white-skinned torso, although taut and muscular, was covered in healed scars, all of them short but jagged. A pair of sturdy legs added to the sense of an impenetrable mass of flesh that could only be described as a human tank.

The deep and heavy breathing emerging from those large black nostrils was intimidating in itself and, as it turned to poke its lumbering head into the room, Harker held his own breath and remained absolutely motionless as he crouched in the dark shadows at the lower base of the wall.

One of the widespread horns briefly caught on the inner doorframe, scraping along it to leave a deep scratch mark. And as its black eyes surveyed the interior of the room, Harker did something that seemed cowardly and pointless. He closed his eyes.

To most this reaction would be considered the response of a terrified person but, even though he was, it was not the reason Harker did so. Over millennia the vision of human beings has evolved to detect a hidden face staring at them, because the most efficient way to evade a predator is to know when it has you in its sights. It is truly a sixth sense that most people possess because when you have that feeling someone is watching you, then most of the time you're probably correct. This thing may not have been human – and truthfully Harker had no idea what it was – but as he sat there hunched in the darkest shadows of the room, he was not about to put that to the test. So he remained still, with his eyes closed, but with his ears working overtime. The moment he heard the creature begin to approach him, he intended to leap back out the doorway he had entered and race back upstairs… and from there who knew what, but regardless that was his plan.

The heavy breathing continued and soon he found himself in need of air. He was just considering attempting to take a breath, when he heard the thing shifting its weight and heading back down the corridor.

Harker opened his eyes and, without losing a moment, stood up and quietly slipped off both his shoes, clutching them in one hand as he approached the doorway, just in time to see the lumbering beast enter another room further along the corridor – and that was when he saw them more clearly. Those massive feet on which it plodded along, but it wasn't the size of them that transfixed him but their shape. They were giant hooves!

He pulled back from the doorway and now back-tracked to the first room where he began to search for the knife again.

This time he spotted it straight away lying near the far wall. Carefully picking it up, he crept back into the corridor, and was planning to return upstairs to the first floor when something in the room directly opposite caught his eye.

At first glance he thought it was a human body but as he edged closer he realised he was looking at a puppet, or rather an effigy, with black buttons for eyes and thick black string crudely sewn into the face to create a smiling mouth and a nose. The simple white, stained dress it wore suggested it was meant to be female, and at five feet in height, stuffed with straw, it was yet another creepy addition to this place's damp and disturbing décor. The doll had been propped up in a sitting position on a torn bale of hay that could only be described as a makeshift bed, with a deep impression in the middle where someone had been sleeping.

'Shit.' he muttered, not just because he now realised he was in that creature's personal bedroom but he had also noticed the bloody carcass of a pig that had been savagely ripped apart and, as he examined it closer, he could make out the bite marks on one of the animal's legs.

The foul sight had Harker retching and, with a hand over his mouth, he now turned his attention to a narrow opening in the wall where surrounding brickwork gave way to solid cement further in. Upon closer inspection he found himself staring along a tight shaft no more than half a metre wide, and with some light only just visible at the far end. With no other options available to him, and realising this vicious game of cat-and-mouse was only going to end one way, he made the decision, put his shoes back on, and thrust himself head first into the cramped tunnel.

It was a tight fit but just wide enough to allow him to crawl through and, although moss-ridden and slimy, it actually felt good to be protected by walls on all sides, and he was already a few feet in and enjoying a sense of relief when a hand grabbed his ankle firmly and began to tug.

Harker looked back to see the creature down on all fours, staring at him as it tried to drag its unexpected visitor back towards it. It let out a piercing bellow and continued to tug wildly. Terror now turned into uncontrollable anger, and Harker succumbed to it and began kicking out at the thing's face and groping hand. He still had the knife but the passage was so tight there was no way he could sit up straight, let alone reach back to the creature, so instead he rhythmically dispensed kick after kick until he landed the heel of one shoe squarely on the creature's fingers.

It let out a deep yelp, immediately releasing its grasp, whereupon Harker immediately scuffled further inside, as quickly as he could, in response to the heavy dose of adrenalin just injected into his system.

The creature was now groaning, one arm outstretched towards him like a child wanting its plaything, as Harker continued pushing frantically along the shaft until finally the beast went silent and disappeared from the opening, doubtless shuffling off to another part of the strange building.

It was then Harker realised that it was probably racing towards where the shaft would open out, and he briefly considered returning to the bedroom – but the half-consumed pig and that creepy puppet convinced him to persevere, pushing forward with all the strength he possessed.

The uncomfortable journey took him no more than thirty seconds and once he reached the opening he warily peered out. Once sure he was alone he tumbled out onto the floor, then jumped to his feet with his knife drawn ready to defend himself.

This new environment looked like a war zone, for it was nothing more than a large open space enclosed by thick crumbling stone walls that in some places had collapsed completely. It reminded him of nothing less than a maze that had long passed its sell-by date and was left to just deteriorate over time. Wisps of dust fell from the wooden ceiling above as he cautiously made his way through this ruin, each step becoming less confident than the last because he had absolutely no idea where he was going.

On an outer wall to the right of him, crumbling plaster allowed thin shards of light to permeate the gloom, thus lighting up particles of dust into shiny sparkles as if offering a brief moment of welcome in this otherwise dismal place.

Pressing forward with trembling muscles, Harker forced his legs back into action, against an overall urge to turn around and return to the safety of the shaft, which was a crazy idea but one brought about by how vulnerable he felt. 'Keep going, Alex. Let's see where this leads,' he muttered to himself as the stench of decay invaded his mouth and throat with each shallow and shaky breath he took. Was this place even linked to the same underground residence he had been in earlier?

Harker gripped the hunting knife in his right hand, glancing down at its tiny little blade that glinted briefly in the strips of light coming through the cracks in the wall and he suddenly noticed the unique shape of its bone handle, which caused him to stop. It was smooth and shaped to fit one's hand but halfway up it a small circle had been engraved onto it, no bigger than a thumbnail. As Harker rubbed this with his finger it dawned on him that it was in fact a release button of some kind, so he carefully pressed it inwards with his forefinger.

A piece of metal flicked out from one side of the handle, like a springing tool from a Swiss Army penknife, and then clicked itself into place. It was a key.

As Harker mulled over its purpose, it became clear what was going on here, even if he didn't yet understand why. *This was a test*. For whatever reason, his being dropped into this nasty little underworld was a test, and he was being given the opportunity to pass it. The key must open a door somewhere and they, the cult of Mithras, were giving him a chance. Either that or a sadistic desire to taunt him with false hope – which seemed far more likely.

Harker clenched the knife firmly in his hand and gritted his teeth. Who, in god's name, were these people and what was this sick little ceremony of theirs? More importantly, what the hell was that infernal creature… could it be an actual demon? Like the one he had seen in his vision? A demon held captive here on earth?

The sheer craziness of these questions was making his head hurt and he clutched the blade and dismissed such otherworldly thoughts. He needed to focus instead on getting out of here – and finding Stefani. Everything else was of secondary importance, and with this in mind he continued to make his way through the dark, forbidding ruins.

Many of the surrounding walls looked like a demolishing team had been let loose with a number of them partially knocked down, allowing a view into a number of dilapidated areas. Brown-stained floral wallpaper dangled lifelessly on all sides, having peeled back over time, and the floors were strewn with every kind of filth from blackened wall plaster to piles of crumbling bricks.

Continuing to survey this squalor, he found himself being drawn towards a heap of dirty grey sticks lying off to the side. And as he squinted in an effort to inspect them further, a cold chill ran right though him. This pile of bones still had shreds of rotting meat hanging off them, and he pulled back sharply in revulsion only to catch his head on a piece of wood jutting from the nearby wall. With a loud crack, the piece of dry timber snapped under the impact, dropping to the floor with a hollow thud. And as Harker massaged the bump now forming on the back of his skull, he froze on catching sight of something moving up ahead.

As the sound of heavy shuffling began to move closer, he now stepped backwards away from the sounds, carefully judging each step so as not to catch a foot in any of the rubble. He crept silently over to another damaged section of the nearby wall, which allowed him a narrow view in the direction of the noises, then huddled up against it as whatever was approaching him got ever closer.

The bull-horned creature came to a stop a few metres away and within Harker's line of sight. Then it raised its bulging head and with its snout began to sniff the air. With each intake of air came a scratchy grunting noise and after the second sniff it lowered its head before turning around and heading back the way it had come and out of sight.

Harker remained still, choosing to stay where he was and listen for any signs of movement, but he couldn't detect any and, as he waited, he began to formulate a plan. Firstly, he realised, there was no way he could take this brute on face to face because it was just too big and, secondly, if it was indeed a demon then who knew what it might be capable of.

The very thought of such an unearthly creature had him shaking his head disapprovingly because the very notion was just ridiculous to his mind, and yet here he was being hunted by a creature with a bull's head and hooves. The rational side of him screamed bloody murder at any willingness to even entertain such a possibility, but he pushed such internal conflict to one side and focused instead on what needed to be done. He obviously had to kill it or else it was certainly going to kill him but, with nothing more than a small hunting knife, was it even feasible? Sure, if he had been Special Forces trained then maybe, but he was an archaeology professor, for Christ's sake!

This last thought suddenly calmed him and he felt an intense feeling of courage and determination. For he wasn't just a professor any more; he was a Templar, and this was far from being his first time in a dangerous situation. Certainly, he had never been up against a real-life demon, with horns and the full power of hell behind it, but, hey, there was a first time for everything.

He was still bolstering his courage with unrealistic reasoning when the strong smell of something unpleasant assaulted his nostrils and he looked behind him just as an oversized hand grabbed him by the throat and pulled him to his feet.

Harker stared into the bull creature's black eyes as it tightened its grip around his neck. The foul stench of rotting meat exuded from its nostrils, making him gag as he was lifted off the ground and held in mid-air. The physical strength of this beast was incredible and, as Harker struggled to breathe, he reacted the only way he could and began stabbing his tiny blade repeatedly into the creature's side. The first two jabs achieved nothing but the third slid past one of its ribs, whereupon it dropped Harker to the floor as it bent forwards to rub at the wound with a loud grunt.

With no time to spare Harker dragged himself to his feet and, in an act of frankly useless defiance, stood his ground with the bloody knife in one hand. But, as he watched the creature still bent over in pain, an idea came to him. It wasn't a great idea but at this point that hardly mattered. He jumped to the other side of a crumbling wall right next to the creature, pressed his whole body against it and continued pushing with everything he had.

The eight-foot high partition toppled over and collapsed onto the wounded beast, sending it to the floor underneath a pile of bricks and amid a flurry of dust. Harker grabbed the nearest brick and straddled the creature with it held high above his head, before he brought it down hard on the creature's snout.

There were many things Harker was expecting after such a blow but what actually happened was not one of them. He watched in disbelief as the snout crumpled inwards leaving a minor dent in the bull's face. Its eyes rolled and eyelashes fluttered, and Harker now noticed the flap where the edge of the bull's head met its shoulders.

This he warily lifted up to uncover a metal collar with a steel padlock to secure the whole construction in place. The whole thing was unbelievably lifelike and had clearly been fashioned out of a genuine bull's head with expertly cut eyeholes that offered the illusion that the wearer's eyes were part of it. In the dim light of this place one would have had to get within a few feet to realise that it was only a head mask and not the creature Harker had taken it for.

He dropped the brick to one side and scanned the ground for the hunting knife, which he swiftly retrieved and then scrambled back over to the creature as it began to revive. He switched the knife around and, as he had already guessed, the key slipped into the padlock with ease and opened it. Then with both hands, one either side of the creature's head, he yanked it off.

The sight that greeted him was disturbing and, even though his muscles ached and his body was still surging with adrenalin, that evaporated in a single moment as he now understood what the puppet had been for. In its place he felt a feeling of tremendous pity and of hatred for whoever had done this.

The childlike features of a mentally impaired boy stared back at him, and offered a tentative smile through the few rotting teeth he had left. By the look of his white patchy skin, all covered in sores, it was clear he had not experienced sunlight on his flesh in a very long time.

Harker smiled back, touching the boy's face lightly, and felt suddenly overcome at what he was seeing. Hastily he pushed some of the heavy bricks off the boy's chest, sending them to the floor with a clatter. This man-child was no more a monster than he himself was, and Harker could only imagine the torment he had experienced. Judging by the state of his body he had been trapped down

309

here a long time, maybe even years, with only a dirty cloth puppet for company. He turned back to the boy's hooved feet to see nothing more than clumpy shoes, made of leather, and stitched into the shape of hooves which must have been uncomfortable to say the least. What kind of sicko could have inflicted such an awful life on another human being, let alone one so vulnerable.

Suddenly to his left, came the sound of rumbling as a section of the wooden wall fell away and a clean, bright light flooded the gloomy interior. Harker stumbled to his feet and held a hand up to his eyes as the figure in front of him loomed into shape. At first everything looked fuzzy but, as his vision adjusted, he began to make out a person's features and, even though nothing made sense at this moment, he recognised them.

'Shit.'

Chapter 32

'That's what you said last time,' David Carter replied angrily, gripping the telephone ever more tightly as he shook his head.

'I'm sorry, David, but I've passed on all your messages and I'm sure he'll be in contact with you the moment he can.'

During the past three hours Carter had left no fewer than eight messages for Sebastian Brulet to give him a call and so far, he had heard nothing. He had of course stressed the extreme importance of speaking with the Grand Master, but was not prepared to reveal the exact nature of his request because he was still unsure how confidential the Mithras information was. If there was genuine secrecy surrounding their very existence – and thus the Templars also – then the only responsible thing for him to do was confer with Sebastian, but this was all taking much too long. And furthermore, there had still been no contact from Harker.

'Can you please get hold of him and tell him I've found something in the archives that could be of serious concern, and he's the only one who can decide it. Lives are at stake here, man!'

This last part was not true, so far as Carter knew, but perhaps it might speed up a reply and therefore he was willing to take that gamble.

'You have my word, I'll keep trying,' the Templar underling replied respectfully. 'But if he's not picking up his messages, what can I do? The last thing I heard, he was in the air, so maybe that could be the problem. Is there anyone else who can help you?'

Carter let out a frustrated sigh. 'No, it's him I need to speak to. Just keep trying, will you.'

'Of course,' came the reply, then the line went dead and Carter dropped the mobile phone into his pocket.

'Damn it,' he yelled before returning to the numerous boxes scattering the floor of the small archive room. The more he read up on the Templars' dealings, the more concerned he got because, from what he had read so far, their encounters with the Mithras cult were even more involved and deep-rooted than he had initially believed. With every new piece of information he sifted through, the more he worried for Harker's and Stefani's safety and, given what he had found out so far, they were both potentially in a lot of danger. The Mithras were a highly dangerous group that the Templars had considered it of crucial importance to dismantle, and Harker's own father had not only been complicit in helping with this but had been the direct reason for their downfall. To find out that the Mithras still existed, after they were deemed defunct for a second time, posed not only a danger to the Templars but a serious threat to Harker himself. Because if they knew who he was, then surely their wish for revenge on the son of the man who had brought them down would be close to fanatical.

Carter pulled out another journal and began to read through it but he was still struggling to fully get to grips with what the Mithras cult actually stood for. From what he had learned so far, they were a serious cause for concern to the Templars, but as to how or why was as yet unknown, and keeping all the details hidden and off the books was truly baffling. And this was even before asking what they had to do with the 'blessed candle' and 'three days of Darkness' prophecy that Harker had become so noticeably obsessed with recently.

Carter scratched his head, raised his arms above his head and let out a huge yawn. So many questions and as yet so few answers – which was why he desperately needed to speak with Sebastian Brulet.

'Bloody hell, Brulet,' he groaned, 'where the hell are you?'

'Right behind you,' A voice answered, and Carter nearly fell of his seat before he spun around to see Sebastian Brulet himself, Grand Master of the Templars, standing in the doorway with his hands casually in his pockets. 'I heard you were trying to get hold of me, David,' Brulet continued with a smile, then held both his hands out in front of him. 'Well, here I am.'

Carter jumped out of his seat and rushed over to shake one hand vigorously. 'About time, Sebastian,' he almost yelled, letting his frustration get the better of him. 'We need to talk.'

'I gathered that simply by the number of messages you left me. So much so, I thought I'd make a detour to the Mont and see you in person.' Brulet maintained a friendly smile as if not responding to Carter's outburst. 'I've not been around lately as much as I should have, but I assure you that all changes as of now. I've rested long enough.'

Brulet had been taking some time off to recuperate after his ordeal at the hands of the Magi months earlier and, considering what the man had been through, no one had ever once questioned that. The six months of torture he'd endured would have destroyed most men mentally but it appeared he had beaten the odds in making a full recovery. The problem was that Carter was still getting to know this man on a personal level and, given how recently he had been inducted into the Templar organisation, he still felt he had much to prove... which of course he did.

'So, what can I do for you?' Brulet asked, peering keenly over at the scattered pile of archive boxes. 'And what exactly have you been looking through down here?'

Carter glanced back at the chaos he had created and winced. 'It looks more of a mess than it actually is but Alex has discovered something we think is... important.'

'Go on,' Brulet replied, now looking ever more concerned, which was difficult to gauge because those unique cross-shaped pupils of his which made him difficult to read.

'The woman Alex asked me to check on, her name is Avi Legrundy.'

Mention of the name had one of Brulet's silver eyebrows raised immediately.

'I did some checking, and she appears to have belonged to a group called the Mithras which' – he motioned to the stack of box files behind him – 'apparently the Templars had a lot of close dealings with some years ago.'

Brulet appeared uncharacteristically shaken and he gazed down at the floor before returning to fix Carter with a stern and steely gaze. 'How much does Alex know?'

It was an unusual reaction from the Grand Master, who was not someone to keep secrets from those he trusted, and Carter sensed there might be a real problem here. 'Not that much at the moment but I'm ploughing through the journals to try and catch up.'

This answer seemed to soothe any concerns Brulet might be having and he smiled once again. 'Good. I would like to discuss it with him myself – just the two of us. Is he here?'

Carter jerked his head back with an expression of surprise. 'He left the Vatican City and arrived in Venice a few hours ago, still chasing a lead on the "three days of Darkness" prophecy. He's still with Stefani Mitchell.'

Brulet looked blank-faced and his head tilted to one side curiously. 'And who is Stefani Mitchell?'

Chapter 33

Father John Davies gazed at Harker with a serenely welcoming look on his face and then slowly nodded in satisfaction. 'Hello, Alex, I can't tell you how long I've been waiting for this moment.'

He stood dazed before this man whose murdering of a mother and child, prior to his own death, had sparked Harker's involvement in this whole bizarre affair some days earlier. He stared back with a stunned expression at the ex-priest.

'It seems you've been on quite a journey, my friend, and I must say you've exceeded all my expectations.'

Harker remained silent, still utterly perplexed, as behind him the oversized man-child pushed the remaining bricks away from his body and staggered to his feet before clutching at the wounds inflicted on him by the short hunter's knife.

'Don't be afraid of him,' Davies urged, indicating the hulking giant. 'He's totally harmless under the right super-vision.'

Harker glanced back at the giant, who appeared to be cowering in abject terror under Davies's gaze. He took a step back and placed a hand reassuringly on the suffering youth's arm.

'Don't touch him!' Davies ordered sharply, and the giant immediately recoiled then limped away like a scared child, heading back into the gloom beyond. 'I know this must be confusing for you, Alex, but allow me to explain and everything will become clear.'

Harker turned away from the dusty, foul smelling cesspit and back to face Father Davies, whose black robe cut a forbidding silhouette against the bright light emanating from behind him. 'What is all this?' he demanded.

Davies beckoned him over with a thin smile. 'Come… let me show you.'

With little alternative except to head back into that underground maze of bricks and filth, Harker stretched his aching shoulders and proceeded through the exit, as Father Davies simultaneously moved backwards as though not wanting to appear threatening in any way.

The room beyond was in such contrast to where he had just been that, sucking in a breath of clean air, Harker paused to take in the sight of the opulent furnishings surrounding him. The black sheep's wool carpet contrasted with the four large, white pillars which rose at the centre of the room to create an inner seating area with fancy red and black velvet sofas placed around a large marble coffee table. On the opposite wall was a large open grate containing a burning log fire, which crackled away merrily as golden flames licked the inside of the chimney overhead it. Above this hung an engraved relief of the now familiar Mithras image with the god wearing a flowing cape while plunging a knife into a captured bull. Images of a scorpion, a raven, a dog and a snake were contained in alcoves set into the walls surrounding this seating area, and red and gold drapes hung from shiny brass curtain rings connected to long poles of walnut timber running the width of the ceiling.

One could be forgiven for thinking they had strayed into the lavish residence of some member of the Roman elite back in the days when their empire was at its height. The most eye-catching aspect of the room, though, was the ceiling adorned with a series of paintings, and Harker quickly recognised a similarity to the Sistine Chapel ceiling painted by Michelangelo. But as he surveyed it more closely, he soon saw that this was where the similarity ended. The separate images had the same general feel, with minor but very significant differences. The outer ones, inspired by the Old Testament, concurred in depicting David slaying Goliath or Jonah and the whale, but some of the inner ones were radically different. Any that might have depicted God as a wizened old man had been replaced with ones that were unmistakably Mithras himself. For instance the famous image where Adam at the creation almost touches fingers with his maker contained instead an image of Mithras with a golden crown and flowing cape, as he towered over crowds of naked, cowering people.

As Father Davies halted and took up his position in front of the fireplace, Harker slowly moved towards the coffee table, and there he felt a shiver of trepidation on catching sight of the symbol etched in its centre. *The overlapping circles surrounded by fifteen swastikas.*

'The two kingdoms,' A voice intervened, and Harker looked over into a corner of the room to see Stefani Mitchell. Wearing a black and red coloured robe, she smiled at him warmly. 'You were right in your theory about that symbol, Alex,' she continued. 'The kingdom of Mithras, the kingdom of hell – and the world of humanity caught between them both.'

Harker felt a bitter-sweet sense of relief on seeing her. But his relief that Stefani was safe was tempered with sheer anger at her obvious betrayal of him. And even though the reasons for her deception were unclear to him, he remained calm and concentrated on what he did know. 'So the death of your father...' Harker began before dismissively pointing in Father Davies's direction... 'and his supposed possession was all fake?'

The pair of them said nothing but, judging by their encouraging smiles, they wanted him to reveal what he had learned for himself.

'And those "blessed candles" you encouraged me to hunt down, and the Prophecy too, they were just... what, some kind of ruse?'

'I'm afraid they weren't nearly as important as perhaps you were led to believe, and nor was the Prophecy.' Father Davies replied, while Stefani now looked almost guilty at this admission.

This reply was about as enlightening as a kick in the teeth, and Harker struggled to maintain his cool. 'I know about the little Mithras cult you have going on here, and I also know that Templars – and my father – helped put you bunch of sick puppies to bed a long time ago. So what's this whole thing about? A punishment for the son of the man who put you out of business?'

Harker was clutching at straws here because the only possible reason he could fathom was revenge but, given the convoluted wild-goose chase he had been taken on as well as the trail of blood left in its wake, it made just as much sense as one of Carter's conspiracy theories. 'If you'd wanted to kill me for my father's actions then you could have snatched me off the streets of Cambridge at any time without killing so many other people in the process. Or are you just a bunch of inbred raving lunatics? You probably all have six toes, don't you? Or perhaps you consider yourselves an extended family, which is most likely just an excuse for some twisted sexual free-for-all!'

Harker knew that he was starting to ramble foolishly, but at this point he didn't care. None of this made any sense to him and, as he let out a frustrated yell, Father Davies took a step closer to the table between them.

'I understand that you're angry, but this is not a punishment for your father's past crimes.'

'So, then, what is it? Some sick endurance test?'

'No, you've got it all wrong, Alex.' Stefani had real sincerity in her voice. 'This was never a test for you… it was an invitation.'

The explanation had Harker dumbfounded, not because he was shocked by it but because he had no idea what she was talking about. As he stood there with a blank expression, a door opened on the far side of the room and a procession of people began making their way in. All were hooded and they wore the same black and red robes as Stefani and, as if rehearsed, they spread out and assumed separate positions around the room. Some sat down on the sofas whilst others stood against the walls, until in the end there must have been close to fifteen of them, who all now stared at him with only their mouths visible under the hoods.

'Why don't you say hello to some friends of yours, Alex?' Father Davies suggested and in unison all pulled back those heavy hoods. As Harker's stare travelled amongst them, noting their smiling faces, he felt his knees begin to go weak and he reached out to the nearest pillar to steady himself.

'Hello, Alex,' Dr Gérald Marceau spoke first. 'It's good to see you again.'

Harker remained silent as he gazed blankly at the others.

'Same goes for me, Professor,' Adonis Anastas spoke next, that same museum curator Harker had witnessed being shot back in Athens.

As Harker stared around, he became increasingly flabbergasted with the recognition of each face. On the far sofa sat Detective Andrea Russo who had chaperoned him back in Italy, and next to him sat Signora Busetto from the Venetian restaurant. Behind them stood the same bald man, resembling Ming the Merciless, who had hosted that crazy marriage ceremony back amid the ruins of the Baths of Caracalla. Beside him all three members of the Order of Tharmis also offered a smile.

'Tharmis,' Harker muttered, only now recognising the significance of that name 'It's an anagram of Mithras.'

'I honestly thought you'd work that out sooner,' Davies declared to a chuckle all around.

Even though all those people now staring at him appeared friendly, even welcoming, this was one of the most unnerving situations Harker had ever experienced. As he racked his head for any rational explanation, it was Father Davies who approached him, with Stefani at his side.

'They call me "Father",' he began with great gravity in his tone, 'and soon all will become clear.'

Harker managed a nod and, at a flick of Davies's hands, the others dutifully lined up and without another word all made their way back out the door they had come in by.

'I'll see you later,' Stefani said, rubbing his arm affectionately before herself exiting the room, thus leaving only

Harker and her father alone amid the crackling sounds of the log fire.

'What I am about to tell you I have rehearsed in my head a thousand times over the years, but it always starts the same way,' Davies began, clasping his hands behind his back. 'At the beginning...'

'That would be good.' Harker interrupted, feeling as if he was smack bang in the middle of an Agatha Christie novel.

'How much do you know about your own father, Alex?'

'Not as much as I would like to,' Harker replied honestly. 'But I know he was a Templar.'

'That is true, and a remarkably effective one at that,' his host agreed. 'But do you know anything about his early life, before he became involved with the Order?'

Doubtlessly Father Davies already knew the answer to this but, given that Harker felt like a rabbit caught in the headlights, he considered it best to play along. 'Up until a few months ago I always thought he worked in a chicken factory so, as you can imagine, his Templar connection came as total surprise to me.'

'Understandable,' Davies agreed, 'since the lies we tell our children can have the direst effects on their upbringing. But do you know the truth about his death?'

The question was delivered flatly and Harker gave a shake of his head. 'I always believed he was killed by an IRA bomb – wrong place wrong time – but given what I've since learnt about his dual identity, I can honestly say I'm not sure any more.'

'Very wise of you, Alex,' Davies pursed his lips together firmly. 'But what if I told you he was in fact murdered by the same people you now hold so dear?'

'The Templars?' Harker exclaimed, with evident disdain for such an accusation.

'One and the same,' Davies replied, ignoring the look of mistrust now on Harker's face as he continued with his explanation. 'And what would you say if I told you I knew it to be a fact.'

'I'd say you would need some really hard evidence to back it up… and, anyway, why would they?'

This defiant response drew a thin smile from Davies. 'Because what you might not yet know is that, before he joined the ranks of the Templars, he was once a member of Mithras.'

This hit Harker like a sledgehammer and he found himself gulping nervously. 'That's ridiculous. I don't believe you.'

His obvious disbelief garnered another dry smile from Davies, who reached into his pocket and pulled out a small square Kodak polaroid photograph. 'But would you believe your own eyes?'

Harker stared down at the picture and suddenly a deep gnawing sensation began to claw at his stomach. The image showed three people standing all together and smiling for the camera. They were maybe in their late teens and, although young, they were still easy to recognise. Liam Harker grinned at the camera, his arm around Avi Legrundy in the middle, with Father Davies on the other side of her. It looked like a typical photograph of close friends having fun and for a few seconds Harker couldn't take his eyes off it, but the more he stared the more he realised this man was definitely his own father. 'That can't be,' He muttered as Davies took it out of his hand and then dropped it into Harker's jacket pocket.

'You can keep it,' he said before giving him a stern look. 'And if you're prepared to listen, then I would like to tell you everything.'

As Harker gazed over at him, feeling nothing less than shell-shocked, he managed a confirming nod and so the ex-priest continued with his explanation.

'The Mithras have been around far longer than you can imagine. In one form or another we were here well before the Romans, before the Persians and earlier even than the Sumerians. We were a religion guiding humans before recorded time itself, and directed empires and civilisations that no one in the modern world even knows existed. The first true faith, born during homo sapiens' fast rise to dominance across the planet and amongst those first few who practised burying their dead.

Davies stepped over to a section of the wall next to the fireplace and pressed it in with his open palm, whereupon a small door slowly swung open to reveal a drinks cabinet and a decanter. 'Our beliefs have survived for thousands upon thousands of years,' he continued, pouring drinks into a couple of crystal tumblers, 'but it was not until the rise of early Christendom that we truly met our match.'

He gathered up the two glasses and returned to Harker and placed one in his hand. 'Russian Standard vodka.'

The fact that this man knew Harker's drink of choice was nothing in itself, but it meant that he had done his homework. Harker took a swig and let the liquid burn his throat before swallowing it greedily in the hope it might combat the numbness he was feeling.

'The early Church realised the power of our religion and it did the only thing it could do to compete... It stole every aspect of it and then repackaged it for its own purposes.'

Hàrker knew what Davies was alluding to but he remained quiet and allowed him to continue.

'And it worked, too. By stealing our beliefs and manipulating them for their own ends, they contrived to make the religion of Mithras obsolete. And so its surviving believers did the only thing they could do... they went underground and waited, biding their time generation after generation, until the moment to rise up again,' By now Davies was grinning with zeal. 'And that time has now come, Alex Harker, and I wish for nothing more than for than you should be a part of it. In fact I want you to serve alongside me.'

These words had Harker coughing on the last sip he had taken, and he wiped his lips whilst busily shaking his head. 'Let's pretend I believe any of this history lesson you're telling me, for what reason would I possibly want to help you?'

'Because it is your birthright.'

'What!' Harker spat out incredulously, but Davies looked unfazed by his reaction.

'There are seven ranks in our church, which is the one true church,' Father Davies began to explain, hardly containing his excitement. 'The first is the Corax, the second the Nympus, third is the Miles, fourth is Leo, fifth is Perses, sixth is Heliodromus... and lastly, the position of supreme patriarch, that of Pater – or Father.'

Davies now stood back and raised his hands in self reverence. 'And your own father was destined to become Pater but, after his defection to the Templars, it fell to me to assume the position and I have done so all these years, working to make us strong once again. And I want you to take your rightful place by my side, as my second, and to succeed me when I retire from my duties.'

Harker barely batted an eyelid but internally he was going ballistic. He couldn't know for sure if his father had had anything to do with this bunch of wackos, because photographs could be doctored. There was also the fact that they only appeared to include a dozen or so members and, given how most religions had been suffering attendance loss over the last sixty years, how on earth this man expected them to usurp the Catholic Church simply made no sense at all. One thing for certain, though, Davies believed it to the core. Not unlike the assuredness displayed by many other mentally ill people Harker had encountered over the years.

'What, so this whole business has been nothing more than a recruitment drive?'

'I wouldn't put it so crudely, Alex, there is far more to it than that.' Davies now placed his hands together and raised them up to his lips. 'What you couldn't possibly know, and even the Templars are unaware of, is that their arch enemies, the Magi, were far from the dangerous entity they were considered to be. They were but unknowing pawns in a deception that we orchestrated long ago. Most of their assets and plundered wealth were given to them by us. All we ever wanted was for them to fight the Templars and in doing so destroy each other through an act of attrition and pave the way for us.'

Davies now smiled as Harker's mouth literally dropped open and the man now crossed his arms and looked towards him deviously. 'The only true way to own the game is get in at the ground floor and we were around long before the Templars or Magi even existed. We watched them both grow in strength before deciding to pick a side and the Magi were always the more pliable; with their total lack of morals and zest for power they proved far easier to manipulate than the Templars ever could have been.'

Harker now only managed a disbelieving shake of his head as the full weight of what he was being told sunk in. 'You controlled the Magi?'

'Controlled is not the right word,' Davies replied, letting out a chuckle and shrugging his shoulders, 'they played in a game that we had created and designed to produce a single outcome… the destruction of both the Templars and the Magi, who were the only true opponents standing in the way of our return.'

Even though Harker was still reeling from the titanic revelation he could see the reality of it. Two organisations, completely opposed, and coerced unsuspectingly into centuries of slowly whittling each other down as the Mithras watched from the shadows, waiting until the moment was right, when they had decimated one another and were ripe to receive the final death blow. 'You're telling me the whole war between the Templars and the Magi has been nothing more than a chess game of your creation?'

'They were always destined to fight amongst themselves Alex,' Davies continued smugly, 'but at every step we have aided in their hatred of one another, for time and patience has always been our weapon; it has also proved our greatest strength and always will be.'

Harker could barely believe it, and as he stood there motionless and perplexed, unable to truly absorb what he was hearing, Davies continued as if the bombshell meant nothing.

'Your father never knew of our true role in all this, and thankfully so given his treacherous behaviour but now, with the true knowledge of what we are and our place in

327

all this, you are ready to take your rightful place amongst us. And you have already progressed further than you realise, and only a single step is left now before you take the position that is your right by blood.'

'A single step!' Harker growled in disbelief, his head swimming in confusion because this whole thing was nuts. 'I haven't even taken a first step.'

A knowing smile crossed across Davies's face and he let out a chuckle. 'Alex, your initiation began days ago.'

During the course of the last few days, Harker had been preoccupied with notions of prophecy, murder, visions, relics, and everything else in between. And also, having only so recently discovered that Mithraism even existed he had not really given much thought to the idea that the sinister group behind everything had been the Mithras cult. An ancient cult, whose only reality and relevance lay buried in the history books! But, as he stood there staring at Father Davies, he began to realise the full significance of almost everything that had happened to him lately, and the stages of Mithras initiation that Davies had explained and that he himself had knowledge of as a professor of archaeology.

'The Corax means the first step in initiation: a baptism.' he muttered as Davies's eyes lit up at his realisation. 'Back in Rome, at your apartment, I was almost drowned. And I remember that boy muttering something I couldn't make out… He was baptising me?'

Davies nodded enthusiastically as Harker continued.

'The second step, called Nympus, involves marrying the god of Mithras like in that strange ceremony back at the Baths of Caracalla.'

'Yes,' Davies concurred with glee. 'You were directly above an ancient Mithras temple which is even now open to the public.'

Suddenly thinking himself back to the museum in Athens, he recalled the crown that Adonis Anastas had so unexpectedly placed upon his head. 'The third step, that of Miles, is being anointed with the crown of Mithras, which symbolises liberation from the bonds of the material world.'

Harker now fell silent as the weight of what he was discovering pressed deeply on his soul. At this point Davies now took over, appearing more thrilled with every utterance.

'The fourth step called, Leo, is the initiation through fire as guided by a representative of Jupiter – Miss Avi Legrundy herself.'

The bizarre chanting Harker had heard Legrundy spouting as he awoke tied up in Dr Marceau's apartment, just before she set it ablaze, now made a twisted sense. Even as Davies continued, he felt sick to his stomach at the deception inflicted on him.

'The fifth step of Perses was an act of faith in vanquishing a gorgon or a true monster, and your defeating of the horned man-child is proof in itself that you are worthy of your new position.'

Harker's revulsion was tinged by the empathy he felt for that lumbering, tortured, disabled boy he had fought against. 'Who was that exactly?'

Davies looked like he could not have cared less. 'That genetic monstrosity was born for one reason and one only, and that was to offer you penance and admission for you when the time came. It is a brute representing all that the Mithras reviles and it has been kept in bondage in those testing grounds for but one purpose – and its reason for existence is now over.'

Up until this point there had been at least a semblance of a normal personality underneath all the psychotic behaviour this ex-priest was displaying, but this cold and heartless statement had Harker not only despising the man but also feeling completely repulsed by him. 'Are you telling me you kept that poor disabled boy in that dungeon all his life just so he could test me!'

Davies's truly deviant nature was displayed further as he looked aghast at Harker's sympathy for what he himself saw as nothing more than a useless entity. 'There have been others tested by that deformed creature, yes, but you were always its main reason for existing. That thing has no place in a superior world, a world of the strong and the pure. It was lucky to have found any purpose at all for otherwise I would have slit its throat as a child, without a second thought.'

The chilling reply now started Harker thinking of the other murders that had taken place on this structured journey of 'enlightenment' the Mithras cult had so fanatically set him upon. 'And that woman and child you mutilated before your own apparent death at the hands of the police? I saw the video of it.'

'Sacrifices must always be made for a higher purpose and, although I will admit they were innocents in all this and, unaware of the miserable fates that awaited them, it was a necessary evil in convincing the Church that the "three days of Darkness" prophecy was imminently upon them.'

'So you murdered a little boy and his mother,' Harker growled in disgust, 'and for what?'

Davies looked shocked at Harker's expression of compassion. 'We'll get to that shortly, but don't forget the boy himself was a verified schizophrenic and so tainted, as for the mother… well, she was too gullible and easily pliable and my standing as an ex-priest offered her a reason to believe in his satanic possession. With a little help from me, of course.'

'So you really once were a priest – at least. Archbishop Federar certainly believed it.' Harker said, still astonished at the level of insignificance which human life represented to this man.

'The road of the Mithras is a long one, Alex, and I had infiltrated the Church long before the Templars even became aware of us. My credentials were genuine, although that corpse with its head blown off, which both the Church and the newspapers believed to be me, was just another lost and useless soul we used for our purpose. A few changes to his dental and blood records, with a little help from Detective Russo, and no one was the wiser as you've seen for yourself.'

Davies now grasped Harker by both shoulders and regarded him as one would do a son. 'We have gone to great lengths in bringing you back to us, after your father decided to deny you your birthright and here you are duly restored to us; to me and your family. For you see, *we* are the same, Alex Harker… because, you see, your father was my brother.'

Harker pulled away from the man's grip, and stared at him in abject disbelief at the disclosure as Davies nodded excitedly.

'Your father believed his siding with the Templars would bring the Mithras to its knees and they even thought that we had been totally destroyed from the inside out. But as you now know it was nothing more than a game within a game and he should have realised that you cannot easily stamp out a belief that has stood the test of time for thousands of years with one single blow of deception. The Templar's arrogance is its greatest weakness; we are still as strong as ever and for the past twenty-five years I knew I would eventually find you. Your father hid you well from us, but once you became embroiled with Sebastian Brulet and those other devilish zealots, I realised it would just be a matter of time until we reached out to you. And now, my nephew, here you are.'

Being identified as kin made Harker feel light-headed and he stared blankly as his 'uncle' continued with the warped sense of logic he had displayed thus far.

'There is so much you have yet to learn about your personal history and importance in all of this, and when I discovered you had resigned your own place within that steaming pile of dung that is the Catholic Church, I knew it was in your blood – your DNA – to resist that same false and deceitful ideology. Catholicism is nothing more than a stolen reflection of the one true faith. Of Mithraism and the millennia of history and devotion that have always behoved us to stay pure and to praise the one true god.' Davies raised his hand towards the painted ceiling and the image at its centre, 'I refer to Mithras, the true lord of humanity and yes, Alex… I am your uncle, and you have now come home.'

Harker now felt in a state of information overload, but that surreal feeling took a back seat to contemplating the complete fantasy that he would ever join a heartless, cold and just plain wicked group as this, regardless of whether he was genuinely related. As he looked up at the man who would be his uncle, now smiling like a Cheshire cat, he realised the fellow was not only a psychopath but clearly insane to boot.

'So, Uncle,' Harker began deciding his best bet for the time being was to play to the man's delusions, 'will you now explain why you had me chasing the 'Darkness' prophecy, the blessed candles, and breaking into the Vatican's archives?'

The use of the word 'uncle' had Davies wagging a finger at him. 'Now, now, Alex. Let's not insult each other's intelligence, since I know how you must feel about all this. You've been kept away from us for too long but, given time, I know you'll come to believe in the truth of what we're trying to accomplish.'

'Ok, Davies, so why the goose chase?' Harker replied tersely, realising this man might be crazy but he wasn't stupid.

'Many of us have felt unsure about the wisdom of bringing you into the fold. Some think you will have become too polluted by your experiences.' Davies pointed his finger upwards, deliberately ignoring the question. 'You found one such upstairs, sharing his bed with a nest of emperor scorpions.'

The remembered image of the swollen blue face of Michael Donitz caused Harker to grimace. 'So that's how you repay those who dare to disagree with you?'

'Yes, but for your sake, Alex,' Davies said sternly, as if Harker had asked for all this. 'All debts must be repaid, and the debt of loyalty is amongst the highest. I doubt he will die, since we administer anti-venom regularly and other medical requirements as necessary. If he survives until tonight, he will have a chance to return to us with a restored sense of loyalty.'

'Or with sheer bloody murder on his mind,' Harker muttered quietly. 'If he has a mind at the end of it all.'

'If we're to fight those that would oppose us, then we must remain strong and united, and absolute loyalty is the lifeblood by which we will achieve that.'

'And what the hell is *that*, exactly?'

'The Catholic Church has become far too powerful to get rid of just like that, but Mithraism has witnessed many other false religions come and go, and yet we are still here. Time is our saviour as it always has been, and in a few thousand years from now who knows how things will have evolved. We have started already to hurt the Church... in fact I had Legrundy remove the entire congregations of two churches only a few days ago, as you might have heard, and that is just another part of our plan to instil fear into the hearts of the masses. We are custodians of the true faith until the time becomes right, and until then we will do exactly what you yourself have been doing over the past few days – by chipping away at the Church piece by piece.'

'And how exactly have I been doing that?' Harker replied, confused by his apparent part in all this.

Davies made his way over to the nearby pillar and with the flat palm of his hand pressed its surface. With a clicking sound a portion of the stone slid away to reveal the two 'blessed candles' sitting in shiny metal holders. 'I'm afraid these little trinkets are barely worth the quartz we had them made from, although I will say they were expertly crafted to make the right impression and the light electrical discharge was a rather ingenious design.' He picked up the two items and held them out in front of him, one in each hand, and then dropped them to the floor where they shattered into a hundred sharp pieces. As

Harker stared down at a chunk which landed at his feet, he could make out a thin wire strip, containing tiny light diodes, running along its length.

'So they're fake! Then what about my vision? You can't fake something like that,' Harker gasped, trying to make sense of an experience that been haunting him ever since it happened.

Davies pulled a tiny vial from his other pocket and gave it a shake. 'Its medical term is scopolamine, better known as the Devil's Breath, and the South Americans have been using it for centuries. It's a highly potent mind-altering drug and I'll admit we've been tinkering with its effects for some time now – well before you even came on my radar. It makes the subject highly susceptible to suggestion and, with added hallucinogenic properties, it allows one to literally lead someone through a "trip", suggesting situations and events which the recipient experiences as being very real. The CIA have been using it for years but we, with some additional manipulation, have turned it into a far more useful compound.'

In truth this explanation made a lot more sense than the vision Harker had been grappling with, and it would certainly account for his cloudy thought processes ever since. Yet it had all seemed so real at the time. 'You're saying it was purely drug-induced!'

'Clever, isn't it?' Davies replied, clearly enjoying Harker's confusion. 'Henri injected you with some of it back at our little temple underneath the Eiffel Tower, which you should know is one of our modern Mithras Temples but with a change of décor. He then led you through the trance step by step, and in the end you never remembered a thing except the trip itself, did you? You never realised how much time had passed either.'

'What time?' Harker demanded, feeling furious at having been tricked so easily.

'You were out for over an hour until the effects wore off, but you never even questioned the time discrepancy afterwards because you were instructed not to and like anyone else under this drug's spell you did exactly as you were told. I've got footage of it all if you want to see. It's quite amusing seeing you laid out on the floor, stoned out of your mind.'

Harker had the urge to punch the living hell out of him right there and then, but Davies was already wagging his finger. 'Don't get silly now or that creature will be back in here to tear you to shreds before you know it. Besides, we used a similar drug on poor Federar, which Stefani injected him with much like you were. But don't worry, the archbishop will have woken up with no recollection at all of what happened.'

He then let out a deep laugh. 'It's all only smoke and mirrors, I'm afraid, just as were the murder of that mother and boy, along with the cryptic message written in blood.'

'They're alive? I thought you said they were dead?'

'No, they did die horribly but,' Davies flicked of his hand uncaringly, 'I certainly wasn't possessed.'

'Why?' Harker rubbed his forehead, thinking back to the grisly image of the mutilated son and mother. 'What was the point any of this? The prophecy, the candles, why?'

Davies now looked distinctly haughty. 'To create a narrative that that would ultimately get you into the Vatican's secret archives and get hold of what I knew was there but never could have stolen myself without getting caught.'

Harker felt a sudden nausea in his throat as he thought back to when he had been fighting for his life against Archbishop Federar and it suddenly occurred to him how long it had taken for Stefani to come to his aid. Clearly she'd had other things to attend to. There they were in a room containing some of the most toxic items that the Church wished didn't exist, and he had managed to get Stefani in there with him. 'What did she take?'

With a smile Davies reached into a pocket of his robe and produced a small leather-backed book which he dangled in front of him. 'A written diary from the first pope ever elected outlaying everything pilfered from Mithraism and incorporated into the early Catholic Church. We've been aware of that secret little vault of theirs for decades and the rumours surrounding it, so when the powers that be saw fit to upgrade its security, I made sure it was one of my associates who undertook the job. I will admit my operative only managed to steal a glance at this diary,' Davies announced, waving the journal at Harker teasingly, 'but, more importantly, he did catch a good look of the three days of Darkness Prophecy. Of course it was only the side facing upwards, but the line *'You are I and I am you. When he is myth and we are reality. This grand deception will be repaid in blood.'* proved crucial in convincing Archbishop Federar that my holy vision was genuine. And gullibly he allowed me to inspect it and thus, as a result, I managed to get a good look at this.'

Davies brought his hand down onto the diary with a firm slap and then slowly shook his head from side to side. 'I have always found using people's own faith against them particularly delicious, and in a sentence, this is proof of all that was stolen from us, and by the time I'm finished the whole world is going to know it.'

'I don't believe you.' Harker shook his head. 'Maybe there were certain similarities in the early religions, and that's always been a matter of speculation, but it still wouldn't have any bearing on the truth and on the story of Jesus Christ.'

Davies was now looking extremely devious and he popped the book back into his pocket. 'There is no smoke without fire and even the smallest doubt can be magnified tenfold in people's minds. By the time I've divulged what lies within these pages, then believe me it will be another nail in the coffin of a religion that's been haemorrhaging followers year on year for decades. Like I said, Alex, time is now our greatest ally and if you destroy enough bricks from the foundations of a house, eventually it will crumble and fall.'

Harker felt all the energy evaporate from his body as he realised how, unknowingly, he had been instrumental in helping the Mithras cult attain their goal. And he felt sickened by it. He had not only been played from the beginning, but he couldn't have done a better job of it himself if he'd tried.

'I can't let you do this,' he protested.

Davies looked unfazed. 'My dear nephew, I know this stings right now, but I promise you that, in the fullness of time, you will realise that what you have done – and what *we* will do together – is not only the right thing to do, but the decent thing.'

'And if I don't?'

'If you don't, then I'm afraid all this effort and my faith in you will have been for nothing. And I will consider it nothing short of a betrayal of your own family, and the greatest disloyalty you could be guilty of.'

That same image of Michael Donitz's swollen features flashed through Harker's mind and, as he stood there deflated and at a total loss for words, Davies slipped past him towards a large pair of double doors over to his right and with both hands flung them open.

Harker looked over to see a large dining room in stark contrast to the Romanesque style of the room he was in. Thick tapestries hung on all the walls and at a long, mahogany table stretching most of the room's length, the now familiar faces of the Mithras group were seated around it. On the table itself had been placed an outsized silver platter with a cover over five feet in length and equipped with multiple handles, and Davies now gestured Harker to enter as Stefani and three of the Mithras followers stood up and reached for the handles.

'Now come, Alex, and take the last step of initiation. Join our ranks and fulfil your destiny along with your brothers and sisters.'

Harker's instinct was to run but he knew not where, so he slowly took a few steps into the dining hall before coming to a stop behind a large wooden chair at the head of the table, as Davies meanwhile closed the doors behind them and made his way halfway along the room.

'Welcome, Alex, for with this banquet we shall let you join our brotherhood. And just as Christian followers of Christ eat his body at every communion… so we eat that of our enemies.'

The huge silver cover was now lifted up, and instantly Harker's eyes began to glaze and his stomach started to tighten – as he looked in horror at the course about to be served.

The dull-grey cooked eyes of Marco Lombardi gazed up towards the ceiling, as he lay there outstretched and his skin brown after hours of cooking. His head had been shaved and his hands and feet removed, his limbs now tied at its ends with thick brown string.

'Ladies and gentlemen,' Davies began with a pleased smile, 'welcome here your brother, for he who was lost to us has now been found.'

Chapter 34

'You're cannibals!' Harker yelled before almost retching at the sight of Lombardi's crisp exterior.

'Of course not,' Davies replied calmly, as Dr Marceau stood up holding a long sharp knife and began to slice away a thin sliver of thigh muscle, 'This ritual has been carried out ever since Mithras's inception and is another rite stolen from us by the Catholic Church.'

Harker looked down at his plate and suppressed the bile rising in his throat. He was wrong: these people weren't insane, they were the devil incarnate. And as he began to breathe deeply and the smell of the baked offering wafted past his nostrils, Davies continued to lecture him.

'Alex, this practice may seem unusual to you,' he said, taking his seat at the other end of the table, 'but it is practised by many of the older cultures all over the world.'

'Maybe hundreds of years ago but not in the twenty-first century,' Harker managed to argue, now focusing his line of vision on Davies at the far end rather than the human shish kebab lying stiff on its oversized serving dish.

'I understand this may be unsettling if you've never experienced it before, so please don't feel obliged to participate if you don't wish to.'

There was not a cat in hell's chance Harker was going to do so but it was still a relief to hear these words. Meanwhile the smell of baked Lombardi continued to permeate the air, and even worse, it actually smelt rather like chicken!

'Gives a whole new meaning to the term having someone over for dinner,' Harker remarked bitterly. 'So what did the evening's entrée do to deserve this?'

'He's the reason you've had so much trouble with Avi Legrundy,' Anastas replied as a plate of man meat was placed in front of him. 'He disagreed with Father's decision to invite you into the family. The idiot couldn't stand the idea of you usurping his position and one day taking your rightful place instead of him.'

Stefani now intervened, 'He tried to convince her to kill you, Alex, and sealed his fate in the process.' she stated flatly and then took a first bite of her prepared meal, which had Harker close to throwing up. He couldn't believe he had found the woman attractive. 'Of course, she told Father soon after but we detained Marco here, and let him believe he had managed in his deception, just to see how far he might go.' A drizzle of Lombardi juice began running down her cheek, which she dabbed at with a white linen serviette. 'He would have had me killed, too, given half a chance.'

This was the most disgusting and surreal situation Harker had ever seen: an entire group of people digging into another human being and yet chatting as though it were over a Sunday roast. Suddenly a thought occurred to him. How could a group of people become so detached from reality as to carry out such a depraved act with little or no emotion?

'You lot are the same children who went missing back at the orphanage all those years ago? And the fifteen swastikas I keep seeing represent all of you.'

'We were lucky,' Detective Russo responded with a nod and sitting to the left of Harker. 'Father offered us a life full of meaning and wealth instead of ending up on the shit heap along with all the other disenfranchised children of this world.'

'Extremely lucky,' Dr Marceau concurred. 'With his guidance and financial help we have all proved successful in our chosen fields and been inspired with the goal of returning the true God to his rightful place.'

'He wasn't so lucky,' Harker replied, gesturing to the oven-baked corpse whose right thigh was now cut away, right down to the femur.

Listening at the other end of the table, Davies swallowed his last bite and flapped a hand in the air. 'With the help of my children here I have continued to build the foundations for the hierarchy of the next generation. And they aren't the only ones, for the people you see here are only the inner circle of but one chapter of the Mithras. We have devoted associates all over the world and with our resources, and the Magi now gone, we can begin to go forth and reclaim our destiny.'

'Ah, yes, the destruction of the Catholic Church would be quite an accomplishment, if you can achieve it,' Harker said bitterly. 'And do your other associates know about your dining habits?'

Harker's sarcasm provoked a look of ambivalence from each of them and Davies's eyes moved around the table warily before settling back on him.

'This banquet is for only our most trusted and, yes, that noble goal is most definitely our long-term aim. But we have another more pressing issue to resolve and it is yet another reason as to why you find yourself here tonight.'

The others eyed each other furtively as Davies pushed his plate forward and stood up. 'There's a good reason why I never got in contact with you after I first heard of your whereabouts.' He stood up and moved slowly past the other guests, lightly touching each one on the shoulder affectionately. 'When the Templars foolishly attempted to eradicate the Mithras all those years ago, it was due to nothing other than their own selfish conviction that they were somehow pure whilst we constituted an affront to their high sense of self-regard. They considered them- selves better than us, and so they used their perceived power to make us suffer.'

Davies finally reached Harker's seat and he put his hands together as if to look noble. 'Avi Legrundy and myself obviously escaped their wrath and then, with no more use for him, they killed your father.'

'Ahh, yes. Where is Miss Legrundy tonight?' Harker asked with a look of distaste and still not buying the tale of Templar murder.

'She's having her face looked at; they were nasty burns.' Dr Marceau informed him and sounding slightly miffed at that fact, 'your overly heroic escape plan almost got me killed too.'

Davies now remained silent and Harker now sensed the unease which his actions had caused. 'Well, she was trying to kill me at the time.'

'It was only an act, Alex,' Marceau persisted, 'I almost choked on the blood pack, and after tossing that pigs tongue in your lap she was supposed to drag me out leaving you to break your own chair, which I had already weakened, so you could escape after us. I almost didn't make it to the back entrance in time. My throat is still raw from the fumes.'

Harker could see this was a real bone of contention for all of them and, as they stared at him menacingly, he realised that his new 'family' could turn from pleasant to vicious at the drop of a hat. 'I apologise, Gérald, but I was under the assumption she had just murdered you, and I was extremely angry about it.'

The hardened stares now began to soften as Davies took that moment to intervene. 'I understand Alex, we all do, and I'm sure you can apologise to Miss Legrundy when she arrives. I think you'll find her most forgiving, given the situation.'

Harker offered a grateful nod, and everyone settled back into their seats, as Davies continued with his pitch.

'As I was saying. We watched as years of designed strife broke out between them and the Magi, which cut down their numbers until recently, when they had managed to do to the Magi exactly what they believed had happened to us, and the time seemed ripe for exacting some well-deserved revenge. But it was most impressive that you, one of our own, played such a pivotal part in their demise. It is with that same fervour that we wish you now to help us.'

It was irksome to Harker to keep being mentioned thus as one of *theirs*, but he gave a nod. 'And what would that be?'

Davies glanced around at his brood and then quickly back at Harker, with a maniacal look on his face. 'I want you to help us destroy those people who killed your father. I want you to help me destroy the Templars once and for all. And I want Sebastian Brulet dead and in doing so we can finally bring this game of ours to a close.'

A low muttering now rippled around the table. 'All debts must be repaid.'

Harker looked around briefly at all the faces focusing on him keenly. 'And how would I do that?'

This reply appeared to encourage Davies who now bent down on one knee, within inches of Harker's face, with the smell of human flesh on his breath. 'You know the hierarchy, you know how they operate and therefore you can get close to them. With you on our side we can put an end to all this, so we now ask for your help.'

Harker stared back into the eyes of his 'uncle', and it just appalled him to think how deluded this man had become. It made sense that his 'children' here had been indoctrinated at an early age, and thus raised to believe in Mithras and their cause unequivocally, but Davies himself? Had the loss of his loved ones and his wish for revenge clouded his judgment so much that he actually believed Harker would participate in such an insane crusade purely because they were related?

As Harker continued to stare at him, he came to the conclusion that he had. And now he sat there silently, as if mulling over the offer, as Davies continued with his wishes.

'Take your proper place with us, Alex, and I promise you a life of wealth and of never wanting for anything, which of course extends to your wife-to-be, Chloe.'

The mere reference to her had his blood boiling, but he managed to retain an expression of composure until, after almost a full thirty seconds of silence, he finally nodded his head. 'I can't deny that I have indeed missed a sense of family over the years, and if the Templars did murder my father, then that changes things. If I do help you though, I need you to make three assurances?'

'Of course,' Davies replied, looking very pleased with himself, his smile a bit overstated. 'Just name them.'

'I want proof that they really did kill my father, and I want it before I agree to do anything.'

'And you shall have it,' Davies replied with a nod.

'Secondly, Mithraism is alien to me, to say the least, so you must allow me to gain experience of it at my own pace.'

'More than reasonable,' Davies replied once again glancing around at those present, who all seemed to find the request acceptable. 'And the third?'

'I will help you in any way I can, but I don't want to be the one whose hand plunges the dagger.'

Davies pondered his nephew's wish, then nodded his head in agreement. 'You help us get to him and I will plunge it myself.'

'Very well,' Harker sat back in his chair and smiled. 'Then if this banquet is not my final initiation, what is it?' Let's get it over with and allow me to get to know my family once again.

Davies clasped a hand on Harker's shoulder and, after beckoning all the others to congratulate their new kinsman, he walked off and disappeared through the double doors.

Detective Russo got to him first, pulled him to his feet and gave him a huge hug.

'Are you even really a Detective?' Harker asked.

'Of course, I am. We've all of us chosen a career in which we can best serve the goals of Mithras.'

'How about your brother-in-law?'

'Oh, that's real, on my wife's side, though. She died a while back, I fear.'

'I'll bet she did,' Harker murmured and as he moved from one hug to the next he couldn't quite come to terms with what a bizarre experience this was. A group of orphans united in a deadly and awful sect with only blood and murder on their minds, yet all of them living normal lives outside it. It was like the Italian mafia where one's family was something to be treasured during the day yet at night those same fathers became homicidal killers and psychopaths. The contrast was frankly unbelievable and yet, as Stefani pushed her way forward to embrace him tightly, he found the whole concept not only terrifying but tragic.

'I knew you'd join us. Father has never been wrong, and family is after all the most important thing in the world. You have to meet the others and I know you'll love Sofia… she is a sweetheart.'

'I know, but give me time, Stefani. I need some space to get my head around all this.'

She pulled back and nodded in understanding. 'It's a lot to take in,' she agreed just as Harker smelt the stench of something god-awful. He turned around to see Davies reappear in the open doorway tugging a leather strap. It was wrapped around the neck of the hulking man-child plodding in behind him.

Although intimidating in size, the poor boy looked absolutely petrified, and the others present now began slapping him mercilessly about the head, mocking him viciously.

'Down on your knees, beast,' Davies commanded and the man-child complied immediately. The others now retook their seats with looks of scorn and contempt towards the giant simpleton. 'This creature, this misfortune of nature, represents all that is wrong with the world we inhabit, which the world now holds up as something to be protected, when instead it should simply be taken out and destroyed. The sick Church of today only offers its flock weakness and pity and we must take pride in the knowledge that our own beliefs are pure.'

As Harker watched the Mithras leader reel off his venomous, rhetorical nonsense he looked around to see everyone present applauding and cheering and his heart sank even lower, if that were possible.

'Alex,' Davies called out to him, slapping the dog lead against his open palm. 'This creature has been raised like cattle for only one purpose: to be slaughtered as an offering to Mithras by one who is true of heart, and as a show of dedication to that which is to be.'

Davies produced the same hunting knife that Harker had been tossed earlier on entering the dungeon maze, and it was now pressed firmly into his hand. 'In the name of Mithras, shed its blood and destroy what it has and always will stand for. I refer to Jesus Christ, the most treacherous betrayer of the human race ever to have existed.'

As the others cheered on with degrading chants, Harker felt his entire throat tighten with anger and he steadied his breathing. They were monsters all right.

'Take your place with us,' Davies encouraged triumphantly as the din subsided and all Mithras's children looked on in excitement, eager for the sick spectacle to begin, 'put this beast out of its misery, for its life now belongs to you and you alone.'

Harker's hands trembled slightly, but not from fear or disgust but rather wholehearted, unadulterated rage. He placed his hand on the man-child's shoulder and addressed him. 'Stand up now,' he ordered loudly and the giant, with fearful tears in his eyes, pulled himself to his feet whereupon Harker untied the dog lead from around his neck. Then, holding the knife up to the boy's throat 'I own you,' he growled. 'And you belong to me.'

Davies looked thrilled at the sudden show of strength Harker was displaying. He even clapped his hands joyfully as Harker leant close to the man-child's face, which was quivering with fear. 'Destroy them!' Harker bellowed, and in that instant the giant stopped shivering. He now only looked confused as Harker bellowed again, 'Destroy them all, that's an order.'

Davies had only just realised what was going on and managed the single word, 'What!' as a huge fist slammed down hard into his cheekbone with a crack, sending him flying against the wall opposite, where he crumbled to the floor in a heap and like a jackpot machine paying out the prized leather backed journal he had been shown earlier, along with his confiscated iPhone fell from Davies's robed pocket and out onto the floor.

The others sat shocked and motionless in their seats as the man-child now, with one hefty movement, flipped the entire table over and began ploughing mercilessly into them with his fists, swinging them left and right and sending anyone they touched sailing off in the opposite direction, like skittles in a bowling alley.

With the cumbersome robes they were all wearing, it meant easy pickings. Harker grabbed his phone and the leather book firstly, jamming it into his pocket and then he snatched up one of the smaller silver platters from off the floor and smashed it hard onto Russo's head. The detective had managed to avoid the man-child's onslaught, but this unexpected assault knocked him out cold.

Harker next turned his attention to Marceau who had initially taken a fist blow to the head but was now staggering to his feet – only to be sent back to the floor with the help of the now dented platter.

'No please…' he heard someone cry out before another hard blow from the giant sent them flying against the wall. Seeing how the youth was making short work of the lot of them, Harker ran back into the other room to grab the brass tongs next to the fireplace and pulled out a burning log, which he hurled up against the wooden rafters of the maze whose doors were still ajar having been opened in order to bring in the human sacrifice.

To the sound of cries and moans of those guests getting pummelled, Harker hurled another burning log and then another, and by the time he returned to the dining room the timbers were already lighting up and starting to burn ferociously.

'Enough. Follow me,' he yelled and the giant ceased his rampage and thundered over to join him.

The scene was chaos and, although none of the Mithras cult looked dead, there were writhing bodies everywhere. To one side he caught sight of Stefani, who bore a big red punch mark on one cheek and was busy screaming obscenities at him.

'You wanted hell,' Harker yelled to her, barely in control of the sheer rage still overwhelming him. 'Well, here it is.'

As smoke began to fill the room, Harker slammed the doors of the dining room, shutting them inside. There was no lock on them which at least gave the Mithras a chance to escape because as much as he wanted to kill them all at that moment, he wasn't a murderer.

He hurried over to the only other door and flung it open, and thankfully saw stairs leading upwards. He paused and looked back to see the giant standing staring at the billowing smoke. 'Follow me,' Harker urged, but the man-child merely glanced at him, then with a smile took off into the burning maze and out of sight.

There was no way Harker was leaving without him, so he rushed after him in close pursuit. All around fire was raging, as he came to a halt at the small opening he had pushed his way through earlier, realising now he had no idea where to go next. Worse still he didn't even have a name to call out so he began calling yelling, 'Come back here... follow me.'

After several seconds, with the heat becoming almost unbearable, the man-child appeared, looming from some side passage, then ran back over to Harker, who now realised what was going on.

The oversized puppet with button eyes hung from his forearm, clutched tightly, and with an understanding nod from Harker they both sped back into the other room and up the stairwell. It ended at a set of double doors fixed above like those on an old-fashioned air-raid shelter.

They bust out through them, both together into the warm night air and without pausing to catch his breath Harker guided them back through the brush, emerging fortunately within yards of the waiting boat he had arrived in.

Harker was first on board and looked back to find the giant looking unsure. It dawned on him that this fellow had probably never even seen a boat before. *Jesus, he might never have been outside before.*

His attempts at waving him on board had no effect whatsoever. 'Get your arse in here now,' Harker ordered, and immediately the giant jumped on board, nearly capsizing the boat in the process. 'Now sit.' He pointed to one of the benches, then started up the engine and began to pull away.

Above the island of Poveglia, smoke billowed up into the night sky in an ever-increasing black cloud, blotting out the stars above. It was impossible to tell if anyone else had made it out to safety, because the entire island was shrouded in darkness. And in truth, as they moved further away and towards the city lights of Venice, Harker really didn't pay it much thought. Honestly, he couldn't care less. Everything he had just learned, the enormity of it all, had him feeling completely numb and at a loss and he found himself gaining solace in only one thing. His position of Jarl, within the Templars. The idea that he was not worthy of the role had been grating on him but, as he looked at the burning island now in the distance, he realised that not only did it serve an imperative function but that he would do all he could to uphold the faith Brulet had placed in him.

As the giant stared up at the stars he was probably seeing for the first time, Harker pulled out his iPhone and peered at the screen. It was cracked in several places but as he pressed the On button, the screen burst into life. He let out a huge sigh of relief and then began deciding what on earth he was going to do next. Where the hell was he going to go, in the company of a gigantic man in rags, wearing hooved boots and clutching a life-sized doll, without attracting unwelcome attention?

Harker finally dialled in a number and waited for an answer.

'David, it's Alex. I need your help.'

Chapter 35

The golden red sunset over the city of Cambridge looked more magnificent than usual as Harker sat lazily on his green garden chair, and he took another sip of his vodka and Red Bull and let it trickle slowly down his throat. It was hard to imagine that fewer than twenty-four hours earlier he had been tussling with a gigantic seven-foot man with a bull's head in the depths of an underground hell hole. His wrenched muscles had begun to ache in the past few hours and, although the drink was helping, the Solpadeine Max and Ibuprofen he had swallowed were only just beginning to work.

The phone call he had made to Carter from the boat had culminated in no less than an all-out rescue campaign. After an hour of waiting off the Venice shoreline he had been met by a large yacht which had taken both him and his new friend to a waiting van, and from there they had been whisked off to a local airstrip, from which a Lear jet had flown him back to the UK. Harker had not recognised the Templar waiting for him on board, but the man had wanted a full breakdown of everything, to be passed on to Brulet. This Harker was happy to do, even if the man had looked increasingly shocked, especially when he got to the subject of cannibalism.

Unfortunately his oversized companion, whom Harker had taken to calling 'Hercules', had needed to be given an anaesthetic to calm him before he could be bundled into the van and then taken to a nearby hospital, under Templar care, which made the idea of coaxing him onto an aeroplane out of the question. Harker had even needed to give himself a jab with the syringe first to reassure Hercules that it was innocuous before he reluctantly accepted one too, out of trust for his new 'owner'. Harker knew he was in good hands and that the Templars would do all they could for him but, given his years of isolation and God knows what else he must have experienced, any possible road to recovery would be long and difficult.

Chloe was there to meet Harker on the tarmac at Stanstead and she had refused to let go of his hand, which was nice to begin with but after the second hour was becoming annoying. All the same, it had been a nice welcome. It seemed she hadn't believed a word of Doggie's story so had spent the past few days seriously worried, and even fearful he might have gone missing for good.

Heading straight back to Cambridge, on receiving a phone call en-route, they had taken a detour to meet Doggie and Carter at the Fox & Hounds pub, where the past few hours had been spent relaxing outside in the beer garden. While enjoying the summer weather, he had brought his friends up to speed on the bizarre sequence of events that had been necessary in order to get him home in one piece.

'That is one of the strangest stories I've ever heard Alex,' Doggie remarked, still bewildered by the account of the Mithras cult and its quest for vengeance against those whom it considered usurpers of its faith. 'Revenge,' he added solemnly, 'is a dish best served cold, indeed.'

'Or in this case hot.' Carter suggested in reference to the blaze that had destroyed the Mithras's cult's underground den hidden deep within Poveglia island.

'Quite,' Doggie replied before turning his attention back to Harker, who was still thoughtfully nursing his drink. 'Have they found any of the bodies yet?'

The thought was unsettling and Harker shrugged his shoulders. 'I haven't heard anything yet except that I know the police are scouring the entire area. Only time will tell; there's a lot to sift through,' he said, 'but knowing that lot's history of beating the odds, I wouldn't be surprised if absolutely nothing was found.'

A silence fell among them the three men as they each pondered the unsettling possibilities, and it was only broken by Chloe's arrival with a fresh round of drinks.

'Drinks, boys,' she chirruped, placing the tray on the round wooden table. Then, noticing how lethargic they all appeared she added, 'Have I interrupted something?'

'We were all just contemplating your husband-to-be's story.' Doggie replied, giving her a grateful nod as he picked up his chilled pint of Guinness. 'That Stefani Mitchell woman really had us all fooled.'

Harker intervened, 'Nice of you to say so, Tom, but it was me she fooled – and she managed it very well.'

It wasn't until getting back on UK soil that he had really begun to consider just how completely he had been conned. And it wasn't so much that she had succeeded in that, but because the Mithras cult's grisly real-life play had been executed with such masterly precision. No, what irritated him most of all was that one simple phone call to Brulet would have foiled the whole charade there and then.

'We could have all done some checking ourselves,' Doggie offered supportively, 'and, anyway, let's not forget that you were drugged for half of that trip. Who knows how it affected your reasoning.'

Harker looked unconvinced at this notion and Doggie hastily took it upon himself to pry further into his friend's apparent vision. 'How real did it seem exactly?'

'Just as real as sitting here with you now.' Harker replied. And if he was honest he still felt in awe of the delusion he had experienced under that manipulative drug known as the Devil's breath. 'I did a bit of checking on it during the flight back and apparently it's used all over South America by gangs and extortioners. Once taken into their system the victims become as compliant and suggestible as is needed. There are common examples of when victims will be driven to their own houses and happily help the robbers empty it of everything not nailed down, only to wake up the next morning with little or no memory of what happened.'

'Sounds like me after a hard night's drinking,' Carter joked with a smile.

'But this weaponised version of it was so potent.' Harker let out a deep sigh. 'It's actually pretty terrifying to think that such a small amount of this stuff can produce such profound results. I mean I felt I was actually floating above the earth, up amongst the stars, and it was so… real.'

Chloe stroked Harker's arm comfortingly, and they all fell silent again.

'Quite a trip,' Doggie remarked eventually, shuffling in his chair and tapping his fingers on the armrest. 'When I was at university, a friend of mine slipped some acid in my drink, and I can tell you it made for an interesting experience.'

Harker looked surprised at the admission and leant in closer to the Cambridge Dean. 'You've never told me that,' he said, impressed by Doggie's candour. 'Was it fun?'

'Depends what you mean by fun,' Doggie replied uncertainly. 'If you consider it fun to be pursued by green aliens with gnashing teeth all the way through the centre of town, all the while screaming like a madman, then yes... it was a hoot.'

The verbal image had Harker bursting out in laughter. 'That sounds bloody awful.'

'Yes, it was, but not as awful as to be found by one's room-mates, sweating like a pig and believing the shower curtain was a forcefield able to protect me from the vicious little buggers!'

Now everyone burst into laughter, and even Doggie himself let out a chuckle. 'That was my first and last experience of using mind-altering drugs... Just give me a good old-fashioned drink anytime.'

The atmosphere now relaxed but the idea of Stefani Mitchell being able to orchestrate such a deception was still gnawing into Harker's ego. 'That woman played it perfectly,' he said.

'I think, deep down, I knew she was a con woman,' Carter said airily, 'I sensed it somehow from the beginning.'

'You never even met her,' Chloe said sarcastically.

Carter gazed at her with his eyelids tightening 'My family was said to possess the gift, as my mother put it.'

'What, the gift to be a pain in the arse?' Doggie said with a snigger, looking smug at his clever retort.

'Hilarious; you're in the wrong profession, Tom,' replied Carter, flicking the Vs. 'No, she said I definitely had the sight.'

Harker himself was trying to not to laugh, because he couldn't tell if Carter was actually being serious. Beside him, Chloe rested a finger lightly upon her forehead and closed her eyes.

'I also have the sight, David... and I'm getting a message. It says... it says you're buying the next round.'

Again the table erupted in laughter again, and they were still chortling when the bartender appeared at the pub door and began to reel off a message.

'Does anyone out here know an Alex Harker?'

Harker craned his head around to face the doorway and raised his glass. 'Over here.'

'There's a phone call for you at the bar.' The man then disappeared back inside.

'I'll be right back.' Harker set his drink on the table and made his way over to the pub door.

'When you get back, I want to hear more about those cannibals,' Carter called out after him, drawing the attention of customers at the tables, who now all stared at him with great curiosity.

'It's all right, I'm a teacher,' Harker announced quickly. 'We were discussing the ancient tribes of Papua New Guinea.'

His response quelled the other drinkers' interest and, after shooting Carter a dirty look, he made his way into the cool interior of the pub and over to the waiting phone. 'Hello?'

'Look out the window and over to your right,' a voice said politely Harker did as instructed and saw a man in a charcoal-grey suit holding a mobile to his ear and beckoning him over to a black limousine parked at the side of the road. The line then went dead and, after an initial moment of hesitation, Harker moved to the pub's front door and made his way warily over to the waiting vehicle.

'Nice to see you, Mr Harker,' the well-dressed man began as opened the car door and motioned for him to get in. 'Someone would like to speak with you.'

The man obviously sensed Harker's uncertainty and he stepped back a few paces, allowing him to peer into the dark interior, where the face that greeted him allayed any further worries.

Sebastian Brulet, sitting on the back seat, removed his dark glasses and stared up at him with those strange crossed-shaped pupils of his. 'Hello, Alex,' he said with a smile.

Without hesitation Harker slid onto the seat next to him and shook the Grand Master's outstretched hand. 'Am I glad to see you,' he began as the door closed behind him, creating the dim lighting that suited Brulet best.

'Are you OK?' were the next words out of Brulet's mouth, and Harker gave him a tired nod. He'd been expecting a call soon from this man, but should have realised that he might turn up in person. There were many things that needed clarification but, before Harker could utter a word, Brulet put a silencing hand up in the air. 'Firstly I am so very so sorry that I kept you in the dark but considering what I know... or thought I knew, I was waiting for the right time to sit down with you and explain about your father, and how he came to be a Templar.'

Harker nodded silently. Even though chomping at the bit to speak, he realised the Grand Master had probably been rehearsing what to say now, and so he waited tight-lipped.

'When I heard your report about what happened, it was as baffling as it was shocking, and let me say that if I had even known for a second the Mithras cult was were still an entity, I would have warned you about them right away.'

'I know you would have, Sebastian, but suffice to say it's been a real eye-opener.'

Brulet looked sincerely regretful at the lack of information he had provided and, after a deep breath, he immediately set about rectifying this as best he could. 'The most important thing you need to know is that your father was a good man, one of the best I have known, and his ties to the Mithras cult were less than solid.'

He then sat back in his seat and his lips twitched briefly as he decided upon from which angle to approach in giving this much needed explanation. 'We became aware of the Mithras group for the first time back in the mid-Nineties as, through all those shared centuries of existence, our paths had never crossed. They were an extremely secretive group who, even though they had been around for far longer than us, had survived as nothing more than watchmen – a lone lighthouse, if you will – who continued from one generation to the next in order to keep the torch alive for their bizarre but ancient religion. They had meanwhile accumulated a lot of wealth and by means of this they did exercise some power, but never as forcefully as, say, the Magi did… or so I thought. In truth we might never have known about them if not for your father because, even though we were unaware of them… they knew a lot about us. And with the information you discovered I now realise they were, and are, more of a threat than we ever could have imagined. I don't mind telling you that we are all still struggling to comprehend their role in not only the Magi's misfortunes but our own as well and it will be something that preoccupies us for a long time to come. Now, if you wish to know more about their activities in detail, that we know about, I'd be happy to go through it with you at length back at the vault because, as David Carter discovered, we had inherited much information on their cult, spanning centuries.

Brulet took a deep breath and raised something that had clearly been weighing on him. 'Of course your latest discovery has turned things on its head regarding the Mithras, but back then and in a nutshell, we believed they had decided that, with times changing, they needed to penetrate the Catholic Church. Their remit – as I suspect you now know already – was not to dominate the Christian faith, as was the Magi's desire, but instead to undermine and destroy it where possible. It's for this reason that the Templars got involved, but not until your father brought it to our attention. You see, the Mithras cult was not a single entity but instead made up of two tribes whose lines can be traced back to the cult's beginnings, and over the generations one side had become far more disillusioned than the other. Whereas your father's side had come to accept these ancient practices as nothing more than a heritage from times past, the other – let us call them the Mithras – had hardened in their belief that their religion was still like a prince in waiting, and that Mithras was a force that would soon become dominant again and we now know this was an understatement of mammoth proportions.'

'So my father was a member of the Mithras then?' Harker asked, now unable to hold his tongue.

'Well, yes, but his family had been pulling away from the more "eccentric" side of things, shall we say, with the exception of his… brother.' Brulet wavered as he watched Harker's expression begin to dull. 'But if you'd let me to give you the whole background first, it might help shed light on that which obviously, and understandably, concerns you most.'

Harker gave a nod and allowed Brulet to explain further.

'There was an internal struggle and it was only then that your father and his clan realised how powerful the Mithras had become and, on behalf of those like-minded, he approached us. Turns out they had been aware of our existence for many years and it was when they realised how serious the Mithras had become in their ambition to destroy the Church that they sought our help.'

To Harker it seemed strange that Brulet actually looked guilty about this story he was telling, before he quickly realised it wasn't because of the story itself but that he had not revealed it to him earlier. 'Sebastian, I admit all this has come as a complete shock to me, but I think I understand why you hadn't yet told me.'

This sympathetic remark appeared to reassure Brulet and he patted Harker on the forearm. 'Let me get all this off my chest and then you'll see why. Your father allowed us to have a meeting with the Mithras hierarchy, but that ended in the death of many Templars and amounted to an all-out assault on us. That was because they now saw us as a primary obstacle in their quest to destroy our Church by any means possible. It was a short and brutal exchange and at the end of it your father was the only one left standing. At the time we believed the Mithras cult was vanquished, for lack of a better word, and their vast resources of wealth were seized and distributed to charitable organizations all around the world – overseen by your father, which seemed the only fair way to do it even if we now know it was only a fraction of their assets. Such was his zeal and diligence that your father was offered the position of Jarl within the Order of Templars… and the rest is history. We continued to spar with the Magi, tit for tat, maintaining a balance, so when your father was killed we came to the conclusion it was perpetrated by them. But…'

Brulet let the sentence hang, whereupon Harker finished the explanation as he saw it. 'But now that you know the Mithras have survived, you're not so sure.'

'Precisely,' Brulet concluded with a look of sorrow. 'Your father though, I see now, was right, because he never fully believed that the Mithras had been completely dismantled, and it was for that reason he kept you, his only child, completely out of the fray, for fear of retaliation. You were always at the forefront of his mind, Alex. And as you were growing up he considered one day inducting you into the Templars, but he really feared that in doing so he would put your life in danger, and felt he could never allow that to happen. When he died very suddenly, the Templars and I watched over you, though keeping ourselves out of sight, and I chose to honour his wishes. For, as you grew and gained your own sense of purpose, it seemed wrong to drag you back into a world he had never wished for you.'

Brulet sat upright as a warm smile appeared across his face. 'Then, as we know, fate brought you back to us and, even though I personally have never been one to believe in the idea of destiny, it's hard not to suspect that your path back to us had not already been laid out from the day of your birth.'

Much of what Harker was hearing he already knew, but now having a more complete picture of his identity and his past was immensely fulfilling, and he felt as if the hazy parts of his past had now been filled in. It was indeed a fairly tragic story and to say his connection with the Mithras was unsettling was an understatement, but it was something he needed to hear even if he knew there would be much further reflection on his part in the days and months to come.

'So John Davies really is my uncle, then?' Harker said with distaste.

Brulet slowly nodded. 'I'm afraid that part is at least true, but he split off from your father's side of the family to join the Mithras faction early on after becoming close with that sick woman Avi Legrundy, who was a small but potent cog in the assemblage of problems that drove your father to approach us in the first place. I assumed they had all died off but given your tales of cannibalism I would dare to say they have since evolved into something unrecognisable. Eating the flesh of other human beings was never in the Mithras mantra as far as we knew because, although being absolute fanatics, even they had boundaries. Of course I realise now that they only allowed us to see what they wanted to, so it is hard to know for sure.'

'I would say that we have only just begun to realise what the Mithras truly are.' Harker replied, happy to get off the subject of his 'uncle'.

'Yes, and a highly worrying one at that,' Brulet agreed, gritting his teeth, 'for a wounded animal is always at its most dangerous.'

This remark had Harker frowning. 'You don't think they died in that fire, then?'

Brulet eyed him solemnly and shook his head. 'The full search will take some time and it's early days, but so far no charred corpses have been found amongst the rubble on Poveglia island.'

The thought was unsettling to Harker as Brulet continued.

'We shall have to play the waiting game, and given Davies's talk of being just one of many Mithras chapters is of deep concern I'm afraid. However, knowing about a threat and in turn keeping vigilant is half the battle.'

There was still one important point that Brulet had so far skipped over and whether it was deliberate or not Harker couldn't say, but it needed to be addressed nonetheless. 'And have you had a chance to look at the diary yet?'

'Ah, yes, your "heist' in Vatican City." Brulet now stared at him with ambiguity in his eyes which had Harker looking sheepish. 'Well, true to Father Davies's words, I have heard that the archbishop doesn't remember anything, although your very being there will be impossible to conceal. However, I've already set some back-channels in motion and I think we can come to a resolution that will put the matter to bed. Best for everyone that way. But, regarding the diary itself, it will certainly be missed so I suggest we return it to the rightful owners, don't you?'

It was asked as an open-ended question and Harker took the opportunity to now make his own views known on such a sensitive subject. 'I would like a look, before it goes back.'

'That's only fair,' Brulet replied, 'but you should know that I've taken a peek for myself and it is far less provocative than Father Davies would have you believe. It contains mainly the first pontiff's own personal thoughts on the inception of the Church itself; it could be used to spin some doubts on the origins of some of Catholicism's formal practices, customs etc, but nothing more. I will, though, have it waiting for you at Mont St-Michel but, after that, it should be returned.'

Harker offered a nod and, even though he was curious to read the diary for himself, it seemed that Davies's wish to use anything at his disposal to 'chip away at the Church', had little to do with truth or fact.

'Any clues on the current whereabouts of Avi Legrundy?'

'No, not yet but like I said, it's early days, and we have their "temple" underneath the Eiffel Tower staked out in case she shows up. Personally, I wouldn't be surprised if she runs for her life. Cowards usually do… but as always, we'll be watching.'

As usual Brulet had a way of soothing Harker's fears and, although it was a major concern, he also felt secure in the knowledge that the Templars were at his back.

'Just a final thought,' Brulet said, clearly wanting now to wrap up his explanation but at the same time unprepared to leave any stone unturned. 'The Mithras files were not deliberately hidden from you in the vault. It's just I wanted to keep them to one side until we'd had this talk. If I'd known the cult of Mithras were still around, I would have had this conversation with you a while back.'

'I understand, Sebastian, I really do.'

Brulet smiled, feeling encouraged by Harker's understanding of his reasons. 'We're good, then?'

'Always.' Harker replied and Brulet gave his seat a gentle punch in relief.

'Well, I've got a flight to catch and some business to attend to, but I'll swing by Mont St-Michel in a couple of days' time. You'd better get back to your friends before they come looking for you… as they always do. You have yourself a good group there.'

Harker nodded as he grasped the door handle and swung it open. 'The best,' he agreed.

After he had exited the vehicle, Brulet threw a final question his way. 'I know you've accepted the position of Jarl already but after all that has happened I have to ask if you're still sure you want it. I know how teaching full-time at Cambridge was a big part of your life and honestly, until we know exactly what the Mithras are, we're heading into the unknown. I fear this battle has only just begun.'

Harker rested his arms on the car roof and lowered his head to the open door. 'I'm going to stay connected to them through the Board of Trust; Doggie will see to that, I've no doubt. But, Sebastian, I'm a Templar now, through and through, and the position of Jarl is needed now more than ever.'

Harker left Brulet and, with a big smile on his face, headed back to the pub garden pausing momentarily to offer a wave as the limo pulled away. He still had many concerns but this chat with Brulet had left him feeling reassured and, even though the Mithras were still out there and more than a force to be reckoned with, the Templars' vault had far more mysteries for him to uncover now and focus on for the time being. As for that assassin, Avi Legrundy, Brulet was right: she would need to possess a death wish to come after him. She was clearly vengeful, but not stupid, and her strong sense of survival would keep her at a distance, at least for now. The Mithras may have been far stronger than any of them could have imagined but the Templars were not to be underestimated. It was unquestionably only the end of the beginning but between them Harker had no doubt they could hold the line. Wherever it may lead.

As he reached the beer garden table and took in the sight of his friends surrounding it, he couldn't help but consider himself the luckiest man in the world and he felt a rush of confidence that together they could take on anything, whatever the future held.

'Where the hell have you been?' Carter demanded loudly, having already finished his latest drink. 'We were about to send out a search party.'

'You're like a bloody ghost, here one minute and gone the next,' Doggie added, as Harker rested his hands on the table and looked around them all genially.

'Everything all right?' Chloe asked, shading her eyes from the bright sun.

'Everything's great.' Harker replied. 'We've got a vault full of historical wonders and artefacts that haven't seen the light of day for a millennium, and who knows what we'll find there.'

'Well said,' Doggie offered and he took another long swig of his Guinness as Chloe thrust a sealed envelope into Harker's hand.

'One of barmaids dropped this off for you. Some girl-friend I don't know about?' Chloe said jokingly, even though there was a slightly uneasy look in her eye.

'Not at the moment. I mean we're not even married yet, are we?'

Chloe landed a firm punch on his arm as Harker ripped open the envelope and retrieved the note from inside.

'You know, that barmaid had one of the strongest Jamaican accents I've heard in years,' Doggie said with surprise, 'and I'm amazed they'd let her into work with that bandage on her face. She should be home, resting.'

Harker felt a chill run down his spine as he read through the couple of sentences written on plain notepad paper, while the rest of them continued with their banter.

> *Today is not the day to deal with you, Alex Harker. First I must respect the day of mourning for my brothers and sisters, but rest assured I'll be seeing you soon.*

Harker sat bolt upright in his chair and scoured the garden quickly for any sign of Avi Legrundy, but the only people he saw were ordinary customers, and with a perturbed glance at Chloe, he went on to read the last line.

> *All debts must be repaid.*